Return to

Ian Wilfred

Return to Luckett Quay
Kindle edition
Copyright © 2020 by Ian Wilfred

ISBN: 9798629982159

Cover Design: Avalon Graphics
Editing: Nancy Callegari & Ruth Nichols
Proofreading: Maureen Vincent-Northam
Formatting: Rebecca Emin

For Ron

Acknowledgements

There are a few people I'd like to thank for getting *Return to Luckett Quay* out into the world.

The fabulous Rebecca Emin at Gingersnap Books for organising everything for me and who also produced both kindle and paperback books. Nancy Callegari and Ruth Nichols for all the time and effort they spent editing the book, Maureen Vincent-Northam for proofreading, and the very talented Cathy Helms at Avalon Graphics for producing the terrific cover.

Finally for my late mum who is always with me in everything I do.

Chapter 1

Hannah was heading back to London after a weekend away with her family. Generally she'd while away train journeys by either chatting away to her boyfriend or by having her head stuck in a book, but this time things were different. There were so many questions which she just didn't have any answers to.

Perhaps she was over-thinking things: the weekend itself had been lovely. Her father had been celebrating his 50th birthday and they'd shared a lot of laughs. Even her stepmother, Susanna, had been on her best behaviour and it was always nice to see her stepbrother and sister. Alfie and Pippa worshipped Hannah and wouldn't leave her alone. At four and six years old, she could do anything with them. She suspected that wouldn't be the case when they became teenagers, but she was enjoying it while it lasted.

Nan was playing heavily on Hannah's mind. She'd been strangely quiet and distant during the party, and when Hannah had asked whether everything was alright, she'd refused to give a straight answer. Perhaps it had something to do with Dad's birthday. Nan might have been reminded of the days when Hannah's mother, Claire, had been around. She had died ten years previously, and even though they weren't blood relatives, Claire had been very close to Nan.

When Robert had met Susanna seven years ago, Hannah had immediately tried to accept her as she wanted her father to find happiness again. However, as time went on, she came to dislike Susanna more and more. She found her to be very manipulative, but her father seemed happy and the joy Alfie and Pippa gave him was so lovely to see that Hannah thought it best to keep quiet.

This weekend had been different somehow. Hannah knew that something was up; she just couldn't put her finger on it. For now it was back to London and the start of another busy week. She knew the first thing to greet her at the flat she shared with Jimmy would be three days' worth of dirty dishes and three days of Jimmy's clothes scattered over the floor, but she was used to this by now. She had always cleared up after him since the first day they met.

She still couldn't believe how lucky she was to have Jimmy in her life. How many people who meet at university actually stay together? Their life together wasn't perfect, both working shifts that could keep them from any meaningful contact with each other for days, but when they got the chance to get away and travel together, they had so much fun.

As Hannah entered the flat, she was in for a shock. What was that smell: air freshener? And a lot of it! Perhaps Jimmy had been trying to disguise three days of accumulated smells before going off to work: but no! There were no dirty dishes, the bathroom was unprecedentedly clean, and as for the bedroom: he had changed the sheets! This was not normal. What *was* he covering up?

A note propped up beside the kettle read:

'Hi, Hanny. Sorry I didn't go with you for the weekend. Love you lots, see you around 11. Jim xx'

He was right to be sorry for not going: he had the weekend off from work, so he had no excuse apart from having to get an earlier train back to be on time for the late shift. Having said that, he would have been bored out of his mind, what with Hannah chattering non-stop to her Nan and Susanna taking every opportunity to get a dig at him. No, it wouldn't have been fair to drag him all that way for that. She found it easy to forgive him, especially now that she had come home to a spotless flat. She could easily become accustomed to this level of service.

Hannah was ready to spend her evening waiting for Jimmy with a glass of wine in front of the telly. First, though, she made a quick call to Nan to let her know she was back safely.

'Hi, Nan, I'm home safe and well! The train was empty: I'm glad I got the earlier one. How are you? What have you been up to today?'

'That's good, darling, thanks for calling. I've not done a lot really. Your dad asked if I wanted to go and have tea with them, but I wasn't in the mood. Much as I love playing with the children. I'm still tired out from yesterday.'

'Yes, I'm tired too. It was late when we went to bed and we were both up early this morning.'

'I think I'll have an early night, Hannah. Thanks again for a lovely weekend. It's always nice to have you stay.'

'No, thank you for letting me stay! Dad and Susanna haven't got the space for me to stay with them. Their house seems so small now that Pippa and Alfie are growing up.'

'Tell me about it. Not a week goes by without Susanna telling me they need to move to a bigger property.'

'I know, but she told me that Dad can't get a bigger mortgage at his age, so they'll have to stay put and make the most of what they've got. Even so, I'm sure Susanna will find a way around that.'

'Oh yes, darling, she has grand ideas about that.'

'What do you mean, Nan? Is there something I don't know?'

'I think it's time for a cup of tea and bed for me, darling. I'm glad you're back safe. Give my love to Jimmy and tell him I missed his company over the weekend. I'll speak to you in the week. Nighty night for now.'

'Good night, Nan. Love you lots.'

Hannah sat back. The television was on, but she was lost in her own thoughts. What was all that about grand ideas? Nothing had been mentioned over the weekend. Could this be the answer to that niggling feeling? She considered phoning her father to ask him, but he wouldn't share anything if Susanna was in the room. All the same, something had definitely upset Nan.

'Wakey, Hanny! What rubbish are you watching?'

Hannah stirred awake, blinking. 'Oh, I must have fallen asleep. What time is it?'

Jimmy leaned in for a quick kiss before answering her. 'It's nearly half eleven. How was your weekend?'

'Good, thanks, but it's nice to be home. Talking of home, how much did it cost to get someone in to clean? I'm only joking, it was a lovely surprise. Everyone sends their love.'

'How did the birthday party go?'

For the next hour, Hannah told Jimmy all about the weekend. She didn't mention her worries about Nan, as he would just say she was over-thinking things as usual. To her surprise, he didn't add to any of her comments about him cleaning the flat: she had thought he'd have taken the opportunity to boast about that.

'I should get to bed,' she announced. 'It's been a long day. Are you coming, Jimmy?'

'Do you mind if I stay and watch a bit of TV to unwind? I'm not tired yet, and I'm not at work until two tomorrow. What shifts are you working next week? I'm sure you've told me, but I seem to have forgotten. Do you think it would be a good idea to get a calendar and put our rotas on it so we both know when we're working?'

'Yes, if you like. I'm off, though. Night, night.'

What was all that about? First a clean flat, now

rotas on the wall? This wasn't like Jimmy at all. True, it was a good idea, as they both worked odd hours: in hotels each week is different from the next, but they had never needed to keep a calendar before. That was something else for Hannah to worry about, and all before work tomorrow, when she could add the hotel's problems to her list of concerns.

By three o'clock in the morning Hannah still hadn't really slept beyond an intermittent doze. Jimmy hadn't come to bed yet, and her mind was hopping from Nan, to Susanna, to Jimmy, and back to the following day's problems at the hotel. Top of the list had to be Nan, because she was the most important person in her life. That was another thing, shouldn't that be Jimmy? No, Nan was the one she had turned to when Mum died. Nan was the one who had supported her in everything she ever did and she wanted her to be happy in return.

It was three years now since Nan had sold her house and moved into her purpose-built two-bedroom retirement flat. It was perfect for her, and they had had so much fun shopping for everything from new plates to furniture. It had been a very special time in both of their lives, apart from the time Susanna had put her two pence in.

'Why do you need a two-bedroom, Betty? It'll just be you living there. When Hannah comes to stay surely she can sleep in the lounge?'

Yes, that had been an awkward afternoon. Dad had said nothing: he was embarrassed, and at first Nan was quiet too. She knew exactly what Susanna was getting at: a smaller flat would be cheaper and then there would be money left over which she would be able to give to Robert, but there was no way Susanna would get the better of her. Nan's answer had shut her up right away.

'Yes, that could be a good idea; what do you think, Hannah? If I had a little money left over from the sale of the house we could go on that cruise we were talking about: a really long one. I wonder if there'd be enough for a world cruise? Thank you for the suggestion, Susanna.'

That had been the end of the matter.

Hannah could hear Jimmy coming along the corridor and pretended to be asleep. The minute his head hit the pillow he was snoring. She lay listening to him and wondering. Perhaps this was a new Jimmy. He might have grown up at last and started to take on more responsibilities. Hannah knew in her heart that, as much as he annoyed her sometimes with his mess, the old Jimmy was the one she would sooner have.

Just as she was thinking that there couldn't be anything else to worry about, she remembered something else Nan had mentioned. She had been talking about the family holiday home in Norfolk's Luckett Quay: could that be what was weighing on her mind? Think, Hannah, what did she say? It was only a quick comment: something to do with the rental agency closing down so Nan would have to find another company to take it on. Surely that would be straightforward? After all, Norfolk was full of holiday lets.

Hannah felt all her worries float away as she remembered all the happy times spent in Norfolk, in that big old house that had been in the family for generations. Every school holiday, winter or summer, was spent there. It was only when she had gone off to university and met Jimmy that she had stopped going. For the first time she realised that she really missed the place and her old friends there, Olivia and Tom, who she had sadly lost contact with. What would they be doing now? Tom no doubt had a high-flying job, and Olivia was probably settled down with a loving husband. Or perhaps they had moved away.

Life had been so much easier when she was a child. Oh, how she missed those days, months, years! Playing on the beach, walking the coastal path to get fish and chips, and (when she was older) buying cider and hiding away to drink it together. It was strange, but the three of them thought they had all the worries in the world growing up, not having a clue what life had in store for them. Perhaps she should try and get in contact with them, but then again Jimmy would never agree to them all meeting up in Norfolk: he hated the place. It was far too quiet for him. No, that was in the past. That was gone, and now it was all about the future: her and Jimmy's future, for ever and ever.

Chapter 2

As the week continued, Hannah started to put her worries about Nan behind her. Even the new Jimmy faded from her mind in favour of worrying about her new hotel manager, who seemed to want to reinvent the wheel. Her job should have been quite straightforward: taking reservations was all she had to do, but no. He now wanted the reservations team to be part of the reception team. To give him his due, he had been quite honest with all the staff and explained that he needed to cut hours: the minimum wage had gone up, so money had to be found from somewhere.

Being on Reception wasn't the problem. Hannah enjoyed talking to the guests and checking them in and out. That was fun. The problem was that the phone kept ringing, and they were missing out on reservation enquiries when she wasn't available to pick up, meaning that bookings were down. The manager couldn't see this, so when the money saved on wages failed to make up for the revenue lost on room bookings, who got the blame? Hannah and her team. She was beginning to hate the job and wondered if it was time to move on. Her CV looked good, and there were plenty of London hotels who might hire her, but first she needed to discuss it with Jimmy. A job which let them both work similar hours would be nice: then they could spend their time off together.

As she sat on the tube heading home, her mind wandered from the job crisis. All Hannah could think about was Luckett Quay, that big house, and it was big; six bedrooms upstairs, two with views out to sea, and a garden that went all the way down to the cliff edge. Luckett Quay beach had been her childhood playground, the site of hours and hours of happy times with her two best friends, Olivia and Tom.

The only time she had felt sad there was when her mum died. Within days of her death, Nan had taken Hannah down to Norfolk while Dad stayed at home to sort everything out. It was the longest period of time she'd stayed there: three whole months. She had even spent the odd day at the village school over in Saltmarsh Quay.

Nan also loved Luckett House: she was always telling stories of when she was there as a little girl. Come to that, everyone she knew loved it there except one: Jimmy. He hated it, but Hannah could never understand why. It was such a beautiful beach. Yes, the house was cold in the winter with no central heating, and if it rained too hard the roof leaked, but when the weather was nice you could take a walk up to Saltmarsh Cliff Hotel and then down the other side of the cliffs to Saltmarsh Quay to sit on the sea wall with fish and chips. What wasn't to like about that?

The half-mile walk to the flat after the tube turned her thoughts from those happy childhood years and towards a meal for one. Jimmy was working yet another evening shift, but one thing was for sure: the flat wouldn't be a mess. He was keeping up this new regime of tidying up after himself. It was all very strange but why knock it? She had been on at him for years about how messy he was, so he was only doing as she had been asking at last.

A ready meal was the order of the day, together with a bottle of wine. The evening was spent looking at job vacancies and trying to prepare herself to repeat the whole thing over again tomorrow. She was fast asleep before Jimmy got home.

*

Sitting at her desk the following morning, Hannah was annoyed at herself for not staying awake until

9

Jimmy came home from work the previous night. She had wanted to discuss the job adverts she had found. It wasn't right to apply for any of them without talking it through with him: they were a team. But they could go through them tonight, as it was Jimmy's day off today and neither of them started work until three in the afternoon tomorrow, so they would be able to have a lie in.

Hannah's first task of the day was to tackle all of her emails. Glancing through the list she saw five new messages from her general manager, Henry. The first four were straightforward requests for reports, but the last one was scheduling a meeting for eight o'clock the following morning. That put paid to her morning off with Jimmy. She would need to be at the hotel for a full 14 hours and she couldn't argue, as her contract stated that she was to work hours 'as required'. That could work both ways, however. They were over-staffed today, so she would take a shorter day as compensation. In fact, once the emails were done she would head home. Jimmy would probably still be asleep: what a lovely surprise she would give him!

Jimmy was in the kitchen when she got back.

'Hi, I'm home! You're up early, it's only eleven o'clock.'

'Hanny! What are you doing here? I didn't expect you until seven.'

Hannah explained about the meeting and suggested a few things they could do with their shared day off: perhaps the cinema, or clothes shopping? Jimmy loved new outfits.

'Right,' she told him. 'You make us a coffee and have a think about what you want to do and I'll go and change out of my uniform. But before we go out anywhere, I want to show you some job adverts and see which ones you think I should apply for.'

Jimmy didn't seem interested in any of the things

Hannah showed him. He was miles away. He also looked nervous. He kept checking his watch and phone, and positively jumped when the doorbell rang.

'I'll get it, Hannah.'

'No, I can. Anyway, what's with the 'Hannah'? You've never called me that, it's always Hanny.'

She opened the door.

'Oh, hello. Sorry, I must have pressed the wrong bell: I'm looking for Jimmy.'

Standing on the doorstep was a girl aged no more than eighteen, dressed to the nines with a large bottle of wine in her hand. She looked like she was off to a party, but it was only lunch time. Hannah was taken aback. She didn't know what to say. Who was this girl and why was she asking for Jimmy? Quickly, say something, speak to her!

'I'll knock on his door for you,' she managed. 'You look very nice, are you off to a party?'

'No, Jimmy and I work together. It's both of our days off today, so he invited me around for a drink.'

'That's nice. So are you Jimmy's girlfriend, as well as a work colleague?'

'Sort of. We've only been spending time together outside of work for a few weeks. It would be nice to be his girlfriend officially, but at the moment it's a secret. Jimmy doesn't want anyone to know we're seeing each other.'

'That's nice. Why don't you just wait here and I'll knock on his flat door.'

'I could do that. I know which one it is. I've been here before.'

'No, you wait here. I'll get him for you.'

Hannah didn't know whether to scream, shout, or cry. All she wanted to do was run away. She went back into the flat without even looking at Jimmy. She picked up her bag and headed back to the front door.

'There you go. He said to just go on up. Have a

nice day together, and if you could just give him a message from me? Tell him it's Hannah now, not Hanny, because Hanny has gone forever.'

Walking out was one thing, but what was she going to do now? She had to think this through. This must be why he had changed. All that talk about writing shifts on the calendar, plus the clean bedding could mean only one thing: they had been in her bed. What could she have done wrong to make him look elsewhere? She could feel the tears rolling down her face.

The next thing she was aware of was sitting in the park, watching the young mums and their children playing on the swings. That was what she had wanted for her and Jimmy, but it wasn't going to happen now. How could she ever trust him again?

Her phone was ringing again: she must have dozens of missed calls and texts from him by now but she wasn't going to reply. Not until she knew what she wanted to do next, at least. But there was one call she was going to make. She needed the person she always turned to when she need to talk.

'Hi, Nan, it's me. It's over. He's found someone else; she's been in my home, in my bed! I don't know what to do.'

'Hannah, darling, slow down. Take some deep breaths. I've got all the time in the world to listen. Now start at the beginning.'

Half an hour later, Hannah had explained the whole story to Betty. Nan had just listened to her, making no comments other than a repeated reassurance that she was there for her. Then they discussed what would happen next.

The one thing they both agreed on was that Hannah had to sit down and talk to Jimmy at some point. Today might not be a good time to do that, but she couldn't put it off for long. Thankfully they only rented their flat, as Hannah knew she never wanted to live there again.

She made a quick call to the hotel to see if there were any staff rooms available for the night. This wouldn't seem too unusual to anyone: staff working late shifts and coming back early the next morning were allowed to stay the night. As for her uniform, she had a couple of spare sets in her locker. She would be alright.

An hour later she was back in central London, sadly wandering from one coffee shop to another, killing time before heading to the hotel. Just one more thing had to be done today: she had to send a text to Jimmy, who was still trying to call her.

'Staying at hotel tonight. We need to talk tomorrow. Hannah.'

No 'love, Hanny' or kisses at the end of the text. It was over. This was the end of the university romance that she had thought would last forever. It was over: time to move on.

Her dreams had disappeared but they weren't only hers, they were his too. They had both worked so hard so that their dreams might become a reality one day: owning their own home and, more importantly, having a family together. How could he do this? What had she done wrong, to make him want to cheat on her? There were so many questions she wanted to ask him, but perhaps it was for the best she didn't know. It was over.

Chapter 3

Hannah didn't sleep well. She was at her desk by six-thirty, emails cleared and ready for her meeting with Henry. She had received a text from the head receptionist Karen, who wanted to know if she had any idea what the meeting was about. Hannah had a good idea, but she wasn't going to say anything to Karen.

'Thank you for coming in early, Hannah, take a seat.' Henry waved her into the meeting room. 'We just need to wait for Karen and then I'll explain everything. Oh, I should mention that Fiona from HR will also be attending.'

That said it all. It was something to do with her contract and more money-saving measures. Hannah wasn't daft; she had thought a few weeks ago that this might happen. Both she and Karen were managers and, now that the reception and reservation teams were being merged, only one manager would be necessary. It was not a job she wanted for herself, especially now that she was cutting ties with Jimmy.

She was right. Fiona did the talking. Essentially, one of them had to go. The roles of Reservation Manager and Reception Manager were being made redundant and both of them could apply for the new position of Rooms Manager, which would cover both job roles. Karen started to cry. She needed this job as she was a single mother with a mortgage.

'I'm really sorry for both of you,' Henry told them. 'I've enjoyed working with you, but the hotel structure has to change. We need to move the hotel forward.'

Hannah cut across his apologies.

'Let me stop you there, Henry. I understand all

that, and I've enjoyed my time working here as well, but it's time for me to move on. I won't be applying for the Rooms Manager position. Please give it to Karen; you know she's the best person for the job. I'll just take my redundancy and go, if that's okay. And while I'm here, I realise I can't go right away and the transition will probably take a couple of months, but I'd like to take some of the holiday that's owed to me from today if that's possible. I need to start planning for my future.'

She could see the relief on Henry and Fiona's faces. This meant no messy interview process to disrupt their work. They would be stupid if they didn't give the job to Karen: she knew the hotel inside and out.

They agreed that Hannah would take two weeks holiday and come back for six weeks after that before being made redundant. It wasn't looking for a job that was on Hannah's mind, however, it was Jimmy. Like the hotel, he was becoming another part of her past, but they had things to sort out between them before she could walk away. It wasn't going to be easy

It was only eleven o'clock when Hannah walked back into the flat. She thought that Jimmy might have been there as his shift didn't start until three, but he wasn't. She made herself a coffee and then set to making a plan of action. Did she really want to discuss losing her job with him? He wasn't going to be a part of her life anymore, so why talk about it? The first thing she noticed as she walked into the bedroom was her suitcase on top of the wardrobe. It didn't take much thought. She knew where she wanted to go: to Betty's. Yes, to her Nan's, her real home, the place where she could plan her future without the added stress of Jimmy being there.

Hannah texted Jimmy from the train: 'Off to Nan's for a few weeks. Hannah.'

When she had travelled in the opposite direction only a few days ago she had been full of questions about her family. This time the questions were all about her. She was worn out. She needed a break and she knew Betty would give her the space she needed to breathe.

'Come on in, darling!' Betty exclaimed. 'I've cooked us a nice roast: your favourite, lamb. And yes, I'm making Yorkshire puddings, and I've thrown together a trifle for afters.'

'You don't throw anything together, Nan. All your cooking is planned and lovely. A roast? Well, that's all my problems sorted out in one meal. I know Yorkshire puddings go with beef, not lamb so thank you for spoiling me. Thank you for letting me come.'

'Darling, this is your home. It always has been and always will be. Now put your case and bags in your room and let me pour us both a gin and tonic. Then we can have a good chat.'

Hannah felt better already. Just being here with Nan helped all of her job and relationship problems seem much smaller than they had in London. Being here would also give her an opportunity to find out what was worrying Nan.

'I've unpacked and I'm ready for that gin! How long until dinner? I'm starving. I can never understand how some people stop eating when they have drama and problems going on in their lives. I'm the complete opposite.'

For the next couple of hours Hannah and Betty chatted about what sort of job Hannah might want to do. They both agreed that finding a job should come before finding somewhere to live, and a lot of hotels would supply accommodation for staff. With her experience she would be able to pick and choose. Did she want to stay in reservation or reception, or make a bigger change and move over to the catering or admin side of hotels? It was a blank page: the world was her oyster.

Finally Hannah sat back from the dinner table with a sigh.

'That meal was beautiful, Nan, thank you so much. I'm so full that I think the trifle will have to wait a bit. I don't think I've got room for it yet.'

'Can I just ask one thing, darling? In all this talk of jobs and finding somewhere to live there hasn't been any mention of Jimmy. Are you really sure you want to count him out entirely? You wouldn't consider giving him a second chance?'

'A second chance would lead to a third and a fourth. No, if he wants someone else and not me I know that time is up. No, it's over. It needs to be a fresh start, not just for me, but for him as well. Perhaps our relationship should have ended when we left university.'

'Good, I was hoping you'd say that. Life would be difficult if you were still together. You'd always have a feeling in the back of your mind that he was up to something.'

'Exactly. So, Nan, now that we've sorted my life out, I think it's time for you to tell me what's on your mind. You're worried about something, I can tell.'

'You can read me like a book, Hannah. There's no hiding anything from you. I'm not really worried about anything, it's just that I have a few decisions to make and I don't want to do the wrong thing.'

'Decisions about what? Is it something to do with your health? Why haven't you said something before?'

'No, nothing to do with my health. It concerns Luckett House. I have to decide whether or not to sell it.'

'Sell Luckett House? You can't! It's been in our family for generations. It's a huge part of our lives, and it's the best place on Earth. Why sell it?'

'Because it needs money spending on it. No

rental company will have it on its books unless I update a few things, and they're not minor things. It will need central heating: a radiator in every room, which would mean a new boiler. We'd also have to install fire doors, a couple of the windows need replacing, and that's all before we do any decorating or re-carpeting. I just don't have the money to do all that. The money I've earned from renting it out over the summer these last few years barely covered the costs. Also, and please don't be angry about this, perhaps it is the right thing to do.'

'Why would I be angry?'

'Susanna thinks it would be a good idea to sell it and give any extra money I make to your dad so that they can buy a bigger house. I think she might be right.'

Hannah was fuming. Who did Susanna think she was? She had no connection to Luckett Quay: she hated the place, and she had always refused to stay in Luckett House. This was the place Hannah had grown up in!

There had to be a solution: no way was she going to let Betty sell it. But if worst came to worst and it had to be sold, Susanna wouldn't get her hands on the money. Anything that came out of that house was Betty's to enjoy, but as long as Hannah was around money wouldn't be a part of the equation. It was about saving Luckett House and stopping it from going on the market at all.

'Nan, there has to be a solution. Surely central heating isn't *that* expensive, and a few doors on top of that... no, I won't let this happen. Between the two of us we will sort this out.'

Once they had gone up to bed, Hannah started Googling plumbers in Norfolk and the average price for central heating installation. It was true, fire doors weren't cheap, but they could surely afford them. Hannah couldn't help thinking that if she was feeling this bad about losing the house, Betty must be feeling worse. The whole situation was so sad, but she would find a way to turn it around. Just how she would do it, well, that was the sixty-million-dollar question.

Chapter 4

'Are you sure we're doing the right thing, Hannah? It's only February and the house will be freezing. I'm not sure if my old car will get us there either. Do you think we've thought this through enough?'

'Yes. The car will get us there. I agree that the house will be cold, but we have enough things packed to keep us warm. Plus, if we light the fires we can move the beds into the living room and it'll be like camping. It's going to be fun, Nan, and once we're there, we'll be able to put a plan of action together. I know one thing for certain: Susanna will not be in that plan.'

'I suppose one good thing is that we'll see the house at its worst in the middle of winter. When were you last in Norfolk?'

'I'm not sure. It must have been at least three years ago, and then it was just for a weekend. Jimmy wasn't a lover of the place. He likes his foreign holidays, like Ibiza: loud music and lots of parties. I enjoyed those holidays we had together as well, but this isn't about holidays, this is about our home, the family home. Look, only another twenty miles and we'll be back in beautiful Norfolk.'

Hannah didn't let on to Betty, but she was worried that she might have made the wrong choice in coming to Norfolk in the middle of winter. They would be camping, and was that a good thing at Betty's age? The house would also look sad in the cold and wet, and not the happy exciting place it always was in the summer holidays. Worst of all, how would they cope if there really was tons of work to be done?

She was still worrying as she turned off the main road towards the sea.

'Almost there, Nan! Do you want to call into the shop in Saltmarsh Quay and get a few things, or should we investigate the house first?'

'I think we'd best get it over with. Let's see it at its worst. I have a feeling we might not be staying long.'

The road down to Luckett House was steep and very narrow. It was the last house in the lane, and Hannah slowed down to look at the other three properties as they passed them by. God, she didn't recognise them! They looked like something you would see on Grand Designs. She remembered them being little cottages but now they were like million-dollar Californian homes. She pulled up at the gate to Luckett House. If the gate's condition reflected that of the house, Betty had been right. It did need money spending on it.

'Can you believe what we just drove past, Nan? When did that happen? Those houses are stunning.'

'Yes, I know. I've had several people contact me over the years to see if I would sell them mine so that they could do the same: knock it down and build something new. It wasn't the house they wanted, just the plot of land. I couldn't sell just to see them destroy it, but perhaps I don't have an option anymore.'

They drove cautiously into the driveway and Hannah held the car door open for Betty. Betty found her keys and in they went.

It felt warmer outdoors than in. Everything inside the house looked dark and gloomy.

The first room they went into was the kitchen on the front of the property. Hannah could feel a lump in her throat as she looked at the big table. It was still there: the table that she had eaten her meals off; the table where both her mum and Nan had spent hours making crafts with her, Olivia, and Tom; the table her father had joked about being the place where Hannah's nappies had been changed.

21

They moved on to the room opposite. This was a room that never really got used except as an extra bedroom if aunts, uncles, and cousins came to stay.

Next they went down the corridor to the back of the house. Light was shining through the window even on this dark, cloudy February day. In front of them, across a huge room, was what this house was all about: the view. Just past the end of the garden and continuing for miles into the distance was the sea. It was choppy, but that didn't take away the happiness that came from seeing it. Not one day that she had spent here was unpleasant to remember. This was a happy place, and suddenly Hannah didn't feel cold anymore. The outside temperature might be freezing but that couldn't take away the warmth the house gave her inside.

'We're home, Nan. This is where we both belong.'

They hugged each other with tears in their eyes, both knowing that Luckett House was not for sale, whatever the price. Once they had taken a look upstairs, lit the fire and unpacked the car, Hannah and Betty both felt that things weren't as bad as they had expected. The rental agency had kept it very clean and tidy.

Even so, they could see that things needed to be done to improve the place. A plan of action was required. Hannah thought it might help her if the agency sent somebody round to point out all the work required. She also needed to find someone to carry out all these renovations, and another downside to being here was the lack of Wi-Fi. That problem could be worked around, however.

'Come on, let's go and get some provisions in. By the time we get back the house will be nice and toasty. I thought we could go up to Saltmarsh Cliff Hotel for a drink while I use the internet, and then we can nip down to the little shop in Saltmarsh Quay for some bits.'

The hotel had been refurbished since Hannah had last been there. They had a snack in the bar, and Hannah noted down some names of local builders from the internet. It felt strange to be here as an adult. When she was a child she had known all the staff by name. The hotel gardens were her playground, half-way between Luckett Quay and Olivia and Tom's homes in Saltmarsh Quay. Looking out from the bar she could see the trees that they used to climb. See, she thought, not everything has changed. The trees live on, and Luckett House will too.

Just as they were leaving, someone called out their names. They turned around and saw Olivia's mum, Jenny.

'Hello, Jenny!' Betty hurried over to her. 'Gosh, how many years has it been since we last saw you? It must be at least ten. How are you?'

'I'm fine thank you, but look at you, Hannah, all grown up! Are you married? How many children have you got? Our Olivia has two! Yes, two little boys, six and four. Oh, wait until I've told her I saw you! We often talk about the old days: you kids playing all day long. That little gang of three, or as you used to call it "the HOT gang"! H for Hannah, O for Olivia, and T for Tom. How times have changed, although not so much for me: I'm still cleaning rooms here at the hotel. How long are you here for? You must go down to see our Olivia and the boys. Sadly there's no husband in the picture, he's gone off and left her. Didn't like the responsibility – but that's another story.'

Neither Betty or Hannah could get a word in edgeways with Jenny; it was like she was on a train, getting faster and faster with no brakes. Eventually they swapped phone numbers, and Hannah promised to give Olivia a call before they left. She had forgotten all about the HOT gang and it made her smile to remember. It had all been so many years ago. She and Betty laughed about old times all the way to Saltmarsh Quay.

They bought enough food to see them through the next few days, but they decided not much cooking would be done that night. Instead, they'd go and eat at the Maple Duck pub on the outskirts of Luckett Quay.

Hannah's phone rang. It was a girl from the rental agency calling to say someone could meet them at the property tomorrow afternoon, a Mr Goring. Tristan Goring. The name seemed familiar to Betty and she soon remembered that he was one of the people that had contacted her about selling Luckett House. What was he doing working for the rental agency? It all seemed very strange to her, but not to Hannah. She suspected that all this business about having to do expensive work to the house was just so that Betty would sell up and go.

'I think meeting Mr Tristan Goring could be quite interesting. I'll be ready for him, but somehow I don't think he'll be ready for me: a woman who's just lost her job and with a boyfriend shopping elsewhere. I think tomorrow could be the time I let all the anger and frustration out. Poor Mr Goring! Something to sleep on, I think. But before sleep, something to eat!'

They had a lovely meal in the pub. It hadn't changed at all over the years, still the same friendly atmosphere. They chatted to a few of the locals and when they mentioned where they were staying they told them it had a new nickname: Millionaires' Hill. One man explained that a development company was gradually buying all the plots up, demolishing, rebuilding, then moving on to the next one as soon as the house was sold. This was just what they wanted to hear. There was no way anyone was getting their hands on Luckett House for any amount of money. There had to be a way of keeping it in the family, and both of them were ready to put up a fight.

Chapter 5

Hannah and Betty both had a good night's sleep. They weren't cold in the night thanks to all the clothes they wore to bed, and a little help from the bottle or two of wine they had drunk after coming back from the pub.

It was almost seven o'clock when they got up. The sea was a lot calmer than it had been the day before, and they shared coffee and toast in front of the big picture window, watching the fishing boats in the distance. Finding a job wasn't remotely on Hannah's mind now. Today would be all about getting to the bottom of why Betty had to do the house up.

'I've been thinking, Nan, perhaps it would be good if I wasn't around when this Tristan chap comes calling. That's not to say I won't be in the room next door listening, of course, but I think it'll be rather interesting to see which hat he's wearing: rental agency rep or potential buyer. What do you think?'

'I think if he says anything out of place he'll soon regret ever meeting you, darling. The pressure cooker you've got inside of you will blow.'

'You could be right. What would you like to do with the morning while we wait? It's no good me phoning any of the potential workmen until we've had this afternoon meeting. Is there anyone you'd like to visit?'

'No, but do you know what I'd really like? A walk around the quay. I know there's not a lot to see, but I was wondering if the little short cut down to the beach was still open at the bottom of the garden, and if we wrap up well I'm sure we'll be okay to try it out.'

Hannah knew every inch of Luckett Quay. When she was young the place had seemed huge to her, but by the time she was a teenager it felt tiny – too small even to be a village. It was little more than eight houses on a hillside, looking out to sea, without a shop or a streetlight to call its own. But now, as they headed out into the February chill, she knew that this was home, regardless of its size, and she would fight tooth and nail to keep it in the family for generations to come.

The path was still there and surprisingly well worn. It looked as if it was used regularly. It was also slippery with mud. They took their time descending, and Hannah was glad that she had insisted Betty bring a stick with her to help with her balance.

Approximately 15 minutes later they emerged from the little wooded area with the sea in front of them, close by the steps leading down from the car park. Hannah could see a few people walking on the beach. She remembered people joking about the word 'quay', asking how this could be a quayside without boats. Many hundreds of years ago there had been a quay here, but now it was as Hannah had always known it: a little beach that let you walk as far as Saltmarsh Quay when the tide was out, where there would be fishing boats, as well as small yachts and little cabin cruisers moored to the harbour wall. She had once called this her beach. She felt a little excited coming down the old path again. Would her cave still be there? The tide was out, so it should be.

They slowly made their way down the beach. Looking back, they could see Luckett House above them. Nothing had changed here. The view brought back so many happy memories of her parents and grandparents shouting to her from the window for lunch or dinner. It felt incomplete, however.

'Is there one missing? I thought there were eight houses on that ridge, but I can only count seven. Are the trees blocking it?'

'No, you're right. Old Mrs Ingham's house has

gone. I knew that she must have died by now, but I thought someone new might have moved in. We can walk back up the steps later and see what's happened. Those new ones do look good up there, don't you think?'

'Yes, they're stunning, but not as warm and welcoming as ours.'

They walked to the opposite end of the beach to the other walkers and sat on a rock. The wind had dropped, and they stayed a while, gazing down the beach. It was the same view they could get from the house, but it had a completely different feel from down here.

'I still can't get over why this is called a quay,' Betty said. 'I know I've been saying it for more than fifty years, but a quayside is somewhere where boats come and go. There's not even a jetty here. This is a cove, or a bay at most. What's so funny?'

'Like you said, you've been saying it for years. Just accept it for what it is – it's historical, not accurate. How many places get called a marina without a boat in sight, or water come to that? Come on, let's make our way up before we get too cold.'

As they walked toward the steps they passed a few other people also heading in the same direction. Everyone smiled, said hello and commented on how beautiful it was here.'

'Are you on holiday?' one woman asked Hannah.

'No, not really. My Nan owns that house up there, but we've not been here for quite a while. It's strange the way you don't realise how much you miss the place until you come back. Are you visiting?'

'Sort of. My family used to own that house up there. Well, not that brand new one, but the plot it's built on. I moved to Sheringham a long time ago but you're right, I didn't realise how much I missed the place until today. It must be all of forty years since I've been on this beach. I'm Josie, and this is my son

Richard. He lives in London.'

'Nice to meet you. I'm Hannah, and this is my Nan, Betty. Would you like to walk in front? We might be a bit slow.'

'Oh, we aren't in a hurry. I can't get over the size of those new houses. Why don't they build little ones, and more of them?'

'Why do you ask? Would you like to move back?'

'It's strange that you ask, but I think I would.'

Josie might have chatted for longer, but Richard wanted to move on before it got too cold. Once they were out of earshot, Betty commented on how sad Josie had looked.

They made their way back up the hill and found that they were right: there was a house missing. There was a metal fence around the plot, and it looked like something new was going to be built on the land.

'I think we're going to have the scruffiest house on the hill,' Betty marvelled. 'If this is going to be like the others, ours will stick out like a sore thumb.'

'Yes, and for the better! All of these look lovely, but Luckett House is special. Now, let's go and get ready for this Tristan chap.'

*

Hannah left the door to the lounge from the corridor wedged open so once Betty had showed Mr Goring in she would be able to nip out of the kitchen and listen to what he had to say. Peeping through the net curtains, Hannah watched a big flash Jaguar pull onto the drive and out he got. He was a handsome man, very smart and respectable looking. She was faintly shocked, but then she didn't really know what to expect.

Betty let him in and off they went into the lounge. Betty did exactly what Hannah had asked her to, making a little bit of extra noise so he wouldn't hear her coming out of the kitchen.

'Thank you for coming, Mr Goring. I really appreciate it. I do understand the problems the house has. I just need to go through the details with you so that I can get it fixed up as soon as possible, ready for the next season.'

'Oh, I wasn't sure you would bother with fixing everything. I thought you might decide to sell instead. You would get a very good price for the property.'

'Do you think so? I don't expect I would get much. Who would want an old house like this?'

'Plenty of people are looking for second homes here in Norfolk and the view you get here is magnificent. I'm sure the money you would get would be significantly more than you could make over many years of rental income. I reckon you could probably get at least a third of a million pounds. Doesn't that interest you, Betty – you don't mind me calling you Betty?'

'No, not at all.'

'And that would be without spending a penny on it. Just think what you could do with that money, Betty. You could treat your family to lots of lovely holidays, and you wouldn't have the worries of Luckett House on your shoulders. I really do think you should give it some thought.'

Hannah was ready to go. She had heard enough. Five, four, three, two, one...

'Hello, nice to meet you, I'm Betty's granddaughter. Thank you for coming along to point us in the right direction. We're novices really and I'm sure you can help us sort out Luckett House.'

'Hello, I was just saying to your grandmother how you could get...'

'Yes, I heard what you said: a third of a million pounds. That's an awful lot of money, and Nan could do so much with it, but one million sounds a lot better. That's what was paid for the plot of land they're starting to build on down the street, and I also know that the old property that has been replaced by one of the new ones at the top of the hill sold for eight hundred thousand. The power of the internet, Tristan, but of course you know that, as you're part of the company that's been involved in the developments. Excuse me if I'm mistaken, but something here sounds wrong. No, wrong's not quite the word. Nan, can you think of a better one?'

'Oh yes, darling, illegal sounds a lot better. Don't you think so, young man?'

'There is nothing illegal about it...'

'Well, Mr Flash Tristan, that might be the case but I'm just glad I've recorded your conversation with this vulnerable seventy-year-old lady. You know where the door is, and I'm counting. You have until I get to ten to be off my Nan's land. One, two...'

The door closed as Hannah got to five. He was gone for now, but she could be sure that wouldn't be the last they would see of him.

'You weren't recording it were you, Hannah? It's a shame. He seemed like a nice young man.'

'Of course not, but he doesn't know that, does he? That was a bit of fun, but it doesn't solve the problem of Luckett House. Things need doing to get it up to standard. That was something he wasn't lying about and to be honest I don't have a solution that doesn't involve a big lottery win.'

They both jumped out of their skins as the doorbell went. Surely he hadn't come back? Hannah went to answer it and there on the doorstep was – surely not! She could barely believe it.

'Hello, Hannah! Welcome back to Luckett Quay.'

'Olivia! Come in, it's so good to see you! Your mum was telling us yesterday that you have two sons, how exciting is that?'

'Exciting is not the word I'd use. Exhausting is probably more appropriate.'

Olivia followed Hannah into the lounge and after hugs and kisses with Betty, started to tell them all about her life. Even though she was living as a single mother she was happy and content with her lot.

'My life's simple. Nothing exciting happens but I'm really happy. My parents are both well, they have the boys a lot, and their other grandparents have them over as well. I'm lucky in that respect. So, tell me about your flash life in London! Big parties with lots of famous people?'

'You must be joking! My life consisted of hours on dirty, crowded tubes, hours on the phone taking room bookings – oh, and hours spent cleaning up after a boyfriend. Nothing so glamorous, I'm afraid.'

Hannah explained about what had happened with Jimmy and the hotel, and how once they got Luckett House sorted out she would start to look for a new job.

'Oh dear, I thought my job was bad! Actually, no. I do like my job, or should I say jobs? I clean, just like my mum does. Holiday lets, mainly, but it's good. People are very kind and generous and with the money the ex gives me for the boys I'm okay. By the way, have you seen Tom since you've been here?'

'No, I haven't, how is he? What's he doing with his life? I always imagined he'd be a teacher, or a top businessman. Why are you laughing, Olivia?'

'Because his only pupils are his plants! He stayed here in the area and he's a gardener. A lot of his work comes from people who are getting older and can't do much for themselves. He cuts grass and trims hedges. He's happy. Had a few girlfriends over the years, but the minute they mention wanting to settle down and have a family he runs a mile. No, I can't see Tom with children, just plants.

'We must have an evening out. I need to go for now, as I've got a flat to clean before I pick the kids up from my mum's. It's one of my easiest jobs, doesn't take long. Do you remember the big houses overlooking Saltmarsh Quay? They're a bit like this one, double fronted. Well, a few of them have been converted into flats: two up, two down. They're very modern, but it still keeps the old character.'

Hannah didn't hear anything else Olivia said. Flats! That was the answer to Betty's problem. Convert Luckett House into flats, sell three, and keep one for herself, with no more worrying about rentals.

'I'm off, Hannah, Betty.'

'Oh, sorry, Olivia, I was miles away. Yes, a night out, just like we used to have. Cans of cider on the sea wall, what do you say to that?'

'I say no to cans, we're old enough to go into the pubs now! I'll give you a call once I know when Mum can have the boys for an evening. It's lovely to see you both.'

'Nan...'

'Hannah, are you thinking what I'm thinking?'

'I think so, but wouldn't you find that sad?'

'Sad? No! The building wouldn't get knocked down: it would look the same from the outside, and we'd still be able to come and stay. It could work; I've seen it done at home. My friend Madge lives in one. The money we make from selling the other three flats will pay for the conversion. So the big question is which one shall we have? Upstairs or down? On the left side or the right?'

'This is exciting, Nan, but how do we go about it?'

'I don't know, darling. Perhaps you need to apologise to Tristan Goring. He might be able to help, as he's a property developer.'

'You must be joking! I never want to see him again, let alone speak to him.'

Betty told Hannah all about the big converted Victorian house that Madge lived in. She had never seen it as one house: it was converted before she viewed it.

33

'She's on the ground floor with a little terrace. Her bedroom is at the front, then the bathroom and a big lounge behind that with a little kitchen on the back wall. It's snug, but not small, and having the ceilings so high up makes it feel big. Her bills are small, as well. It's perfect for her.'

Chapter 6

The following morning Hannah and Betty were up early. They were excited but didn't have a clue how to go about anything. They didn't even know which questions to ask, let alone to whom. Betty's suggestion of apologising to Flash Tristan would be a last resort.

Hannah did have one idea. If they walked around Saltmarsh Quay to look at some of the conversions, there might be builders working on one, you never knew. It might also be worth asking Olivia who had cleaned conversions. This was a real adventure, but at least both of them were on the same page. There were exciting times ahead.

'Darling, I was thinking we could walk to Saltmarsh today. I know it would take a while, but we could get a taxi back. It's not raining, and the wind has died down. What do you say?'

'If you think you're up to it, it's okay with me. We could stop at Saltmarsh Cliff Hotel for a coffee, which would break up the walk. Also, I'm quite interested to see if there's any building work going on as we head down from the hotel into the quay.'

The previous night they had walked around and around Luckett House planning what sort of conversion could work. They wanted both a two bedroom and one-bedroom flat upstairs and the same downstairs. All four flats would have their lounges at the back of the house and would have a sea view from the bedrooms at the front. A bathroom could go in between the two rooms and, as the lounge would be big, the kitchen could be put in one corner of it. That kind of detail was what they were struggling to figure out. This was where it would be good to look at some that had already been converted. Hannah wondered if she would be able to have a look at the one Olivia cleaned.

Notebooks in bags and phones charged they set out on their mission. Once they made the top of the hill the hotel was just a few hundred yards down the other side. Coffee and bacon sandwiches sounded like the perfect start to their day. Betty ordered, while Hannah logged on to the hotel's Wi-Fi.

'What are you looking at, darling?'

'Properties for sale in the area; I just wondered if there were any converted houses. You never know, we could get some ideas from them. Bingo! There is one! It's actually two flats in the same house. I'll give the agent a call and see if we can view it today.'

'But we don't want to buy one. Isn't that a bit cheeky, Hannah?'

'Yes, no – I don't really know.'

'Two coffees and two bacon sandwiches, sorry it took so long. We're a bit short staffed today.'

'No problem, thank you. This looks lovely, well worth the wait.'

Hannah showed Betty some photos on her phone. The flats were empty and it looked like they had just been converted, which was good. They both realised there would be a lot more to getting the conversion right than the building work itself. Firstly they needed architect's plans, then planning permission. Most importantly, they needed the money to do it. Once the three spare flats had been sold there would be money, but they needed it at the start of the project, not the end. There were so many questions and issues to sort out.

'Do you think we're just running away with this idea?' Hannah wondered. 'Does it all seem a bit of a dream to you? Oh, there's my phone ... Yes, thank you ... We appreciate that ... three o'clock then, thank you.'

She hung up and turned back to Betty. 'That was

the estate agent. They'll meet us at three o'clock at the house, so that gives us four hours to walk around the quay.'

'Yes, and at least Saltmarsh can be called a quay. It has boats, jetties, even a fish market.'

They paid the bill, put their hats and coats back on and headed for the nice bit of the walk down the coastal path into the quay. They knew it like the back of their hands. They had walked it hundreds of times. When Hannah was little the treat when they arrived was fish and chips eaten on the sea wall. It was too cold to stop and sit on one of the seats on the path and the view wasn't that good today without the sunshine. The breeze was getting up as well, but once at the bottom they would be sheltered.

'Nothing's changed. Some houses have had a lick of fresh paint but there are no new ones. It's a shame we ate those bacon sandwiches, we could have had fish and chips for lunch.'

'Yes, but we could have them for tea if we stay over here long enough.'

'That's a deal. Now comes the hard part. We'll take a walk around all the little streets, looking for houses that are being worked on, builders' vans with phone numbers on, or For Sale signs. We're going to have a day of being detectives or, to put it another way, being nosey.'

'That's not a problem for me, darling, I've had nearly seventy years' practice.'

To their joint surprise there were plumbers' and electricians' vans aplenty in Saltmarsh Quay. Everything was written down in their notebooks. There were a few little cottages for sale as well, all with the same estate agency who was selling the flats they were going to view. Sadly their office was in nearby Well Next the Sea.

As they turned the corner into one of the side streets Hannah stopped in her tracks. There was someone digging up a front garden ahead of them – it was Tom! He hadn't noticed them yet. How could she surprise him without frightening him to death? A tap on the shoulder? A clap of her hands? No.

'Excuse me, aren't you the T in HOT, young man?'

He turned around and the smile on his face was as huge as it had always been. He looked the same, just a little older with different hair.

'Hello, Hannah! And Betty, it's so lovely to see you both! What brings you here? Oh, silly of me: Luckett House, of course. I bet you've noticed a difference over on the hill with all those flash new properties. I'm surprised yours hasn't been snapped up by the property company doing all the building. They've taken over Luckett Quay. Do you know what the new nickname is?'

'Yes, Millionaires Hill. But as for selling Luckett House, you must be joking! Talking of that property company, do you know anything about them? I think they sound a bit ruthless.'

'I will say, Tom, one of them was nearly killed yesterday when he over-stepped the mark with Hannah.'

'Let me guess, it wouldn't be someone by the name of Tristan? You wouldn't be the first. How long are you here for? We must have a night out. Have you seen Olivia yet? She's got two kids, really lovely boys, and she's doing a marvellous job bringing them up on her own. I try to help with the boys' stuff, you know: football, making dens, that kind of thing.'

'Yes, we saw her last night. A night out would be grand. You might also be able to help us with a few questions if you've got a spare hour or so.'

'What sort of questions?'

Hannah explained the situation with the house and what they were up to today. Tom said he had lots of contacts that they might want to consider getting in touch with. He could pop around to the house tomorrow if they liked. He also thought that getting planning permission would be easy so long as they weren't changing the look of the property from the outside. Apparently the local council was getting fed up with all the flashy new builds. They were more into preserving the traditional appearance of Norfolk flint homes. Thanking him, they said their goodbyes and headed off along the road.

'Now that young man would make a lovely boyfriend for someone, don't you think, Hannah?'

Hannah ignored her. Tom was more like a cousin to her. They had grown up together. She couldn't look at him in a romantic way and he would definitely feel the same about her. Anyway, Olivia had said he didn't want kids and she wanted a dozen. Well, two or three would do, but it was still a far cry from the life Tom would be after.

'Come on, best foot forward. Let's get up to the property. If we get there early and hang around someone from the other flats might start chatting to us.'

The house conversion was nearly at the top of Saltmarsh Quay. It was a detached house in a row of five similar builds with fabulous views down into the harbour. One flat had curtains up and another one looked like it was being decorated.

First of all they walked around the back to see how much garden there was. Why they did this they didn't know, as they had no intention of buying the place. Then they took a look through the downstairs windows. These flats were laid out the opposite way around to their plans for Luckett House, with the lounges at the front. No one came out so they just had to wait for the estate agent.

Finally a young girl arrived. She was obviously just an office worker who had been asked to show them around as she hadn't a clue how to even get in the house.

'Good afternoon, I'm not late, am I? My boss said three o'clock. I'm Emmi, by the way.'

'No, we are early. Thank you for the appointment at such short notice.'

She showed them into the first flat on the ground floor. It was very basic and straightforward. The bathroom was between the lounge and the bedroom just like they wanted to do, but in this one they had cut part of the lounge off to make the kitchen a separate room. Neither Betty nor Hannah liked that idea.

The upstairs flat was a bigger one. This had two bedrooms and the kitchen was against the back wall with an island unit separating it from the seating area. This was it. Betty and Hannah were smiling. This was just what they could do at Luckett House.

Emmi spent the whole time on her phone texting. She wasn't a bit interested in whether they wanted to buy it or not and never once pointed out any of the features, let alone tried to sell them one of the flats. That was just as well, as it meant they didn't have to make up stories as to why they were viewing the property.

'Thank you, Emmi, I think we've seen everything. Just one question: could you tell us the name of the building company that did the conversion?'

She looked completely blank, like they had asked her how to get to the moon. Eventually she phoned her office and they told her it was Fern and Fern. It seemed an odd name: you would think it would be Fern and Son, or the Fern Brothers.

'Thanks again. We will be in touch.'

'Sorry, why will you be in touch?'

'If we decide to buy the property?'

Could anyone be that thick? They laughed all the way back down to the quayside but they were feeling good. The kitchen in the lounge idea would work.

Now to Google Fern and Fern and find out their phone numbers.

'We've earned our fish and chips, Nan. It might be a bit early still, but the pub's bound to be open. Two gin and tonics, I think.'

She looked at the sign on the chip shop door as they passed. It said they opened at five pm, so that gave them an hour: probably enough time for two gins!

They found a little corner in the pub and read over the details of the flats that Emmi had given them. They gave the dimensions of the rooms, so once they got back to Luckett House they could measure them to see if the same was feasible there. They had to be careful to remember that the bathrooms had to come out of the front bedrooms' floor space. This was exciting but, and there was always a but, they hadn't figured out how to pay for it.

As they were discussing this, the door of the pub opened and in walked Josie and Richard who they had met on the beach yesterday.

'Hello again, another nice winter's day, isn't it? Not as clear a view as yesterday, though.'

'You're having another day over here?'

'Yes, this time we're viewing some properties here in Saltmarsh. I've made my mind up to move back after all these years.'

'Have you seen anything you like?'

'Not really. They're all a bit too big and I realise as I'm getting older perhaps I should be looking at properties without stairs. A flat, perhaps, as long as it's got two bedrooms, but its early days yet.'

Hannah and Betty looked at each other. They were thinking the same thing, but should they say something? Would they be jinxing it? Betty spoke first:

'We've just viewed two flats at the top of the

village. Both are very nice, perfect for one person.'

'So are you thinking of moving here from Luckett Quay?'

'Oh no, but since I've started this conversation, and we would appreciate it if you don't repeat this, I'm hoping to convert Luckett House into four flats. It's very early days. We don't even have planning permission or a builder yet.'

'So you would be selling some of them? I'd be very interested if you do. Like I said, that was where I was born and lived until I had to move away.'

'You had to move away, Josie?'

'No, I meant chose, sorry.'

They chatted about the flats for a while. Richard seemed really interested and they exchanged phone numbers. There would be one problem: the house would only have two flats big enough for two bedrooms and Hannah was sure that Betty would want one of them. But as they all said, it was very early days and it might never happen. Having said their goodbyes, it was time for fish and chips.

'Tell you what, Nan, I'll nip up to the little shop and see if they have any chalk, then get us a bottle of wine and book a taxi before we get the fish and chips. And one other thing I need to do is the thing I've been ignoring for days: answer Jimmy's texts to let him know where I am, and that I'm okay.

As they waited for the fish and chips to be cooked she texted Jimmy to tell him she was with Betty in Luckett Quay and she would contact him again once she was back in the Midlands. As she pressed send it crossed her mind that this was the first time she'd given him any thought all day. Come to that, he hadn't even entered her head. Was she actually over him? More importantly, was she ready to move to on a new life? A single life, that was what she needed: no boyfriend, just herself.

Back at Luckett House, neither of them knew

what they were most excited about, diving into the fish and chips or getting stuck into marking out floor plans for the flats. Fish and chips came first, since they were best eaten hot.

'You can't beat seaside fish and chips,' Betty declared. 'They are the best. I could eat them every day.'

'Yes, but that wouldn't be very sensible. Right, are you ready? Where shall we start: flat one, two, three, or four?'

'You've named them already? Which is which?'

'I think number one has to be the one you'll own, don't you think?'

Over the next five hours they marked out each room with the chalk. They laughed so much; it looked like a crime scene with all the markings on the floors, but it worked perfectly. As long as the bathrooms could go in-between, everything else should be straightforward.

Hannah was able to get in touch with Fern and Fern, and a Brian Fern agreed to pop round the next day. She hadn't told him what she had in mind, just that she needed a quote for a little bit of building work. Then she went off to phone Jimmy, as she felt her text had been a bit abrupt.

Betty poured another glass of wine and pulled her chair around to look out the window as she waited. It was dark, so she couldn't see much, just some flickering lights out at sea from fishing boats coming and going in the night.

Hannah was some time, and apologised as she came back in.

'Sorry, Nan, I couldn't get him off the phone. He kept saying how sorry he was and could I forgive him but like I kept telling him, it's not about being sorry, it's about moving on. We've outgrown each other. You must be tired. I know I am, but I feel like the fresh air has done me good. Are you ready for bed

43

yet?'

'Yes, I think I am, but first of all I have something to tell you, something that will solve our problem.'

'What, the Jimmy problem? That's not an issue; he's out of my life.'

'No, the one thing that could hold us back from sorting out Luckett House: the money. I have an answer.'

'I don't understand.'

'It's quite simple. I've made up my mind to sell my flat in the Midlands and move to Luckett Quay permanently. This is going to be my new home for as long as I've got left.'

Chapter 7

Hannah didn't sleep well. The thought of Betty living here by herself all year was a worry. She wouldn't have Dad, Susanna, and the children a minute or two away if she needed anything. What would happen when she couldn't get out and about for shopping anymore? Wouldn't she get lonely? There were so many reasons why she shouldn't do this, and not many advantages. Hannah needed to have a really serious talk with her. She worried about the loneliness most of all. Betty loved company and since Grandad had died she had joined so many little groups. No, this was madness, Hannah decided. She ought to just keep it as a holiday flat.

Betty had other ideas, however.

'Morning, darling, I'm guessing you didn't sleep well worrying about me here all by myself. You don't need to, I'll be fine. I'll have my food delivered from Sainsbury's so if the weather's bad I won't need to go out, and if we can persuade Josie to buy one of the flats I'm sure we can keep each other company.'

'Yes, that would work. You could have one of the two-bedroom ones and she can have the other.'

'Why do I need two bedrooms? Your dad wouldn't stay over with Susanna and the children. Even two bedrooms would be too small for them.'

'What about me? Where will I stay when I come to visit?'

'Why would you need to stay with me when you've got your own flat?'

Hannah was confused until Betty went on to explain that there would only be two flats for sale. She was giving one of the flats to Hannah.

'You might as well have your share of your inheritance while I'm alive. That way I'll be able to see you enjoying it. Then when I've departed this earth, which, fingers and toes crossed, will be a while yet, my flat can be sold and that will be your stepbrother and sister's inheritance. As you youngsters say: "sorted!"'

Hannah burst into tears. It had never crossed her mind that this would happen. Oh, she loved her Nan so much! The thought of having a little bolthole here where she had spent the happiest times of her life was so unbelievable. And being a flat, it could just be locked up without any worries.

After lots of hugs and tears, they began looking to the more immediate future. They had to get a plan together before Brian the builder arrived. For one thing, they didn't want to be ripped off, but they knew he had made a good job of the property in Saltmarsh Quay. They also had lots of questions: how long planning permission would take, what the cost of the conversion would be, and most importantly, what time scale he could offer for getting the work done.

Hannah also found Josie's phone number and gave her a call to see if she wanted to come around at some point and have a look at the house. The more they could keep her and Richard in the picture the more likely that she would stay interested and hopefully buy one of the flats.

'Are you ready, Nan? I can hear someone pulling up on the drive.'

A knock at the door followed, but as Hannah opened it the smile was knocked right off her face. It wasn't Brian the builder but Flash Tristan.

'What can we do for you? Haven't we made it clear that we aren't up for sale?'

'That's not why I'm here. I wanted to follow up on your viewing yesterday. I was sorry I wasn't able to show you around the flats. I just hope Emmi was able to answer all your questions. Can I come in, or are you going to count to ten again?'

Hannah was a little bit taken aback. This was a different side to Tristan. He wasn't trying to persuade her to sell, and she could tell he knew what they had been up to by visiting the flats.

As they walked into the lounge, Betty appeared.

'What's he doing here?'

'That's what I'm waiting to find out, Nan.'

'I'm here to find out whether you want a second viewing on the flats.'

'You know the answer to that. It's a no, thank you very much. And if you don't mind me asking, just for future reference, are you involved in any other businesses we might come into contact with? Just so we don't bother. Rental agencies, property developers, and now estate agencies, please tell me you have nothing to do with the fish and chip shop in Saltmarsh Quay! I couldn't bear not going there if you owned it.'

'Very funny, but no, I have nothing to do with any bags of chips.'

'Good, I'm pleased. As for the flats yesterday, they were lovely, but might I suggest that if you want to sell them you don't send that young lady to show people around? If you do, you won't have a cat in hell's chance of selling them. Perhaps her typing skills are better than her selling skills, but if not then I'm sure she's good at something. I'm guessing you employed her for at least one of her talents.'

With that, the doorbell rang. Hannah nipped off to answer it. Tristan's face said it all: he was enjoying the banter with Hannah and, if she was honest, so was she. He was good looking and very flirty.

'Hi, you must be Brian, come in.'

'Sorry, but I don't think I will. I'm not interested in the work you need doing.'

'Why? I've not explained any of it yet.'

'No, it's just that I don't do any work that's

connected to the owner of that car, I'm sorry.'

'I can assure you, Brian, the owner of that car invited himself here and he's just leaving. Isn't that right, Mr Goring? Ten, nine...'

Tristan was gone in seconds, without a goodbye or a smile, and Hannah explained that they had viewed the flats yesterday and he had come to see if they were interested. She also mentioned how he had tried to get Betty to sell Luckett House. Brian wasn't a bit surprised by any of Tristan's actions, hence why he wouldn't do any work involving him.

'That's good to hear. We converted the house into flats for a private client and as there are only a couple of estate agencies in the area he went with Tristan's company. But that young man has upset a lot of people with his wheeling and dealing in the past. Now tell me what you want done. I just need to go to the van and get my notepad. Is it alright if my son comes in to help?'

When Brian came back in, there following him was a hunk of a fella about the same age as Hannah and the complete opposite to Tristan. He wore scruffy work clothes but over such a fit body! He had beautiful blond hair and blue eyes. Hannah could feel herself blushing. He was hot but he didn't realise how good looking he was. He was shy, not even managing a smile for Hannah. That was probably good: the last thing she needed was to meet a fella like that, but he was very nice. If she was using the flat as a weekend place he would certainly be something very nice to look forward to, but the way he looked he no doubt had a dozen girlfriends.

'This is my son, Carl. Carl, this is Betty and her granddaughter Hannah.'

The next three hours were taken up by explaining their vision for the house. Brian said he wasn't fazed by the project. Over the years he had converted lots of similar properties, and the good thing was that the house had been very well built and not many internal walls had to come down. It was mainly a case of building stud walls.

The biggest job would be the plumbing. The whole building would need new boilers: four, to be precise, central heating, and of course it would all need to be rewired. Hannah was paying attention and asking lots of questions. She was also trying to get Carl involved, but he didn't go for it. At one point she actually tried to flirt, but he didn't pick up on it. Betty did, though, and had a big smile on her face.

'The planning permission should be straightforward, ladies, and I can do all of the paperwork for you. I'm one hundred per cent sure you won't be turned down, especially as you say they will be permanent homes and not holiday flats. The council are trying to discourage holiday lets. You're saying there will only be two for sale?'

'Well, we think we might have only one for sale actually, as someone is very interested in having one. We should know within a few days. Why do you ask?'

'It's just that my uncle has died. He was the Fern who started the business. I'm his nephew, the other Fern. The thing is, my aunt is looking to sell up and move somewhere smaller. I'm sure this would suit her down to the ground. Do you mind if I mention it to her?'

'Of course not, it would be perfect. Don't you think so, Nan?'

'Yes, three old ladies and you to keep us young and on our toes!'

They all laughed, even Carl, and that showed his perfect teeth. Hannah was like a little schoolgirl.

Once Brian and Carl had left, Betty made them each a coffee and they sat looking out to sea.

'Chalk and cheese, Hannah.'

'Sorry, what do you mean?'

'Chalk and cheese: Tristan and Carl. One flash

49

man with a suit, a little bit weedy, with dark hair and eyes, and certainly not to be trusted. And the other is the boy from next door: friendly, helpful, and strong. But one thing they did have in common, darling. They were both very sexy.'

'I don't know what you mean.'

'Oh, yes you do. It's your old Nan you're trying to kid!'

They laughed about it. Betty was right; they were both sexy in their own way. But enough of men, all her attention had to be on the property.

No sooner had she determined that, there came another knock at the door.

'Who is it this time?'

'Another good looking man, I expect. They say everything comes in threes.'

'Very funny.'

But Betty was right; it was another young man. This time it was Tom. Hannah had forgotten that he was coming around. He came bearing gifts, which gave him a point over the other two: cakes from the bakery.

'Come on in. It's Tom with cakes, Nan, what do you say to that?'

'Like I said, everything comes in threes.'

The afternoon was taken up with telling Tom about their plans for Luckett House. He was pleased and agreed with Brian that they would get planning permission quite easily. Hannah also explained how she had split up with Jimmy and at the same time been made redundant.

'So what's the next stage with the property development?' Tom asked Betty.

'That's the difficult part. I need to go and tell Hannah's dad what I've decided to do.'

'Will he be alright with it?'

'Oh yes, I'm sure he will. He just wants me to be happy. The problem is going to be my daughter-in-law. She's not going to be a happy bunny.'

'That's your Nan sorted, so what are your plans, Hannah? Now that you've been made redundant, you could always move here as well. That would be nice, wouldn't it, Betty?'

'I think Hannah would be bored here full-time. She likes a life with lots of excitement and I don't think the pub in Saltmarsh Quay holds that much attraction for her. Having said that, things might have changed a little after today.'

'What do you mean, Nan?'

'All I will say is that everything comes in threes. You have your choice.'

Hannah didn't engage with Nan's joking and jumped back into asking Tom how he had got into gardening. He explained that university hadn't interested him when he left school, and he had loved the idea of working by himself. He wasn't part of a team and he had his own business. True, he didn't make a lot of money: more in the spring and summer than in the winter when everyone's gardens had gone to sleep, but he earned enough to live on. And every now and then a design project came up. He loved the design aspect: delivering something for a client that had all started on a blank piece of paper.

'Thank you for the tea, it's been lovely catching up with you both. It brings back all the happy memories of when we were kids. They were special times that I will never forget.'

On that note, he left. Hannah and Betty sat there looking out to sea for a minute or two before Betty eventually spoke.

'So, my darling, we've seen the bad boyfriend, Tristan; the gorgeous one, Carl; and now we've seen the perfect one, don't you think?'

Chapter 8

'Come in, come in, good morning! Well, a horrible one really: wet and windy, and it looks like it's settling in for the day. So nice to see you again, Josie, and you, Richard. Nan's in the lounge, follow me.'

Richard helped Josie off with her coat. 'Thank you, I was just saying to Mum, what a horrible day to be viewing properties.'

'Well, I'm sorry we haven't a lot to show you here. We haven't even got any plans drawn up.'

'Yes, but we have marked out the rooms with chalk. Very professional, don't you think? It looks like a scene from a murder film, I'm afraid!'

They all laughed and for the next hour or so they walked around the house trying to visualise what the flats would look like when they were finished. Richard kept going back to the idea of one of the two-bedrooms. His only reservation was that one was upstairs but, as Josie said, it would be possible to put a stair lift in as the staircase was very wide, not like the ones built these days. The two-bedroom flat would really suit her. Josie looked happy and Richard was far more relaxed than before, especially when Betty said that Hannah would be having one of the other flats.

'So if Mum decides to buy one that means there would only be one other for sale.'

'Yes, and as Nan and myself want a nice quiet life hopefully we would be in a position to be choosy about who we sell it to. Another older retired person would be nice, don't you think?'

'So what do you think the next stage is?'

'For my part I have to go back to the Midlands, tell my son what I've decided to do, and put my flat up for sale. In the meantime, a builder we've had in to look at Luckett House is going to work out an estimate for the cost of converting the place and we'll take it from there. The trouble is I don't have any patience. Now I've made the decision I want it done right away.'

'The time will fly by,' Hannah reassured her. 'And the wait will give you time to think carefully about whether it's right for you, Josie. If it's not, that's not a problem. Hopefully you'll find somewhere that's more suitable.'

'This is suitable. It's perfect: the one place in my life I would never have dreamed I could come back to.'

'Yes, I think it would be the ideal place for Mum. By the way, is the builder local? Have you seen some other work he's done?'

'Oh yes, it's Fern and Fern.'

At that, Josie had to grab the back of a chair to stop herself falling. Betty wasn't daft: it was the name Fern that had caused that to happen, but why? What was Josie's connection to the building company?

'Are you okay, Josie? Can I get you a glass of water?'

'I'm fine thanks. I think I turned too quickly.'

That was a lie; she hadn't moved. This was something from the past that Josie was either scared of or wanted to forget. Betty thought it could be something to do with her reasons for leaving Luckett Quay: what was it she had said in the pub about 'having to move away'? Richard obviously knew what it was all about. Why had she had to move away? Was it a family thing? One thing was for sure: Luckett Quay held a lot of memories for Josie, but were they all happy ones?

Richard cleared his throat. 'Right, I think we should be off. Thank you so much for showing us the house. We have each other's phone numbers, so perhaps when the ball gets rolling you could give us a call with an update.'

'Of course, and like we said, if you aren't interested in the end, there'll be no hard feelings. I'll show you out.'

Once they were gone Hannah brought up Josie's funny turn to Betty. It had to be something to do with the Fern family. Perhaps they needed to check them out: were they bad workmen? Did the company have a bad reputation, or was it something personal between Josie and the Ferns? As they were talking, Hannah's phone went off.

'Please don't let it be Jimmy again ... oh, its Olivia! Hi, lovely, how are you? ... That would be lovely, let me just check with Nan. Its Olivia, she wants to know if I can meet up with her and Tom tonight. It means you'll be here by yourself, do you mind? It will only be for a couple of hours.'

'Of course it's fine. I love my own company. I can have a practice run and pretend I'm living here.'

'Nan says that's fine. Where shall I meet you both? ... That sounds nice, yes, and food as well? I'm definitely coming! See you at around seven-thirty then.'

'Are you going somewhere nice?'

'Yes, a bar meal up at Saltmarsh Cliff Hotel. Olivia said we can talk better up there than in the pub as that gets quite noisy. It will be fun, the first get together of the HOT gang for years. Now, what are we going to do for the rest of the day? It's not lunch time yet, and it's too wet and cold to go for a walk.'

'Why don't we just stay here and have a quiet afternoon? I suppose we could nip out for some food. We still need to decide how and when we're going to go back and explain everything to your dad.'

'That'll be the easy bit, Nan. Just wait until Susanna hears about it. Look, I'll take the car and do a food shop. It would be stupid for both of us to get wet. What do you fancy? How about a big fry up for lunch: bacon, sausage, egg, the full works?'

'Perfect. Could you get me a little ready meal for tonight and a bar of chocolate, please?'

Hannah thought she could get most of those things in Saltmarsh Quay's village shop and save driving any further. She was right.

'Is that everything? Are you on holiday? Sorry about the weather, it's gorgeous here in the summer.'

'I know, I grew up over in Luckett Quay.'

'I expect you've seen a lot of changes over there with all the flash new houses. I think they're starting on another one soon. I've seen that the old house has been knocked down. I'm Rob, by the way. I own this shop. And you are?'

'I'm Hannah. That will be everything. Thank you, goodbye.'

As Hannah was picking up her bags she saw someone familiar walk into the shop out of the corner of her eye.

'Hello, how are you today? Working indoors I hope, not building out in the rain.'

'Dad and I have a little plastering job in a cottage up the hill. I've just come down for a sandwich. Are you and your nan staying long?'

'No, I think we'll go back up north tomorrow. But hopefully once your dad has some information for us we will be back soon. Perhaps then we could go for a drink.'

'I'll mention it to Dad.'

'No, not your dad, just me and you.'

Carl went bright red. He dropped his keys and the sandwich he had taken out the fridge. Hannah smiled, he was so sweet and innocent.

'Happy plastering, Carl, and I'll see you for that drink when we come back!'

Hannah laughed all the way back to the house.

Carl really was so shy, but so gorgeous. She wouldn't be surprised if he'd never had a girlfriend. She would have to question Olivia about him tonight.

Back at the house they had their fry up and chatted about all things house, looking out the windows at the view and planning their futures. Hannah thought it would be a good idea to find work in London that came with accommodation. That way she wouldn't have two sets of bills. Perhaps when she was up at the hotel tonight she could make use of their internet and see what work there was. She should be nervous but she wasn't, just very excited.

It had stopped raining by the time Hannah left for her night out, which was a relief.

'I was thinking that we could stay here tomorrow and go home the following day, if that's okay with you?' she asked. 'That way I can have a few drinks without worrying about driving tomorrow.'

'Perfect. I'll text your dad, invite him and Susanna around for an evening, and we can let the cat out of the bag.'

'Cat? More like a huge tiger, I think.'

Hannah was at the hotel before Tom and Olivia. It was very quiet. She ordered a gin and tonic and found a little corner table for the three of them. She checked her phone as she waited. There were more texts from Jimmy and one from Henry, her boss, to thank her for making his job easy. He had given the Rooms Manager job to Karen, which was nice. He also wanted her to give him a call at some point as he had something to tell her which she would probably be quite happy about. She texted him back to say she would phone tomorrow. Another text came through, from her dad this time, asking what Betty was up to. He had a message from her asking for a family meeting. She ignored it: this was Nan's affair, not hers.

'Hello, it's Betty, right? We met at the flat the

other day.'

'Hi, no, Betty was my nan. I'm Hannah.'

'Sorry, I get mixed up. Oh, here comes my boyfriend! Tristan, this is the lady that I showed round the flat.'

'Hi, Tristan. So, your girlfriend, Immy...'

'No, it's Emmi, but Immy does sound nice.'

'Here come my friends, you'll have to excuse me. Have a lovely evening. Are you celebrating something?'

'Yes, Tristan and I have been going out for six months today, so it's a little celebration. We're meeting my mum and dad here, aren't we, Tristan?'

'Can I ask what your dad does for a living?'

'He owns the rental company and estate agency we both work for.'

'Really, that's very interesting. Have a lovely evening. I'm sure you will.'

She could see that Tristan was fuming. He knew that Hannah was miles ahead of him on the score card. Oh, he was a slippery snake, but he wasn't going to say anything in front of his girlfriend.

'What are you laughing about?' Olivia asked.

'I've just pulled Tristan down a peg or two, that's all. You look lovely, Olivia, and here's Tom, all dressed up as well! I'm glad I made the effort.'

Tom went to the bar and got them all a drink. Hannah could see Emmi's parents arriving and Tristan was all smiles, getting the drinks, holding the chairs out, a real salesman. Yes, that was the word. He was selling himself as the perfect son-in-law to be. What a stupid fool he was.

'Here we go, three gin and tonics. This is a little bit different from the old days, sneaking cans of cider and hiding out around the quay. They were fun days. In a way I miss them. Sometimes it's not as much fun being an adult.'

'Tell me about it, two kids and no husband is no

barrel of laughs. No, I'm lying. I wouldn't be without Sam and Ben, they're the best thing that has ever happened to my life.'

Tom raised his glass. 'Here's to the first meeting of the HOT gang, after all these years, and hopefully we won't leave it so long next time. The lady behind the bar is going to bring the menus over to us. She's having a few problems at the moment.'

'Yes, that's my mum's boss, Glenda. They have a huge staff problem at the moment, practically no staff, to be honest. A new hotel has opened around the coast and several of the staff have left to work there. By the way, Hannah, perhaps we should change places.'

'Why?'

'Because a certain Tristan can't take his eyes off you.'

'Really? That's interesting. I think I'll stay here. Something tells me he's annoyed with me, and that's the way it's going to stay.'

'Hi, I'm really sorry, but we aren't doing bar food tonight. You're more than welcome to go into the restaurant to eat if you like.'

They agreed that would be fine, so after ordering they headed in. This time the seating was the other way around: Hannah was facing towards Tristan, but the back of his head was to her, which must have been very frustrating for him.

The food was lovely, and they had lots of wine and chit chat. Oliva talked a lot about her boys and how she was glad the husband had gone, not that they were divorced yet. Tom explained all about his gardening work and how he would love to get into garden design in a bigger way. His dream would be to design a garden at the Chelsea Flower Show.

'So that's our news. Now it's your turn, Hannah. Tell us all about the bright lights of London.'

'No bright lights, just lots of dirt and smelly

people on the tube every day. It's not as glamorous as people think, but I might be leaving it all behind now that I've been made redundant.'

'Come and live here,' Olivia suggested. 'I'm sure you could get a job here in the hotel, and you've got the flat. It will be just like the old days: the HOT gang back together again.'

With that, Glenda came and cleared their plates.

'Glenda, I was just saying to my friend Hannah that you would give her a job. She's been made redundant from a huge hotel in London.'

'Name your price, you can start tomorrow! Start now, if you like. I'm serving the food, running the bar, I'm on Reception, and no doubt later tonight I'll be the night porter! Joking aside, if you're looking for work why not pop in for a chat tomorrow? I'm sure we could find something for you. Excuse me; I can hear the phone ringing.'

They laughed about what Glenda had said but perhaps it would be a good thing to look into, even on a short-term basis while the house was being converted. Hannah would give it some thought, but she couldn't see herself living here full time. It was so quiet. There was so much she would miss.

'What would you miss, Hannah? Name me three things.'

'Well, to start with, shops, but lots of other things as well.'

'You don't need shops. I've got two kids, that's what the internet is for! Anything you can buy in London, I can get online. Come on, Hannah, it'll be fun. Not just for me and Tom, but Betty too. You'll be able to help her with settling in. And if you're bored, there's always Tristan to have a bit of fun with.'

'I don't think so. He's not my type and anyway, I've no money he would be interested in. My dad doesn't own lots of companies.'

'Does that mean you *could* be interested in him?'

'Don't be silly, Olivia, I've just got rid of one boyfriend, I don't need another. Having said that, half an hour with Carl the builder would be quite nice. He's really fit.'

With that, Tom got up and went to the toilet.

'Now look what you've done, you've upset Tom with all that talk of Carl. You're right, he is gorgeous, but so shy. To be honest, and I can't put my finger on why, he's different. Not in a bad way, in a nice way. He's a hard worker, but I sometimes wonder if he's happy being a builder. Come to that, if he's happy being here in Norfolk.'

'Why would I upset Tom?'

'You really don't know, do you? He's always fancied you and something tells me that now you've come back he thinks he's in with a chance. I've never seen him dressed like he is tonight, or as happy as he is, to be honest. Tristan's not the only one who can't take their eyes off of you.'

Chapter 9

Hannah was feeling a bit rough. She had a headache after all that gin and wine but it was worth it. The three of them had had a laugh and in some ways it did feel like the old days, which was nice. Looking at her phone she saw that it was gone nine and she'd only just woken up.

'Morning, Nan. I'm sorry I overslept.'

'Not a problem, darling, we're on holiday! Did you have a nice night? If you don't mind me saying so, you do look a little...'

'Rough is the word. We drank too much, but we did have a laugh. That was, until I put my foot in it. Olivia reckons Tom's got a soft spot for me, but I've never looked at him like that. He's always been more like a cousin to me.'

'Oh dear, not to worry, I'm sure you can put him straight. By the way, I messaged your dad.'

'I know. He wants to know what you're up to. I think you've got him worried. Would you like another coffee? What do you fancy doing today? It doesn't look as windy out there as yesterday, and it's stopped raining. We could go for a walk; help me clear my head. Oh, by the way, I was offered a job last night. I don't know what the job is, but it's up at Saltmarsh Cliff Hotel. They're very short staffed and it might be perfect what with all that's going to be happening with the house.'

Two large black coffees later, Hannah was feeling a bit better. She told Betty all about her night out and how she had annoyed Tristan. Betty found that hilarious. They decided it would be warm enough to walk down onto the beach and it would do them both good: just what they needed before heading back to the Midlands the next day. Hannah also decided to go up to the hotel and see what Glenda had to say. She hadn't got anything to lose and she needed a job once she had finished working out her redundancy period.

'Damn, that's what I have to do, I need to phone Henry. I forgot all about it.'

The doorbell rang.

'Can you get that, Nan, I won't be a minute! If it's Tristan, just start counting out loud, he'll soon go away.'

Hannah went into the other room and spoke to Henry. It was fabulous news: as she had been so kind and not caused a fuss over the restructuring at the hotel they were going to pay her the six weeks' pay but she didn't need to go back and work those six weeks! How fabulous was that?

'Who was at the door? Please tell me it wasn't him. Oh, hello, sorry.'

'This is Margaret, she's Brian's aunt.'

'Hello, it's nice to meet you.'

'I'm sorry to just turn up like this, but as I was saying to Betty, Brian was sure that you were heading home today so I wanted to catch you before you left. The thing is, I need to downsize. My husband has died and Brian and his wife Jane are moving into my property now that he's taken over the business. There's lots of storage there for his materials and vehicles and I just need something small. I know how properties can get snapped up very quickly and I was wondering if I could put my interest forward for one of these once the work is done.'

'You're more than welcome to look around and I'm sure Nan would be over the moon to sell you one. There's a possibility there will only be one available as Nan's keeping one of the single bedroom flats and I'm having a two-bedroom. We also have a lady who's very interested in the other two-bedroom one.'

'I would only want one bedroom. The most important thing for me is a sea view. I can cope with almost anything else as long as I can see the sea.'

'We aren't off back to the Midlands until tomorrow. We'll need to speak to my son about everything there, and obviously we'll need to talk things over once your nephew has given us a quote, but if everything goes ahead you are more than welcome to purchase one if the price is right for you. I'm sure we would get on well living here together, and the other lady interested in the place is lovely as well. Everything has happened so fast. It's exciting; I just want it all to happen now! Let me show you around.'

Hannah left Betty to do the talking. She could tell she liked Margaret just as much as she had Josie. This would be a perfect set up. They were all around the same age and they all shared a real love for the area.

'Can I get you a tea or coffee, Margaret?'

'I'm fine thanks, I've taken up enough of your time already. I must get off. Thank you again, I'm sure you'll be more than happy with my nephew's work, he's very good. My husband taught him well, they worked for many years together. He's more like a son to me than a nephew. My husband Frank and I never had any children, you see. I would have loved a daughter, but Frank didn't want any. But that's another story; I mustn't keep you any longer. Thank you again.'

Hannah showed Margaret out. She was so happy: she just knew Betty, Margaret, and Josie would get on well together.

'She was very nice, Hannah, and I think she would be perfect. I'm sure Josie would get on well with her. So now we just need it all to come together. Tomorrow would be good!'

'Tomorrow would not be good. We have to go

63

back to face Dad and Susanna. Come on, we can worry about that later. Let's go for a walk and then I'll pop up to the hotel to see what job Glenda has to offer. It could be pot washing!'

There was no one else down on Luckett Quay's beach. The tide had just gone out, so the sand and pebbles were wet but without a single footprint anywhere. If ever there was a reason Hannah should get a job here it was this. It was a bit too cold to sit on the rocks but a slow walk from one end of the beach to the other was lovely.

'Are you sure you're doing the right thing? Shouldn't you wait until you get home to decide? You have a lovely full life there, and there must be things you'll miss.'

'Of course there are, but look at this place! Imagine waking up each morning to this view. My health will surely be better with so much fresh air, and think how safe this is, miles away from any city. Who couldn't be happy with their lot living here? No, I'm seventy and this is where I want to finish out my days, there's no doubt about that.'

They walked back to the house, poured themselves some hot chocolate and sat in the bay window. There was nothing either of them craved more in the moment than this.

'This says it all, look at the view. Anyway, do you think I should move here?'

'Yes. And perhaps I should too. Speaking of that, I had better get up to the hotel and see what Glenda has on offer.'

'Good luck; I'll keep my fingers crossed for you, darling.'

The meeting went well. Hannah had a tour of the hotel with a running list of the problems that Glenda was facing. They talked about everything to do with the day-to-day running of the place. The only thing that was not mentioned was what job was on offer:

was it bar work? Reception? Hannah didn't have a clue, but she didn't want to say anything in case that showed what level of job she was looking for.

Glenda had asked her what experience she had over the years, which was easy to answer. She had worked in most departments. Some she liked more than others, but she did find it easy to adapt.

'So, do you think you would enjoy working here? Do you think there's any department you would like to be in more than another?'

'Yes, I think I would enjoy my time working here. There are parts of the hotel I would get more out of than others but you have to take the rough with the smooth. Just because I don't enjoy it as much doesn't mean I won't still give it my all.'

'Hannah, I would love for you to come and work here. I know you're going home tomorrow, but the job's yours if you want it, and you can start whenever you like. Very soon would be preferable.'

'I'm sorry to sound thick, and I think I may have missed something, but what job are you offering me exactly?'

'The job I would like you to accept because I think you will be brilliant at it and bring so much to it is Catering Manager. That would also mean being a Duty Manager, which at the moment we would share. It's not going to be easy at the moment: we are scraping the bottom of the barrel, but I'm sure we can turn things around. What do you say?'

Chapter 10

'You what, Betty? Did you hear that, Robert? You have to stop her. There's no way she can do this. We need a bigger house, and how much is all the conversion going to cost? You should be selling the house, not renovating it! Say something, Robert, don't just sit there!'

'Mum, are you really sure you have thought this through? Luckett Quay is very remote and you aren't getting any younger. How will you manage for shopping and getting around in the future?'

Hannah sat there, not saying a thing. She was waiting for Susanna to finish her rant before she brought all the positive things to the table. She could tell that her dad was embarrassed and once she was allowed to have her say he would see the positive aspects of the situation.

'Susanna, I own this flat which my late husband and I worked very hard between us to buy. The house in Luckett Quay has been in my family for generations. I'm selling off half of it: two flats, and when I die my flat will be passed on to Pippa and Alfie as their inheritance. In the meantime, after this flat has been sold to pay for all the building work and the two flats are sold, if – and I'm not promising anything – if there is some money left, then we can discuss the possibility of you and Robert borrowing some of it.'

There was silence in the room. Hannah could tell that her dad was thinking things through. Also, from the looks he had given Susanna he obviously wasn't impressed with her rant. But there was more to come. Neither of them had yet to pick up on it, but, oh yes, here goes, the penny's dropped.

'Mum, you said you were selling two flats, but the

house was being converted into four. Are you going to rent the other out as a holiday let?'

'No, that's going to be Hannah's flat and yes, before you ask, I have given it to her just like I will Pippa and Alfie. That's her inheritance.'

'But why does she need a flat in Norfolk when she lives in London?'

'Because I'm moving to Norfolk. I've taken a job in the local hotel.'

Hannah explained all about the Catering Manager job. Robert was very happy: he had always worried about her being in London, and he knew how happy she had always been in Norfolk. There wasn't a word out of Susanna. As annoyed as she was, she knew she couldn't rock the boat any more without jeopardising her chances of getting the money that might be left over. That bit about Nan and Grandad both working had also struck a chord with her. Now that her children were at school there was nothing stopping her from getting a job, even if it was only part time.

'So what happens next, Mum?'

'First of all this place will go up for sale. I'm hoping the builder will come back with a quote very soon, and then we can apply for planning permission. That should be straightforward and, fingers crossed, the work can start as soon as that's in place.'

'But what happens if this sells before the flat is finished?'

'I'll just have to cross that bridge when I meet it.'

'And I'm very lucky as the hotel has staff accommodation. It's not brilliant, but it will do in the short term. I just need to get the rest of my stuff from London and store it all here at Nan's, then I'll be off to Norfolk to start the job.'

The rest of the evening ticked over peacefully, everyone just taking in what was about to happen.

Robert and Susanna soon headed off. Once they had gone, Betty joked that she wouldn't want to be in that car. No doubt Susanna wouldn't be stopping to draw breath.

'I'm sorry, I hadn't given any thought to you still having things in London. Would you like me to come with you?'

'No, to be honest it's only clothes. The flat came furnished, so there's not a lot to bring, and I think I'll get rid of a lot of the clothes. The thing I'm not looking forward to is seeing Jimmy, but even though he is the one in the wrong it seems only fair to see him face to face and get a bit of closure. I'll text him and see when he's around. Could I borrow the car?'

'Of course, and as for the car, when we're both living in Luckett Quay we can share it. It's pointless you getting one when I'll only be using it on odd occasions.'

'Thanks, Nan. Right, let's get this text over with.'

*

'Come in. You didn't need to ring the bell, you have a key.'

'No, Jimmy. It didn't seem right to just walk in.'

Hannah followed him into the flat. It was clean and tidy but probably for her benefit rather than some girl he was going to entertain. He looked sad and thin: he had lost a lot of weight for such a short period of time.

After a bit of general chit-chat Jimmy went to make a coffee. Looking around, Hannah was shocked to find that she didn't miss this place. The flat didn't evoke any sentiment. She reckoned that was a good thing, but seeing Jimmy again was a different matter. She realised now how much she had missed him, but she couldn't show him that.

'Here you go, just as you like it, two sugars. I'm so sorry, Hanny. I was stupid. I hadn't realised what I had to lose if we...'

68

'No, Jimmy, there's no 'we' anymore. It's over. Please don't make this more difficult than it is. Both of us need to move on. We're still young. Go and have some fun. What we had was good while it lasted; let's both look back on it with fond memories. But that's all it can be now: memories.'

'But surely everyone can be forgiven for making one mistake? Please give me a second chance.'

'I didn't want to ask this, but *was* it only one mistake, or were there others I didn't find out about? If there were, I don't want to know. Come on, Jimmy, we had some fabulous times together. Let's end this in a friendly way.'

Eventually Jimmy dropped it and they talked about the house in Luckett Quay and Hannah's new job at the hotel. When Jimmy went to the shop to get something to make a sandwich with Hannah went through her clothes, making one pile to take away and another for the charity shop. It didn't take long as she wanted to get on her way and not hang about. As much as they had got on over the last couple of hours she didn't want to drag it out.

'Your favourite, Hanny: cheese and pickle on granary, and not forgetting a packet of crisps.'

She hated him calling her Hanny now. He always had, but it just didn't seem right anymore. She decided not to say anything, though.

There had been no mention of the young lady who knocked on the door that day. Had she left the scene? Sandwich eaten, the car was loaded up with Jimmy's help. He had agreed to drop the bin bags of clothes she didn't want off at the charity shop. Clothes, some books, CDs, and a few photos all in the car, it was time to say goodbye forever. He would stay in London, the busy city that he loved, and she would soon be on the coast in Norfolk.

'Hannah, it was a one-off. There had never been anyone before her, and hasn't been since, come to that. I was so stupid. I know it was wrong and it will be the biggest regret of my life. I really wish I could turn back the clock and make it so it had never happened, I do, but all I can do is say I'm so sorry for breaking your heart. You know I'd never do anything to hurt you, so this is it. I know where you are if I have to contact you, and if I end up moving from here I'll text you my new address.'

'Fine. Look after yourself, Jimmy, and promise me you'll have fun. Go enjoy yourself. Go after the things you really want in life. Follow your dreams.'

'I will, and I'm sorry. I wish I could turn back the clock but I can't. Even more so I wish I could make things better between us. Perhaps one day. Drive carefully, and remember that I'll always love you.'

As she drove away her heart was breaking. At the first opportunity, she pulled over and sobbed like she had never cried before. The thing that hurt was that she knew he really meant what he said. He was sorry, but so was she because she could never forgive him for what he had done. It was time to put her life with Jimmy behind her. She had a new future to look forward to and he wasn't any part of that.

Chapter 11

'Morning, Hannah, and welcome to your first day at Saltmarsh Cliff Hotel! How's your room? I know it's on the pokey side, but like you said, it's only until your Nan's house is ready.'

'Everything's fine, thanks. It's a palace compared to some of the places I've lived in.'

'Good. Let's go through to my office and start your induction. I'm sure you want to get stuck in as soon as possible.'

Glenda ran Hannah through the recent history of the hotel. A few years ago it had been bought by the famous American actress Devel Devonshire, who had also fallen in love with David, the hotel manager. That had given Glenda her extra responsibilities.

'You see, Devel and David split their time between here and her home in Hollywood so I run the hotel when he's away. Mind you, never a day goes by where I don't have David's support, either on the phone or via emails. He's still in control of the major decisions, but the day-to-day running of the hotel is down to me and, from today, you. So that's the who's who. Any questions so far?'

'Earlier you said that you were short of staff. Which departments are struggling?'

'I'm coming on to that. The housekeeping department is running perfectly, no staff issues there. Our Housekeeper is Annie and she has a wonderful team working for her. Reception is struggling, mainly because I'm being pulled in every direction and can't focus on it. Hopefully now you're here I'll be able to give some time to sorting that out.'

'So that just leaves Catering.'

'Oh, don't swear! I hate that word so much at the moment. The head chef left us, and as I haven't

71

found anyone suitable to replace him, we have to use agency chefs. It works out very expensive this way, but once we get a good head chef in the kitchen we'll bounce back.'

'That just leaves the restaurant, then.'

'Another swear word! To be honest, it's not that bad. I just need to find someone with a bit of enthusiasm and plenty of go in them. That was tricky, but I think you're just what we need. Why don't you tell me what you're looking to get out of the job? It's completely different from what you've done before. I don't mean to say you won't be good at it, but I'd like to know where you see yourself going with the job.'

They talked about Hannah's last role at the London hotel and splitting up with Jimmy, as well as her time spent here on the quay in her youth. Hannah was very honest with Glenda. She wasn't sure if she would get bored with the quiet life, but she was up for a challenge.

'Let's go for a tour of the hotel and then we can draft out a training programme. I'll also introduce you to all the staff on duty today. We'll start with Annie. She's worked with David and me for years. There's nothing she doesn't know about the hotel staff and our regular guests.'

As they walked through Reception to the stairs Hannah spotted a familiar face: Tristan. Unfortunately today she wasn't in a position to be rude or sarcastic to him as he was a paying guest at her workplace. He hadn't seen her, which was good. They were out of his view when Glenda stopped and asked in a low voice:

'Did you see that man going into the lounge? Well, that is...'

'Tristan.'

'So you know him?'

'Sadly, yes. Please don't tell me he comes here a

lot.'

'Every day, Hannah. This is where he does his "business". None of the staff like him, but being that he spends a lot of money here, we have to be polite. More importantly, his future father-in-law, who I must say is lovely – not a bit like him – spends a fortune with us. Ah, here comes Annie. Morning, my love, can I introduce you to Hannah?'

Annie was lovely, just like Glenda had described her. She made Hannah feel very welcome. She was introduced to a few of the housekeeping team then followed Glenda down to the kitchen. The staff members there were all very young. She could tell that they needed a leader to keep them in line.

Back in the office, Glenda summed up.

'That's about it. It isn't a big hotel but it is a very busy one. What do you think of everything you've seen so far?'

'It's all good. I really think I'm going to enjoy myself here and it's clear that the catering side is where you need me most. It's been years since I so much as waitressed, but I think it will be fun. I'm ready to throw myself into it!'

'I am so glad you've said that, Hannah. I was worried that as you've come from a reservations and reception position you might have a few misgivings about jumping in to Catering from day one.'

The next couple of hours were spent going through the fine detail of the Catering department, from the strengths and weaknesses of its staff to service hours and menus. Hannah had a lot to read up on but she was excited to start. Glenda's look of pure relief said it all; she was delighted that this would be Hannah's baby from now on. Starting tomorrow, she would throw herself into three shifts a day but as it was now five-thirty, Glenda insisted that she finish for the day and make the most of an evening away from the hotel while she could.

Switching her phone back on as she walked up to her room, she received a voice message from Betty saying that a couple were interested in buying her Midlands flat. There was also a text from Dad wishing her luck with the new job and one from Brian the builder, explaining that Betty had suggested he contact her about the building work since she was living locally now. He had a quote for her and wanted to meet her at Luckett House to run through his proposals on site. She gave him a call.

'Hi Brian, it's Hannah. When would you like to get access to the house? I'm not sure of all my shifts yet and I don't want to mess you around. I will know more tomorrow.'

'Are you free now? It'll only take half an hour. I can't meet you there but Carl can. I will give him a list of the things I need to know from you.'

'Yes, that's fine thanks, Brian. Give me half an hour to get changed and walk there.'

Seeing as it was going to be Carl, not Brian, Hannah took a bit more care with her appearance than she normally would. He was cute, even if he didn't know what to do with it, but it could be fun seeing him without his dad. Would he be any different? She called Betty to fill her in on the new job and to find out about the couple viewing the flat before heading down the hill to Luckett House.

'Hi, Carl, sorry I'm a bit late, I was on the phone to Nan. Here, let me open the door.'

He wasn't so different without Brian around. He was still quiet, but today he wasn't wearing his usual work clothes. He had obviously gone home from work and showered before arriving. He smelt lovely and the jeans and t-shirt he wore clung to the firm lines of his fit body.

'What do you need to do?'

'Dad needs the measurements of the bay windows on the front of the house. We'll have to fully replace all four, so we want exact numbers to price that up for you.'

Hannah kept out of the way while he got on with it. There was nothing worse than having someone watching you as you worked. She decided to go to the part of the house that would become her flat. This was the first time she had been here without Betty, so she could take time to plan it all out in her head: where her bed would go, how her kitchen would be laid out, it was all so exciting!

'That's all the measurements I need. Thanks for coming down.'

'That was quick. So, what have you got planned for tonight?'

'Nothing much, I'll probably find a film to watch on TV later.'

'Do you fancy going for a drink, then? Have you eaten yet? No? I'll treat you to dinner at the pub, then.'

'You don't have to do that.'

'I know I don't, but I want to. Starting tomorrow, I'm going to be tied to the Saltmarsh Cliff Hotel twenty-four-seven, so I must make the most of not being there tonight.'

Hannah could tell he was nervous. She had never met a boy as shy as Carl before. They got into his car and drove back up the hill and around to Saltmarsh Quay. She tried to make conversation with him, but he only gave her yes and no answers. It was hard going and she began to think that this might not have been such a good idea.

As they walked into the pub she could see people looking at them and putting two and two together. They found a table and she suggested it might look better if he went to get the drinks, which he smiled about. He could smile, thank goodness.

She had a gin and tonic, and Carl a pint of lager. Hannah thought she could guess what sort of meal

75

he would order, and she was right: steak and chips. She decided to have the same. By the time the food arrived they were on their second drink and Carl was looking a lot more relaxed.

'I remember when you used to come here on holiday. I always saw you hanging out with Olivia and Tom. It was like you had a special club or something.'

'We did. It was called the HOT gang. We thought we were so cool.'

Carl thought that was hilarious. The food came, and they enjoyed it while Hannah talked about her time in London and at university. He was interested, as he had never lived anywhere other than Saltmarsh Quay.

'It was pretty much taken for granted that I would go and work with Dad and Uncle Frank when I left school. I'm not complaining, it's a lot better since Frank... well, he's dead now, but since he stopped working and Dad took over. I'm allowed to do a lot more than when Frank was in charge. All I did for him was fetching and carrying but Dad's taught me a lot of real skills.

'Frank didn't think I was capable of anything, you see. He was always putting me down and Dad was too scared to speak up for me. He was an odd man and didn't treat his wife very well, which was especially bad considering that it was her dad that gave him the building business in the first place. He would have been nothing without her but he treated her like she was always in the way. Everything about the business is better now that the men who work there aren't always on tenterhooks, just waiting for Frank to explode over something. People who would never have hired the company before are now coming around to us just because he's gone.'

'He sounds horrible. It's so sad, because Margaret is so lovely. Nan and I both really hope she buys one of the flats.'

Over the next hour they chatted about all sorts of things, but Hannah couldn't get any details on how Carl spent his spare time. There was no mention of any girlfriend and, come to that, no mention of any mates.

'I don't know about you but I feel fat and full,' she announced at last. 'It's time for me to say goodnight and walk back up that hill to the hotel.'

'I'm sorry, I could have driven you up, but I think I've had too many pints to drive. I can walk up with you, if you like?'

'No, you're okay. It's not too late and I have my torch. It doesn't take too long from here. It's been a nice evening; we will have to do it again some time.'

'Yes, I'd enjoy that.'

They left the pub and walked a bit further down into the quay. Hannah had to go in the opposite direction to Carl but there was just one more thing to do before she said goodnight to him: something she had wanted to do all night. He was just about to say goodnight when she went in for the kill.

She kissed him. Not on the cheek but full on the lips. She could tell he was shocked: he went all rigid, and he didn't join in. It was just Hannah doing the work – if kissing could be called work. It felt good, but very odd. She had never kissed anyone who did not respond to her before. It was all very strange and something she regretted doing.

'Goodnight, Carl, and thank you.'

'It should be me thanking you, you bought the meal.'

'I was thanking you for the kiss. Goodnight.'

Walking back up the hill, she struggled to figure him out. Her mind also turned over what he had said about Margaret: what a sad life she had spent with Frank! That would certainly change if she bought the flat; Betty was fun to be with and with Josie there as well they would never have a dull moment. That would be those three sorted. Now for the huge task of putting Saltmarsh Cliff's catering department in order: where on earth was she to start?

Chapter 12

It had been just over five weeks since Hannah had planted that kiss on Carl's lips, and it had been the same length of time since she'd had a day off work. She was loving her new job and was beginning to feel that she had broken the back of it, so today she finally felt able to leave the team to run everything without her. She was having a day off; not just a morning or an evening but a whole day away from the hotel and was going to spend it with Olivia and her boys on the beach. It was still only spring, so coats and hats would be needed but perhaps the boys would play with their fishing nets in the rock pools leaving her to catch up with Olivia's news.

'Sorry I'm a bit late, Olivia, I just wanted to make sure the breakfast shift went okay without me.'

'Switch off from the hotel; it's your day off! Mum's been telling me how hard you've been working, seven days a week and everything. She says you've really got the place sorted out. Are you happy there?'

'More than happy. I love it, far more than I ever thought I would. Enough about the hotel, how are you and the boys? Look at them over there. They have a wonderful place to grow up in, just like we did.'

'Yes, they're really happy kids, but these days all I do is talk about parenting with the other mums; it's one big child-rearing bubble. I want to escape from that today. I want to know your news! What's happening with the house?'

'I've loads to tell you. Nan's sold her flat. That's all going through but, like everything else, it's taking its time. The planning permission we need to convert Luckett House into flats looks like it will go through without a hitch. I think that's because they're not holiday lets, the council are just happy to preserve the look of the place.

'There's not a lot of furniture Nan wants to keep so next week I'm going down to move all the bits that are going to charity shops into one room and all the things she's keeping into another. Once it's all gone, Brian and his team will start knocking down walls and dividing it up into flats. It's getting very exciting. Dad seems happy with it now that he knows I'll be staying here in Luckett Quay because he won't have to worry about Nan being isolated when she starts needing extra help.'

'So you really will be staying long term? You're not going to get bored with the quiet life here?'

'Oh, I'm staying. The job's great and I'm getting a good team together. I've promoted a couple of the waiting staff to supervisors so that they can run shifts while I have days off. It will be good to have some time to myself.'

'Time to find a man, then! Speaking of men, I think you've upset one of them.'

'Who? No, don't tell me, it's Tom, isn't it? I thought something was wrong. I've seen him twice when I've had to pop down to Saltmarsh Quay on errands. I tried to talk to him, but he was in a bad mood both times. I didn't think it had anything to do with me, though. What have I done wrong?'

'You were spotted a few weeks back coming out of the pub and kissing a certain builder. Tom found out somehow and now he's jealous.'

'How ridiculous! We went for a meal, had a few drinks, and kissed goodnight, that's all. I've not seen or heard from him since. Haven't people got anything better to do with their lives than gossip? As for Tom, the last thing I need is for him to get all worked up every time I talk to someone else.'

'You're not in London now; this is a small

community and everyone knows each other's business. Any snogging has to be done in private. I know that from experience, but that's another story. By the way, a little word of warning: watch out for Carl's mum. She's very protective of her little boy.'

'Boy? He's a man, and a very fit one at that. If Tom wants to get worked up about my social life he can come and talk to me about it instead of sulking. And talking of men, there's another one I could do without seeing again, and that's Tristan. He's in the hotel all the time, meeting up with all sorts of people, and he's so demanding! Clicking his fingers at people, expecting my staff to drop everything and see to him first. I've lost count of the number of times I've had to bite my tongue over it. Besides, he's always winking at me as though we're friends.'

'What do you think of Emmi? She's a little bit, how can I put it...'

'Thick? No, that's unkind. I feel sorry for her. He's only using her to get at the inheritance she's got coming, but that's never going to happen. Her dad's not stupid. Mark my words, Olivia, one day Tristan will meet the real Hannah and then he'll wish he hadn't.'

'So you'll have a busy social life on your days off, what with Tom, Tristan, and Carl to contend with.'

'Shut up, the last thing I need in my life is a man. I learnt my lesson with Jimmy. That relationship went on far longer than it should have done. No, I have my new job and the excitement of my new home, I don't need a man – or a boy – to share it with, thank you very much. Anyway, how about you? Your mum was telling me that the boys don't see their dad. Isn't it about time you started looking for a man?'

'You must be joking, what man would want to take me on? Remember, it's not just me, it's Sam and Ben as well.'

'Yes, but they could do with a man around to kick a ball and do other boy things with.'

'Oh, they've got that. There's my dad and Tom: he sees them at least once a week and thankfully wears them out for me.'

'I didn't think Tom wanted kids? Anyway, enough talk of men, let's go and help the boys find some crabs in the rock pools.'

The rest of the morning was spent playing on the beach. Once the tide was out they walked around to Saltmarsh for lunch. The four of them sat on the harbour wall to eat fish and chips. Come three o'clock the temperature had started to drop, so they headed back to Olivia's for a cup of tea. They stopped off in the village shop for sweets for the boys and wine for themselves on the way. It had been a lovely day, especially being outdoors in the fresh air. After all those weeks cooped up in the hotel, it was the perfect day off for Hannah.

They got cosy and played board games until it was time for the boys to go to bed. Then it was time to open the wine and relax. Hannah had been relaxed all day, but it was lovely to just switch off.

'They're in bed and absolutely exhausted. You're really good with children, you know. You'd make a fabulous mum.'

'What's with you? First you're encouraging me to find a man, and now you want me to start a family? No thank you. I have the hotel staff; they can be my children for the next few years. I didn't think I would get on with them as well as I do, seeing as most of them are just out of school. And then I have Glen; he's like a big brother figure to me. One of my favourite times of the day is sitting down between the breakfast and lunch shifts for a coffee and a chat.'

'Yes, I've known Glen for years, he's so funny. He was at the hotel when I waitressed for a few years before having the boys. I always laughed at how benignly two-faced he was, laughing and joking with the guests and the complete opposite in the kitchen. We always joked about him "taking his smile out the drawer" for the visitors.'

'I think once the kitchen is sorted out the hotel will be working like clockwork. Glenda was telling me that David and Devel are in London for a few days and he's set up a meeting room to interview for a head chef. I've been trying to persuade the agency chef to take the job but he loves the flexibility of agency work. He doesn't want to be tied down in one place.'

Hannah was starting to feel tired. Whether it was the fresh air, too much wine or, just being able to finally relax, it felt like time for bed. She was loving having Olivia back in her life, and her two boys as well. She knew that they were only joking about her having a family soon, but deep down she did want one someday. Not yet, though. A few more years of single life sounded good.

'Thanks for such a lovely day. I've really enjoyed myself; we must make it a regular thing, especially as we head on into the summer and can start having picnics and full days on the beach. Right now I should get to my bed. I think I'll walk back to the hotel. I have a torch in my bag to walk the costal path. It will only take twenty minutes or so.'

'Are you sure? I would offer to drive you but I can't leave the boys alone, and I think I've had too much wine.'

'Don't be silly, I need the fresh air. Thanks again, and I'll keep you updated with the goings on at Luckett House.'

'Not just at the house, but in your heart as well! Who will win you over: Tristan, Tom, or Carl? Or could there be a mysterious fourth contender?'

'I think you've been reading too many romance novels! That or it's been too many glasses of wine.'

On the way down into the quay, Hannah was laughing to herself: men! Admittedly, it did feel quite nice to be getting some attention though.

It wasn't as late as she had thought: only nine-thirty. In London, she and Jimmy would only now be getting ready to go out, but walking through the village it looked like everyone had gone to bed. Well, all but one. She bumped into Tom walking beside the sea wall, and he scowled at her.

'Hi, off to the pub to meet someone?'

'Not that my social life is any of your business, Tom, but no. I've spent today with Olivia and the boys and now I'm on my way back to the hotel. Besides, if I was off to meet someone that would be my business. Why are you being like this? We're mates, and have been for years. One of the things I was most looking forward to coming back here was the chance to spend time with you and Olivia, just like the old days.'

'But these aren't the old days. Olivia has her little family, you have your new career, and I have... Well, we've all grown up and gone in different directions.'

'Yes we have, but that needn't stop us from being friends! We went from childhood into our teens together. Surely we can be adults and still be friends.'

'There's a problem with that, Hannah. I want more. I just don't want you as a friend; I want you as my other half. That's something I've wanted for the last God knows how many years, and you moving back here has just confirmed that I'm in love with you. I always have been.'

Chapter 13

'Hi, Hannah, how was your day off?'

'Morning, Glenda. It was great, thank you. I spent it with Olivia and the boys. We had a good laugh, Sam and Ben wore me out, we gossiped, ate the wrong food, and drank too much wine. The perfect day off.'

'Good, I'm happy you were able to switch off from the job. Any news on the house?'

'Yes, fingers crossed things should start happening soon. I need to go down and sort out the old furniture and stuff, but I'll be able to do that between shifts. By the way, how did everything run without me yesterday? I didn't see anything urgent in the handover book, and the staff said they thought it went okay.'

'Yes it was all fine on your side. I think the kitchen staff saw an opportunity to mess around with the waiting staff while you weren't here, but hopefully that will be sorted soon. David's done loads of interviews and two chefs are coming up to do a trial with us. We can see if they're any good and also if they like it here: the quiet Norfolk lifestyle isn't for everyone. Apparently one of them has applied because he knows the area. He's stayed in Luckett Quay a few times.'

'That's great, the sooner the better! Right, I'd better go and look at the diary to see how many are booked in for lunch. I'll catch up with you later.'

'Yes, I'll let you know which days these chefs are coming. It's important that you meet them, as you'll have to work very closely with them.'

The new chefs weren't Hannah's top priority at the moment. She was worried about Tom. She hadn't had a clue he felt the way he did, and she needed a way to get it across to him that the feeling wasn't mutual.

Oh, this was all she needed! Tristan appeared, walking into the hotel as if he owned it, as per usual. Well, today *she* would go to him when he next clicked his fingers or whistled at one of the staff. Money or no money, that behaviour needed to stop.

Sure enough:

'Woof woof!'

'Sorry, what did you say?'

'I said, "woof woof!" That's what you get if you whistle: a dog comes running.'

'Are you trying to be funny? I was trying to get the server's attention.'

'If that's the case, I suggest you do what every other guest of this hotel does, and politely ask for what you require. From today my staff have been told not to answer to whistles or clicking of the fingers.'

'I am a paying guest! I will do as I like to get their attention, do I make myself clear?'

Hannah just walked away. She knew that if any other guest had talked to her like this she would have given in, but not for him. He needed to be taught a lesson. She headed out toward Reception, where Glenda was giggling to herself.

'Good on you, Hannah. We've put up with his nonsense for far too long, and I'm sure David and Devel wouldn't stand for it either.'

Not much later they saw him leave the hotel, swearing away to himself. Hopefully he would get the message.

Tristan pulled out of the car park just as Emmi's dad, Raymond Dove, drove in. Hannah had noticed earlier that he had booked a table for lunch.

'Good morning, Mr Dove, how are you today? I've reserved a nice quiet table for you. It was for four, wasn't it?'

'That's right. I'm a bit early, so I'll sit in the bar. Could I get a coffee while I wait? By the way, was that Tristan I saw driving out at such a speed?'

'Yes it was. Take a seat and I'll fetch your coffee myself. I won't be a minute.'

Should Hannah mention why he had rushed out? She wondered whose side Mr Dove would take: hers or Tristan's. The last thing she needed was to upset him, as just today's lunch bill would probably come to over a hundred and fifty pounds.

'There you go, one pot of coffee. Is there anything else I can get you?'

'No, I'm fine, thanks. How are you settling in here? I will say that the restaurant seems a lot more organised since you've started.'

'Thank you, that's very kind of you to say. I'm really enjoying the job, and the staff are lovely to work with. I should apologise about something, actually; I was the cause of Mr Goring speeding off like that. Perhaps I should apologise to him but it's difficult, because I feel I need to stick to what I said for the sake of the staff here.'

Raymond frowned. 'Please take a seat and explain. I'm confused.'

Hannah told him about the constant clicking fingers and whistling, and the way Tristan expected everyone to jump to the minute he appeared. She could see that she was right to have mentioned it. Mr Dove's face said it all. Perhaps she could take the conversation a little bit further? Oh, Tristan, you've started to hang yourself.

'You see, Mr Dove, it's such a fine line and the last thing we want to do is upset guests who spend money here every day. What with all the people your future son-in-law entertains here, he has been a good advert for the hotel. I'm hopeful some will come back again.'

'I'm still confused, my dear. You say Tristan is

here every day? Doing what, and who with? He should be working. And I can assure you that he will never be my son-in-law. There's no way I would allow my daughter to marry the likes of him.'

She knew that would be the end of Tristan's regular visits, whistles and all. Of course, once he had had his telling off from Mr Dove he would know who had caused it. Bring it on! Hannah would be ready for him.

The lunch shift was over by two o'clock. Since everything was prepped for dinner ahead of time, Hannah decided to walk down to Luckett House for an hour or two and start to empty cupboards and drawers. The house felt so familiar, and so huge compared to her little staff room at the hotel.

She started with the kitchen. There was nothing in the cupboards Betty wanted to keep, as she had all the crockery and utensils she cared about at her flat. She would bring them with her when she moved in. All the stuff here was off to the charity shop.

Hannah was on her fifth box and feeling really pleased with what she had achieved when she heard a knock at the door.

'Hello, Margaret, come in.'

'Are you sure? I was just coming back from walking on the beach and I could see movement through the window. I thought Betty might be down here visiting.'

'No, it's just me. I'm packing up all the stuff we don't want to keep. How do you fancy a cup of tea? I brought some milk with me from the hotel. There, take a seat and excuse the mess. I'll put the kettle on.'

'Are you and Betty getting excited? Brian tells me it won't be long before he gets started on the building work.'

'Yes, Nan's flat sale is going through okay, so it's all systems go! By the way, there's no rush for you to make a decision on whether you want to buy one of the flats. You have to be happy with the decision you make and your current house must have so many happy memories that you would be leaving behind.'

As Hannah was handing Margaret the cup of tea, she could see Margaret was getting upset. Perhaps she shouldn't have mentioned her house. It wasn't long since her husband had died, and there was so much for her to take on.

'Are you okay? I'm sorry; I didn't mean to upset you.'

'You haven't – well, I am upset, but it's nothing you've said. As for leaving the house, that's not a problem for me. It has no real happy memories.

'Come sit beside me, Hannah, and if you have a minute I'd like to tell you something before you hear it elsewhere. You see, my marriage wasn't a happy one. Frank had a problem, and it was me. Well, it was more about his guilt, to be honest. I'm sorry, I'm not explaining this very well.'

'It's alright. Just take a deep breath and start at the beginning.'

'Frank was just a lad when he came to work for my father. He taught him everything he knew. They got on really well together but I was an only child and didn't have many friends, let alone boyfriends. Then when I was around twenty Frank started to show an interest in me. I was confused, as he had loads of girls after him – very glamorous ones, and there was me, just a Plain Jane. My mum and dad encouraged it, so we started dating. It was nice. I was happy, but Frank was always a lot friendlier to me when my parents were around. We dated for three years, and then one day he proposed to me. I was shocked but very happy, and my mum started to plan the wedding. Frank wasn't interested in any of the arrangements. He became a lot quieter too, except when he was out with his mates.

'My parents bought us a house as a wedding present. My dad could afford it, but my goodness, a house without a mortgage! It was a lovely day. Even Frank seemed to enjoy himself.

'We settled into our new home and life ticked along. But I could tell that Frank was restless. He spent a lot of time in the pub with his mates, which I didn't mind to start with, but within a couple of years it was clear we were growing apart. I sank into myself, kept my mouth shut, cooked, cleaned, and ran a nice little home. I always believed that it must be my fault.'

'How sad! Couldn't you have talked to anyone about it?'

'No, but everyone else was talking about it around me. People were saying they had seen Frank here, there and everywhere but I just shut myself away. By this time my mum and dad had died and Frank was running the family business. Not that it had much to do with family anymore.

'Then, out of the blue, everything came out. After all those years of frustration building up inside of Frank, the final straw was when my oven went wrong: funny how it took a stupid oven to bring all of our problems to a head. I burnt a meat and potato pie and he went mad. He stormed out of the house and didn't come back for four or five hours. When he did get back he laid into me: how dare I burn his food? Surely I was capable of cooking a pie? And then he said it. The thing he had been so screwed up about for so many years. He just came out with it.'

'Margaret, you don't have to tell me. This is obviously distressing for you.'

'He told me the only reason he married me was that my father promised him the house and business if he would be my husband.'

'That's terrible! I'm so sorry.'

'The awful thing is, it wasn't just Frank I stopped

loving at that moment, but my parents as well. To think that they... no, I don't want to. But I had to tell you, as there are still people living around here that know that story and if I do move into one of the flats they will be itching to tell you and Betty.'

'Let them tell us, and I will tell them where to go. This house has always been a happy home and I can assure you, even when it's divided up into four flats it's still going to be a place of happiness. We'll make it a new start for us all, filled with fun, laughter, and lots of gin. The rest of the world can sod off, what do you say to that? I say here's to Luckett House, the home of new beginnings!'

Hannah had already known that Frank hadn't been a nice person from the things Carl had said, and now all this had come out. What a very sad family they had been.

That got her thinking about how lovely her own family life had been when her mum was alive. She could never have a comparable relationship with Susanna, not that she would want to replace her mum, but she could hope for her dad's happiness. That relationship had been out of her control, but she did find herself missing another relationship, one that she had had higher hopes for. She had loved Jimmy, and their time together before it went so wrong: at university, on those amazing holidays, even spending their days off together. Stopping to think about their past only made it hurt more. Oh, Jimmy, why did you mess it up?

Chapter 14

It had been just over a week since Margaret had told her story to Hannah. She had cleared the house, and the charity shop staff had been over the moon with all the donations.

Brian and his team had moved in, and Luckett House looked like a bomb site. Hannah had been chatting to one of the older builders about how fast things were moving, and he joked that Brian was eager to get the flats finished because once Margaret moved in he would be able to move into her house.

But today wasn't about the renovations; it was all to do with food. The first of the chefs was due to come and look at the hotel and show how well he could manage the kitchen. Glenda and Hannah were both nervous as they knew they had to get this hiring right. They needed a good team leader who could take away the worry of the kitchen from them. They also needed the person to fit in well with them, as they would be the three main people in charge of the daily running of the hotel.

'This chap is called Mark,' Glenda told her. 'He's thirty-four and has quite a bit of experience. I offered him a room at the hotel for last night but he preferred to drive down this morning. The chef coming for tomorrow's trial will arrive later this evening.'

'I hope at least one of them will be okay. I know the cooking and organisation skills are important but I just want someone to take control and stop all the messing around. At thirty-four, Mark's not a kid, so that might help.'

'Yes, the one coming tomorrow is only in his twenties, but he's the one who was particularly keen to move to the area. Well, we'll soon see, and if neither of them is any good we keep looking. The last thing we want is someone who doesn't fit in. By the way, Hannah, I think you did the trick with Tristan. He's not been near the place since you spoke with him, but Mr Dove and his wife have.'

Mark arrived dead on time. Glenda sat and had a coffee with him while she explained about the history of the hotel, and then showed him where to change into his chef's whites. That was where Hannah took over. She took him in to the restaurant, went through the menu and heard his suggestions for changes. Then came the important part: introducing him to the kitchen staff. This was crucial. She wanted to see his reaction to them and vice versa. Was he a people person? It was only a small team, so they had to gel.

Some hours later, Hannah burst into Glenda's office like a small whirlwind.

'One word, Glenda: disastrous. If that man worked here we would be advertising for every other job in the kitchen. Just who did he think he was? It was bad enough him talking to his team the way he did, but to swear and cuss at the waiting staff as well...'

'And he was only here for four hours! I suppose we should be grateful that he saved us the embarrassment of having to chat to him about how the day went.'

'Yes, but it was his own fault. You don't mess with forty-year-old gay men: they've spent their lives fending off nasty remarks. It was so funny. I think every member of the restaurant team were in the kitchen to witness it. To be fair, Glen had put up with his grumpiness and snapping for over two hours, but when Mark called him a poof, that was it.'

'What were his exact words?'

'He just said "I might be a poof but that didn't worry you last night when we were having sex."

Everyone knew it was a joke and screamed with laughter, but obviously Mark didn't. He didn't say a word, just put all his chef knives in a bag, went and got his clothes, and drove off. Not even a goodbye or a request for his expenses! Perhaps I should give the money to Glen as a thank you for getting rid of him, what do you think?'

'Well, we now know what to do if we don't like the next one: have a quiet word with Glen.'

'Oh, don't joke! Tomorrow's has to be better. We need an easy life. Well, not too easy, but easier than this. Tomorrow's another day and another chef, we'll just have to wait and see. Hopefully he'll be the right one.'

The rest of the day went smoothly. Both waiting and kitchen staff laughed all the way through dinner service. Glen was loving all the attention, but that was nothing new.

The last customer left the restaurant at ten-fifteen, and once everything was laid up for breakfast all Hannah had to do was balance the evening books. She joined Glenda at Reception and finished the day up with a gin and tonic.

'All finished, Hannah? It's time to hand over to the Night Manager. I'm a bit disappointed that tomorrow's chef hasn't arrived yet. I wanted time to suss him out before we go through it all again, but he phoned to say he missed his train and was catching a later one, so he probably won't get here until after twelve.'

'Never mind, we can stare at him while he's having his breakfast. Do you think we should let Glen serve him? We might not need to go through with the trial!'

'No way, we need a head chef urgently. The way I'm feeling right now, if he has two hands, two feet, and can cook, the job's his.'

Hannah was the first in the restaurant for the

breakfast service. As it was midweek, it was mostly older couples and a few businesspeople, no families. Everything was going well, although there was no sign of the chef. Apparently he had asked for a couple of bottles of beer from the night porter when he arrived and asked for a wake-up call for seven-thirty.

Glenda spotted her scanning the dining room and wandered over.

'Morning, Hannah, we won't be able to suss him out after all, he's asked for room service. Please don't send Glen with it, we don't want him frightened away! I've told him I'll meet him in Reception at ten and then once I've chatted to him we can meet up around ten forty-five.'

'That sounds perfect. Breakfast is nearly over. I've just got to nip down to Luckett House and see Brian for half an hour. We need to discuss plug sockets.'

'That sounds fun, I don't think. Having said that, if Carl's there you might have a good time.'

'Don't mention him. He's avoiding me, I don't know why. Perhaps he thinks I'm going to eat him.'

'I thought that's what you wanted to do?'

'I might, but I have the problem with Tom to sort out first. Why are men so stupid? Right, I'm off. See you in a couple of hours.'

Sadly there was no Carl that morning: he had gone to the builders' merchants to get materials. To be honest, it was a bit of a waste of time her going down. Brian had marked out where he thought all the sockets should go before she got there, but it was nice to see the progress. Internal walls were starting to go up, the bathrooms were all marked out, and work on the plumbing was well underway.

'It's looking good, Brian. Are you happy with how it's going?'

'Yes, really pleased. There is one thing I wanted

to ask you, though. Each of the downstairs flats will have a back door to access the rear garden and the upstairs ones will use the old back entrance at the end of the corridor. But we haven't discussed separating up the garden: is it going to be communal?'

'I've not really thought about that. Also, since speaking to Margaret I was thinking that it would be nice to have something in the garden where everyone can meet up.'

'What do you mean, like a summer house?'

'That was my first thought, but whatever it is it will be used more in the winter, and that might be cold and damp. Do you have any suggestions? What do you think your aunt would like?'

'Yes, a communal room would be good. How about a conservatory on the back? It won't be cheap, but it would be quick and easy to do.'

'That's a brilliant idea! I will mention it to Nan. That would mean they could sit and chat with a cup of tea together, rather than sitting by themselves in their flats. Leave it with me. I'm going to have to get off now, I've a chef to interview! Give me a call if you need anything else. Oh, and by the way, how's Carl?'

'He's fine, thanks. Still being wrapped in cotton wool by his mother but that's mums for you. I think he'll still be living at home when he's fifty! It's going to be a few years yet before she'll untie those apron strings.'

*

Glenda met Hannah just as she was hanging up her coat.

'Perfect timing, Hannah! James has just gone to get changed into his chef's whites. I think he might be the right one. He's very polite and keen. He asked lots of questions, and when one of the waiters brought us a coffee he was friendly towards them.'

'So just give him the job! He sounds perfect. No

need for a trial, ask him when he can start!'

'Shush, here he is! James, this is Hannah, the—'

'Jimmy? What are you doing here?'

'You know each other, then?'

'Yes, sadly we do. James – or Jimmy, as I know him – is the reason I left London.'

'Hi, Hanny, how are you doing?'

Chapter 15

'I'm so sorry, Glenda. I hope I didn't leave you with too many problems yesterday, it was just the thought of being there with him...'

Glenda shook her head.

'There's no need to apologise. It was an understandable reaction, and everything was okay here. The lunch shift was quiet and last night they only served twenty-four guests. He's gone now.'

'I know, I phoned the hotel before I came back to check. Why was he here in the first place? We talked about James the chef and how he knew the area; how did I not put two and two together? I'm so mad at myself!'

'Look, go and sort breakfast out for now. There are only a couple of tables booked for lunch, so that will give us a few hours to go for a walk and have a talk after you set the wheels in motion. I'll catch up with you in a couple of hours and between us I'm sure we'll able to sort things out.'

Hannah was getting the coffee on when it hit her: sort things out? What was there to sort out? Jimmy had gone and he certainly wouldn't be coming back, unless... and why a walk? Oh, surely Glenda didn't want to give him the job?

Breakfast service went smoothly. She wanted to ask the waiting staff about Jimmy but no doubt they had heard who he was to her by now. He wouldn't have kept that a secret. Who would be the best one to ask?

*

'Sorry to leave you all in the lurch yesterday, Glen, I had something urgent to sort out. How did the chef do? Did he get on with all the kitchen staff: no situations like the day before?'

'No, the complete opposite. He was polite to everyone and there was no messing around. Everything was very professional but in a fun way. He showed the younger workers in the kitchen how to do things in a way that gave them a real confidence boost. I know you don't want to hear this, but he seemed like the perfect person for the job. He is just what this hotel needs: between the two of you, this could become the best place in this part of Norfolk to eat.'

'I was worried that would be the case. Did he mention me at all?'

'Sort of: he was very discreet and clever. He realised that with me being the older one and gay, I'd be quite friendly with you and repeat everything back, so do you want to hear it? He knows he messed up. He was flattered by the attention from that young woman, and he regrets it. He misses having you in his life, and he's sorry. I know I only met him for a few hours yesterday, but he did genuinely seem sorry. I know none of that was what you wanted to hear, but that's all I have.'

'I appreciate that. None of it surprises me, in any case. No doubt he went out of his way to impress Glenda, too.'

'I think they did get on quite well, sorry.'

So Jimmy was the best man for the job, and Glenda knew that. Hannah could tell that their little walk and talk would be all about that. The hotel could go for months looking for another suitable chef. What should she say?

If Jimmy were to come, he would probably get bored: he never liked Norfolk before. And surely one day it would click that she was no longer interested in him. Having said that, Hannah might be the one to get fed up and want to move on. There were other jobs to be had in the area, and she could still live in her new flat. Yes, she would make it easy for Glenda.

He could have the job.

'Are you ready? I thought we could walk down to the beach seeing as it's such a lovely morning. You could show me your new flat on the way.'

'Yes, I think the builders will be there but that doesn't matter. I need to check a few things with Brian anyway. By the way, I'm going to make this easier for you; I don't have a problem with it if you want to give Jimmy the job. We will act like professionals. Of course, I can't promise that he will stay once he realises I'm not interested in having a relationship with him again.'

Glenda explained that, for Hannah's sake, she had half-hoped he wouldn't be any good, but he had been. He had brought so many menu ideas, and the staff liked and respected him. He gave them confidence and encouragement to reach up to his level. Obviously she had brought up the subject of their relationship with him, and he told her that the breakup was one of the worst things that had ever happened to him. He realised that what he had done was wrong and stupid, and he wanted to prove he had changed.

'Right, tell Jimmy the job's his. I'm okay with it, but let's not talk about him any more today. Let's get down to Luckett House and my new flat instead. It's so exciting!'

A lorry was parked in front of the house as they approached. It turned out to be delivering some doors: not the best-looking ones in the world but they were fire doors, which was the important thing. There was no sign of Brian's van but a few of his workmen were busy plaster-boarding the stud walls. After a few hellos, Hannah led Glenda upstairs. She showed her Josie's two-bedroom flat and then Margaret's. Even with the bathroom cutting into the bedroom the rooms were big, and as for the kitchen and lounge, the views were to die for. Downstairs,

Betty and Hannah's flats were very similar. Once some of the trees and shrubs were cut back, the views would be as equally as nice as the ones upstairs as well.

'Of course, some shrubs will go entirely, because we're – oh, hi, Carl! I didn't see you there. This is Glenda, we work together at the hotel. Is your dad around?'

Carl went bright red: even Glenda noticed it.

'Dad's gone to arrange the bathroom tiling at the builders' merchants. He should be back soon.'

'That's alright. I'll just have to catch him later. But I was saying about the garden...'

Hannah explained that she and Betty both liked the idea of a conservatory and that they wanted a quote from Brian for one that would stretch the full width of the house so that each flat would be able to access it through French doors.

'You see, I think it's important that there's a place where Nan, Josie, and Margaret can meet up. If someone else moves into the flats in years to come, they just need to put a dividing wall up and the upstairs flats can use the front door to get around to the garden.'

'What a great idea. As they get older they can keep an eye on each other as well.'

'Yes, Nan's really excited about it. We'll just have to see if the budget stretches that far. Come on, let's get down to the beach. Would you like to come with us, Carl? Get a bit of fresh air and run around on the sand? We can play kiss chase.'

Poor Carl was so embarrassed! Glenda scolded Hannah for teasing him but they both had a laugh about it later.

They were the only ones on the beach. It was peaceful, and they both agreed that they missed being able to come down here now they were so busy at the hotel. Hopefully that would change if Jimmy agreed to take the job: as if he wouldn't! It was nice not to be only chatting about hotel stuff. As the weeks and months went on they were becoming more than just work colleagues, but good friends, so much so that Hannah explained about Tom.

'So let me just get this clear; Tom fancies you, and so does Jimmy. You fancy Carl, but he's not interested, and that's not even taking Tristan into consideration.'

'What's he got to do with it? I can't stand the man.'

'Yes, but he flirts with you and there have been times I can tell you've enjoyed it. Oh dear, Hannah!'

'Enough of this! Come on, back up the hill, we have a hotel to run! As I said before: the last thing I need in my life is a man.'

'That might be what you think, but do those four fellas realise that? All I'll say is I'm watching this space. I think that before this season's over, one of them might be a lot happier than the other three. Let the best man win!'

Win? This was no competition, and she wasn't a prize. One thing was for sure: life was going to get a lot more complicated with Jimmy here. She would have to be professional. No, that wasn't the word: she was going to need to be strong. She knew he would throw himself into the job and make a really good effort at turning the kitchen around. If only this opportunity at the hotel had come a few months ago, how different their situation might have been...

Chapter 16

Jimmy accepted the position at Saltmarsh Cliff Hotel. He gave a months' notice at his old job, and now three weeks of that had passed.

Hannah had got her head around it all and to be honest her mind was more often on the house renovation than anything else. There was something more pressing she had to deal with today, however, and it was sitting in the bar waiting for her.

Tristan was here. It was his first visit since he had stormed off that day, and he had asked if she could spare him a few minutes. She had agreed, although she did leave him to sweat for half an hour. That might not have been the wisest move, but she was feeling petty.

'Sorry I've been so long, I needed to sort a few things out before the lunch shift starts. What can I do for you?'

'I want to know what you've said to Raymond Dove about me. Apparently I need to come and apologise to you and all the staff. Apologise for what?'

'He asked what had happened to make you drive off in a hurry, so I explained I was rude to you and why. So perhaps I owe you the apology.'

'You know that's not true. And I am sorry about the way I treated the staff. It's just that I get so busy that I don't always realise what I'm saying.'

'Apology accepted, but you need to understand that it wasn't so much what you said as the way you said it: always demanding things, with no please or thank you. All the same, if you really are sorry that's enough for us this time. We will look forward to seeing you at Saltmarsh Cliff Hotel again. Now, is there anything else I can help you with?'

'Yes, actually, as a way of making it up to you, would you have dinner with me? Obviously not here, but somewhere else.'

'That would be lovely, when are you thinking of?'

'So you will? I'm shocked; I thought you would tell me to get lost.'

'Don't be stupid, it will be nice! I can't wait to meet Emmi again. It will be fun, just the three of us, don't you think?'

'No, just the two of us. Emmi won't be there and she doesn't need to know either.'

With that, Hannah got up and left, not saying another word. She had suspected that was what he had in mind, that's why she had gone along with the idea. But to actually spend an evening with him? Oh no. And as for sitting and chatting with Emmi, the girl couldn't hold a conversation to save her life!

As she walked back towards Reception she could see Tristan leaving by the front doors. What would his next move be, she wondered? She laughed to herself. He was so silly.

The lunch shift was busier now that the weather was getting warmer and the sun was out. Lots of visitors to the area were walking the coastal paths and stopping off for bar snacks or a drink. This was the start of the season, so rotas and staffing levels needed to be kept an eye on – no more single-waiter lunch services. Perhaps she ought to look into creating a day-time team. It was something to talk to Glenda about. The last thing she wanted to happen was for lunch to run into dinner with all the clearing up and preparing overlapping. The same went for the kitchen: she would discuss it with Jimmy when he started. Having a chef on duty in the afternoons might be a good idea. Her head was full, if she wasn't thinking up ideas for the hotel, she was ruminating on Luckett House.

She was in her own little world, laying up the

tables for dinner, so she didn't notice the two people standing at the restaurant door. When she finally looked up, she realised it was Josie and Richard.

'Sorry, I was miles away! How are you both? What brings you here?'

'Mum and I wondered if we could have a quick word with you, if you have time.'

'Of course, why don't you take a seat in the bar – no, the lounge? There are a couple of women in the bar who – let's just say they must be celebrating something. They are a bit loud. I will get us a drink: tea, coffee, or something stronger?'

'Tea would be lovely, thank you. You are sure it's no trouble?'

'Tea it will be, just give me two minutes.'

Hannah went off to the kitchen to make tea. She was desperately hoping that they hadn't come to say Josie didn't want the flat after all. She would be the perfect company for Margaret and Betty.

'Here we go, tea and some homemade biscuits. Now, what is it that you want a word about?'

'We might have a problem. Mum still wants the flat, and she's got a buyer for her house, but would she be able to bring a dog with her? She's only just got him. One of Mum's friends has just died and while she was ill Mum walked Bonkers for her – that's his name. Then when Mavis went into hospital Mum had him at her house.

'When Mavis got very poorly she told Mum that she wasn't worried about dying, her only fear was what would happen to Bonkers. Mum could hardly say no, so when Mavis passed the dog came to live with her permanently.'

'I can't see that being a problem. Nan and I would love a dog around the place, and I'm sure Margaret won't have a problem either.'

'Who's Margaret?'

'Oh, sorry, Margaret's the lady who's buying the

other flat. You'll like her: she's a similar age to you and Nan. Her husband's just died and she wants to move somewhere a lot smaller. She's from the area: you never know, you might know her!'

At that, the colour drained from Josie's face.

'Do you think we can go now, Richard? I'm feeling a little warm. I need some fresh air, I think. I'm sorry, Hannah, thank you for the tea.'

Richard looked confused, but he followed her out. Hannah didn't know what to think. It must be all to do with Margaret. There must be loads of women by that name but how many in this area who had just lost their husbands? This was the same way Josie had reacted when Fern and Fern had been mentioned: she had had to hold on to the back of the chair. What was the connection between Josie and the Ferns that caused her so much distress?

It looked like they would have to find someone else to buy the flat. By the look on Josie's face, she was ready to run a mile from the place. Hannah just had to wait for the phone call from Richard to say his mum had changed her mind. Never mind, perhaps she might get a little more money from the next person, and that could help with the cost of the conservatory.

It was now half past four and she had two hours before the dinner shift. She needed an hour's sleep, a shower, and a quick something to eat.

As she was locking the restaurant door, she could hear the two women from the bar ordering a taxi from Reception. That was good: there had been a fear they would stay all afternoon and into the evening. The bar bill was good but they probably would have upset the other guests.

'Ha, you over there! Are you the new bit of stuff from London? You must be, I've not seen you around here before.'

Hannah ignored the shout, although it was

obviously referring to her. She thought about cutting through the kitchen but it was too late, the woman was already in her face.

'I'm talking to you, don't ignore me! I have a bone to pick with you.'

'Hello, I'm Hannah, the Catering Manager. How I can help you?'

'Help me? I know exactly who you are and what you've been up to! Moving down here, thinking you can do what you like with who you like, well, we do things differently here in Norfolk!'

'I'm sorry, madam, I don't have a clue what you are talking about. Do you think you could keep your voice down a bit? We have other guests in the hotel and I think you and your friend have had a little too much to drink. Perhaps you wouldn't mind waiting outside for your taxi?'

'I'll wait outside, but first I need to do what I came here for and that's to tell you to keep your dirty claws off my son! He doesn't need to get involved with some cheap tart like you.'

At this point Hannah just wanted to hit the woman. Who was she anyway? Oh no: she should have realised. It had to be Carl's mum. She had been told his mother was possessive, and here was the proof. There was no way Hannah would let her get away with this but standing here in Reception wasn't the time or the place for that.

'I think your taxi has pulled up outside, ladies. Let me show you to the door.'

'We aren't leaving until I have your word you'll keep your hands off my Carl!'

'You have my word my hands won't go near him. Come on, the taxi's waiting.'

Hannah ushered them out of the hotel and into the taxi, but she couldn't let this woman have the last word. Just as she was about to close the door she leaned in for a parting shot.

'You know, I promised to keep my hands off your son, but I can't promise the same for my lips. Goodbye, ladies!'

Well, it was turning out to be one of those days. Tristan and then Carl's mum, who would be number three? Hopefully nobody; Hannah didn't really believe in that superstition.

Reception paged her. She had a phone call waiting.

'Hello, Hannah speaking, how can I help ... oh, hi, Jimmy.'

Setting down the phone an hour later, she felt that the whole conversation had been a waste of her time. She didn't know why Jimmy had bothered to phone. She was fed up with hearing about how sorry he was every five minutes, not to mention his fussing over the things left in the flat as he moved out. She didn't want any of the CDs they had bought, nor any glasses or towels. She thought she had made that quite clear already. She had taken everything she wanted from her old life when she left.

As for him being 'excited to be working with her', that was nonsense. He should be excited about the job, the challenges ahead of him, not her face in the background. She did let her guard down once by telling him she thought they would make a great team. Hopefully he realised that she meant a working team and nothing else.

Still, as she poured herself a coffee, it did cross her mind how nice it had been to hear his voice again. It just went to show that not all things that come in threes are bad after all.

Chapter 17

Jimmy was due to arrive today in readiness for starting his new role tomorrow, but tonight he was moving into the staff accommodation. Apparently a mate was bringing all his stuff down from London. Hannah was ready. Once he had settled into his room she would take him down to Saltmarsh Quay for a drink and something to eat and set out some ground rules.

First, though, she had something to sort out with Brian at Luckett House. She wasn't sure if she should mention his wife's visit to the hotel. Perhaps he would already know. In any case, Hannah was focused on conservatories today. She needed to decide what style she wanted, what height, and what type of roof to top it off with. Who would have thought it could be so complicated?

She wasn't even certain it was still a good idea to have one. She hadn't heard from Josie or Richard, so couldn't be sure whether Josie still wanted the flat. Surely if she didn't she would have let her or Betty know by now? And should Hannah question Margaret about Josie? If she did, she might end up with two flats to sell.

'How are things going? The place looks amazing: just as if it had always been four flats! Now that the walls are plastered the rooms look great. I'm so excited for Nan to see them too.'

'Yes, it's coming along great guns. The lads have nearly finished the pipe work for the central heating, and connecting all the radiators won't take long. All the bathroom things arrive the day after tomorrow and the kitchen cupboards and worktops ought to be here by the end of next week. But about the conservatory: you don't need planning permission if you don't extend the house too far, which is good. That leaves you to decide which design you want and how you want it: just about every part of a conservatory has options.'

For the next two hours they went through every option they had. Betty was on the phone with brochures in front of her and between them they came up with three favoured options.

With the help of masking tape and cardboard boxes they marked out how each would look. One of the options had to be discarded because the doors would be in the wrong place, but it was coming together. Betty and Hannah's priority was to have a table that would seat at least eight people on one side of the conservatory, and chairs and sofas on the other, arranged in view of each other and overlooking the garden as well.

The decision was finally made; they would have a little wall about two feet high on the sides of the conservatory which met the house. The wall the conservatory backed onto would be plastered and the front edge of the conservatory looking onto the garden would be all glass with two sets of French doors, one set on either side. Now that everything was marked out there was only one option for the roof: it had to be a pitched roof.

Betty and Hannah were happy. Brian told them he would get a good deal on the frame as the conservatory company wouldn't have to fit it: he and his team would put it up. They said a quick goodbye to Betty on the phone and, just like that, it was time for Hannah to get back to the hotel.

'One last thing I need to ask you, Brian: does Margaret like dogs? Would she object to the lady who buys the other flat bringing a dog with her?'

'Just the opposite! She would love to have a dog around the place. She always wanted to have one, but my uncle wouldn't allow it.'

'Yes, I got the impression that he could be a little difficult. It sounds like Margaret didn't have an easy time with him.'

'A *little* difficult? That's an understatement and a half. He was horrible: carried a huge chip on his shoulder all the time I knew him. I bit my lip around him for years.

'Don't get me wrong, I am very grateful for all that he taught me. He was a master craftsman and he left me the company. Saying that, all I got were the tools and machinery. It wasn't like there was a building or much in the way of stock. There wasn't exactly a queue of people wanting work done either; between you and me, business has been better since he died. He treated me better than a lot of his workers, too. He always acted as though they owed him a favour for employing them, which was rubbish. Any one of us could have left him and got work elsewhere.

'Even so, the only time I really fell out with him was over Carl. He treated that lad badly, especially when I wasn't around to see it. To be honest, I still don't know the half of it. Carl's never talked to me about it, so I only know what the other chaps have passed on.'

'But Margaret, why did she...'

'Stay with him? I don't know. Times are different now, thank God. Women don't have to put up with all the things they suffered years ago. I'm pleased that she's moving here, not just because I'm buying her house, but because she'll have people to talk to. Now you've decided to have the conservatory, it's even better. She'll be very happy here, and it's nothing less than she deserves.'

'But why did Frank have such a big chip on his shoulder? Everything was handed to him on a plate. He had the business, and as for being given a house as a wedding present... he should have been the

111

happiest man alive!'

'Yes, but perhaps he wanted something or someone else. It was too late to take it back if so, he had made his bed and that's where he had to lie. But that's in the past. We're looking to the future and I know Margaret's going to have a wonderful time living here.'

As Hannah walked back up to the hotel she felt that everything was coming together nicely. Her day had been all about the house, but the people she was working for were more important: these three women, coming together in the latter part of their lives. She still wanted to know what had upset Josie and whether they needed to have that discussion before going any further with the flat purchase. On the subject of things she wished she knew already, how was she going to feel when she met Jimmy again? Would he be waiting for her when she got back?

*

'Hi, Glenda, is it time for me to paint on the welcoming smile yet?'

'He's in his room, I think. The friend who brought him down has just left. It's going to be okay, stop worrying.'

'I'm not worried, I just want to set some ground rules. Once we get that out of the way things will be fine, that is, until it clicks that I don't want him. We've just got to hope that won't happen until the summer season is over. Speak of the devil, here he comes!'

'Thank you, Hanny.'

'First of all, it's Hannah. Not Hanny, Han, or anything else. And secondly, thank you for what?'

'Sorry, Hannah it is. Thank you for giving me the job. I knew the final decision would be yours.'

'No, it was down to the staff. Everyone enjoyed working with you, and we need a good chef. That's why you got the job; the staff would never have forgiven me if I had vetoed you. One in particular would have given me the cold shoulder for weeks.'

'Oh yes,' Glenda laughed. 'You have an admirer before you've even started work. Glen is really looking forward to working with you, though I don't know if your cooking skills impressed him as much as the uniform!'

Jimmy laughed too; that was the ice cracked, if not fully broken. Hannah was still wary – she knew he would be on his best behaviour until he had his feet firmly under the table, but she was determined that he was never going to touch her table again.

He liked the idea of going to the pub and Hannah was secretly looking forward to it as well. They planned to meet in an hour, after Hannah and Glenda had finished the day's closing admin.

'You wouldn't like to come to the pub as well?' Hannah asked her.

'No, it will do you both good to talk freely. Set the ground rules and get tonight over with, because tomorrow the last thing that will be on his mind is you. Once he sees the mountain he has to climb in the kitchen, romance will go right out the window. Between you and me, if he does get everything in order quickly, I will just keep giving him other problems to solve for us. There'll be no time for anything else, I can assure you.'

The pub was busy. There was a local band on later, which had brought in a few extra patrons. The food was good and most of their conversation was about the hotel. Hannah had made some notes for him on the staffing problems in the kitchen and notable functions that were coming up over the next few weeks.

It turned out to be a very productive evening. They both decided that it would be better not to stay for the band, as that might turn it into a late night –

not what Jimmy needed to have before his first day.

'Right then, Jimmy, shall we make a move? We'll head back up the coastal path I think.'

As they got up to leave, Hannah saw Tristan coming through the crowd towards them. He looked drunk. That was just what she didn't need. She knew he would say something embarrassing, but he was blocking their way out.

'You might have turned me down once, but you just wait and see! When I'm rich and powerful, you'll be begging to go out with me!'

Hannah didn't answer, just pushed firmly past him followed by a confused Jimmy. She was just getting herself together heading for the door when Carl stepped through it.

'Oh, hi! I'm sorry about my mum. She didn't mean anything by it. I think she heard an exaggerated version of what happened from some gossip. I did try to tell her that all they saw was a kiss goodnight. I'm sorry.'

Jimmy's face was a picture. His jaw was practically on the ground, but there was worse to come. As they walked through the pub car park they were greeted by Tom heading the other way. Before Hannah could say anything to him, Tom demanded:

'You told me he wasn't in your life anymore! What's he doing here on the Quay?'

Hannah completely ignored him and carried on walking. She couldn't care less whether Jimmy was keeping up. She knew he would catch her eventually – he was sure to have something he wanted to say.

'What on Earth was that about? You've certainly been busy! Three unhappy chappies already?'

'Four, counting you! I'm living my life as I want to now. I'm in control and I do what I want, when I want. No man is going to make me change who I am ever again!'

Chapter 18

Jimmy's first week at the hotel had been fine. Hannah had set the ground rules and he was getting stuck into the job, putting lots of hours in every day. It was all very impressive. The younger members of the kitchen team were excited to be learning new things, and it was like a ton of bricks had been lifted off Glenda and Hannah's shoulders.

They were finally able to take days off from the hotel, but it wasn't just the hotel Hannah needed a break from. She needed a day away from Luckett Quay, both hotel and house, so she had decided to go to Sheringham and visit Josie. They were going to meet up at Josie's house. Hannah wanted to put her straight: not that she doubted Josie had already realised that Margaret was the person buying the other flat.

On the way to the bus stop she spotted Tom walking towards her. After his outburst outside the pub she really didn't want another confrontation. It had been weeks since he made his little speech about wanting more than a friendship and she knew she shouldn't have left it so long to chat with him again, but now wasn't the time. Still, it was best to be polite.

'Morning, Tom, how are you? I'm off to Sheringham for a day off.'

He ignored her, not even managing a hello. Hannah felt a little offended; the least he could have done was acknowledge her, even if he was in a hurry. That was his problem, though.

She felt more relaxed once she was on the bus, although she still wasn't sure how to broach the subject of Margaret with Josie. It was a lovely journey along the coast, passing all the different villages. Everyone who got on the little coast hopper said good morning. It was completely different to travelling in London, where you were scared to make eye contact with people, let alone speak.

There were two stops in Sheringham, one at the top of the town and one down by the harbour. Josie had offered to wait at the harbour stop so that they could have a little walk together before heading back to hers for some lunch.

'Good morning,' she greeted Hannah, 'and what a beautiful one it is! How was your bus journey? It does take about three times as long as driving yourself, I'm afraid.'

'It was good and to be honest it doesn't take that long. And who are you?' Hannah directed her attention to the bundle of energy at Josie's side. 'Just look at that tail wagging! You are gorgeous!'

'Hannah, meet Bonkers. I know it's a silly name but it does suit him.'

'It does! So, Bonkers, are you going to show me the sights of Sheringham?'

They walked along the harbour wall. It was quite busy, with lots of other dog walkers. The tide was out, though, so everyone was well spaced out. There was no mention of Luckett House on the walk; Hannah talked about the hotel and mentioned Jimmy turning up. After an hour or so, they turned around and headed back into the town, looking into a couple of the little gift shops' windows on the way.

'I must apologise for the state of my house,' Josie said as they began to climb the hill. 'I've started to pack. I've tried to keep all the boxes together. I've got rid of so much stuff I should have thrown out years ago – you forget half the things you own while they're hidden in the cupboards. I counted over thirty dinner plates: why? It's only me, and sometimes Richard, so I've cut it down to eight. Here we go, we can cut up this side street and that's my house there on the corner.'

'What a lovely position! I bet you can see the sea from upstairs.'

'Yes, I should have changed my bedroom into a lounge to capture the view. That's the thing I'm looking forward to most in Luckett Quay. To be able to sit looking out that huge window watching the fishing boats come and go, all snug in my armchair even in the winter. Here we are, let me take your coat. I'll put the kettle on; that's something I haven't packed yet!'

Hannah took a seat in the lounge. On the way in she had noticed the 'for sale' board outside saying 'under offer'. So, Josie was still up for moving to Luckett Quay, but Hannah had to talk with her about Margaret before getting back on the coast hopper.

'Here you are, a cup of tea. Help yourself to a biscuit. Sorry they're not like the ones at the hotel; these are from a packet. I've made a cottage pie for lunch, will that be okay for you? It will be about another hour.'

'That will be lovely, thank you. This is a lovely little house. Surely you'll miss it when you move. Sheringham is such a nice place as well; are you sure you're doing the right thing by moving?'

'Of course I'll miss it. I've been here so many years; this is where Richard grew up, this was our family home, and there are so many memories here. But you can take memories with you wherever you go. They don't stay behind, they are with you forever.'

'I'd never thought of it like that. Strangely, it's the complete opposite for me and Nan: we're moving back to where we had our happiest memories, bringing memories from the Midlands with us.'

'Yes, but I'm moving back to Luckett Quay, where all my childhood memories are from, and I'm so looking forward to it. I am a little nervous but in a good way.'

'Why have you chosen to do it now, Josie? I'm sorry; I know it's none of my business.'

'Don't be sorry, if I don't tell you then someone else will. When I was young and having a good time down in Saltmarsh Quay, I met a man. We had fun and both found each other very attractive, so we started seeing each other. It was good, and we could both see ourselves staying together, but there was a fly in the ointment.

'He essentially had to choose between his head and his heart. I was the heart, but he chose the head. I was out of the equation, and that would have been the end if I hadn't found out I was pregnant. I told him, it was his right to know. He could still have followed his heart and married me. I know it would have been a good marriage.

'Let's just say he followed the pound signs. The grass was greener on the richer side and he made the better financial choice. So there I was, pregnant and alone in Luckett Quay. My mum had a sister here in Sheringham and I moved in with her after Richard was born. She looked after him so that I could go out to work. This was her house that she left to me.'

'Oh dear, I'm so sorry.'

'Sorry? I've had a lovely life with a fabulous son, so there's no need to be sorry. I've been really happy here. But that doesn't answer your original question of why I've chosen to move back now and not before.'

'I think I know. Was Frank Fern Richard's dad? Now he's died, there's nothing keeping you away.'

'Yes, dear old Frankie. It's sad; by rights he should have had the perfect life and me the not so good one, but it was the other way around. Give him his due, he did give me money to help me bring up Richard, but Richard never had any contact with him. I did, on and off. It was usually when he had had too much to drink and he was feeling guilty. I don't have any hard feelings, it's just sad to think of

118

what he could have had but missed out on.'

'It is sad, but Richard doesn't seem to have needed him.'

'No, though I think it would have been nice for him to have had a dad. Whether Frank would have been any good at it, we will never know.'

'That does still leave us with a little dilemma over the flats.'

'I know, but I don't hold anything against Margaret – I presume she is the one who wants to buy the other flat. Richard was well on the way before Frank did his deal with Margaret's dad. By the way, "deal" is not my word; it was the word Frank used to describe what he had done.'

'Does Margaret know about Richard? If so, what do I do? She needs to know that you are the one buying the other flat. How do you think she will deal with that?'

'Yes, she knows. It didn't take long for people to work it out. We've never mentioned it to each other, but all these years we've been perfectly pleasant to one another whenever we met. It is quite ironic that we could both be living under the same roof; I wonder what Frank would have to say about that? I've heard stories over the years that suggest he wasn't a good husband to her, and he certainly wasn't a good boss to his workers, but I have a lot to thank Frank for. If it wasn't for him, Richard wouldn't be here. So for something that looked so sad and wrong, it actually worked out perfectly. I never felt any guilt because I didn't do anything wrong. All I ever did was fall in love with a man and have his baby. If he didn't want to stay and raise him, that was his problem, not mine.'

Chapter 19

Over the next few weeks, Hannah got on with balancing the job and the house conversion. She had yet to see Margaret, but she knew she couldn't put it off for ever. The sooner everything was out in the open the better.

Her other little problem, Jimmy being at the hotel, wasn't such a problem anymore. He had become one of the kitchen team, going for drinks with them after work, and the hotel was running really smoothly. Glenda was more than happy. She hadn't seen Tristan either, but every time Raymond Dove was at the hotel he always made a beeline for her with the same question: how many times had Tristan been up to the hotel?

Today was her day off and she was off to see Brian at the house. He had something to show her and he said it was a surprise. First, though, she wanted to nip over to see Olivia at one of the flats she cleaned. She wanted an idea of how to lay the furniture out, and what sort of furniture she and Betty should be buying in the first place. She also wanted to know if Olivia had seen much of Tom and what she knew about him ignoring her.

Hannah arrived just as Olivia was finishing up, and Olivia showed her around.

'So this is it: quite simple, not a lot of furniture, and the same wooden floor all the way through. The girl who lives here is young. She works in Norwich.'

'I really like it. She's been very clever to match the colour scheme all the way through the flat, so that if, say, the bedroom door is open, the same white walls with burnt orange accessories flow through all the rooms. Thanks for letting me see it. I will let you get on with your cleaning, although there

120

is one other thing...'

'I know what you are going to say. It's about Tom. I don't know why he's so screwed up over you. I've tried to explain that there's nothing between you and Carl, but no joy. And now Jimmy's on the scene it's made him worse. I think you're going to have to talk to him. Now, when are you coming around again? The boys had such a good time with you. They keep asking if we can do it again.'

'Next week, I promise. I will check which is the quietest day for me to have off. Love you lots, see you later, and tell the boys I'm up for a game of football, okay?'

'I'm not sure they'll let you! Football time for them is with Tom. Hannah, please talk to Tom.'

Hannah knew she had to, but what could she say? Only the truth that she didn't fancy him: he had to understand that.

The tide was out so she could walk to Luckett Quay via the beach. It was warm out, and lots of holidaymakers were picnicking on the sands. This place hadn't changed in years and that was a good thing.

Now to see what Brian had got to show her. She was a bit earlier than she had said, but hopefully that wouldn't be a problem. Perhaps she should wait a bit? No, sod it, she was excited.

The new windows were looking good – she had seen them from the beach – but that couldn't be the surprise. She had seen them going in over the last few weeks. Getting closer, she noticed that Brian's van wasn't there but other workmen's cars were. Over time she had got to know them all very well, laughing and joking and taking the mickey. Especially old Len – he was past retirement age but still managed to keep up with the younger men.

'Hi, Len, how's it going?'

'Everything's fine, but I've had instructions not to

let you in the house until Brian gets back. He shouldn't be long now; he's nipped out to get some materials.'

'Come on, I won't tell him if you don't. It won't hurt.'

'It will. I'm sorry, but you aren't going in.'

'So what are we going to do while we wait?'

'We can chat. Tell me about the hotel; how are you enjoying it? Are you excited about moving in here? It's getting close now.'

'Is that what the surprise is all about? I know what we can talk about, tell me about Carl. Why's he so shy?'

Len shrugged.

'I feel sorry for the lad, really. He doesn't like the job much, although he's very good at it. He keeps himself to himself, mostly because his mother doesn't let him breathe without her permission. Good looking lad he may be, but he's never had a girlfriend that I know of.

'Still, now Frank's not around to keep putting him down he might get a bit more confidence in himself. And who knows what's in store for him now he's learnt how to kiss? In fact, perhaps I'm shy and need to be a bit more confident. How about a kiss for me, Hannah?'

'Very funny, Len. It was only a peck on the cheek to thank Carl for a nice night out. And look, here comes Brian. You've completed the task of keeping me out. Thanks for the chat.'

Brian parked his van and headed over.

'Hello, you're not been in, have you?'

'No, the security guard hasn't let me. If I'd given him a kiss he might have given in, eh, Len? I'm getting excited, or maybe nervous.'

'Come on then.'

Hannah followed Brian. He headed straight upstairs. Apart from a few minor changes it looked the same as ever: no surprises here. She was thinking that she must have missed something until the look on Brian's face gave away that he was having a bit of fun with her.

He grinned. 'Sorry, wrong flat.'

Back downstairs they looked into her flat, which was also no different from the last time she had seen it: it was still full of boxes and tools. This was being used as the storeroom for all the building equipment. Brian was grinning ever wider and finally led her into Betty's flat. She was taken aback.

'Oh how fabulous, Brian! What a surprise – you and the team have worked so hard!'

There in front of her was Betty's new kitchen, all fitted, shiny and new. The room was nearly finished. It just needed painting once the plaster was fully dried and the wooden floor fitted, then Betty could move all her furniture in.

'Do you think your nan will be pleased? I'm so happy she's gone with this kitchen; I know the doors are darker but it makes a statement. The bi-fold doors into the garden, or possibly the conservatory, are a great choice as well. If I was living by myself I would love this flat.'

'Yes, she's going to love it. Thank you so much.'

'There was one other thing I wanted to show you. Just have a look in the bathroom.'

Hannah didn't want to take her eyes off the kitchen. Her first thought was that she had to persuade Betty to buy some new modern furniture, but she was sure she would anyway. The internal doors caught her eye as she moved to the bathroom. It had certainly been worth spending a little more on them to get a better quality door.

Brian had switched the bathroom light on from the outside and she could hear the extractor fan going. Even though she knew what to expect from the layout and the fixtures it was still a huge surprise. She was glad they had gone for the corner shower cubicle rather than a bath. It gave a lot more floor space and considering that there was no window, the lighting was perfect.

'Pleased? More importantly, will your nan be pleased? All we have to do is put the wooden floor down and she can move in. That is, if she doesn't mind living on the building site while we finish the other flats. Speaking of the others, which one should we start work on next?'

Hannah didn't know. As much as she would love hers to be done, it would make sense to do the upstairs ones first. She threw the decision back to Brian so he could choose another lovely surprise for her.

She said her goodbyes and decided to take a walk along Luckett Quay beach for some peace and quiet instead of walking back up to the hotel. Finding a little rock away from everyone else she started to contemplate how much her life had changed in such a short time.

She didn't miss London at all. The air was fresh and clean here, and as for the old job, no way could she go back to that. She loved living in Norfolk again. It was great to be reunited with Olivia, and when Nan arrived they were going to have some great times together.

There were downsides, of course. Jimmy was one of them. She knew he was playing by her rules at the moment but that wouldn't last long. She couldn't afford to let her guard down where he was concerned. Then there was the problem of Tom. She badly wanted him as a friend, but that was all.

She spent a lot of time thinking of how to furnish her apartment. She would go very minimalist: white walls and a grey sofa, with pops of yellow throughout. That way, when she got bored with it she just needed to change all the yellow to another colour with matching rugs, cushions, duvet cover, and ornaments.

Hannah couldn't believe that two hours had passed. She was starting to feel cold, so decided to head back up to the hotel. The beach was quiet and empty apart from a couple walking towards her, hand in hand. They hadn't seen her; they looked all loved up, kissing and cuddling. She recognised the girl. Katie worked in her dad's pub down on Saltmarsh Quay. She was a lovely girl, always friendly, but who was she with? Hannah couldn't believe it. What was she doing with him? This was going to be embarrassing, but not for Hannah.

'Hi, Katie, how are you? And hello, Tristan.'

Chapter 20

'Good morning, Hannah, did you have a good day off? How's the house coming along? There are three messages for you in the handover book when you're ready.'

'Yes, really good thank you. Let me guess, is one of the messages from Tristan Goring?'

Hannah explained to Glenda that she had seen him with young Katie down on the beach. There was no way she would be returning his call. Let him sweat it out. There was a message from Margaret asking her to call back and one from her dad saying it wasn't urgent, but could she give him a call? Once the breakfast shift was over, she would call Margaret and her dad. First of all, however, she was going to text Tom: something she should have done weeks ago. She needed to sort his problem out, for both their sakes.

'Tom,' she wrote, 'we need to talk today. I will meet you in Saltmarsh Quay by the old boat house at 3pm.'

Sorted. Now to get this breakfast show on the road.

*

'How was breakfast? It looked quite steady. I didn't want to call you out, but Tristan has rung back twice saying it's very urgent. I told him you were tied up all day with meetings and restaurant opening times but I don't think he will take no for an answer.'

'Good, let him turn up. Then I'll see what he wants.'

Hannah was a little confused after calling her father. He was bringing Nan down to see the work on the house and stay for two days, which was good news. Even better, Susanna wasn't coming with them. He had also said he would need Hannah's help, but he hadn't specified why.

There was still no text message from Tom to say whether he would meet her, so she decided to just go down at the appointed time and see if he turned up. Next up was a call to Margaret.

'Hi, Margaret, it's Hannah, how are you?'

'I'm fine, thanks. I'm sorry to bother you, but I wonder if we could meet up one day this week? There is something I'd like to talk to you about.'

'Of course. I can't today as I'm working three shifts, but tomorrow I'm only doing breakfast and dinner so I'll be free in-between.'

They decided to meet up at the Maple Duck pub for lunch the next day.

Hannah got back to work, on her guard for Tristan. She was actually looking forward to seeing him. She wanted to know what excuses he would come out with this time. But looking at the lunch bookings in today's diary, she realised he wouldn't be coming over yet. Raymond Dove was booked in for lunch, and Tristan wasn't that daft. He would have checked beforehand. The last thing he needed right now was to be seen skiving off work for this.

Lunch was busy, so Hannah only managed a quick chat with Raymond. Tristan's name wasn't even mentioned, only the weather and how good the food was.

She left the team to clear up and prepare for dinner, as she only had twenty minutes to get down to Saltmarsh Quay. Tom had better turn up or else she would be even angrier than she already was.

*

'Hello, how did you know I would be here? I didn't answer your text. What do you want, anyway?'

'Thanks for coming, Tom. Let's take a walk.'

There was no way forward other than honesty.

'Look, I want us to be friends. I miss not having

you in our little HOT gang. I can't help how you feel about me but you need to understand that I don't feel the same way about you. I'm sorry if that upsets you but honestly, I don't feel that about anyone right now. Yes, I kissed Carl, but he didn't kiss me back so there's no future there.

'As for Jimmy arriving here … we are getting on well, but that's our working relationship. I didn't want him to move to Luckett Quay but for the hotel's sake I'm glad he's here. The two of us are never getting back together again, whether he realises that yet or not. It's not my problem, and it needn't be yours. Please, Tom, let's be friends. We have the whole summer ahead of us. We can all still have a great time together.'

Tom didn't answer. They kept walking in silence for the next half an hour. It was awkward, and Hannah was beginning to think that she had done the wrong thing. She wasn't saying he needed to get over it immediately, she just wanted to say goodbye and head back to the hotel.

Just then she saw two boys running towards her. It was Sam and Ben! Thank goodness for that. They were just what she needed to break the ice. Olivia was following behind and waved to them.

'I'm glad I've seen you both together at last! There's something I want to do.'

'What's that?'

'I'll tell you what I want, Tom. I want to bang both your heads together to knock some sense into the pair of you!'

All three of them laughed. It was still an awkward moment, but much more relaxed with the boys there jumping around and shouting.

Oliva explained that she wanted to arrange a night out for the three of them at the pub. Her mum would have the boys overnight and she intended to have a lot to drink. Hannah agreed that it would be good to do, she just needed to check the rotas to see if she could get a dinner shift and the following morning's breakfast shift off. Tom eventually agreed as well.

After a quick kick around with the boys they said their goodbyes and Hannah headed back to the hotel. It was time to get herself ready for the dinner shift.

There had been two more calls from Tristan which she refused to return, but somehow she expected to see him tonight. She was ready for him but to her surprise, by ten-fifteen he still hadn't turned up. Dinner was over, the restaurant was all laid out for the following morning's breakfast, and all that was left was to take the shift's paperwork to Reception.

Time to call it a day then – but no. Tristan's absence during dinner had been too good to be true and now there he was. He must have been outside waiting for the restaurant lights to be switched off.

'You had better take a seat in the lounge. I will just be two minutes tidying up here. Coffee? Or something stronger?'

'Coffee would be good, thank you.'

Hannah finished off the paperwork and made a pot of coffee. As she walked back to the lounge she could see that he looked worried and quite rough: not at all the dapper Tristan she was used to seeing.

She poured two coffees, handed him one, and explained that his life was no concern of hers. She was here to run the hotel and as long as he showed some respect to the staff he was more than welcome to come into it.

'What you saw yesterday wasn't what you thought it was. I was just...'

'It's none of my business. You can have a dozen girlfriends for all I care, but until you choose one of my friends I won't say a thing. If girls are silly

129

enough to believe everything you say that's their problem.'

'You think I'm a joke, don't you? Well I'm not. I don't stop and settle. I want to make something of my life. I will be successful one day, just you wait and see! Why are you smiling like that? You might be content with a boring job in some little hotel in Norfolk, but that's not me. If you want to get somewhere in this world, you have to...'

'Find a businessman with an impressionable daughter? Fill her head with promises in the hope that you'll end up with her father's business one day? I'm sorry, I thought the girls were thick to fall for your stories, but you're the stupid one. It's not the girls you have to convince, it's their fathers, and somehow I think they can see right through your little games. You're so sad. I hope you see that before it's too late. I would hate to think of you ending up in some boring job in Norfolk.

'Goodnight, Tristan, and all the best. I hope you find what you are looking for before you lose your looks and cheesy charm. You'll have no hope after that.'

He left. He was such a sad character, to think that if he didn't behave that way his life could be really good! Hannah often wondered how he had ended up like this.

She returned the coffee cups to the kitchen and almost jumped out of her skin when Jimmy appeared behind her.

'Sorry. I was going to ask if you fancied a drink, but then I saw you with your friend. Is he coming back?'

'First of all, he isn't my friend and never will be. Secondly, yes, he will probably keep coming back, always trying to impress somebody new. He's just a very odd, sad young man. Finally, yes, please. I would love a drink: one nice large gin and tonic.'

Jimmy fetched drinks and they sat by the window looking out at the sparse scatter of lights on the sea. He explained that he was slowly falling in love with that view, and with the area. If only he had listened to Hannah when she talked about how special Luckett Quay was, he might have come around to it years ago. He couldn't believe how little he missed London.

'You know I came here to try and win you back, but it's not just that. I really think this beautiful place has made me grow up and appreciate my life. It's made me realise how much I've got, but it has painfully emphasised what I've lost, and that's you. I'm sorry. I want my Hanny back.'

Chapter 21

It was set to be a busy day for Hannah. On top of her usual duties at the hotel, including the weekly planning meeting, she was meeting Margaret at Luckett House and getting ready for Robert and Betty's arrival tonight. Fortunately for her schedule, they would be staying at the hotel. Tomorrow the three of them planned to meet up with Brian to discuss the conservatory.

She was glad to see a text from Olivia saying that her chat with Tom seemed to have done a world of good. Apparently he was looking forward to a good night out together.

For now, though, it was time to get the show on the road. The guests would be down for breakfast any minute but the shift should go smoothly, as she had three staff on duty and one of them was Glen. The restaurant was his stage and he was ready to perform as soon as he walked through the kitchen door.

She was right. Breakfast went so well that Glen pulled her aside before the end of it and said:

'Look, we're nearly done here. There're only two more rooms to come down for breakfast, so why don't you go early? I can finish this up. Give my regards to Carl if you see him at the house.'

'Ha! I've already scared him off, God knows how he'll react if I pass that on!'

'You never know, he might be flattered! Now go, or it'll be time for the lunch shift already. But I should tell you before you hear it elsewhere: last night Jimmy was spotted out with one of the local girls, Britney, in the Maple Duck and let's just say they were checking out each other's throats. With a bit of luck, maybe he'll leave you alone now.'

Hannah quickly changed clothes. She felt a little jealous after what Glen had just told her but he was right that she had wanted Jimmy to move on. It was better not to dwell on it.

She headed down to the house. Margaret hadn't arrived yet, but Brian and the other builders were busy with the second downstairs flat. The bathroom was being plumbed in and the last radiator was being installed. Upstairs, the plastering was finally finished and they were putting together the kitchen base units.

Hannah smiled to herself when she saw Carl hard at work. She was tempted to tell him what Glen had said, but she didn't think he'd appreciate it.

Margaret arrived, and Hannah showed her upstairs to her flat. Most of the workmen there knew Margaret, but none of them seemed very comfortable in her presence. They were perfectly polite but, one by one, discovered a sudden excuse to do something elsewhere. Margaret noticed it too.

'They don't know what to say to me. One thing's for sure, they will be happier working for Brian than they ever were under my husband. How some of them put up with that treatment for so many years I will never know. But then I suppose I was putting up with it as well, and I stayed.'

The view from upstairs was stunning. In some ways Hannah wished she had one of the upstairs flats, but once most of the trees and bushes were cut back the view from downstairs would still be nice. It would also be great to have the conservatory connecting her to Betty's flat.

After some chit-chat about fixtures and fittings with Brian they went down to see Betty's finished flat. The wooden floor had been laid down since Hannah's last visit. She couldn't wait for Betty to see it tomorrow.

'Hannah, have you got time for a little walk?

Perhaps we could go down to Luckett Quay. That's what I'm looking forward to most about living here: opening the door and having that beach just five minutes' walk down the hill.'

They talked about the flats and how Hannah was getting on at the hotel, but that wasn't why Margaret had wanted to have a chat. They walked to the rocks and found a quiet place to sit. Then the conversation finally came around to Josie. Margaret wanted to know if she knew Margaret was buying one of the other flats.

'She does, and neither she nor Richard have a problem with it. To be honest, I think she got over Frank before you were even married. She had her son and he was so special that all her emotional energy went towards him. It still does, I think. As for Richard, I get the impression that Frank was never part of his life, so he has no bad associations with you. You will like him: he's very sensitive and quiet.'

'Yes, I know a lot about Richard. He's been so successful in his career! But that's another story.'

'Why, what does he do? I imagined he worked in an office of some sort.'

In actual fact, Margaret explained, Richard was a top fashion designer with a big fashion house, although she seemed to think he was cutting back on his work for them. Hannah couldn't understand why Margaret would know all this. It was quite odd, but she didn't think it would be right to ask her.

'So, given that Josie doesn't have a problem with you being there, do you have any doubts about her? The last thing Nan or I would want is for either of you to be unhappy. We'd totally understand if you wanted to change your mind and not move in rather than have to bump into her most days.'

'None at all. This is a new life for me and I mean that. There'll be no more pretence. I have no hidden secrets left to come out in the open. I just want the

134

last part of my life to be enjoyable, and I hope as time goes on Josie and I can talk about Frank together. Somehow I think we'll find we have something in common: a lack of respect for Frank. I would also like to talk to Richard about his dad sometime, if he's willing. But that's for the future. For now, let's head up the hill; you will have a restaurant full of people waiting to be fed soon. Thank you for this, Hannah. I know that Luckett House is going to be a very happy home for us all.'

*

Hannah was back at the hotel in time for lunch service. Glen had got everything organised and, as there weren't many tables booked, it was a very relaxed shift.

After lunch she had the heads of departments' meeting with Glenda, Annie, and Jimmy to discuss the following week's business.

'That seems to be about it,' said Glenda, consulting her agenda. 'We've covered the functions, VIP guest rotas seem okay, staffing levels are good, so that just leaves Any Other Business. Let's go round the table: you first, Annie.'

'Not a lot from me, Glenda. I've had a rep from our new toiletry supplier visit us and I'm looking at getting a better quality soap and shampoo for the suites. I'll let you know if anything comes of it.'

'Great. Hannah?'

'Everything's okay in the restaurant. Glen will be running a few more shifts for me. He's really good, so that will give me more time to spend on training new staff.'

'Thanks. How about the kitchen, Jimmy, anything new to report?'

'No, it's going well. I've got a new lad doing pot washing who's very keen to learn. I think if we get a quiet shift soon I'll put him with Mark to train on cold starters and we'll take it from there. Are you still

135

looking for waiting staff, Hannah? Because there's a girl down in Saltmarsh looking for work. Her name's Britney. She seems nice and very keen, I'm sure she would fit in well with your team.'

Hannah wanted to say something sarcastic, but this wasn't the time or the place. She told him to get her to fill out an application form but she knew there was no way she would be giving her a job. Britney! No doubt she had blonde pigtails. What would happen when they fell out? Would he expect Hannah to sack her? On your bike, Jimmy!

Once the meeting was over with, it was time to get ready for dinner. Betty sent Hannah a text to say that they had left and should be at the hotel by eight o'clock. That would suit Hannah – by the time they were booked in and ready to eat the restaurant should have quietened down and she would be able to join them.

*

'Look at you, or should I say look at that tan! See how well she looks, Robert?'

'It's all the fresh air, Nan. I walk everywhere and with the sea breeze and a little sunshine I soon get tanned. Let's get your room keys from Reception and I'll show you up to your rooms. I've booked us a table for nine, but come down whenever you're ready and have a drink in the bar.'

After showing them up, Hannah went back to the restaurant to give Glen a break. It occurred to her that something had seemed off about her dad: it was like he didn't want to be here. It was all very strange, as she had assumed being away from Susanna and the children for a while would be exciting for him. It would be a little bit of freedom. No doubt she would find out what was bothering him before long.

'Are you sure it's okay for us to eat in here?' Betty asked. 'We could quite easily go to the pub.'

'Its fine, this is one of the perks of working here.

136

You take a look at the menus and I'll be back in a moment to take the order.'

After the main course they all decided they were too full for a dessert. Hannah went off to get coffees for her and Robert. They had chatted non-stop about Luckett House and Betty couldn't wait to see it tomorrow, but for now she was going to bed. She was tired out with excitement and nerves over tomorrow. This was a big step for her but she knew it was the right thing to do.

With Nan gone, it was time for Hannah to clear the air with her dad. What did he want to discuss? Whatever it was, most likely it would have come from Susanna. Sadly, he was often reduced to being her messenger.

'Dad, are you okay with Nan moving here? You don't think she's doing the wrong thing?'

'No, this is definitely the right thing for her. I was worried at first, but now I know you're settled here, I'm happy. I think she's going to love it here, and having those other old ladies living in the same building will be perfect for her.'

'I'm pleased, and I'm sure she is too. So then, if it's not Nan moving here that's bothering you, what is? You can barely look at me tonight. What have I done wrong?'

'What do you mean? You've done nothing wrong! I'm very happy for you and the hotel. You really seem to love the job, and after all the organising you've done down at Luckett House you should be so proud of yourself.'

They changed the subject and chatted about nothing much for another hour. A couple of times Hannah thought Robert was building himself up to say something but changed his mind. It was a little uncomfortable. The last time he had been anything like this was when he was trying to break the news to her that he had met Susanna. Perhaps they were splitting up?

They said goodnight and Robert went up to bed. Hannah nipped into Reception before following suit. She wanted to see what tomorrow's bookings looked like.

She went through the paperwork in her pigeonhole and noticed that someone had taken a call from Emmi asking if Hannah had time to meet up with her. That was frustrating: the last thing she needed was to get any more involved with Tristian's love life. This needed nipping in the bud right away. It might be nearly eleven, but the message did say to phone back when she saw it.

'Hi, Emmi, it's Hannah. What can I do for you?'

'I need to ask you a question and I'd be grateful if you could be honest with me, as there's something I need to know.'

'Ask away, what is it?'

'Are you having an affair with my Tristan?'

Hannah couldn't help it, she laughed out loud. She apologised and reassured Emmi that she wasn't doing anything of the sort. Emmi didn't seem too convinced, so Hannah decided to lay it on thick and tell her what she really thought of her boyfriend. She knew that if Emmi went running to her dad about it he would only find it funny.

'Look, Emmi, you're a very nice girl and for what it's worth, I think you deserve a lot better than Tristan. He's extremely rude, arrogant, and selfish, and on top of all that, he's very sly.'

That ended that conversation. As Hannah was finishing off her duties for the day she wondered how she had been drawn into this business with Tristan. It was starting to really get on her nerves. Perhaps she shouldn't have said those things but she didn't have anything nice to say about him, except that he was very good looking, and Emmi knew that all too well!

138

Chapter 22

She was still laughing the following morning. To think that Emmi actually thought she and Tristan were having an affair! He would be the last person in the whole world to tempt her like that. True, he was good looking and very fit, but once he opened his mouth and all those smarmy comments came spilling out, the attraction was lost.

There was one thing that bothered her about her conversation with Emmi and that was village gossip. If Emmi thought that something was going on, how many others had reached the same conclusion? This was a very small community and everyone knew everyone else's business. She didn't like to think of everyone talking about her in that way.

If the gossip had connected her to Carl, that would be a different kettle of fish. Mind you, then the phone call would have come from Carl's mum and that would have been a lot worse.

She had two main things on her agenda today: show Nan her new flat and find out what her dad's problem was. First, though, she had a bacon sandwich in the staff room. Jimmy had finished his own breakfast already, and walked over to her on his way out.

'Good morning, is it today your Nan's here? It must be exciting for her. By the way, I left Britney's application form in your pigeonhole. I think she'll be a hard worker.'

'I'll take a look at it tomorrow. I need to spend today with Dad and Nan sorting house things out. I'm not promising anything, though. It's not just me; she has to fit in with the rest of the team. You've been here a while now yourself, are you still enjoying it? You're not missing London?'

139

'I'm enjoying it a lot more than I ever thought I would. Creating new dishes is great fun, and when the summer season ends and we go into winter I can create a whole new menu. It does feel strange, though. In most places I've worked I've been the kid in the kitchen, but here I'm the boss and one of the oldest. That's a big responsibility, but they're a great bunch of boys and girls. Because it seems such a short time since I was in their position I can remember the things that wound me up and stop that from happening to them. We're a great little team. How about you? I think this hotel was made for you, Hanny – sorry, Hannah.'

'You could be right, but I'm also excited about my flat. I've been really lucky and I want to enjoy my time here with Nan and Olivia. We were good friends once and now we are older what we have is even more special. There are lots of fun times ahead for us, I'm sure.'

'Wasn't there a third person in that club? How's he coping now you're back?'

'Don't go there! He has some sort of crush on me. Apparently he always has, but I've never known.'

'Well the few times we met up with them I could certainly tell. He could never take his eyes off you. He was so jealous of me, and even now when I cross his path in Saltmarsh Quay it's like he's snarling at me. God help you when you get a boyfriend, he's not going to be happy. Can you believe we're here discussing this? Twelve months ago...'

'Twelve months ago our lives were very different, Jimmy. We've moved on.'

'We might have moved on but in one way we're still together: we are both together in this hotel and even living in the same staff accommodation.'

'Yes and it's working very well, far better than when we were together don't you think? I need to be off. I'm looking forward to interviewing Britney and

140

getting to know her a little. It will be good to find out what her interests are outside of work and what really excites her. See you later, Jimmy.'

*

Betty was ready and raring to go. She couldn't wait to get down to Luckett House and meet up with Brian. Dad was still quiet. He only had today to get whatever it was off his chest; he would be heading back to the Midlands at teatime, leaving a very excited Betty here for the week.

Robert kept telling Betty to slow down on the hill but she was having none of it. Hannah knew that Brian would be just as excited as Betty; he was so proud of what he and his team had created. Hannah's only worry was that Betty would want to bring all of her old furniture – she would love her to buy some modern pieces.

'It looks no different from this side,' Hannah pointed out as they made their final approach, 'Apart from the windows, of course. They're the same sash type but new, and the grey colour against the white walls will look stunning. Brian said that painting the outside will be one of the last jobs because of all the dust from their lorries and vans. Nan, you're biting at the bit! Go on in before you burst with excitement.'

For the next two hours the three of them went around the house with Brian. Unsurprisingly, they kept going back to Betty's flat. She was over the moon, and there was no need for Hannah to worry about her old furniture: she was having a new sofa, chair, and small dining set as well as some rugs. She also suggested finding some modern artwork for the walls. Hannah could see that her dad was genuinely happy about everything they saw. Perhaps he had just been concerned about Betty seeing her flat and Hannah had been worrying over nothing.

Brian was right about the conservatory: it had to

be built so that in years to come it could be divided up if necessary. He also thought that the patio in front of the conservatory should also wind around the sides. This would be helpful in case of a windy day as at least one side would be sheltered and could be an escape if it got too hot inside.

Everything was sorted out. There was just one more question for Brian to answer:

'When can I move in?'

'Whenever you like! Obviously the men will still be working here for a few more weeks, but just you give me the nod and I'll have it cleaned through.'

Betty was delighted. A shopping trip to Norwich was on the cards for her and Hannah: they needed furniture, new bedding, and curtains. The only things she would bring with her were a few sentimental things, her clothes, and kitchen equipment which would all be hidden in cupboards.

The three of them left Brian to it and headed down to Saltmarsh Quay for some lunch before Robert made his way back to the Midlands. He had gone all quiet again, so there must still be a problem to be solved in the next couple of hours. Hannah wished he would just come out with it.

As they were walking towards the Maple Duck they bumped into Margaret. Betty invited her to join them for lunch. It would be good for them to get to know each other better, she said. Robert didn't look happy about it and didn't speak much all the time they were eating.

'Nan, why don't you and Margaret have another drink while Dad and I take a little walk? Some fresh air will do him good before he drives back.'

'That's a good idea. I'm sure we will be okay on our own, don't you, Margaret? We might get chatted up – that would be nice!'

Hannah and her dad walked along by the sea wall. It was a lovely sunny afternoon and Hannah knew a seat looking out over the harbour. This was it. She was ready to clear the air.

'So what's wrong, Dad? Get it off your chest, it can't be that bad.'

'It is, and there's no easy way to put it. Susanna thinks it would be best if your flat was sold and we took the money it makes to help buy a bigger house. You could eventually have Mum's flat when something happens to her. I'm sorry, I know you're so excited about moving there, but like Susanna says you have your room at the hotel to live in so you don't really need the flat.'

Hannah was fuming, but not with her dad. She was angry with Susanna, so to start shouting just before he had to drive back to her wasn't a good idea. At the end of the day, he was talking to the wrong person. It was Betty's flat and Betty's money. He had to deal with Betty, she told him, whether he found the courage to do it today or waited until Betty was home again. Hannah gave him the option, but she knew he would have to do it today rather than go back to Susanna without an answer.

Re-joining Betty, they said their goodbyes to Margaret and walked back up the coastal path to the hotel. Hannah suggested a pot of tea on the lawn and left Betty and Robert at a little table under the tree to talk. She took her time, not wanting to get involved in their conversation. She knew Susanna would have been more than happy to let Betty sell Luckett House. With that money plus the money from selling their house she and Robert could buy a posh four-bedroom house on the outskirts of a nice town. She would be able to lord it over her friends then. But Hannah knew Betty would be thinking of that as well.

'Here we go, tea and homemade biscuits.'

Robert stood up. 'I'm sorry, darling, I don't think I'll stop for tea. I'd better get off. Thanks for letting us stay at the hotel, it's been lovely. I'll be back in a week tomorrow to pick Nan up. I'll text you when I'm home. Bye, Mum, have a nice week here and don't overdo it! We're all here to help and support you.'

Hannah and Betty waved goodbye and walked back to have their cup of tea. Hannah wasn't going to say anything as it was none of her business, but Betty looked like she was in deep thought. Hannah knew she would never want to hurt her son, her only child.

'The flat's still yours, darling, there was never any question of that. I will help your Dad and Susanna out once Josie and Margaret have paid me for their flats. There'll be enough money there for a nice semi-detached house on a nice estate. I have told your father to relay that to his wife. I've also told him to tell her that if she gets off her backside and earns some money by doing a day's work for once she can have her manor house. But something tells me he won't tell her about that bit of the conversation. Oh, these biscuits are to die for! I can see me popping up the hill for tea and biscuits on a regular basis. Now, when can you get some time off to go shopping? We've got two flats to furnish!'

'Thank you, Nan, I love you so much.'

'I know you do, darling, I really do.'

That certainly wouldn't be the end of the discussion. Susanna had always managed to get what she wanted regardless of anyone else's feelings.

Apart from that, today had been lovely. To see Betty's face as she walked into her new home was something very special and Hannah would never forget it. The love and attention Brian and his team had given the property was special as well, but the thing that had really made her day was seeing Betty and Margaret getting on so well. Luckett House was going to be a home filled with love.

Chapter 23

It had been an extremely busy week for Hannah and Betty. They'd visited every retail park in about a 50-mile radius. There couldn't be a single chair or sofa they hadn't sat on but, tiring though it had been, it was exciting. Orders had been placed, and there was news from Brian: the kitchen and bathrooms were finished in all the flats, leaving just bits and pieces to finish off.

There was still a lot of snagging to be done, and next week they were starting on the conservatory, but tonight Hannah had an evening away from it all. She was off to the Maple Duck with Olivia and Tom. Before that, though, she had an interview with Britney. She couldn't wait to meet her and find out what she looked like and whether she would mention her new boyfriend.

Hannah took a quick look at the reservations as they set up the restaurant for lunch and noticed that Raymond Dove had a table booked for four. Hopefully it was a business lunch and not a family one with Emmi and Tristan involved. A quick briefing with the kitchen to check the daily specials and any shortages, and it was show time. Without Glen, this time: Hannah had given him some time off as he had covered lots of shifts for her during Betty's visit.

'Good morning, Mr Dove. Your table is ready; I've given you your usual one in the corner. If you and your guests would like to follow me this way?'

That was a relief: a business lunch without Tristan. She ran through what was on and off the menu with them, fetched pre-lunch drinks and left the wine to breathe. She was just walking to the door to greet some other guests when she saw Raymond

Dove stop at the service station on the way back from the toilet. Hannah's heart sank. She didn't want to be questioned about Tristan again. For one thing, she didn't want to tell the truth, but she didn't want to lie to him either.

'How can I help you, Mr Dove? Is everything alright with the table? I'll be over shortly to take your order.'

'Everything's fine, thank you. I just wanted a quick word. My niece Britney is coming here for an interview today and I'm asking you to employ her if you can. She's my sister's daughter and she's not had it easy in life. I'm sure just a couple of shifts a week would help to build her confidence, and it would be such a relief to the family to see her settled down doing something productive. I hope you don't mind me mentioning it, but I've found in this world it's not what you know, but who you know.'

Hannah smiled, but as he walked away she swore under her breath. How could she say no? Just two shifts a week couldn't hurt, even if she was awful. The hotel needed Raymond's business, and it could be worse – he could be asking for a job for Emmi! Now that *would* be a problem.

'Please come through, Britney. I thought we could sit in the snug as it's a lot nicer than my office. Take a seat. I've looked at your CV and there's not a lot on there, so why not tell me about yourself?'

'I've lived in Saltmarsh Quay all my life. I enjoyed school and I have lots of fun with my friends from there still. That's about it really.'

Hannah was getting nowhere. There must be something, but Britney seemed to have no ambition to do anything. She wouldn't leave the Quay to go to university: apparently she had learned all she needed to know here. She wouldn't like getting the bus every day to go to a bigger town to work, but she did like to spend time on the internet looking at clothes.

'So, Britney, one last question: what is your dream? By that I mean what would you love to achieve in life more than anything else?'

'That's easy. I want a nice house, a lovely husband, and four children.'

'That sounds lovely, but don't you want a career first?'

'Oh no, I want to be married and be a mum in a years' time.'

Hannah had to stop herself from laughing, not at Britney but at Jimmy. Just the thought of him settling down with four children... She realised that there was no need to carry on the interview. She had to offer her the job, after all. She was probably going to be useless, but if it meant keeping Raymond Dove happy it would be worth it.

'Well, you sound perfect for the job. We run three shifts a day here: breakfast, lunch, and dinner. Weekends are our busiest times, so I suggest that you pick a couple of days next week and come in for a trial. Not just for us to see how you do, but to see if you like it as well.'

'Thank you, that would be nice. I'm afraid I can't work weekends as that's when I see my friends, and I don't like getting up early in the morning so I wouldn't be able to work a breakfast shift. How about a Tuesday or a Wednesday?'

'That's perfect. Shall we say next Tuesday lunch time? If you get here for eleven-thirty am on Tuesday and then five-thirty on Wednesday to do the dinner shift, would that be okay?'

'Yes, that's good. It won't interfere with me seeing my friends.'

'Great, I think that covers everything. You will need to wear a black skirt and a white shirt on Tuesday, so I look forward to seeing you then! Oh, by the way – have you mentioned your dream of being married and having children to your boyfriend? If

147

not, I think you should, because I'm sure he'll be as excited as you are and want to start planning the wedding.'

'Do you really think so?'

'Oh yes, Britney, the sooner the better.'

Hannah showed her to the door, and how she kept a straight face she would never know. Should she wait for Britney to mention the children, or should she say something herself? Either way, there wasn't time now. It was almost time to get ready for the bright lights of Saltmarsh Quay, but she popped into Betty's room first.

'Hi Nan, what are you up to?'

'Nothing really, just staring out to sea. I think it's going to become a habit once I'm here full time. I have a date to move out of my flat: three weeks from tomorrow. Isn't that brilliant timing? I'll be living here within the month! I also heard from your dad. He won't be staying overnight when he comes to pick me up. He wants to do it all in one day. I presume that's Susanna's idea. I think that before I leave the Midlands I'm going to have to have a word with that woman and set her straight on a few things.'

Hannah was ready to hit the Quay. She had a quick chat with Glen on her way out; making sure that everything was ready for dinner.

'I'm all sorted, don't you worry. Go off and have fun! Go and kiss lots of fishermen, that's just what you need, Hannah!'

'Very funny! But you are sure everything's okay?'

'Go! Oh, Jimmy was asking if you were around. He wanted to know how the interview went with his so-called friend Britney.'

'Now that's a long story. I'll fill you in tomorrow, but I will say that I think it will be something different. I'll pop in and let him know before I go.'

Jimmy was in the staff break room when she found him.

148

'Jimmy, you were looking for me. Everything went okay. Your friend's coming in for a couple of trial shifts next week. She's a nice girl, such a shame we can't train her up to become a supervisor. By the time she's fully trained it would be time for her to leave and have her first baby.'

'What are you talking about? Baby, what baby? Are we talking about the same person? I'm on about Britney.'

'Yes, Britney; she mentioned that within the year she was planning to be married with her first child on the way and a lovely little house – no doubt big enough to prepare for the other three children. Isn't that what you wanted too? Anyway, I must be off now. See you tomorrow!'

Oh dear, what had she said? And how would Jimmy get out of this one? Hopefully once he gave her the push she wouldn't bother to come in for the trials. But enough of that, time to have some fun! She was keeping her fingers crossed for Tom to be in a good mood.

Hannah walked down the coastal path. It was busy: the beach was full of people having an evening swim and children playing in the rock pools. Her stomach was rumbling. She felt hungry but not necessarily in a drinking mood.

She was just heading off the beach towards the pub when her phone rang. It was Richard, asking if he could come and measure up Josie's flat for furniture. He was doing it as a surprise, so she wouldn't be with him. He was coming from London just for the day. They arranged to meet at Luckett House the day after tomorrow. Betty would have gone home, so Hannah would have some free time.

'Come on, we're waiting!' Olivia called out to her. 'Put that phone away, the hotel can manage without you for the evening!'

'It wasn't the hotel, it was about the flat. My

round now, who's drinking what? I'm starving.'

Thankfully Olivia wasn't in a drinking-to-get-hammered mood either, and Tom didn't drink much anyway. The food was good and down to earth: steak, chips, mushrooms and peas, followed by apple tart and custard.

Hannah filled them in on Luckett House, Olivia chatted about her boys and Hannah was conscious of the need to bring Tom into the conversation. She asked him about his gardening jobs and whether he would be free to help with landscaping up at the house once the conservatory was built. She suggested that it might be good if he got together with Josie, Margaret, and Betty. The garden would be something that brought them all together. Tom was actually very excited about it, although he would like to see the plot first so that he could come up with some ideas before he met them.

The time flew by. Hannah realised it must be getting late when some of the chefs from the hotel came in for last orders. No Jimmy, which was unusual. She had noticed Britney and her friends hanging out in the corner by the pool table.

'Right then,' Olivia declared, 'back to mine for a night cap. Mum's got the boys, so we can play some music just like the old days.'

They headed up the hill to Olivia's, laughing and joking like they always used to. Hannah was pleased; Tom was almost back to his normal self. They were just turning into the little estate where Olivia lived when a taxi pulled up outside one of the bigger houses. A few moments later, Tristan came out, got in the car and drove away.

'Who lives in there, Olivia? It's a nice house, and that's a lovely car on the drive.'

'That's Marie's house. She owns a hairdressers' somewhere posh, I think. She's a lovely woman but she's got terrible taste in men, and I do mean men;

there's been a lot. I think she falls for their charm, but most of them are looking for a meal ticket. It's strange how she can be a good businesswoman, but so stupid where men are concerned.'

Once at Olivia's none of them fancied any more alcohol and they all had a coffee. The atmosphere was thankfully light, with lots of talk about Sam and Ben. Tom was reminiscing about all the things they did together: day trips, football, and not to forget swimming. Olivia laughed and said her life would be far more hectic if she had to do all those things with them. She was also thankful that when Tom brought them back they were always so tired out.

After an hour or so, Hannah decided to make a move back to the hotel. Tom offered to walk part way with her, so they said their goodbyes to Olivia and headed off.

'Olivia's very lucky to have you, Tom. You're far more than just a friend to her.'

'Yes, I get a lot of pleasure from being with the boys. I'm just thankful her ex isn't around. He wasn't a nice person.'

'If you don't mind me asking: what happens if and when Olivia finds a new man? Would he take over your responsibilities?'

'No, because she's made it quite clear that her family is complete with just the three of them. She's adamant that there'll never be another man in her life.'

'Is that so?'

As she walked the final stretch by herself, lots of things were going through Hannah's head. Olivia had never mentioned to her that she didn't want another man. It was very strange.

Chapter 24

Hannah wasn't working until the dinner shift. She had arranged it that way, just in case she drank a lot the night before, but she was up early. Betty wanted to go down to Luckett House one more time before Robert arrived to take her home. She had also asked if Brian would be around: she wanted to discuss installing some shelves.

They made a quick breakfast and were off down to the house. It was a strange feeling, seeing fewer and fewer vans each time she visited. Most of the tradesmen had finished their work by now. Brian had said before that this was his favourite part of a job: adding the finishing touches before handing it all over to the client.

'Good morning, how are we both today? Isn't it today you're going home?'

Betty smiled. 'I am home, Brian, but I know what you mean. One last trip back and when I return it will be for good.'

On the subject of shelves, Betty explained that she had seen some thick shelves set into an alcove and painted the same colour as the walls in a magazine, and wondered if it would be possible to do that here. She wanted three shelves above the TV unit to display a few pieces of old pottery that had been in the family for years. Brian said it wouldn't be a problem. He would get Carl to start building them tomorrow. Once they were made and painted he would take a photo and send it to her on her phone.

'Anything else, Nan? The last thing we need to do is upset Dad any more by being late.'

'No, I'm sorted. Thank you, Brian, I'm so grateful. I don't think any other builder would have done such a good job as this. You've got a lovely team of men working for you and Carl's such a lucky lad to have you to teach him everything.'

'Yes, he's a good lad and he works hard. He always does a hundred-percent job, but I don't think his heart's in it. I can't put my finger on it exactly but I think he would sooner be doing something else. I don't know what, but he's too polite to let me down when I ask him to help out. Perhaps one day he'll work out what he wants out of life, and then I can support him in return.'

Back at the hotel, Hannah helped Betty carry all her bags to Reception, and then walked out to the lawn, where they waited for Robert to arrive.

'Here he comes, Nan. Oh no ... he's not by himself. He has a passenger.'

'Who, not Susanna? Please, no! Just the thought of driving all the way back with her in the car − I'll have to pretend to be asleep.'

Susanna stepped lightly out of the car and smiled at them both.

'Hello, I hope you don't mind but I thought I would be company for Robert on the way down. How's the new life going, Hannah? Is it as exciting as London down here?'

'More exciting! We have bingo on a Friday night over in the village hall. I never had that much fun in London. Now, if you'll excuse me, I need to get some work done before they end up sacking me. I've booked a table in the restaurant for twelve-thirty so you can have some lunch before you travel back. I'll see you then!'

Why was Susanna here? What was her game? Perhaps she *had* just come for the ride and to keep Dad company. No, Hannah knew she was up to something. As much as she didn't want Nan to go, she wished Robert and Susanna would. Thank goodness she didn't have to sit down with them for lunch!

'Hi, Hannah, the lads said you were in the pub last night. How did Britney look?'

'She looked pretty, Jimmy, all dressed up like she was waiting for someone. A lady doesn't like being stood up, you know.'

'Oh, don't take the mickey! What am I going to do? I don't want a wife, let alone kids.'

'Excuse me, but don't you think you should have told me that a few years ago? I know you don't want her, and I certainly don't want her working in the restaurant, but we can't upset our best customer who happens to be her uncle, so what do you suggest we do?'

'I don't know, you're the one with the brains! I'm just...'

'The one with something a little too twitchy attached to his body, right? This is your problem, Jimmy. I have enough on my plate today with Susanna here. To be honest, I think I might rather have your problem.'

Lunch was busy and Hannah kept out of the way of Betty's table, leaving it to the other staff. She just had to say goodbye when they were finished and they would be off. Nan came by her station as one of the waiting staff cleared their plates.

'We'll be off now, darling. I'm just making a quick visit to the loo first.'

This is where she will grab me, Hannah thought, when Nan and Dad are in the loos – look busy! No, she's gone in as well.

Hannah decided to walk them to the car, keeping close to Nan because Susanna wouldn't dare say a word if she was there. She was so focused on staying with the group that she forgot about Nan's bags.

'Your dad's just coming with me to get my bags, are they behind Reception?'

'No, I'll get them, it's okay, Dad...'

Too late, they were gone. Wait for it...

'So, I expect you're feeling very proud of yourself, conning an old lady into buying you a home. It's disgusting, but you've not heard the last of this. We'll hire a solicitor and they'll prove you are manipulating her! That's your father's money tied up in that flat, not yours, and he needs it. So I wouldn't get too comfortable, because it's not going to be yours for very long, mark my words.'

Hannah didn't say a word. She wasn't going to bring herself down to Susanna's level. She would just keep counting to ten in her head and Nan and Dad would be here soon with the bags.

'Bags are in the car. Are you all ready, Mum? It's been lovely to see you, darling, and the next time will be when Mum is moving in! Look after yourself, and don't work too hard. Come on you two, into the car.'

'Actually, do you think we could spare a couple of minutes? We could go and sit at that picnic table.'

Robert frowned. 'We haven't got a lot of time, but I'm sure a minute or two will be okay.'

What's Nan up to? Hannah wondered as they followed Betty over. She seems very serious. I think something is brewing, and by the look on Susanna's face, she's nervous.

'Right, this won't take long. I wasn't going to say anything until we were back in the Midlands, but I can guess from your faces that Susanna's just had a go at Hannah, so why not clear the air now? I can only imagine what you had to say and to be honest I'm not interested to know. What I am interested in is facts and figures, so here goes.'

Robert tried to butt in, but couldn't get anywhere. Susanna just sat there, red faced. Nan was on a roll and she was not going to stop until she had got everything off her chest.

'The flat I've given to Hannah is her inheritance but because I have the money to do it now she's getting it before I die. When I do go, my flat and any money I have left will go to your children. Hannah will have had her share already. I'm sorry that there's no money for you as such. Everything goes to the grandchildren. But once my house in the Midlands is sold and I get the money for Josie and Margaret's flats there should be some money left, even after I pay Brian what I owe him. That money I *will* give to you and Robert to buy a bigger property: not enough for a mansion, but plenty for a four-bedroom house on an estate. That subject is closed, but I haven't finished with you yet. What you need to do—'

This was Nan's punchline. She had given with one hand and now she was taking back. This was the part Susanna wouldn't like.

'Now that the children are older you need to get off your backside and go out to work. Help to pay the bills and make life a little easier for your husband. Work in a shop or clean rooms in a hotel, and perhaps then you can earn enough to buy the manor house you want. We're not a rich family. We've all had to work hard to get what we have. Why not do the same? Right, now that's been said, I won't mention it again. I'm ready to go home.'

Hannah could only imagine the atmosphere in the car going back to the Midlands. If there was any more trouble from Susanna, Betty would not be forking out for anything. She had really stepped over the mark with her this time.

Before the dinner shift Hannah wanted to catch up with Glenda, tell her the Britney saga and plan the Duty Manager rotas. Between her, the Night Manager, and Annie the housekeeper they were all struggling to cope with covering the hotel 24/7. The question was, would David agree for them to have a trainee manager, someone to be the responsible person if none of them were present? Glenda was normally very good at predicting David's reactions but this time she wasn't sure. In her opinion he might suggest Glen, but would it all become a bit frantic and dramatic if he was left in charge? She would mention it to David when he called next.

'Before you go, Hannah, how are the Tom and Jimmy situations going? Any improvement?'

'I can confirm – figures crossed, of course – that they are both okay and moving on without any intention of having me romantically involved in their lives. Hopefully that will give me a little time to work on Carl! He's just so shy and I don't know why. I haven't been able to suss him out yet.'

Chapter 25

Hannah had a call from Betty apologising for her outburst, and a text from her dad to say they had made it back okay, but no mention of Betty's speech from him. But that was yesterday, and the stress of the house conversion and the move must have affected everyone.

Today was another day. Hannah could do without meeting Richard down at the house. She had a pile of paperwork to get on with and she needed to spend some time sorting out the next year's budget with Glenda. There were also a lot of things being delivered at different times down at the house. If the builders would be there at the time it wasn't a problem, but if they weren't she needed to make sure she was. Margaret was also itching to move in as soon as everything was sorted with the solicitors, and if Jimmy came to her one more time about this Britney business she would scream.

First things first. She would get the breakfast shift over with, leave lunch to Glen, and then be back for dinner.

Mid-morning, she got a text from Richard to say he was running late. The traffic was bad and part of the motorway had been closed. He did apologise.

To top off her manic morning, Hannah watched Tristan pull up outside the hotel. He had an older lady with him. Hannah's first thought was *surely not another one,* but she was really old. That couldn't be it.

'Hannah, may I introduce you to my grandmother? Would it be possible to have coffee in the lounge? She's staying here tonight. I know her room won't be ready yet, but I've just picked her up from the train station.'

'It's very nice to meet you, Mrs Goring.'

'No, my dear, Goring is the other side of the family. I'm a Van Lincoln and very proud of it! I don't think the Gorings could say the same.'

Hannah arranged for them to be served coffee and headed out to Luckett House. She knew she would be early, but she could start getting a feel for her flat. She couldn't wait to move in and leave the hotel behind. Both living and working there made it very difficult to switch off.

There weren't any vans as she came up the drive, thank goodness. She had brought a key but the door was open and the radio was on. Someone was singing along to a Kylie song. They had quite a good voice! She walked towards the singing but waited for the song to finish before clapping.

'Oh! I'm sorry, Hannah, I got carried away.'

'I could hear that. I've never heard you so excited! So that's the answer: put the radio on, and Carl comes to life! I forgot that the shelves were being made today. Don't they look good! Nan will be so pleased, they are so chunky – the shelves, that is, not you. But then you are chunky! Sorry, I must stop teasing you, but you are so serious! Come on, Carl have some fun. There will be lots of time to take things seriously when you are older.'

'I'm sorry, but I need to get on. Len's working in your flat if you want to go and chat to him.'

Well, that was her told. Hannah didn't know what else she could do to make Carl lighten up. Perhaps it was just her he didn't like? That sounded like a car approaching, it must be Richard.

'Hi, sorry I'm late, the traffic is really bad today. Thanks for meeting me. This shouldn't take long. I just need to take measurements for some units in the lounge and plan how to lay out the bedroom. I want to surprise Mum. All her furniture will look too clumsy here. This needs to flow.'

'She's very lucky to have you.'

'I know that I'm very lucky to have her! She was such an encouragement to me when I decided to move to London. It was a huge decision all those years ago and she did loads of jobs to support me. Thankfully after a little bit of success I've been able to repay her with holidays and treats and she loves coming to London. When she stays with me we go to the theatre and exhibitions which we both enjoy.'

'I gather that you have a very exciting job.'

'Sort of exciting: no one ever guesses, and when I tell them they look quite shocked. I design women's clothes. I work for Gina Le Gina fashion house, so my name's not on any of the garments. God, I've been doing it for over forty years now. Nearly time to hang up my tape measure and scissors, but that's another story.'

'I'm not surprised you do something like that; you are so stylish, and your mum has some lovely clothes which really suit her. I bet a lot of that is your doing.'

'I might have had a hand in it, yes. Now, I mustn't keep you long – oh, there goes your phone. I will get on upstairs and get measuring. Will it be okay if look around the other flats as well?'

'Of course. Excuse me while I answer this. Hi, Glen, what's wrong?'

Richard nodded and walked off. It was just as well, as Hannah was rather distracted.

'She what? Who does she think she is? Just say no for now, and I'll deal with her when I get back. I should be with you in about an hour. To be honest, I suspect her bark is worse than her bite.'

Hannah went looking for Richard. He was measuring for a sideboard and a couple of armchairs to go in the bay window.

'The flats are really looking good, Hannah. They're far more complete than I thought they would be. The last time I was here it was a building site but now it looks like it's nearly time to move in. I know that Mum's going to be so happy here. You are definitely sure the dog will be okay here? He's not a barking dog but he will lick everyone to bits.'

'Yes, we're all sure. Don't worry about Bonkers. What do you think of the other flats? I can't wait for the conservatory to go up. It will be the perfect place for Nan, Josie, and Margaret to sit and natter away the day – and Bonkers, of course, running in and out of the garden. That reminds me, I need to let Tom know there's a dog coming. He's a friend of mine and a garden designer. He's coming up with some landscaping ideas.'

'I think you're right: the conservatory will be like a community room. The builder was showing me the plans for it; he's really pleasant and chatty.'

'Which builder?'

'The gay one that's fitting the shelves.'

'Sorry, gay? Oh, I've been so stupid! Are you sure he's gay?'

'Yes, why? Just because he's not camp and loud? Some of us are quite...'

'Richard, thank you so much! You've solved a huge mystery. Not that it's a problem. Yes, Carl's a lovely lad. He keeps himself to himself, but – there's my phone again, sorry.'

'I'm done here anyway. I need to be off to sit on that motorway again.'

'Okay... Hi, Glen – I'm on my way back, just leave her be and I'll sort it out. Give me ten minutes.'

Hannah waved Richard off. She was so tempted to go in and see Carl. Everything made sense now. He was kind, sensitive, thoughtful, and very shy but she knew she wanted to help him.

Now wasn't the time or the place, however. She also needed to go back and sort out Mrs Van Lincoln. What was it with that family? Who did they think they were?'

'Hi, Mrs Van Lincoln, I've been told you have a little problem. How can I help?'

'There were two things wrong with that sentence, young lady. For one thing, you do not say "hi" to a guest, you say "hello". Secondly, it is not a little problem, it is a huge one. I have asked the staff to move that little table in the middle of the big window and replace it with a large one. I hate sitting at a poky table, and they have refused to do it. Come on then, don't just stand there! Instruct them to do it.'

'Please excuse me a minute.'

Calm down, Hannah told herself, before you say something you will regret. There was no way she was going to start moving tables around. For one thing, she would have to lose three other tables to do it and the restaurant was small enough as it was. All this fuss before Mrs Van Lincoln had even seen her bedroom: would she expect them to move beds and wardrobes as well? This just had to happen on Glenda's day off.

'Hello again, Mrs Van Lincoln, I've looked at the bookings for dinner and I'm afraid it will not be possible to change the whole restaurant around today. I will have a look at it tomorrow and see if it will be possible for the rest of your stay. Housekeeping have informed me that your room is ready; if you would like to follow me, I will show you to it.'

And breathe! Hannah wasn't sure she had taken a single breath throughout that speech. Mrs Van Lincoln mumbled something but Hannah ignored her: at least she was following her.

Half an hour later, Hannah was back in Reception. Surprisingly, Mrs Van Lincoln had been happy with the room. Having her bags and suitcase unpacked for her might have helped the situation. Thankfully she planned to have a nap until it was time to get ready for dinner, which looked set to be a difficult experience.

Hannah spent the rest of the afternoon doing paperwork in the back office, but her mind was on Carl. It was wrong of her to think he needed help, but there must be something she could do to make him happier with himself. She didn't need to interfere with his life; he just needed pointing in the right direction. Looking at the clock, she saw that she had just enough time to get down to Luckett House and back before dinner. What she would say or do when she got there, she didn't know, but she went anyway.

*

'Hi, Carl, I was telling Nan on the phone about the shelves and she has no patience. She wanted me to come back down and take a photo of them straight away. You've done a really good job: they are stunning.'

'Thank you, I'm pleased with them.'

'Good, and thank you for explaining about the conservatory to Richard, it was a big help. He's nice. I didn't realise he was a fashion designer until just recently. When I first saw him I thought he would work in a bank or something like that, but then I'm normally wrong about people. I'm always putting my big feet in it.

'He said he had to move away from here to follow his dreams. I don't think he would have got very far with that career here in Norfolk. He seems like a happy chap, content with his life and that's good. I'm starting to feel like that, more so here than I did in London. I think it's best to be happy with yourself, even if your family and friends don't understand to start with. They normally come around.'

She could tell he knew what she was getting at but he wasn't visibly uncomfortable or trying to escape the room again. Hannah dropped the conversation and started to take photos of the shelves to text to Betty.

'Right, I need to get back to the hotel and put the smile on for dinner. Thanks again, Carl, have a lovely evening.'

'Thank you. I suppose it takes all sorts to make a world. It's just a question of where you fit in. I think the hardest part is finding out where you *want* to fit in.'

He smiled: a real smile, not false at all. All these months she'd been trying to suss him out and now she knew at least one of the answers. Was she starting to see the real Carl? She hoped so.

Chapter 26

The hotel staff had escaped the wrath of Mrs Van Lincoln last night. She had decided to eat in her room and have room service because the tables in the restaurant couldn't be moved around to suit her. That came with its own problems, of course. One member of staff was taken up with her all evening, so in a way she had the last laugh: her own personal butler!

This woman meant business and today she had requested a meeting with the General Manager. That was Glenda, but as she was away it fell on Hannah to go: not something she was looking forward to. Still, it had to be done. There had to be compromise and Hannah wasn't going to give in completely. Mrs Van Lincoln was booked in for two weeks which would be a nightmare if boundaries weren't set now.

'Come in ... oh, it's you. I was expecting someone more senior. You had better take a seat over there so that I can see you properly.'

What Mrs Van Lincoln wasn't aware of was that Hannah had spoken to David, who had the last say over everything to do with the hotel, acting on behalf of the owner, Devel Devonshire. So now she had a couple of tricks up her sleeve.

'Good morning, I hope you slept well and everything was comfortable for you? What is it that you wanted to ask me about? I'm afraid that Glenda the General Manager is away for a couple of days. How can I help?'

'You probably can't help but seeing as you are the person I have to deal with you will have to try. First of all, I didn't sleep well. I would like to be moved to a bigger room. Secondly, has the table problem been sorted out for me?'

'The room I am unable to improve, as this is one of the biggest in the hotel. I can move you to another one if this really is uncomfortable, but if I do the new room will be a lot smaller. I'm afraid I can't accommodate you with regard to the table question either. We are in the middle of the busiest part of the season and we can't afford to move three tables out of the restaurant to create the layout you have asked for. What we can—'

'I knew you wouldn't be able to help. You're just a glorified waitress! I demand to speak to the owners and tell *them* the problems I'm having with this hotel and your bad attitude.'

'Excuse me, but if you would just let me finish: I have spoken to the owner because we always like to go the extra mile for our guests, and they recognise that the restaurant situation is a huge problem for you. What they suggest is that, if you are more comfortable having your meals in your room we will assign a staff member to provide a butler service. Of course there would be a charge for this: thirty pounds per night.'

'But you say there is no charge for room service.'

'Yes, room service is bringing one tray of food to the room, not a service like you received last night where the waiter had to come up six times. If that will be all, I should get on. If you need anything else, don't hesitate to phone Reception and they will page me.'

That went well, but Hannah was sure that wouldn't be the end of it. There were still thirteen days to go before she left. Still, fingers crossed, she might leave early! For now, she would put Mrs Van Lincoln's problems aside: she was not the only guest here and Hannah had plenty of problems of her own to deal with!

Jimmy was still on her back about not wanting to work with Britney anymore. He hadn't given her the elbow, still just making excuses about not being able to get time off to see her. But the problem Hannah wanted to solve most was how to help Carl become Carl.

As she headed back to Reception, in walked Tristan. He didn't look his normal confident self. He was still smart, but the way he held himself was different.

'Good morning,' she greeted him. 'How are you? I've just been chatting to your grandmother; are you off up to her room? We're having lovely weather today: perfect for a walk.'

'A walk would be lovely, but I fear that's not what my grandmother will have in mind.'

Hannah smiled to herself. What a strange family they were! It was nice to see Tristan knocked down a peg or two.

*

The next couple of days went without any hiccups. Mrs Van Lincoln came down to the restaurant every night and didn't complain at all. This was not what Hannah and the rest of the staff had expected; she hadn't asked to see Glenda when she came back. The one thing that Hannah had noticed was that Tristan came to visit every morning and took her out and exactly three hours later she returned to the hotel. It was a very strange routine – not that Hannah was concerned, she was just being nosy.

One thing she was excited about was an upcoming date with Carl. Well, it wasn't a date as such; he was driving her to a furniture warehouse in the firm's van to pick up some pieces she had ordered online. Apart from short messages to arrange this, she hadn't spoken to him since their little chat about finding out who we really are. So as well as fetching the furniture Hannah had another little plan, which would hopefully be helpful.

First, though, she was meeting Tom down at

Luckett House. He wanted to take some measurements in the garden. He was taking this little project very seriously and wanted to come up with lots of suggestions for Betty to look at. Also, the slab of concrete had been laid for the conservatory foundations, and Hannah hadn't seen that yet.

'That's huge, Brian! Have we done the right thing? Should it have been smaller?'

'No, it's perfect. Look, come and stand where the big windows are going to go: the view is incredible. Now imagine you are sitting on a sofa looking out. It's glorious, uninterrupted sea.'

Hannah still wasn't sure, so Brian suggested that they get some empty boxes, break them up, and place them where furniture might go. He said the space would soon fill up, and he was right. With two sofas, a dining table and chairs, and not to mention some sort of unit, it was going to be a real social space.

Tom had finished his measuring and Hannah was keen for him to see where the best places could be for seating areas: she wanted one sheltered from the wind and one to catch the winter sunshine. The garden needed to be able to be used all year round, if it wasn't raining. She did wonder whether all this would cause a problem for him, not having a blank page to work on.

She needn't have worried. Tom was eager to get as much input as he could.

'This is so exciting! When's your Nan next down here? I can't wait to show her all my ideas. I'm glad I've been able to see it with the conservatory base down, as I realise all the planting has to be down near ground level. I don't want anything to block the view. Right, I've got all I need, so I will be off.'

Carl walked in just as he was leaving, not in his work clothes but dressed casually. They greeted each other as they passed, but Hannah could tell Tom

168

wasn't happy to see him. She sighed. She had thought they had moved on from that. If only he knew that he would probably have more of a chance with Carl than she would... but she wouldn't be telling him. If Carl wanted to keep his life private, that was his business.

They said their goodbyes, Hannah found the warehouse address on her phone and put it into the Satnav, ready for the off. It was now twelve-thirty, and it would take a few hours to get there as it was on the outskirts of London. Although in the back of her mind Hannah knew what she was planning might not work, she also knew that for it to have a chance once they got to the warehouse she had to look surprised.

The journey went well. Hannah did most of the talking, telling Carl all about her old life in London. She even touched on her mum dying, which was something she rarely talked about. Susanna and her stepbrother and sister also came into the conversation, but the one thing she didn't do was ask Carl any personal questions, just one about work.

She could tell that he did love his job and took pride in it. Hopefully one day it would be his business. He did mention how controlling his mum was, always trying to protect him and checking up on him: what was he doing, who was he seeing, and so on. It caused a few problems with his dad, who kept telling her that she needed to cut the apron strings. Hannah did find herself wondering if she behaved like that because she knew he was gay.

'That was good timing,' Carl said as they drove through the warehouse gates. 'The car park is empty. Come to that, it looks like the whole place is shut up.'

'If you pull over there, I'll get out and have a look.'

There was a note on the door: the same note that the company had posted online to say they were closing at lunch time today so that the staff could attend the funeral of another employee. She stood and read it carefully, then walked back to the van and explained the situation. Hopefully she looked convincingly surprised.

'I'm so sorry, Carl, we've come all this way! Look, it's nearly four o'clock; we will get stuck in the teatime traffic if we go back now. Why don't I see if there's a cheap hotel around here? I'll get us two rooms and then we can come back here first thing in the morning when they open. We should make it back to Norfolk before lunch. What do you say? Just give me a few minutes to see what's nearby.'

Carl didn't protest. Of course, Hannah had already sorted out where they would stay; this was all part of her plan. She just needed to confirm the rooms in the Travelodge.

'Sorted, how do you fancy something to eat? Would a pizza be okay? Here's the postcode for the hotel. And if we pass a Tesco or Sainsbury's, could we stop in? I'd like to get some toiletries.'

They followed where the Satnav took them, heading towards Central London. Carl spotted a Sainsbury's and Hannah suggested that he wait in the van while she bought them each a toothbrush, soap, and so on. This was part of her plan as well: hopefully they would have a decent shirt she could buy for him and something for her so that they didn't have to stay in the same clothes.

On her way back to the car she looked at the other businesses in the retail park and saw that there was a Pizza Express. Back at the van, she suggested that they eat before going to the hotel, as she didn't want to be sat in a hotel room for hours. Carl agreed and they walked to the restaurant together.

*

'For a big hunky lad, you don't eat a lot. Sorry, I mean you eat healthily, not like me.'

'I try to, but I don't exercise much. The job keeps me fit but it does help that I like vegetables and salad. That salad was beautiful.'

Hannah could tell that he was really relaxed and not fazed by the overnight stay. If anything, he seemed to be enjoying himself.

'Right, let's find this hotel. It shouldn't be too far from here.'

The hotel had an underground car park. Hannah got her bags together and they walked up to Reception. She did the checking in and got the key cards.

'Here you go, you're 506 on the fifth floor, and I'm 408 on the fourth. You had better take this. I got you some toiletries and a clean shirt: I hope it fits. Why don't we each have a quick shower and then meet down here in Reception? Say around seven o'clock? We can find a little pub and have a couple of drinks.'

She didn't give him time to answer but by the look of him there wouldn't be a problem. Up in her room she emptied out her huge handbag. She couldn't believe how much she had squeezed into it: her phone charger, spare underwear, perfume, deodorant, even a change of shoes (hopefully he wouldn't notice them). She also had her new top, which she really liked. Hopefully Carl would like his shirt too. She checked which way the pub was on her phone. It was only about a ten-minute walk away.

Showered, with her hair and makeup done and her nice new brightly coloured top, Hannah was ready to hit the town. Hopefully so was Carl. She was nervous because she didn't like lying to people, but this wasn't really lying. Apart from her knowing that the furniture store would be closed, this was more like an adventure that was planned but kept a secret.

'Oh good, it fits: you look very smart! Just one more thing – I need to ask the receptionist something. I won't be a minute.'

Now this wasn't in her plan, but hopefully she would get lucky. After a couple of minutes spent laughing and joking with the male receptionist he went through to the back of Reception and handed something to Hannah. Carl wasn't really sure what was going on.

'Here you go, we are in luck. The lad behind the desk had some aftershave in his bag and he's kindly let me borrow it to give you a squirt. Even better, it's a good one!'

The job was done and the bottle returned to the receptionist. Now all she had to remember was how to get to the pub. They passed a couple of nice ones on the way, and Hannah had to make excuses to avoid them. They turned a corner and she could see the one she was looking for.

It was quite empty as they walked in, with no more than a dozen people in the bar. Having said that, they were all men and it was early, not even half past seven. Hopefully it would get busy later. Carl went to the bar and got himself a pint and Hannah a gin and tonic. She found a table to sit at: this had to be given some careful thought as she wanted Carl to be sat where he could see everything. She could see him laughing with the woman behind the bar, so he must be relaxed in here.

'One G&T,' Carl announced, sliding it towards her. 'The woman behind the bar said they've got a drag act on later who is a bit of a comedian and a singer. She suggests that if we don't want picking on we ought not to sit in the front row.'

'No, we're okay. The little stage is in the corner over there.'

Carl was taking everything in. Every time the door opened he looked over, but saying that everyone coming in turned and looked at him. It was nearly nine o'clock. They were on their third drink and the pub had become busy. Quite a few groups of people had come in together and were sitting near the stage. There was a mixture of all sorts of people of various ages.

Carl was loving the music being played and Hannah had noticed something else, especially when Carl went up to the bar: the amount of blokes giving him the eye. She could see he had noticed but it didn't seem to be a problem. An older man who obviously had a few drinks in him had passed their table, looked down at Carl and said, 'Fresh meat?'

All three of them had laughed and Carl replied, 'Very fresh!' which caused a bigger laugh.

At around ten, the pub was getting ready for the entertainment. Hannah and Carl stood up and moved a little closer to the stage but far enough back not to be picked on. That was when it started to happen: fellas acknowledged Carl and got into conversation with him. Everyone was friendly and there was a lovely atmosphere.

One lad told them that the act did two slots and would be back on for the second part at eleven-thirty. This was to keep people in the pub and drinking, but he also said that some people would travel right across London to see him.

He was brilliant: the pub was cheering and laughing throughout the act. Hannah and Carl had loved the evening as much as anyone, but for Hannah it was time to leave.

'Another drink? It's my turn.'

'Not for me, I'm heading back to the hotel. I'm tired and I've had a few too many gins. You stay and have fun. Wait for the second performance. I will get a taxi and see you in the morning. Text me when you are up; we don't have to be out of the rooms until eleven o'clock.'

'No, I've had enough, we can both go back.'

'Don't be daft, stay and have some fun! You're

enjoying yourself, I can tell.'

'Okay, if you really don't mind, but let me see you to a taxi first.'

They went outside and waited for a black cab to drive down the road.

'Thank you so much, Hannah. I can never repay you for tonight. You must have put so much into planning this, and there's so much I want to talk to you about. This has not just been a lovely evening; it is the start of my new life. Well, not here in this pub but in my head. And one more thing, if I wasn't gay you'd be the perfect girlfriend for me, you really would. Thank you.'

Chapter 27

Hannah hadn't seen Carl since the morning after their night in London when they had successfully picked up the furniture and driven back to Luckett Quay. The evening's events had been well discussed on the way home, both of them agreeing that it had been a great night out. Carl didn't mention any more about being gay, and he didn't need to. He was different: relaxed and confident. Hannah was looking forward to seeing what the future held for him, but more than that, she was looking forward to having more fun nights out with him!

These last few days had been busy for Hannah, not just with decisions about Luckett House, but also at work. Worrying things had happened. More precisely, she had seen things that she knew she shouldn't have seen. What should she do? Could she just turn a blind eye? That would be wrong, but then how she came to know about it was also wrong.

It had happened yesterday and involved Mrs Van Lincoln. Housekeeping had contacted the restaurant to say that there were a lot of dirty dishes in her room and could someone please come up to collect them? As everyone else was busy, Hannah went up. Mrs Van Lincoln was out with Tristan, so there was no a chance of bumping into her.

The housekeepers were cleaning the bathroom as Hannah entered the room. When she went to the desk to collect the tray of crockery, she saw some paperwork in a pile next to it. It looked like estate agent's details for farmhouses with lots of land, while another pile contained house builders' details. There was nothing strange about that. Lots of people who stayed at the hotel were there while they were looking for a house to buy. What concerned Hannah was another piece of paper: a photograph of Luckett Farm with a handwritten note across the top reading '7 four-bedroom houses, 5 three bedroom, and 3 five bedroom = total 15 houses'.

Back at her desk, Hannah couldn't switch off from what she had seen. House building wasn't a problem, as it would bring more business to Saltmarsh and Luckett Quay. The difficulty was getting to the farm: there was only a narrow dirt track at present, so obviously a road would have to be made. The only place to build that would be straight through the riding stables. She knew Mrs Van Lincoln was thinking the same thing, because she had had a map on her desk with a big red cross drawn right through the stables.

All she remembered about the stables were the happy times she had spent there as a child. When she had walked past it since moving back there had always been people coming and going. She needed to find out more about it, and planned a visit for the same afternoon. She smelled a rat.

Chatting to the staff at the hotel, she found out that the old lady who used to own the stables had died a couple of years ago, and her son Clive was running it as a livery yard for horse owners to stable their horses, coming and going as often as they liked. It wasn't open to the public for lessons anymore. By all accounts he wasn't a very nice person, but he was smart enough to invest in good stables to keep the money coming in.

'I'm off for a walk, Glenda. It's past time I got a bit of fresh air. By the way, how much longer before Mrs Van Lincoln checks out?'

'Three days and four hours, not that I'm counting! She has been enquiring about availability next month, though.'

'We are full! We have no room for at least four years! Oh, please tell her that and don't book her in again.'

'I wish I could but sadly that's not true. Do we know what's she's doing here? Where do she and Tristan go every day?'

'I've no idea. Perhaps she's having a little holiday with her grandson.'

*

Hannah headed up to the main road and turned down the little track just beside it. She could see about eight horses in one field and three in another. There were a few cars parked nearby and people visible mucking out stables. This was completely different to the place she remembered visiting as a child. Those had just been wooden stables, but these were very posh. She wouldn't think it would be cheap to stable a horse here.

'Can I help you? This is private land. Are you looking for something?'

She had to think quickly and come up with a story. This must be Clive and she knew immediately that she didn't like him.

'Hi, I'm looking for the person in charge. I want to enquire about what's on offer here.'

'I'm in charge, but I'm afraid we are full. We aren't taking any more horses, and even if we were I doubt that you could afford it. We are very expensive, goodbye.'

'You're probably right, sorry to bother you. I'll just carry on down the lane and take a look at the farm that's for sale.'

He just glared at her, apparently confused. She didn't look back or say anything more.

The farm was quite a way down the lane. One of the staff at the hotel had said it was empty. The farmer had gone into an old people's home and all the animals had gone when he retired. That was why it was up for sale. She could see from the farm gate that it was a huge plot and, if houses were to be built there, they would have fabulous views.

As she walked back up the track she saw someone coming towards her on a horse. They stopped a few paces away and leant down to speak to her.

'Hello, Hannah! What brings you up here?'

'Hi, Emmi, I was just enquiring about the horse riding but apparently they don't give lessons anymore. It's such a shame, I use to love coming here as a child.'

'So did I, that's when I fell in love with riding. You're right, there's been no lessons since Mrs Oliver died, but if you were that interested why not get a horse and stable it here?'

'I thought I might, but there are no empty stables. The place is full.'

'Rubbish, there are at least four free! Who told you that?'

'The chap in charge.'

'That's weird; he's normally keen to have the place full to the brim. Clive's a bit of a money grabber.'

Hannah said goodbye and headed back to the hotel. The stables weren't the only thing on her mind: tonight was Britney's first shift in the restaurant, which she wasn't exactly looking forward to. Thankfully Hannah wouldn't have to get involved as Glen was going to train her. He had the patience of a saint until someone crossed him. It was also Jimmy's night off: what a coincidence!

*

'Good luck, Glen. Would you like me to tell her to button her shirt up a bit more? As for the skirt – I will mention that it needs to be at least six inches longer than it is. The businessmen are in for a treat tonight, I think.'

Two hours later, Hannah could see that Glen was pulling his hair out. She was slow and could only carry one plate at a time: not even one in each hand!

He had stopped her taking drinks to the tables after she had dropped a tray of wine glasses, and to top it off she was forever going into the kitchen to chat to the chefs.

'Hannah, does she realise that she's here to work? Fair enough, it's all new to her, but on your first shift you should be keen to learn. She has to go. Please sack her, do something! Why are you laughing? It's not funny, I've aged twenty years tonight! Don't ever ask me to train someone again!'

'I'm laughing because – no, see for yourself. Look at table five!'

Glen turned around and even he had to laugh. He had never seen this happen before! Britney had sat down at a table with two businessmen that were eating there. They had poured her a glass of wine and she had even called to one of the other waitresses to bring them another bottle.

'Oh dear, Hannah, we've had people work their first shift and never come back but this really takes the biscuit. It's just a shame Jimmy's not here to see it. Good luck getting rid of her, somehow I don't think she realises she's doing anything wrong. I suppose at least she's getting them to order more wine!'

'Shut up. When and if she gets up from the table, send her to my office.'

As she headed back into Reception she saw, sat in the corner of the lounge, Mrs Van Lincoln and Clive, the owner of the stables. This made Hannah feel a lot better about what she knew, as anyone who saw the two of them together could quite easily begin to put two and two together.

Clearing a couple of coffee cups away from another table, she saw Tristan coming back from the bar with two glasses. Once he had placed them down, Mrs Van Lincoln dismissed him as if he was one of the waiters. Hannah smiled, but got caught out by Tristan, who wasn't amused.

'Something the matter, Hannah?'

'No, not at all, why do you ask?'

Tristan fumed. 'You think you're so special! Running around this hotel giving out orders as if you owned the place: I think you forget that you work here and we pay your wages! Over this last couple of weeks my grandmother has spent hundreds of pounds in here, so I would just watch your step if I was you.'

'You're right, I do work here, and your grandmother's bill *has* helped towards paying my wages. Yes, your grandmother, not you, and as for watching my step, I think it's your step I'm watching. Mrs Van Lincoln has just dismissed *you,* so it looks like it's you stepping away from her, not me. Goodnight.'

Chapter 28

The following day their little problem with Britney was resolved. She had handed in her notice, saying, in her words: 'I think I'm too good to be a waitress.' The restaurant staff had a little giggle over that. Sadly the chefs weren't as happy as she had been good eye candy, but it was a huge relief for Jimmy.

Today was a big day for Hannah as a furniture van was arriving to bring all Betty's possessions and such furniture as she was keeping to Luckett Quay. The new sofa, chairs, table, and bedroom furniture had already been delivered and Hannah was going to spend the day arranging the flat for Betty's arrival tomorrow. She wanted to unpack all the kitchen things and sort all of Betty's clothes into two wardrobes: one for winter and the other for summer. Moving the furniture in would be alright as a few of Brian's builders were still on site building the conservatory.

First, she had a quick handover with Glenda. She was in two minds over whether she should mention what she had seen in Mrs Van Lincoln's room and the hotel lounge, but as it was none of her business she decided against it.

Hannah spent half an hour with Glenda going through the following week's events and VIP guests at the hotel. Then, with her bag full of cleaning materials, she took a quick look at her watch. It was nearly ten o'clock, so she had a good twelve hours to get everything done.

She walked out through the hotel car park. She noticed Tristan and Mrs Van Lincoln driving out, but just pulling into the hotel was Raymond Dove.

'Good morning, Hannah, got a day off?'

'Yes, my Nan's flat's finished and I'm off to get it

ready for her. It's all a bit overwhelming, but very exciting! I can't wait for us both to move in.'

'Putting down roots, eh? That's a big thing, but apparently you're not content with one property! I hear you were viewing another one yesterday, the old farmhouse at the top of the hill. Emmi said she saw you up there, have you won the lottery?'

'No, though that would be nice! I was just being nosy and, well, perhaps I was putting two and two together and not quite making four.'

'That's very interesting because, as you know, I'm in property and for some reason the farmhouse has come off the market this week. No one's saying why. Perhaps if you tell me what you know I might be able to make it up to four?'

'It's only gossip, so I wouldn't like to repeat it. Oh, by the way, Tristan is being very kind, taking his grandmother out every day.'

'Yes, he's had a couple of weeks off to take her sight-seeing.'

'That's nice, because there are a lot of lovely properties to look at – sorry, I don't mean properties, I mean the beautiful sites around Norfolk. We have beaches, villages, even riding stables if she's into horses.'

'Thank you, Hannah. I hope you have a good day sorting everything out for your nan. I owe you one.'

Problem solved! Mr Dove was now on the case, and there was no way the stables would be coming down if it was left to him. Upset his daughter like that? I don't think so.

Oh good, the furniture van was already at the house. If Hannah got them to move everything into her flat, she could unpack the boxes there and carry everything across the corridor to put away in Betty's place.

'Morning, Brian! How's everything going?'

'Just fine. Come and look at the conservatory; the

brick work's finished and tomorrow the frame goes in. It's just a shame it couldn't be finished before Betty arrived.'

'That's not a problem; she will enjoy watching it all come together. By the way, can I be cheeky and ask to borrow one of your lads for half an hour later on to help me move some furniture?'

'Of course, Carl's around, so he can help you. He's upstairs dealing with some snagging in Margaret's flat.'

'Okay, thanks.'

'Can I ask you something? No, actually, it doesn't matter.'

'I don't mind, what do you want to know?'

'You know when you and Carl went to get your furniture? Did he say anything about ... well, I don't exactly know what it is. Since he came back he's been different and his mum and I can't put our fingers on why. I will say that he does seem happier, but like I said, he's different.'

'I'm not the person you should be asking. Perhaps you should be talking to him.'

That was the end of that conversation, but it was good to hear that Carl was okay.

Now to get stuck in: the kitchen boxes first, as there were so many. Hopefully everything would fit in the cupboards. Then, if she got Carl to help move the bed and wardrobes, she could pack Betty's clothes away and leave all her nick-knacks for Betty to arrange herself. This was so much fun: Hannah couldn't wait to be doing this for her own flat!

'Good morning. Dad says you need a hand moving some furniture?'

'Hi, Carl, you look different! Is that a new haircut? It looks nice.'

'Thanks, it's not just a new haircut, but a new me. I'd like to talk to you about it when the rest of them are not around, if that's okay.'

'Of course, I will look forward to that! Now, would you be able to help me move those two wardrobes, please?'

They moved all the furniture into place and then Hannah made the bed up, put the new towels in the bathroom, and cleaned for England. All the kitchen things were put away, and the sofa looked lovely, especially with the brightly coloured cushions. It had taken her nearly all day but she was happy with her work. Now that the builders had left, Hannah had a look around the conservatory. The doors leading into it from her and Betty's flats were perfect and once in there the view out to sea was magnificent.

A knock at the door startled her; she had been miles away. It was Carl, bringing a welcome offering.

'Hi, I've fetched some fish and chips and a bottle of wine. I thought you would need a break. It's nearly eight o'clock.'

'Gosh, where has the time gone? I think I've been day-dreaming the last couple of hours away. Let me get two plates and a couple of glasses from Nan's kitchen, and we can sit out in the garden.'

It was a lovely evening and not a sound from anywhere. Hannah saw that Brian was right: Carl *was* different. She almost wanted to say he seemed confident.

'So, Mr New Haircut, what else is new? What have you been up to?'

'Where do I start? Well, I've had a night out in Norwich, which was nice. Not like the one we had in London. This was a gay pub, and it was quite quiet but that was good. I could chat and find out a bit about the gay scene here in Norfolk. Believe it or not, there's quite a lot going on! I'm excited about it.'

'I'm pleased for you. So does that mean you won't be running off to the bright lights of London? I thought you might.'

'No. London's fun, and perfect for the odd

weekend away clubbing, but no. Norfolk's my home. That's something else I want: my own place.'

'What will your mum say about that?'

'I think she'll be fine with it. I reckon she has known all along that I'm gay and that's why she's always been so over-protective of me. But since I came back from London everything's fallen into place in my head. I accept who I am and that's it, really. Do you know, Hannah, I never thought a gay person could be a builder? I always thought that if I came out I would have to move away and do something else, I don't know what. I love my job. It's a great family business. Why would I want to give it up just because I go to bed with men? And I—'

'I'm so pleased for you, I really am, but eat your fish and chips before they go cold!'

They chatted about the people Carl had met in Norwich and the different groups he could join if he wanted to. He was different, and it wasn't just about him being gay, it was about the family business: he felt ready to work with his dad to make a bigger success of it. But life was not going to be all about work: he had several years of fun to catch up on!

'Come on,' he told her, 'let's lock up and take the rest of the wine down to the beach. I might just go to the van and find another bottle.'

The evening had rushed by and it was getting dark. The sky was clear, the stars and moon were shining, and they were both so happy. They knew that this was going to become a special friendship.

'That's me sorted out, so how about you, Hannah? Will it be Jimmy or Tom now that I'm out of the equation?'

'What do you mean? Neither, of course! Jimmy cheated on me, and as for Tom, he's more like a cousin to me.'

'Yes, but everyone makes mistakes in life. Couldn't you forgive Jimmy? He has given up his life to be near you: surely that says something.'

'Yes, it does. It says that he's not to be trusted, and I'm not about to be hurt by him again.'

With that, Carl dropped the subject. They spent the rest of the evening chatting, laughing, and getting to know each other a lot better. This friendship was just starting, but it was something that they both knew would continue for many years to come. He wasn't a bit concerned about the relationship he would have with his mates and work colleagues once they found out he was gay. As he said, if they weren't happy with it, they weren't worth having as friends.

It was starting to get very late. They had both drunk too much wine and Hannah had a busy day tomorrow with Betty arriving. They headed back up the hill. Carl was going to leave his van at the house and walk back down to Saltmarsh Quay.

'You see, Carl, this is the friendship I want with Tom, but I don't think it will ever be like this. He always wants more. If he would only accept that I don't, we could be having a great time together. Thank you for a lovely evening, I'm so happy for you – no, for us! Friendships are very precious.'

'I know, but there's one more friendship you need to sort out: the one with Jimmy! I somehow don't think he's ready to give up on you yet.'

Chapter 29

It was the big day: Betty was arriving this morning. Hannah had a bit of a bad head after last night's wine on the beach with Carl. She didn't even bother to go into the main hotel; she went straight out of the staff block and down the hill to Luckett House. A supermarket online delivery would be arriving at ten o'clock and hopefully Robert and Betty would be there in time for lunch.

There were no workmen at the house: Brian had suggested that his men work on one of his other projects today as it could be quite an emotional day for Betty. Hannah still couldn't get over the fact that this was going to be her home as well. She couldn't wait to move in, and she did wonder why she hadn't already done it. The furniture was there: all she had to do was move her clothes and other bits and pieces down from the hotel.

The delivery was on time, and soon all the food was packed away. The flowers she had ordered for Betty were delivered and made ready: it was just a question of waiting for her to arrive. A knock at the door surprised her: were they early?

'Oh, sorry, Tom, I thought you were Dad and Nan. Come in!'

Hannah's phone rang as she showed Tom into the hall and she answered it.

'Hello, Dad, are you nearly here? You're only just leaving? No, I suppose it's not a problem, I'll see you in a few hours. Drive carefully!'

'Is everything okay?' Tom asked.

'Yes, but they're only just setting off – something to do with my stepmother, apparently. It doesn't matter. Have you come to look at the garden?'

'Yes, but I thought Betty had already moved in. I

wanted to discuss some ideas with her. Perhaps I'll come back later in the week.'

'Could I ask a quick favour, if you've got half an hour to spare? It's just that, since I'm stuck here twiddling my thumbs until they get here, I might as well bring all my stuff down from the hotel.'

'Yes, of course. I've got nothing else planned for the day.'

They went off up to the staff block. There was no furniture to move, just clothes and bits and pieces which Hannah threw into black bin liners.

As they carried the last few bags to Tom's van, Jimmy appeared from his room. They said a quick hello, but there was no real conversation. It didn't bother Hannah. She was over him and if he wasn't over her, that wasn't her problem.

'That was a bit awkward.'

'You mean me and Jimmy? Relax, that's in the past. I've moved on.'

'No, I mean me and Jimmy.'

'I don't get it.'

'I thought you would know already. A few weeks ago I had some drinks in the pub while Jimmy was in there with some of the hotel staff. I don't really know how it started but we ended up arguing and there was a fight. We were both thrown out.'

'Arguing about what?'

'About you. He was talking about how he was going to win you back and I said you wouldn't because of his cheating. Then I might have said a few other things because of the drink.'

'I don't want to know any more. Believe it or not, none of that has anything to do with me. I'm simply single and enjoying being by myself. That's the last of the bags. I will clean the room and get rid of the rubbish tomorrow. Are you ready?'

There wasn't a lot of talking as they unloaded the van. Hannah got Tom to leave the bags in the lounge.

Once it was all done she just wanted him to leave but as he had put himself out for her she thought she had better offer him a coffee. She could tell he couldn't wait to go either. He looked very uncomfortable.

'I had better get going. Tell your Nan to give me a call when she has time to chat about the garden.'

'Will do, and thanks for doing this today, it's been a huge help. You and Olivia must come round one night and we can have a mini house-warming party.'

'Yes, okay.'

Oh dear, he wasn't a happy chappie for some reason, and why would he get into a row with Jimmy? One good thing about moving out of the hotel was that she would see less of Jimmy.

Setting that aside, Hannah set to tidying her clothes away before Robert and Betty arrived. Two hours later, everything was packed away. Hannah had taken a few things out of Betty's fridge into her own, and finally felt that she had moved in. This was it: her new home!

As she opened the doors to what would eventually become the finished conservatory she became even more excited. This was going to be a lovely space for her and Betty to enjoy, and hopefully Margaret and Josie would enjoy popping down as well. Whoever would have thought that she would end up living in the house where she had spent all her happiest times as a child?

Robert texted her to say that they had stopped at a supermarket but would be with her in half an hour. Hannah was a little worried as this was a huge step for Betty and no doubt would be so emotional for her: leaving the Midlands behind and starting a whole new life in Norfolk. By the time the car pulled onto the drive her stomach was doing somersaults.

'Come in, Nan, here's the key to your flat, and before you go in: if you aren't happy with where I've placed any of the furniture, we can move it. I'm sorry but it will probably take you weeks to find all of your kitchen things. I just put everything away in the easiest cupboards and drawers.'

Hannah could see that her dad was nervous too. He was obviously thinking the same things as her. Betty took the key and turned it in the lock.

'Oh my goodness, how fabulous is this? To think what this used to look like! I'm so excited, and I don't want to change a thing! Now show me to the kettle, Hannah. Robert can nip out to the car and get the rest of my things and I will make us a cup of tea.'

Hannah went and helped her dad with the bags. Neither of them could believe how calm Betty was being: she was nothing but excited.

'And to think, Dad, I was worried sick over how Nan was going to react.'

'Me too, darling. I'm sorry we're late. Susanna needed me to do a couple of jobs and to be honest it was easier than getting the backlash for not doing them. She's still mad about all this and I can't get her to understand that it's Mum's money, not mine. Hopefully as time goes on she will see what I mean. Right, this is the last of it; let's see if that tea is made.'

The tea was made and Betty had taken it out into the garden with some cakes she had bought at the supermarket. They sat down to drink it, but every so often she would get up and wander back into the flat to look at something. They chatted about how unrecognisable the building was, the conservatory, and the stunning view. When Betty came back out for the fifth time, she was carrying a bottle of champagne and three glasses. Robert took the bottle from her, opened it, and poured.

'Mum, Hannah, I'd like to toast both of you: here's to the start of many happy hours spent in this garden, and no doubt with a lot more champagne!'

Hannah raised her glass in return.

'Thanks, Dad. I just hope I'll be able to keep up with Nan, Josie, and Margaret! Something tells me that wine o'clock will come around on most days!'

They laughed, and then Hannah saw a change on Betty's face. It had to happen: there had to be an emotional aspect to this move.

'Are you okay, Nan?'

'Yes, and I would just like to do a little toast of my own. Here's to the people who aren't here, who have been a huge part of Luckett House's story. My dear parents who brought me to this magical place over seventy years ago, your father and grandfather, who fell in love with it just like us. And your dear mother, Hannah, who loved it as well. She left us far too early and I know she'd be so happy for us both being able to live together here.

'I'm not sad about leaving that little flat in the Midlands. I was upset moving into it from our family home, but this has always been home for me, as long as I can remember. The building has changed so much, and for the better, but the feel of it and the memories are still here.

'Here's to you as well, Hannah, to your dreams. You have your whole life ahead of you, and what a wonderful place to plan your future in! Top the glasses up, Robert, and let's toast Luckett House, the most important part of our pasts, present, and future.'

Chapter 30

It had been nearly two weeks since Betty and Hannah had moved in, and today was a very special day. There were no builders left at Luckett House: the work was finished!

The conservatory was looking great. It just needed to be furnished and both Hannah and Betty knew exactly how they wanted to do it. So much so that they had already ordered the furniture: two huge, comfy three-seater sofas, a dining table that would seat ten, and a large sideboard.

The only job left was the garden and Hannah wasn't getting involved in that. For one thing, she didn't know a thing about plants, and she also didn't want to encourage Tom any more than was necessary. No, she was leaving the garden design to Betty.

The last couple of weeks had been great fun. Betty had rearranged her kitchen cupboards and given Hannah lots of her kitchen equipment. They had spent countless hours down on the beach, taking picnics and sometimes even going down there in the evening with a bottle of wine to watch the sunset.

The builders' leaving wasn't the only excitement about today, because Josie was finally moving in! She and Bonkers the dog would be installed by the time Hannah got home from work. Betty and Hannah were quite nervous: it wasn't like someone moving in next door. This was someone who would share their front door and garden. There would have to be a bit of give and take from all of them.

'Isn't it strange not seeing any building equipment or skips on the drive?' Hannah wondered. 'I suppose this is it now: the place is our own. I do hope that Josie fits in with us, and Margaret, come to that. I am nervous now. I really want us all to get along.'

'I know what you mean, darling, but I'm sure everything will be fine. Once the conservatory furniture arrives we will all have a place to sit and get to know each other as well. By the way, I've spoken to Tom on the phone and arranged for him to come up when you are at work tomorrow.'

'Thanks, it's not that I'm avoiding him, I just don't want him to get me involved with the garden. I've had a text from Richard to say that he and Josie will be here by mid-day. He has organised everything with the furniture removal men, so you and Josie can leave everything to him. I'm not sure what time I'll be back, but probably quite late. The hotel is rammed this week and with the evenings being so lovely, people are eating a lot later. Are you sure you have everything you need here?'

'Yes, and if I haven't I can walk down to the shop in Saltmarsh Quay. Please, don't fuss over me. Let me do things for myself while I'm still capable.'

'Okay, I'm sorry. Have a nice day and give Josie my love! I've left a little card and present for her up in her flat.'

Hannah knew she had loads to do today: the paperwork had piled up over the last few weeks due to her spending more time with Betty. Now Josie and Margaret were moving in over the next few days, she felt more comfortable leaving them to get to know each other. She took a quick look in her pigeonhole on her way in. Catching her eye on top of all the other paperwork was a note asking her to phone Raymond Dove before twelve o'clock today.

'Hello, Mr Dove, it's Hannah from the Saltmarsh Cliff Hotel. I received a message to phone you this morning, how can I help? Of course, that's not a problem ... yes, I see in the diary that you have a table for four booked in at one-thirty. After the dessert, you say? Of course, I will make sure that it's me that serves, that won't be a problem. Well, we will look forward to seeing you at lunch time! Goodbye.'

What was that all about? Why insist that Hannah serve them? Perhaps he knew he could trust her to be discreet if she heard a private discussion? There went her chance to make a hole in the paperwork backlog today. Still, there was always tomorrow.

She popped in for a quick chat with Glenda to see if there was anything she needed to know before getting stuck in.

'Any news? What delights have I missed? Any gossip? Scandal? I must say, it does feel strange coming up here to work rather than just crossing the courtyard from the staff block.'

'Not a lot. We should exceed budget for the month, and the bookings for next month are looking good as well. Glen has everything under control in the restaurant and Jimmy seems to be doing okay, although I think he's missing having you around in the staff block. I wouldn't be surprised if he soon gives up trying to get you back and finally decides to move on.'

'I was thinking the same thing, but on a positive note he has sorted the kitchen out and put loads of great procedures in place.'

'I agree. Talking of your admirers, can we mention another one? You know old Harry, the gardener? Well, he's way past retirement age and he's decided to stop work altogether. He was only coming up a couple of days a week anyway, and he has suggested Tom as a good replacement for him. What do you think?'

'Perfect, I'm indoors in the restaurant and he's outside, so that's not a problem and I think he'll do a brilliant job. If I plan it right, he could even do the garden down at Luckett House when I'm up here and vice versa! Right, if that's everything, I had better get ready for Mr Dove and his guests.'

Glen greeted her as she came into the restaurant. She should catch up with him soon, though no doubt he had everything organised perfectly, down to the last teaspoon.

'Hannah, you were wrong!'

'Wrong about what? Look, Mr Dove's just parked outside. It's not businessmen he's entertaining for lunch, it's his wife, daughter, and Tristan. Why are you smiling? What's funny about that?'

'Nothing – well, not yet.'

Hannah didn't have time to press him.

'Good afternoon, Mr Dove. If you and your guests would like to follow me, I have a table for you right in the window.'

Hannah led them to the table and took their drinks order before explaining the daily menu options. She smiled as she walked away – Tristan had ordered an orange juice! He must be trying to impress Raymond by acting as if he didn't drink alcohol during the day. It was starting to look like this could be a very interesting lunch.

Every time Hannah went back to the table poor Tristan was trying to impress Raymond. He was always very flattering towards Mrs Dove, but it was so noticeable how he was ignoring Emmi. Sadly she wasn't aware of it, if she was, by now he would be long gone from her life.

'Ah, the desserts, thank you, Hannah: my favourite, crème brûlée.'

'There we go, one cheese and biscuit platter for you, Mrs Dove. Can I get you anything else?'

'Not for the moment, thank you.'

This was when the excitement started to build. Hannah just had to wait for them to finish and then serve what Raymond had asked for. There was no question that this was going to be a surprise, but for who? It was now getting on for three o'clock. Most of the tables were empty and the staff were laying up for dinner. Hannah helped out, keeping one eye on Raymond.

'When you are ready, please, Hannah.'

This was it, the moment she had been waiting for.

'Champagne, Daddy? What are we celebrating?'

'All will become clear once Hannah has opened the bottle and poured... Oh, I suppose I could tell you while she's doing it.'

Hannah realised by the look on his face that he wanted her to hear what he had to say.

'Emmi, your mother and I have been chatting for quite some time. We both realise that you don't really enjoy working in the office, and we wanted to help you find something that you loved doing, so—'

Hannah had never been so slow at opening a bottle of champagne. She was even slower at pouring it. She didn't want to spill it, but she also didn't want to take her eyes off Tristan. He had a fixed smile on his face, as if to say that this was not just Emmi's future under discussion, but his as well. Hannah could sense that there was a fall coming. Everything was slotting into place. Hurry up, Raymond, spill the beans!

'—since we know where your heart lies, we've bought the riding stables for you.'

'What? Daddy, are you serious? I'm going to own the stables: my own business?'

'Not just the stables, but the farm cottages as well.'

'You can't have, it's sold! There's going to be houses built on that land.'

'Sorry, Tristan, but you are right in a way, it is sold. I exchanged on it yesterday, and there aren't going to be any houses on it, just horses.'

'But I ... um, please excuse me. I forgot, I have an appointment. Thank you for lunch.'

With that, Tristan ran to Reception and ordered a taxi. His face was a picture, but his wasn't the face Hannah really wanted to see. That was Mrs Van Lincoln's when he told her what had just happened.

'Oh look, he didn't stay to drink his champagne. Why don't you join us and drink it, Hannah? It would be such a shame to waste it. Now let's talk horses, Emmi. That will be the perfect end to a very successful lunch; don't you think so, Hannah?'

She agreed and left them to talk horses, smiling to herself. She and Raymond Dove were becoming a good little team. Having said that, she knew her place and would never overstep the line with him.

It had been yet another disappointment for Tristan's hopes. Surely his and Emmi's relationship couldn't last much longer? Mr Dove would make sure of that, and somehow Tristan didn't seem the horsey type of guy.

As the Doves left, he apologised for getting her to employ Britney. She had told him the same thing as she had told Hannah: that waitressing was beneath her. He wasn't impressed with that attitude and joked that perhaps Tristan and Britney could get together, as they would have something in common.

'What's that, Mr Dove?'

'Oh, that's not for me to say. She's my niece and he's an employee. I will let you make your own mind up. Thank you for a lovely lunch, Hannah, it's one I'll remember for years to come.'

Chapter 31

Hannah was still smiling the following morning. Poor Tristan, he didn't have a lot of luck in life. Perhaps if he concentrated on his work instead of how to use people to get what he wanted, life would be a lot kinder to him.

It was only six-thirty, so the house was quiet. Hannah hadn't seen Richard, Josie, or Betty when she came home last night.

She decided to make a flask of coffee and take it down to the beach. It was something she had become accustomed to doing if she was up before Betty. It set her up for the day.

She was disappointed to see, as she stepped from the coastal path onto the beach, that she wasn't the only one here today. She didn't want a conversation with anyone – this was her special time. She started to walk in the opposite direction, but hearing someone call her name, turned round and realised that Richard was walking the dog on the beach.

'Hi, Richard, you're up early!'

'Yes, Bonkers was restless all night. Something about being in a strange house, I think. I finally gave in and got up, and to be honest I'm glad I did. It's so beautiful down here first thing in the morning.'

'Yes, coastal walks have become one of my favourite pastimes. I'm dreading not being able to do it in the winter when it's wet and windy. How did yesterday go, by the way? Has your mum settled in okay? More importantly, is she happy with the flat? How about you, Bonkers? I can already tell I'll be borrowing you to go on long walks with me. I think we have a lot of adventures ahead of us!'

'More than happy with the flat, and she's over the moon to be back living in Luckett Quay after all these years. I'm so happy for her and really looking forward to staying here.'

'That'll be nice for her. I expect it feels good to get away from your busy, exciting life in London now and then.'

'Oh, it's certainly busy, but not as exciting as it used to be. I'm getting too old for the job, I think. You have to keep your finger on the pulse twenty-four-seven because the fashion industry is changing so fast these days. I think it's time I bowed slowly out of it, leaving by the back door where no one will notice me go. It used to be an awful lot of fun, juggling new ideas every week. It was a blast in its day, but now ... well, now I'm losing interest. That's something I never thought I'd say, but there we are.'

'So what next? You're still young.'

'Thanks for saying that, but I'm not. I'm fifty and then some. Now Mum's sorted it might be time to organise my life a bit better too. It's time to get out of the fashion industry: always best to leave while you're still on top, although I never reached quite that far.'

'I'm afraid I don't know much about the designer world; all of my clothes come from the high street! Well, that's not entirely true. They may be high street brands but I find them on the internet.'

'I wouldn't expect you to know much about my area: it's not like I get to sign my work. Anything I come up with is simply Gina Le Gina.'

'Gina Le Gina I do know. They're too big not to be aware of them.'

'The lovely thing is, I was there at the beginning. It's been so exciting to see it grow and flourish over these last thirty years. Of course, now there's no Gina behind the brand, only the company still using her name. Times have changed.'

'How on earth did you go from a little old Norfolk town to the bright lights of London?'

'It's a long story, really. It all started with a friend of my mum's, Clare. She lived in London and was going to work for this new fashion house as a seamstress. Before the job started she came to Sheringham for a couple of weeks' holiday. I'd just left school and was working in one of the ice-cream shops, not yet knowing what I wanted to do with my life.

'Clare was so excited about her new job. She had a feeling it was going to be big. She always encouraged me whenever she came to Norfolk and on this occasion she took an interest in my artwork. She felt I had a talent and told me that I should try to pursue it once the summer season was over.

'She loved the job, and wrote to my mum every week telling her all about it. That winter, when all the businesses had shut or downsized and I was bored, Clare invited Mum and me up to London for a week. She lived a few miles out from the city, but we would take the tube in and visit museums and exhibitions or go to a show. It was always a busy week whenever we went to see her.

'On one day we had planned to meet Clare at her work. We waited outside the building and she came down to tell us that she had been asked to finish a garment off before she left, but that it wouldn't take long. We were allowed to wait inside where all the deliveries came and went.

'There was a man in a smart suit going through some paperwork in the same area. He was polite, but seemed upset about something. Then he swore over one of the papers and instantly apologised. He explained that the person responsible for checking stock in and out of the building had just been sacked for not keeping the books up to date. He jokingly said, "I don't suppose you want a job?" and without thinking, I said yes.

'The next day I went into work with Clare. I

sorted the paperwork out in under a day. To be honest, it was easy. All the delivery and despatch notes were dated, so I just had to be logical about it. Just before it was time for me to leave, the chap who had been struggling with it the day before came to see how I was getting on. He was very impressed, and he offered me the job at a higher rate than the other person had been paid. So that was the start of my career in the fashion industry.'

'But how did you go from checking goods in to designing clothes?'

'Luck, really. I was in the right place at the right time. Part of my job was taking deliveries to whichever floor or designer needed them, and once I left the basement I was in a fantasy land, surrounded by glamourous, chic men and women. I wanted to be working up there more than anything. I didn't know how I could manage it, but I was determined to make it happen.

'The paperwork part of my job I could do in my sleep. To be honest with you, I went in early to get it out of the way so I could spend my day in the rest of the building chatting to the cutters, seamstresses, and anybody and everybody who would talk to me.

'I was asked if I could work on one particular Sunday, as there was a big delivery of fabric arriving from one of the ports. As it had come a long way and cost a lot it needed checking off before the lorry could leave. This wasn't a problem for me, as it would mean extra wages. There had also been a buzz about this fabric in the building: apparently it was different, very modern, with very bright colours. Everyone seemed eager for the chance to work with it.

'You have to remember that these were the days before mobile phones. I was just told that the lorry would leave the docks at six in the morning, so I would need to be there early. I had a key to the basement, so that wasn't a problem. I picked up a couple of Sunday newspapers and a bacon sandwich on the way in and settled down to wait.

'I'd only been there about half an hour when there was a knock at the door. I opened it, thinking it was far too early for the lorry, and there was Gina! I'd never seen her in the flesh before. There were photographs of her all over the building, but even though I walked all over with my deliveries I never went near her office.

'She could tell that I was nervous, but she tried to make me feel at ease. She knew my name and apologised for not meeting me sooner. She joked that she had never been to the basement before and asked me to show her what I did on a normal day. I think she was just trying to be polite. She was there because she was so excited about the fabric that she couldn't wait until Monday to see it.

'I offered to make her a coffee from the staff room and when I came down she was sitting in my little cubbyhole where I kept the files and a little desk. It was a trestle table, really, but I used it as a desk. I could see that she was looking at the drawings I did to occupy my time.

'I had a big sketch pad that I would doodle clothes on. It was a little game I played with myself: when a new fabric came in I would design a blouse or a skirt that could be made with it. Sometimes I would be adventurous and draw coats or dresses as well. I was embarrassed to see her flicking through them, but before she could say anything I heard the lorry pulling up outside.

'I called out the codes on the labels as the fabric rolls were unloaded and Gina checked them against the delivery note. It was all correct and the driver left after about an hour. Then Gina asked if I would mind carrying a few rolls up to the cutting room. I did as she asked, obviously, and as I was heading down for the last couple of rolls she looked at me and said, "I think you should bring your sketch pad up too, if you've got some time to spare." Did I have time? Of course I did: this was only Gina Le Gina asking to see my drawings!'

'Oh, how exciting! You said it was luck, but I don't think so. You had a talent and she noticed it. Carry on, what happened next?'

'It was thirty-odd years ago, but every minute of that day is still clear in my head. It was the day my life changed forever. By the time I got back up with the last of the fabric, Gina had undone the packaging and laid the cloth out on four cutting tables. I remember looking at the clock and seeing it was one-fifteen. Do you know what time we left the building? Nine-thirty at night! It was and always will be the best day of my life. We laughed and bounced ideas off each other while she cut out fabric, then we went up to the sewing room and carried on talking as she stitched things together. It was so special and a week later, after I had trained someone to take over my job, I was up there again. I wasn't just working with the designers, I was one of them! That's when the hard work started. I had so much to learn about that world, and it didn't come easy. It took years to master, but every day was so exciting that I never wanted to go home. I often joked that I would have worked that job for free.'

'It sounds absolutely wonderful – oh! Look at the time; I need to get to work for the lunch shift. I've really enjoyed listening to you. I know you must have lots more stories to tell. I'm sure Nan would love to hear them too. One last question before I go: did you never want to have a range with your own name on? Surely that's the dream for every designer.'

Richard laughed. 'That's another long story, so I think we'll have to save it for later.'

As Hannah got ready for work she thought how

modest Richard was about everything. What great achievements, and what an exciting life he had had! But she couldn't dwell on that for long: she had a hotel to run. In a way she felt similarly to Richard; she loved her job, and even in this short time she had worked miracles for the hotel, working with Glenda and Jimmy to turn everything around. Yes, she was in a very happy place.

Chapter 32

A few days had passed. Josie had settled in and Richard had gone back to London. Another week and Margaret would be living in Luckett House as well. The conservatory furniture had arrived and it was all perfect. They had done the right thing by having it built across both flats. The views were stunning and once the garden had been landscaped everything would be finished. Hopefully that would start today, as Tom was coming round to show Betty his ideas.

'Morning, Nan, are you okay?'

'Yes, I was miles away. Would you like a coffee?'

'I'm okay, thanks. I need to be getting up to the hotel. I've a busy day ahead but that's a good thing. You said you were miles away? Where would that be?'

'Oh, just soaking everything up. I remember years ago I did yoga and meditation for a short while and once the class was over I always felt light. My head was clear, and that's how I feel every morning I wake up here. It's a lovely feeling.'

'I know what you mean. I don't miss anything at all about my old life, apart from – no, I don't.'

'What were you going to say, Hannah?'

'I sometimes miss the happy times I had with Jimmy. We used to laugh a lot and have nice days out. But that was before he went and messed it all up. There's the door, I'll get it.'

It was Tom. He'd parked his van in the drive.

'Hi, Nan's waiting for you. She's very excited: a whole garden from scratch! Oh, sorry, I thought you were by yourself.'

'Oh, right. This is Steve. He's helping me out because I've got a couple of other jobs on, and I've managed to get the contract up at the hotel as well.

You probably knew that already, seeing as you work there.'

'Congratulations, I'm really pleased for you. Nice to meet you, Steve. Nan's around the back in the conservatory. It might be easier if you go through the gate: better than having two gardeners walking their muddy boots through her new flat! I'll say goodbye for now, I'm off to work. Have fun. We need to arrange that night out with Olivia soon: perhaps you would like to join us, Steve?'

I can't believe I said that, Hannah thought as she walked away. It was obviously the wrong thing to say: the look on Tom's face! Steve certainly is very handsome, but look what happened when I made eyes at the last hunk in this house! I got it all wrong and he turned out to be gay. I know Steve's not gay, though, not with the way he eyed me up and down just now. Oh no, he's interested enough.

She shook her head. She needed to pull herself together and get into work-mode. Although, thinking of the hotel: would Tom let Steve help up there as well? Steve with a shovel in his hand ... not a bad view to look at when you were working.

*

'Morning, Glenda, another hot day I see. Anything I need to know before I start?'

'Yes, you have a visitor waiting for you in the lounge. He doesn't seem very happy.'

'I'll head straight down there. How unhappy?'

Glenda shook her head. 'Good luck.'

Who else could it have been?

'Hi, Tristan, how can I help?'

'You can help by telling me how you got Raymond to buy up the riding stables. Emmi may be a little thick and not know what she's talking about most of the time, but she happened to mention that you were up there snooping around while my grandmother was staying here. That seems a bit suspicious to me.'

'I'm sorry, but I wasn't snooping anywhere. I went to the stables to enquire about riding lessons, and why is your grandmother relevant to this discussion? I have a lot of work to get on with, so did you want to speak to me about anything else?'

'Not now, but I suggest you work fast, because if my grandmother finds out you stopped her from buying the stables you'll be looking for a new job pronto! She'll make damned sure of that.'

'Thank you for the terrible advice, Tristan. That was pure rubbish, apart from that bit when you said Emmi was thick: I think she must be, or she would never go out with a scumbag like you. If you will excuse me, I have a hotel to manage.'

Hannah felt good. At last, she had got one over on him. She did feel awful for saying that Emmi was thick, though. She didn't deserve that.

Something told her she hadn't heard the last of Tristan and Mrs Van Lincoln, but there was work to be getting on with. It was going to be a long week as Glen was on holiday. On some days she would have to work three shifts again.

'Morning, Jimmy, I'm just checking in. Do we have everything that's on the lunch menu?'

'Yes, apart from the scallops, but I'll have them in time for dinner service. Have you settled into your flat okay? It's strange not having you around here as much. I'm looking forward to Glen's holiday period as I'll get to see more of you!'

Hannah smiled and walked away. If she was honest with herself, she missed seeing him around as well. She poured herself a coffee, grabbed her paperwork and took it out to the garden. She found a quiet seat under one of the trees where there was a nice cool breeze. How many people could say they had an outdoor office looking out to sea?

Taking a glance back at the hotel she saw that

someone was standing in the restaurant window looking out at her. It was Jimmy. He looked sad. She was surprised by how long he had stayed. Was it the job that had captured his interest, or was it her that was keeping him here?

'Hello, Hannah. Reception said you were out here. I'm sorry to bother you. What a lovely place to be doing paperwork!'

'You're not bothering me, Margaret, how are you? Getting excited about moving in, yet? Do you fancy a coffee?'

'I am, and no thank you. It may be a stupid thing to worry about, but I wanted to see you to ask if Josie has moved in okay. It must be so strange for her, coming back to Luckett Quay after all these years, and with me moving in soon as well.'

'Josie's fine, and Richard too, come to that. Things might be different if Frank was still alive, but this is a new start for all of us, myself and Nan included. It's a clean slate; leave everything behind and take up a new beginning.'

'I wouldn't think that a young girl like you would have to start again just yet. You don't have a past to forget the way we do.'

'That's where you're wrong. Can you see the person looking out of the window back there? That's my past, and he seems to think that by moving here and working with me he can be part of my future as well.'

Hannah went on to explain the whole Jimmy story, including how he had followed her here. This was the first time she had told that story from her heart and not her head.

'Oh dear, what can I say? My story is very similar, with both our partners cheating, but you were the brave one. You left him, while I stayed with Frank. I never had the guts to leave and oh my goodness there were so many times I should have. To be honest, I shouldn't have married him in the first place. Once I found out about Josie and baby Richard that should have been the end of us, but in those days things were different. It feels like an easy excuse but it was harder to leave in the face of the social stigma and everything that goes with it. I sometimes think that if Frank had been with Josie he would have been a nicer man. At least he wouldn't have been so bitter, and perhaps he would have actually liked himself. That's what it all came down to: he really despised himself. There would have been nothing he would have loved more than to be a part of Richards's life.'

'That's so sad for all of you.'

'Yes, decisions made in haste can shape our whole lives. They have for your Jimmy: he was stupid, and he obviously knows that. But you have to give it to him, Hannah; he's fighting to get you back. Of course, whether he wins that fight is entirely up to you. Thank you for the little chat, I will leave you to get on with your paperwork now.'

After a couple of hours Hannah hadn't achieved much beyond moving paper from one pile to the next and back again. Her mind was on Jimmy. His being sorry wasn't the issue. She believed that he was genuinely sorry, but that didn't excuse what had happened. But she also couldn't let go of the question: would she be as happy living here if he wasn't around?

Chapter 33

It was Margaret's moving-in day, and Hannah was getting anxious.

'I think I just heard Josie go out, do you think that's because Margaret will be here soon? I hope we've done the right thing. I know both of them have said it's not a problem, but what if it is? The last thing we need is an atmosphere. It's not like being next door neighbours; they have to share a garden and even a staircase!'

'Calm down, darling, everything will be fine. She's probably just taking Bonkers for a walk. Now, we still need to make a decision about the garden. I know we've gone over Tom's ideas together already, but just come outside and give me your opinion.'

'Don't get stressed over it. It's just the garden.'

'I know, but it has to be right for all four of us and Bonkers.'

'Well, you've answered your own question. Let everyone have a say. It could be the perfect ice breaker after Margaret moves in. Leave it to me, I'll give Tom a call and arrange for him to come round at a time when we're all here. Oh, that sounds like a van. It must be Brian with all of Margaret's furniture.'

It was two vans: Brian in one and Carl with Margaret in the other. Hannah went out to meet them and say a quick hello, then left them to get on with everything. It wasn't really a day off for her, as she had to work on a pile of hotel paperwork. She could achieve much more working at home with fewer interruptions, and Betty seemed a lot more relaxed knowing that the garden design decisions weren't going to be left entirely up to her.

Sometime later, she had a welcome interruption.

'Hi, Hannah.'

'Hello, Carl, how are you doing? Is everything moved in alright?'

'Yes, we're done with the furniture and most of the boxes. Dad's just taking Margaret back to get her clothes.'

'Have you got time for a coffee, then? I'm ready to take a break from this paperwork and you can tell me what you've been up to. I've not seen you around much lately, does that mean you've been going elsewhere to socialise?'

Hannah made the coffee and they took themselves out to the garden. Carl couldn't wait to tell her all his news: he had met up with a group of lads in Norwich for drinks and they had invited him to go away for a couple of weekends to London and Brighton. He had entered a whole new world, one that he fitted into. He felt more normal than ever before in his life.

'So aren't you tempted to move away?'

'Not at all, I'm enjoying my work here more than ever. I'm discussing jobs with Dad, giving him my opinions, and we're growing closer than ever before. That's not to say I don't enjoy my times away. They're wild, and that's not something I ever thought I'd say about my life!'

'So have you met anyone nice?'

'I've met lots of nice people, but I know what you mean. Yes, there's one guy I've seen twice: once in London and once when he came and surprised me here in Saltmarsh Quay. His name's Brett, he's two years older than me and he works in an office designing things that sound very complicated to me. He wants me to go on holiday with him so that we can get to know each other better.'

'That will be lovely! Where are you thinking of going?'

'We haven't decided yet, but before I get into

211

anything too serious I think I need to speak to Mum and Dad. Not about the holiday but about being gay. I'm not worried as they're both very open-minded, but it will probably come as a big shock to them. I really wish I had come out years ago but I can't put the clock back.'

'I'm so glad you aren't moving away. I would really miss you. I don't laugh as much with Tom, he takes everything so seriously. Speaking of Tom, have you seen his new assistant? If so, what do you think?'

'I think Steve's very nice, in more ways than one! From what I can gather he's just moved here and is staying with some relation down in Saltmarsh. I think he and Tom went to college together. But be careful, Hannah, you know what happens when you start kissing men! They end up being gay.'

'I can assure you there is nothing gay about Steve, and before long I'll find out for certain! There's just the small problem of jealous Tom to sort out first.'

They were laughing and joking and didn't hear Brian and Margaret come back until there was a knock at the door.

'Are you still here? I thought you were leaving.'

'My fault, Brian, I offered him a coffee and we got chatting.'

'It's not a problem. To be honest, Carl's been a lot more alive since you moved here. I don't know what you've done to him, but he seems to have discovered the art of conversation. He's spending his money like mad, too: new clothes, going away for the weekends ... he's a different person altogether!'

Carl reddened. 'I'm standing right here, you know.'

Hannah smiled. 'He's not wrong, though. The question is, Brian, is it change for the better?'

'Of course it is. He's a lot happier now, right, Carl?'

'Yes, I am. But right now I think I should be getting on before I'm sacked for loitering.'

Moments later Margaret appeared with some empty boxes that Brian was going to take away for her. Josie and Bonkers arrived back as they were loading them into the van. To Hannah's surprise, Margaret and Josie hugged each other, which was a lovely thing to see. Carl and Brian left and Betty invited everybody else inside.

'I think now that we are all moved in, it's time to toast Luckett House together. How about I open a bottle of something and we go into the garden to drink it?'

'If you give me a minute to wipe Bonkers off, I have a bottle of fizz in the fridge waiting for us,' Josie replied.

The afternoon was spent out in the sunshine with champagne, wine, nibbles, laughter, and lots of talk about the garden. Hannah was just hoping that the final design would look something like one of Tom's drawings.

As it was getting close to seven o'clock and they were all a little merry, Hannah suggested cooking something. They all agreed on a pasta dish that would be easy to cook. She left the three of them in the garden and went to get started, followed by Bonkers who had no doubt heard the word 'food'.

As she was waiting for the pasta to cook she stood in the conservatory looking out at the three of them. It was as if they had been friends for years. She was so happy, not just for them but also for herself. She had had the perfect day: a catch up with Carl in the morning and an afternoon of giggles with the girls. Norfolk was a special place, and these new friends had become very special to her as well. There were exciting times ahead for everyone.

Chapter 34

A few days later, and it would be fair to say that Hannah and her new Luckett House housemates had not had a sip of alcohol between them. Truth be told, they were still recovering from christening the house.

Today was the day of the big garden debate. Cakes were laid out, the kettle was on and the four of them were awaiting Tom's arrival. One thing that had happened over the last couple of days was the marking out of sections of garden with sticks, string, and plant pots. All the plans were on the table in the conservatory. Hopefully Tom wouldn't be too disappointed with what they had come up with.

Betty heard him pull up on the drive and went to meet him at the side gate.

'Come in; please don't be frightened by what you see in the garden. This is Josie, Margaret, and of course you know Hannah.'

'Hi, I've brought Steve along. He will be helping with the work, if that's okay with you.'

It was perfectly fine with Hannah. Steve was giving her the eye again, and she felt herself blushing.

He had a cut above his eye that hadn't been there before: trust her to fancy a bloke that got into fights!

Margaret went into the conservatory to get the plans Tom had produced, then the three of them started to go over what parts they liked. The main difference was that they didn't want a lawn. Tom had put it there for Bonkers to run around on, but Josie said the beach would do for that. It was all about easy maintenance.

'If that's the case, why not go for raised beds around the edges? I can see that you've given a lot of thought to this.'

'We have, and we love the idea of three or even four seating areas.'

Hannah interrupted to offer tea and coffee. She asked Steve if he would help her carry the cakes and tray out. He jumped at the idea, and because Tom was so engrossed in the garden he hadn't noticed.

'That looks like a nasty cut, have you been fighting?'

'Of course not, a branch of a tree we were cutting down hit me earlier today. It was my fault, I was in the way. Why, you don't think I get into fights, do you?'

'No, but I think you need to get that cleaned up before it gets infected. Come here; let me find you a plaster.'

Hannah washed the cut and put a plaster on it while Steve stood there in silence. She was shaking, not because she was nervous but because she was physically excited to be so close to him. Annoyingly, the feeling didn't appear to be mutual. Hannah recognised how confident he was, even cocky, so full of himself that there was a female drooling over him. That might work with some of the girls in Saltmarsh, but Hannah didn't want to be one of those girls.

She made her decision too late: just as she finished pressing the plaster on, he moved his face towards hers and kissed her. This wasn't a little thank you peck but a full on lip-to-lips smacker. If she wasn't very much mistaken there was a tongue in it as well. She knew exactly what she ought to do: pull away, but did she? Of course not, she stayed right there and enjoyed every moment of it.

Steve was the one to pull away, saying: 'I think we'd better take the tea out before they come looking for us, don't you?'

He had controlled the whole situation, even leaving Hannah wanting more. She was so mad at

215

herself for falling for it and there he was, carrying the tray with a huge smile on his face. Thankfully the four outside were so engrossed in the garden details they didn't notice how long they had taken to make the tea.

'Nan, what have you done?'

'We haven't done anything, it was Tom. Once he realised we didn't need the lawn he cut up all the designs, so we could mix different elements together. What do you think of the colour scheme? We'll have grey fences and black and white pots and troughs. It's so exciting; we would never have come up with all of this by ourselves! Tom's so clever!'

The cake was eaten, the tea drunk, and the garden began to be properly mapped out. Margaret seemed the most excited and in a way very emotional, but she covered it up well. Lists were drawn up of the plants they wanted, and now all Tom had to do was go away and work out how much it was going to cost. All the while, Hannah tried to keep her distance from Steve, not even catching his eye. On the one occasion she did, he looked like a cat that had got the cream.

'Right then, Betty,' Tom announced, 'give me a couple of days and I'll come back to you with a price and a time schedule. We should be off now. Thanks for the tea and cake.'

'Yes, thank you,' Steve agreed. 'I look forward to more cake when we're doing the garden. Oh, and thanks for taking care of my cut, Hannah. I think I'll have to have a few more accidents, don't you?'

She could feel herself going red again. Tom hadn't picked up on what Steve had said, but Betty, Josie, and Margaret had. There would doubtless be questions later. The men left, and Hannah and Betty cleaned the cups and plates away.

'That was nice,' said Josie. 'If you don't mind, I'm going to take Bonkers for another walk on the beach.'

'Can I join you?' Betty asked.

They left together, Bonkers bouncing between the two of them. Margaret insisted on helping Hannah wash up the cups and plates. She was very quiet, and Hannah felt that she ought to say something.

'Are you okay, Margaret?'

'Oh yes, I'm just grateful to have been involved, that's all.'

Margaret explained that this was the first time in her life someone had asked her opinion when creating a garden. When she was living with Frank he had decided on everything, right down to how many bedding plants there would be and of what colour. She was allowed to do the weeding and watering, but it was his garden, just like it had been his house.

'I'm just so overwhelmed by everything. This probably sounds stupid to most people, but after he died I struggled for several weeks over what to eat every day because I had never made decisions before. I wasn't allowed to. And to be there today in that garden, being asked whether I would like this or that was hard for me, but it felt good to be in on that dilemma.'

'Margaret, I'm so sorry. No one should have to put up with what you've had to. It's not right.'

'I know, but I could have left and I didn't, so it was my fault in a way.'

Once everything was put away they headed back out into the garden and talked about the different seating areas for different times of the day. By the time Betty and Josie got back it was starting to get a bit breezy, so they all decided to move into the conservatory.

'I'm going to have to love you and leave you, ladies. I'm afraid the hotel late shift is calling. I've just got time for a quick shower, and then I'll put my face on and go to face the public.'

'Oh dear,' said Josie, 'I was just thinking of cooking something, but I need to feed Bonkers first. Margaret, Betty, how do you fancy a chicken stir fry?'

'Sounds good, I wish I was staying! Have a lovely evening and not too much wine. I'm not sure we've recovered from the day you moved in, Margaret!'

Hannah got herself ready and headed up to the hotel. It was another full house and the majority of the residents would eat in the hotel tonight. A quick chat to Glenda and a briefing with the kitchen, and it was time to get the show on the road.

The evening started quite normally with the seven o'clock rush. This was mostly elderly couples who ate quickly and didn't hang around long. As they left, the next batch of residents appeared. These filtered in slowly, never liked to be rushed, took their time over dinner and chatted a lot more to the staff. There were a few non-resident bookings for nine o'clock as well: two tables of two and a table for six.

By nine the table of six had arrived: a lovely family on holiday in Saltmarsh Quay. A young couple celebrating their first wedding anniversary took the first of the two-person bookings. Hannah was just taking some of the evening's paperwork to Reception for the receptionist to put on the computer when she noticed Olivia standing in the lobby.

'Hello, you look nice! I didn't realise you were coming up tonight. I'm busy for another hour and a bit, and then we can catch up in the bar.'

'I'm here to eat, actually. I'm on a date. It's all very last minute. To be honest, I'm very nervous, as I don't know the man.'

'How exciting! I'm so pleased for you, where is he?'

Hannah really was pleased for Olivia. That was, until her date approached.

'Oh hi, Steve.'

'Do you two know each other?'

Hannah explained that they had met because of Tom and the garden at Luckett House. Apparently it had been Tom who set Olivia and Steve's date up. That was very convenient, and he wasn't daft: anything to stop Steve chatting her up!

'In that case, if you would like to follow me, I will show you to your table. We have a nice quiet one over here by the window.'

*

After taking their drinks order and going over the menu, Hannah decided to make herself scarce and leave the serving to the other staff. The really annoying thing was that they were sitting the wrong way round. Olivia had her back to everything but Steve could see all that was going on. That was a problem because every time Hannah passed into his eye-line he focused on her: not really the thing to be doing while you were on a date with someone else! If only Glen had been on duty she could have left him to close up, but there was no way she could leave yet. She had to stay to the end of service.

She avoided serving the starters and the main course, but it got to the point where there were only two tables left occupied in the restaurant. She could hear someone calling her name and knew she couldn't ignore it. She counted to ten under her breath and headed over to Steve and Olivia.

'Is everything okay? Just let me clear these plates and I will fetch you the dessert menu.'

'Could we also have some more drinks, please? A pint of lager and another white wine. The meal was lovely. I think I'll have to come up to the hotel more often: there's a lot here I like!'

The smarmy sod, winking at her as he said that! He clearly had no interest in Olivia whatsoever. Hopefully she could see through him. But then, once he got what he wanted from Hannah, he would probably move on from her as well. As Hannah took

219

their desserts up to the table, Steve headed to the toilets.

'Are you having a nice evening, Olivia? Was the food okay?'

'The food and wine were lovely, shame about the company! Talk about full of himself, and that's when he actually decides to speak to me. Tom has a lot of questions to answer: what made him think we were suited for each other? When I mentioned Sam and Ben he practically turned white with fear!'

'I think Tom was thinking about me. He noticed Steve take an interest in me when they were down at Luckett House planning the garden, and as we know, Tom is jealous of any man I talk to. He's on the way back – enjoy your dessert!'

Eventually they were the only couple left. Steve was looking at the bill when Jimmy came out from the kitchen to check that the evening had gone okay and all the customers were happy. Hannah explained about the chap with Olivia and suddenly thought of a way to wipe the smile right off of Steve's face. But was it the right thing to do? She would have to make clear to Jimmy that she was only doing it to make Olivia feel better.

'It's just to shut that smarmy, arrogant sod up. Please don't read anything else into it, okay?'

Jimmy was all for it, of course. Any excuse would have got his agreement. As Steve and Olivia stood up from the table and headed towards them, Hannah put her hands on Jimmy's face and went in for the kiss. She made it a nice, long, slow one, so that Steve would have to stand there waiting for her to finish with the bill in his hand. That was game, set, and match to Hannah and Olivia.

Chapter 35

The following day Hannah phoned Olivia and they had a good giggle about the night before. Apparently Steve was fuming. He claimed it was because two staff kissing at work wasn't right, but truthfully he knew they had been taking the mickey out of him. It didn't help that Olivia had been laughing about it at the time. Their walk back down to Saltmarsh Quay had been taken in silence. But one thing Hannah didn't share with Olivia was how much she had enjoyed kissing Jimmy.

Once off the phone, Hannah could hear voices in the corridor. It was Betty, Josie, and Margaret. Tom had just arrived to take them to a garden centre to look at plants for the garden.

'Good morning, ladies, are you ready? More than that, are you excited? Hi, Hannah, are you coming with us?'

'No, I'll leave this one to the experts. My plant knowledge is nil, but thanks for the invitation. You all have fun. I'm having a quiet morning with coffee in the sunshine before I go to work this afternoon.'

Hannah had noticed that Richard's car was on the drive, but he wasn't in sight. He must be out walking Bonkers. She was just getting comfortable with her coffee on the sun lounger when Bonkers came bounding over to her, followed by Richard.

'Hi, I'm sorry; you'd think he would be worn out by now! We've walked for miles but just as you think he's ready for a sleep he gets a second wind. Having said that, I could have stayed out walking all day. I think that Luckett Quay is my new addiction: I just can't get enough of it!'

'Yes, I know what you mean. I've just made a coffee, would you like one?'

'That would be nice. I will just nip up to the flat and change out of my walking boots, give me a couple of minutes.'

Hannah made the coffee, but Richard seemed to be taking ages over his boots. When he did make it back down he was reading a note and carrying a very old-looking suitcase. He looked miles away.

'Are you okay, Richard? You're not leaving just yet?'

'No, not leaving, and I think I'm okay. Margaret has left this outside the flat door for me. Her note says that she didn't want to give it to me in front of Mum in case it upset her. She thought that as they're going to be out for a few hours it would give me time to digest everything. Somehow I don't think I will like what I find in here. It's a little scary, and it's very heavy.'

Hannah tried to make light conversation while they drank their coffee. This was the sort of moment when she needed Bonkers to be playful, but he had fallen asleep in the shade. She was intrigued about what was in the case. It obviously had something to do with his father. Perhaps it was some keepsakes or mementos. Still, Richard's feelings were more important than her curiosity.

'You don't need to open it now. Why don't you put it in the boot of your car and then when you are back home in London by yourself you can think about taking a look?'

'No, the last thing I want to do is take anything of his to London. He's never been a part of my life and I don't want him to start now. No, I need to get it over with. To be honest, even if Margaret thinks I should have some of his possessions, I don't want them.'

'Then I'll leave you to have a look in peace and quiet.'

'No, there's no need for that. Let's see what's in the case. Hopefully it's not clothes. I'd hate to touch

222

anything he's worn.'

He put the case on the table and opened the stiff lock. It looked like this case hadn't been opened for quite a few years. Richard and Hannah puzzled over the contents. It was full of books: not ordinary books but big scrapbooks. The one on the top had a date on it. Before Richard would look inside it, he took all of them out of the case and placed the case on the ground. They all had dates on them.

'Where do I start? Should I go to the one with the oldest date on? It's the year I was born – you don't think he was—'

'Are you okay? I think you could be right, but you won't know until you open one up. I don't know what to advise you. Are you sure you don't want to do this in private? Somehow I think this is going to be very personal.'

'No, stay. This is getting a bit morbid. You choose, pick a book.'

Hannah looked at them, spread out over the table. Which one should she go for? The books all had different covers, and had obviously been bought individually over many years. The one that stood out to her had a yellow and black design and a label on the front reading: 1974 – 1979.

'This one, I think. Are you ready to go back to the seventies? I've chosen, so now you open the book.'

Richard moved the other books aside and turned the cover. There on the first page was a newspaper cutting with a picture of two models on a catwalk under the headline 'Bold Colours Come to British Fashion Week'. Hannah could see Richard smiling: something had made him happy.

She wanted him to savour the moment, so she headed back into the house to make them another coffee. She took her time, but peeking from the window she could see that he was looking in a couple of the other books.

'Here you go, a fresh coffee. How are you getting on? Can you make any sense of it all?'

Richard explained that Frank had kept scrapbooks of Richard's life, starting with the photos Josie had given him: baby pictures, school photos, even pictures of events he had been involved in as a child over in Sheringham. Perhaps she had hoped this would bring them together, but that had never happened.

The most interesting items followed Richard's career: clippings from fashion magazines with his name mentioned in passing, right up to his own collections being presented under the Gina Le Gina name. There were pictures and write-ups of fashion awards and celebrations. As Richard put it:

'Everything is here: my whole career. He's followed my life. It's strange. Most of this was before the internet took hold, so he would have had to search out all these things on his own. It must have taken a lot of time. I don't know what to say, other than it looks like he was interested in me.'

'To me it looks like he cared. How does it make you feel?'

'I don't know, but it has brought back so many happy memories that I had forgotten. The childhood times with Mum are always fresh in my mind, but the clothes! Goodness me, how have I forgotten so many of the collections? Some of those over-the-top dresses ... they were wild, but in their day they were the thing to be seen in. Those are happy memories resurfacing, and I suppose I can thank Frank for that. He's still Frank: not Father, not Dad, just Frank.'

For the next few hours they went through the scrapbooks together. Hannah was fascinated by the stories behind the dresses and which celebrities were wearing them. She couldn't stop asking questions. She wanted to know everything: from where the inspiration for a design came from, to how long it would take a garment to get from a sketch to the shops. She could tell how happy Richard was to talk about his career, and she encouraged him.

After a while spent laughing and joking over the books, Richard suddenly went quiet. It was as though he had seen something to take the wind out of his sails. He started to close the books, putting them in a careful pile before opening the suitcase to put them away.

'Is something wrong? You look so down suddenly. You should be so proud of what you've achieved, look what a fabulous working life you've had!'

'Yes, and "had" is the operative word. Did you notice when the scrapbooks finish? Two years ago. Frank wasn't daft, and he could see what I knew as well. I've had my day. I stopped getting recognition because my time was over. I was mentioned in a few publications, but not as a designer, just as "consultant" or some other obscure title. Frank left me on top. He didn't want to follow me into the downturn, and do you know, that makes me realise that he cared? It wasn't just a question of sticking anything with my name on it into these books. No, he was showing pride in his own way. It's very touching.'

'It is. This man that everyone thought was hard and miserable, and who wasn't really liked did have a heart. These scrapbooks prove it. But the most important thing is not just that he was proud, but that he loved you.'

Chapter 36

It had been a couple of weeks since Hannah and Richard had gone through all the scrapbooks together. He needed time alone to fully get his head around everything so had told Hannah not to mention it to Josie. That was the last time Hannah had seen him as he hadn't returned to Norfolk.

The garden project had commenced and Betty, Josie and Margaret had wholeheartedly thrown themselves into it. It was just like the three of them had been friends for years. In contrast, Hannah had kept well out of the way of the garden. Every time Tom and Steve were there consulting and discussing plants, borders and colour schemes, she'd made sure she was at the hotel. Tom also had a set contracted rota for working in the hotel grounds. Knowing that in advance made it extremely easy for her to avoid him, or simply take time off. Hannah was annoyed with both of them – firstly Tom for organising a date for Olivia, and secondly, Steve for his arrogance.

It was now the weekend, Hannah's time away from work, and an opportunity to go out and enjoy herself. She was treating Olivia to a weekend break in London while the boys spent time with their grandparents. Carl was also coming with them, and Hannah was looking forward to the three of them having fun in the capital. Another reason why she didn't want to be in Luckett Quay was that her dad and Susanna were visiting for a few days. She would have welcomed her father coming alone, but really was not in the right frame of mind to cope with Susanna. Luckett House was now completed, and as Betty now had a clearer idea of her finances, they would all be discussing money. It was not a conversation Hannah wished to be a part of. She'd been kind enough to let them have her flat for the weekend, and this was the perfect chance to spend time with her friends.

Carl was due to pick her up in about ten minutes; just time to say a quick goodbye to Betty.

'Right, Nan, are you sure you'll be okay? Susanna will obviously have a figure in mind as to how much she wants, but please don't let her bully you?'

'I'll be fine, darling, don't worry about me. You really deserve a great weekend away as you've hardly stopped working since you got here, what with the new job and sorting out the flats. Sounds like a car outside, it must be Carl. Now, don't forget, I can cope with Susanna, so off you go and party.'

'Okay, Nan. See you Sunday night, but promise you'll phone me if Susanna upsets you in any way.'

'Yes, I promise; now off you go.'

Hannah fetched her case and closed the front door behind her. However, it wasn't Carl outside, but Tom arriving to work on the garden. His face positively lit up when he saw her.

'Off on holiday?'

'No, just a weekend break. Ah, here comes my lift. See you, Tom.'

Tom wasn't happy, he would have liked longer with Hannah, but there again he was lucky she hadn't given him a piece of her mind for trying to organise her and Olivia's love life for them.

Having set off on their journey to London, next stop was to collect Olivia.

'Can't wait to meet your friend Brett. By the way, have you booked a holiday yet?'

'Long story, Hannah, but there'll be no holiday and no Brett either. We've stopped seeing each other, so this weekend it's just three single friends off to have some fun. Hopefully, that'll involve some men. What do you say to that?'

'I'd say, lead the way!'

Two hours later they were pulling into the car park of their London hotel. The journey had been smooth, and it was still only lunch time. Olivia wasn't particularly happy with Hannah for booking a room to herself, she would have preferred a twin room to share, it would have been far more fun. However, Hannah had jokingly remarked about it being awkward if either one of them picked up a fella for the night. Keys collected from Reception, they planned to meet back in the lobby in 15 minutes.

'So you two, top of my list is something to eat. I'm starving hungry and could really do with a lovely healthy meal washed down with a large glass of wine.'

'Hark at him! I'm the complete opposite. No way am I going out clubbing without a full stomach.'

'Clubbing? Did you say we're going clubbing?'

They walked a short distance to the vibrantly busy Covent Garden area with its quaint boutiques, eateries, gift shops and bustling market. True to his word, Carl had a healthy lunch with a gin and tonic, and the girls shared a large pizza, garlic bread, bottle of wine, ice creams and chocolate brownies. They were full! A good walk round the shops should help work some of it off though.

Hannah had received a text from Betty to say that Robert and Susanna had arrived. They'd left Pippa and Alfie with Susanna's mum for the weekend, and surprisingly Susanna seemed to be quite happy to go along with everything. Hannah had no need to worry.

'Everything alright?'

'Oh, yes. Just Nan letting me know that Dad and Susanna have arrived in Luckett Quay. Right, let's hit the shops, we need to go clothes shopping,'

They had a great afternoon selecting clothes for each other to try on, but only Carl had actually bought anything. Two shirts and a pair of jeans, in fact. Making their way back to the hotel, they stopped off at a nearby supermarket for a couple of bottles of wine to drink while getting changed for the evening. The plan was to shower and change and then all meet in Hannah's room to finish the wine before going out.

'Look at you! Very smart! The men will be drooling over you later. Hopefully, it'll be the same for me and Olivia too.'

'Oh, I can't be bothered with romance. I don't have the time for any of that.'

'Who said anything about romance? Tonight's all about sex.'

The three of them finished the wine, and now rather merry, set off for their evening out. Carl knew of a steakhouse he'd been to on another recent visit to London, so they opted for a quick meal there before going to one of his favourite pubs. It was primarily a gay pub, but did attract quite a mixed crowd, and being Friday it was karaoke night. Not that any of them had any intention of singing, but it did give the pub a far more appealing vibe.

By the time they got to the pub, the evening was in full swing. They made their way to the bar passing by the karaoke singer. He was really quite professional, not your normal drunk Friday night pub singer at all. These singers meant business!

'Let's stand over there, we'll have a better view of the stage.'

Olivia and Hannah followed a very outgoing and confident Carl. He was acting just as if this London pub was local and he was a regular.

'Hey, what do you two find so funny?'

'You. You're almost a different bloke to the one we left in Norfolk.'

'I know, but as much as I love coming here for a break, I don't think I could live here. Just look around at some of the guys here. It must have taken them days to get ready, and all in the hope of finding love or even sex.'

'Well, yes, but that's not just reserved for gay men, is it? Everyone's the same, dressed up to the nines in case they meet someone. That was me before I met Jimmy, you know. I felt really bad because I hadn't got a fella, but things change. Some people get back out there, and others just tend to give up.'

'I'm in that boat. It's exactly what I did when my ex left me with the boys. Once Sam and Ben are in bed and I've cleared up the chaos they've left behind, that's me done I'm afraid. I just want to relax in front of the telly with a nice cup of tea and a packet of biscuits. I can't see myself being romantic with anyone. These days I'm just not in the mood for romance.'

'I must admit that since splitting up with Jimmy, I've felt like that too but hopefully that will all change one day. How about you, Carl? What are you looking for?'

'Well, there's only one thing on my mind at the moment, and that's having fun with you two this weekend. I might do a bit of flirting, and get a few phone numbers but that's as far as it'll go. Now, come on, I know that chap who's about to get up and sing. Follow me...'

Hannah and Olivia followed Carl thinking they were getting nearer to the front of the stage as part of the audience, but the next thing they knew was that Carl had pushed them actually on the stage as backing singers! They'd had far too much wine, and were now belting out Diana Ross songs. Come the fourth one, there were about a dozen people on stage; it was like one huge party.

By the time they left the pub it was nearing one o'clock in the morning, and they were all still singing as they happily wandered along on their way to a club. They had to queue up, but didn't mind as it gave them an opportunity to get some fresh air, but eventually they were allowed into the nightclub. The atmosphere was exactly the same as the pub with people enjoying themselves, but the music was so loud they couldn't hear each other speaking.

Carl was heading straight to the dance floor, and this greatly surprised Hannah. She thought it would be the last place Carl would want to be, but he was in his element, not just dancing, but flirting away and getting a lot of attention in return.

Hannah and Olivia made a quick trip to the ladies, and as they were walking back they noticed Carl talking to a very handsome chap. Rather than interrupt him, they thought it best to give him a bit of space and go and do their own thing. Eventually when they did go looking for him, they were absolutely amazed to find him in exactly the same spot. However this time he wasn't just talking, he was kissing this attractive young man. After a few coughs and warning noises, they did get his attention, and told him they were leaving. It was now four in the morning, and they were going to head back to the hotel.

'Okay, just give me a few mins, I'm coming too.'

'No, don't worry. It's your weekend too, why not stay with your friend and we'll catch up with you in the morning?'

It's our weekend together, remember, so just give me a few minutes to say goodbye to Mike and I'll be with you.'

The fresh air hit them as they came out of the club. It had been a lovely evening and both Olivia and Hannah had told Carl that he should have stayed with his new friend, Mike. He did admit that he would have liked to, but if Mike was interested in him, then there was bound to be another time.

It was about a twenty-minute walk back to the

hotel, and an opportunity to sober up rather than just get a taxi. There was still a lot of laughing and giggling going on, but all three were tired. It had been a very long day, and now it was time for bed.

'You could have stayed, you know. You didn't need to come back with us.'

'I wanted to, so don't worry. Anyway, if Mike's interested in me, let him wait. I know I've only been out for a short time, but I've learnt so much very quickly. When I came to London before with a few of the lads from Norwich, I met someone who I thought was a really lovely guy. One thing led to another and I ended up going back to his flat. We had a great time together, and yes, I really mean great! We exchanged phone numbers and I sent him a couple of texts during the week.

Anyway, I thought I'd surprise him the following Saturday night. I knew he went to this club regularly so I turned up to find him. Would you believe he acted as if he didn't know me at all, just wasn't remotely interested? I was obviously only a one-night stand to him. There he was looking for someone else. That was such an eye-opener to me and I've no intention of being used again. Yes, I might be missing out on a lot of fun, but I don't want a different bloke each week. Now, what have we planned for tomorrow? More shopping, eating and drinking, I imagine?'

Hannah and Olivia were impressed. They were glad to know what Carl wanted out of life, but even more so what he didn't want. Come to that though, what did Hannah really want, and where was her life heading? Her new job was going well, and her flat was perfect, but in all honesty Betty didn't need her now she had Josie and Margaret. So how would her future pan out? She remembered how nice it had been to kiss Jimmy the other week.

Should she give him another chance?

Chapter 37

All three of them set their phones for an alarm call so they could be down in Reception for half past ten. Hannah had been up before the alarm even rang, as she wanted to phone Betty to find out how things were between her father and Susanna. She knew she should really have sent a text to ask if it was convenient to call, but stupidly she went ahead and phoned her. Betty didn't seem quite herself.

Oh, hello, darling, are you having a nice time? Yes, we're just having a coffee in the conservatory before we head out for a walk. Not sure where we're going yet, Susanna's going to make the final decision. Okay, I'll let you get on. Thanks for phoning. See you tomorrow evening when you get home from London.'

Well, that was short and sweet, if not to the point. Or was Hannah reading too much into things? A final check in the mirror and down in the lift to meet Carl and Olivia. A text had come through from her father, Robert, to say that Betty was fine and not to worry. He had everything under control, but what did that mean exactly?

'Morning, you two. I could die for a greasy fry up for breakfast. Did you both sleep well?'

'Morning, Hannah, yes great thanks, although it does seem strange waking up and not having the boys jumping into bed. I'm a little hungover, if truth be told, and yes, I could do with some food too. Whose phone is that?'

'Mine. It's a text from Mike.'

'Oh, and who's Mike?'

'Mike from last night. He's keen, Carl!'

'Yes he wants to know if we'd like to join him for lunch.'

'All three of us?'"

'Yes, what should I say?'

'Tell him yes, but first I really could do with some breakfast. Tell him we can't meet until after one o'clock. By that time I'll be hungry again.'

Carl texted him back and they all headed off to find some breakfast somewhere. A couple of minutes later another text came through, this time with Mike's address on it.

'We'll probably need to look at the map as I've never heard of the area. You've worked in London, Hannah, so you'd probably know. Ever heard of Holland Park?'

'Ha, very amusing, Now, seriously, where does he live?'

'I'm telling you it's Holland Park. Here take a look at my phone; it has the address and postcode.'

Hannah looked at the text and stopped dead in her tracks, explaining to Carl that Holland Park was one of the more expensive parts of the capital. She reeled off a list of celebrities and famous stars who lived there. Who was Mike exactly, and what did he do for a living, Hannah wondered? Carl didn't know anything about him, apart from the fact he was great at kissing.

'You two were talking for ages, Carl. He must have told you something about his life, surely?'

'No, nothing at all. He was asking me about myself and that's all we got round to discussing.'

'Well, you must have left a good impression. Oh, look, there's a café across the road, and I can smell bacon cooking!'

They each had a huge fry up, washed down with lots of strong coffee. All they could talk about was Mike, who he was, and what he did for a living. They did joke that perhaps he had a tiny bedsit in one of the large mansions. Wouldn't that be a let-down? One thing they did agree on was that after breakfast they needed to return to the hotel and change out of their casual clothes. Holland Park was a very salubrious Central London district, smart clothes were called for!

'Do you think we ought to take a gift with us? Flowers, chocolates or wine perhaps? I think perhaps it's a bit rude to arrive empty handed, don't you?'

'Olivia, you're beginning to make me rather nervous. Just think, if I hadn't come back to the hotel, I might have been waking up in Holland Park this morning!'

An hour and a half later, dressed to impress, they were waiting for a taxi to take them to Mike's. It wasn't that far, and they could easily have taken the tube, but as they were running slightly late owing to Carl having difficulty deciding which shirt to wear, they decided to take the quickest route. The taxi eventually drew up outside an impressive detached house situated on a street with about a dozen similar looking properties. Carl, Olivia and Hannah stood silently on the pavement, totally in awe of the decadent mansions in front of them.

'Carl, he's your friend, not ours. Go on, ring the doorbell then.'

There was no need. Before Carl or any of them even got close to the door, Mike had opened it and was there to greet them. Hannah did notice that the house was divided up into separate flats, each of them with their own doorbell.

'Hi, everyone. Do come through. The weather's so beautiful today that I thought we could go out into the garden.'

With that, Mike led the way down a long corridor and straight out into a huge, yet divided up garden, separated by ornamental hedges. They turned into a small well-maintained garden area complete with gorgeous outdoor furniture and the most colourful plant pots you could ever imagine.

'Take a seat and help yourself to some nibbles while I get us all a drink. Won't be a minute.'

From where Hannah was sitting, she had a good view of the lounge, very modern, almost minimalistic with lots of white and chrome. They all sat in silence as if they were waiting for an important appointment, but each of them was taking it all in. What a home!

'Here we are, red or white? Sorry, I'm presuming you'd all like some wine. I do have some soft drinks too.'

'We're all a little hung over today actually, and I'm not really used to it. I've got two young sons, so I don't get very much time to myself. Hence, when I do, I tend to be led astray.'

Olivia and Hannah chatted about themselves, their friendship, the hotel and Luckett House. In fact everything apart from the subject of what Mike did for a living. Nobody seemed brave enough to broach that topic. After about half an hour, Mike asked if anybody was hungry. He hadn't prepared any lunch as he wasn't sure of their preferences, but when they all said they were fine, Hannah decided to take the bull by the horns and raise the question.

'Mike, you certainly don't have an apartment like this without having a career to match. So, what exactly do you do for a living?'

'My job's quite boring I'm afraid. It involves juggling a lot of money around within the IT department of a city bank. I wouldn't say I like it, but it does pay well.'

He then explained how he had inherited the flat from a rich and generous uncle. In a way, it was something of a relief to the three of them. Mike was down to earth and similar to them; he certainly wasn't wealthy or pretentious. The rest of the afternoon was spent chatting, laughing and enjoying a barbecue in the garden.

When it got to nearly four o'clock, Hannah discretely mentioned to Olivia that perhaps it would be a good idea for them to leave. Mike could then spend some time with Carl alone. Olivia agreed. They said their goodbyes and arranged to meet Carl back at the hotel the next morning, ready to travel home.

'What a lovely afternoon, and a really nice guy too. Very suited to Carl, but I just hope he's genuine. I bet they're already at it like rabbits, even though we only left twenty minutes ago. Anyway, what do you fancy doing tonight, Olivia? Did you want to go clubbing?'

'I'm not bothered about going out dancing, or drinking come to that, but a nice quiet meal with a couple of glasses of wine would be perfect.'

They walked back towards the hotel, chatting about Mike and Carl, both of them agreeing how well suited they seemed. They also agreed that it would be a shame if Carl moved down to London, as he was now becoming a part of their little group, and actually he was far more fun than Tom.'

They chose a quaint, Italian restaurant and ordered some pasta. There was an interesting atmosphere, full of young families, laughing and enjoying being out together.

'Don't you miss having the boys' father around, Olivia?'

'Oh, no, not at all, and to be honest, the older they get, they become less bothered about it. He was hardly at home when we were together and towards the end of the relationship, I was positively encouraging him to go out of an evening. I do believe he was part of my life for a reason though, and that was to help me produce two lovely sons.'

'I'm with you on the sons bit, but wouldn't you love a man in your life?'

'I don't really know, but you can talk, Hannah. You haven't got one either. At least I've got Ben and

Sam for company. Wouldn't you even consider giving Jimmy a second chance? And what about Tom? You know he fancies you.'

'I'd say a big fat no to either of those options. Anyway, Tom doesn't really fancy me. He may think he does, but you know him better than I do. We really wouldn't be compatible for long.'

'But, Hannah, he's a good bloke underneath it all. He was there for me when my ex left me, and the boys adore him. They always have such a fantastic time when Tom takes them out to football or comes round to tea. He's got so much patience with them. He'd really make some girl a wonderful husband, you know.'

'I'm beginning to think I don't want a husband. I'd prefer to just have fun.'

'Well, if that's the case, you should hook up with Steve.'

'Right, that's it, no more man talk. Do you know, I've only ever come into contact with one man worse than Steve and that's Tristan up at the hotel. Come on, let's pay the bill and go and find somewhere for a good old boogie. It's Saturday night, and we don't have to be up early in the morning. You don't have the boys, so let's go and hit a dance floor.'

*

'Oh, look at the state of you two. Now, I'm not saying you look bad, but let's just say I've seen you looking better. Was it a heavy night or something? Oh, and if you're going to be sick, try and ensure it's before we start on our journey home.'

'Very funny, Carl. We were only going for a quiet meal, but then Hannah persuaded me to go dancing, and we stayed until half past three this morning. It was well worth it though; we had a great night, didn't we?'

'Hey, you two, less of the chat. I need some food, or actually I think some paracetamol would be better. What's the time?'

'It's two-thirty in the afternoon. How about some lunch and a little walk in the fresh air before we head home? That'll do you two the world of good.'

'Listen to Mr Chirpy there. I suppose you stayed off the drink and had an early night?'

'You're dead right. I was in bed by five o'clock.'

'Evening or morning! We didn't leave Mike's until gone four!'

'Yes, my dears, last night, and we didn't get up until nine this morning. Enough said, except that I'm feeling on top of the world. Shall we have a singsong as we walk along? We could skip as well.'

The girls couldn't help but laugh. They were delighted for Carl, and even though they both felt quite rough, all in all it had been an enjoyable weekend.

Chapter 38

As it was late when they got back from London, Hannah hadn't had a chance to catch up with Betty, but today she was up early and keen to find out what happened with Susanna. She made herself a coffee and headed out into the conservatory. As she opened the bi-fold doors, she saw a note had been left on the table. 'Hi, Hannah,' it read. 'Was up early. Gone for a walk, love Nan.'

Hannah didn't think anything more about the note. Betty loved going for her walks, so it really wasn't unusual. She checked her phone and got ready for work. Glen had agreed to do the breakfast shift, but now it was his time off so it would be an extremely busy couple of days for Hannah. Two shifts today and then three for the following two days.

Walking towards the hotel she could see Tom's van parked in the car park. She had forgotten he'd be working in the hotel grounds, and that meant that Steve would also be there too. She went in the side door, avoiding the pair of them. She'd also failed to remember that Glenda was also having time off. A quick check of the handover book, and there it was, a note to say that the Night Manager had phoned in sick. She would have to sleep in, as the porter couldn't be left in charge. Hannah was beginning to pay the price for her long weekend away.

'Hi, Glen. Everything, okay? Anything I ought to know?'

'Not really. How was your weekend away? Manage to snog anyone?'

'We had a lovely weekend, thanks, and no, I didn't kiss anyone. Now, you go and have a fabulous couple of days off, and perhaps make up for what I missed out on, a good snog with someone.'

'Very funny. You know me, I'd sooner have a cheese sandwich and a packet of crisps, but you never know, if that gardener was available, I might be inclined to give in.'

'You mean Tom?'

'No, not Tom, he's yours! I was talking about his fit assistant, Steve.'

'Tom's not mine and nor will he ever be, and as for Steve – well, you're more than welcome to that arrogant chap.'

Hannah checked the rest of the restaurant team were organised and getting ready for the lunch shift. There were only a few tables booked, but tonight was going to be a busy one. The hotel was full and there were also some non-residents eating. A quick check with all the other departments at the ten o'clock meeting and then an hour or so catching up with the paperwork. Hannah hated the meetings when Glenda wasn't there, as Jimmy had a habit of staring at her as she went through all the daily business agenda of the hotel.

'Morning, everyone. It's a busy day ahead for us all, so I'll try and keep this as brief as I can. The hotel's full tonight and Ken, the Night Manager has phoned in sick. I'm going to have to sleep here tonight, so can I have a room made up in the staff block, Annie?'

Each department updated her on their schedules. There was nothing to worry about, but Hannah did notice Jimmy's face light up when she said she was staying overnight. Any ideas he might have would be totally wrong. The kiss was just for Olivia's sake, and to knock the smile off Steve's face.

The rest of the morning passed by very quickly. Lunch was over and the restaurant re-laid for dinner. There were a few people coming in for afternoon tea, giving Hannah a couple of minutes free to phone Betty. She wouldn't have time to pop back to Luckett

House and it would be so helpful if Betty could bring her some toiletries and some clean clothes.

Hannah had an inkling that something was not quite right. Betty didn't seem very chatty, subdued even, but she was probably tired after her morning walk. As she put the phone down, she could see Tom's van pulling out of the car park. She breathed a sigh of relief, knowing she wouldn't need to make small talk with him or Steve, but another vehicle was pulling in, in its place. Someone else she wasn't in the mood for. Time to get back to her office and hopefully avoid any confrontation with Tristan.

In little more than half an hour, Hannah had managed to devise rotas for the next four weeks. She was now at a bit of a loose end looking for other things to do, but from the office window she could still see Tristan's car. She couldn't avoid him for much longer, but quite honestly, why should she have to? She hadn't done anything wrong. Just then her pager bleeped, telling her to phone Reception.

'Hi, you wanted me? Okay, not a problem.'

However, it was a problem. The night porter had just called in with the same sickness bug as Ken had. That meant Hannah would have to stay up all night.

'Hannah, there's a lady here asking to see you personally. She said she'd wait outside as she's got a dog with her.'

'Hello, Josie, what can I do for you?'

'Betty's asked me to drop a few things off for you.'

'Oh, thank you so much, Josie. Sorry to have put you to all this trouble.'

'It's no trouble at all, dear. I was taking Bonkers out for his walk anyway. By the way, is Betty alright? She didn't seem her normal self today. Normally we have a cup of tea or coffee together, but I found it difficult getting two words out of her. Also, I found it rather strange that she asked me to bring your things up. I would have thought she'd have preferred to come here herself. I wouldn't go so far as to say there's a problem, but I am a bit concerned.'

'To be honest, I haven't seen her since I came back from London at the weekend, but she was out early today and she didn't say much on the phone either. Anyway, thanks, Josie, but I'll have a good chat with her tomorrow.'

Josie left to return to Luckett House, leaving Hannah to have a good think. There was definitely something on Betty's mind, and more than likely something to do with Susanna. Her thoughts were interrupted; someone else preying on Hannah's mind was Tristan, walking through the hotel lounge deep in conversation with Steve. How did those two know each other, and more importantly, what on earth were they discussing so intently?

'Excuse me. Could we have two more beers over here?'

Ignore him, continue walking, he's just trying to impress Steve, she thought to herself.

'I think she's in a rush to get to the kitchen. You do know how she and the chef just can't keep their hands off each other.'

'Right, that's it. You've both overstepped the mark. I'm in charge of this hotel, and I won't be spoken to like that by anyone.' With that, Hannah found one of the waiters to serve them, although yes, she was going to the kitchen, but only to see if everything was progressing to schedule for the dinner service. It did give her an opportunity to calm down a little. Tristan always seemed to annoy her and right now she was certainly not in the mood to answer him or Steve. It wasn't the right time or place – that would no doubt come in due course.

The dinner shift flew by without any issues. Hannah loved nights like this as the staff all seemed to enjoy their work; the food was coming out of the kitchen in good time and the customers were satisfied. There had been a beautiful sunset that evening, and everything looked quite picturesque. The downside was that as the evening wore on, Steve and Tristan had both drunk far too much to safely drive home. The barman had just phoned a cab for them, leaving Hannah to say goodnight to the last customers and get some drinks for the chefs. As she was passing through the lounge, she noticed Tristan and Steve leaving. What a relief!

The kitchen staff were all in good spirits, and certainly appreciated the drink that Hannah had brought them. Jimmy wasn't with them though. Apparently he'd gone off to take a shower after finishing his duty. Hannah guessed that was because he knew she was staying the night. The barman had found a mobile phone while wiping the tables down, and handed it to Hannah, saying that it was at the table where Tristan was sitting.

Perhaps she could use this to get back at him for his crass remarks, but for now all she could think about was the responsibilities she'd found herself with – both the Night Manager and night porter being off sick at the same time presented many challenges. One of the cleaners was due to come in extra early to cope with the hoovering and dusting which the night team normally did. The kitchen porter was helping to prepare the breakfast trays for room service, leaving Hannah to organise the food. The list for newspapers had been emailed across by the receptionist who had also printed off the next day's arrival cards. Everyone was pulling together to help her out, and Hannah really appreciated their efforts.

She was just turning out the lights in the bar and restaurant when in came Joe, a taxi driver from Saltmarsh Quay. Hannah knew him well as he was the only taxi driver in the area and regularly drove guests to and from the hotel.

'Hi, Joe. What can I do for you? I don't think anyone's waiting for a taxi, unless they've called from one of the rooms.'

'Oh, I'm not here to collect anyone. I've been sent to pick up a phone which has been left behind by one of your guests. Bit drunk the chap was, he said he either left it in the bar or the lounge.'

'Sorry, Joe, but nothing's been found. If it comes to light, I'll keep it behind Reception.'

As Joe left, Hannah felt slightly guilty. What made her tell such an outright lie? After all, she didn't want Tristan's phone and she had no inclination to look through it. It was now 11.15pm. Would Tristan return and demand they start looking for his missing phone? Surely, in his drunken state, he'd have either fallen asleep or passed out by now. Hannah knew he'd be back sooner or later though, his car was still in the car park, but suddenly she had a brilliant idea. Look in the restaurant diary where phone numbers were written next to bookings and she'd find the number she was looking for. She'd text first, after all it was getting late, and she didn't want to wake someone up if they were already asleep.

'Hi, Mr Dove. Sorry to bother you so late, but Tristan was up at the hotel today and he's left his phone here. I don't know any other way of contacting him. Hannah.'

Seconds later Hannah's phone rang. Raymond Dove confirmed that he'd pick up Tristan's phone early the next morning. Job done. No more reason to feel guilty about lying to Joe. Now there was a long night ahead. Time to lock the main door and walk around the building, checking that windows and doors were shut and locked. Then she heard footsteps...

'Thought you might like some company. I've made us both a hot chocolate just like I used to, and I've brought some biscuits too.'

'Thanks, Jimmy, that's really kind of you. Just let me lock the front doors first.'

Hannah and Jimmy sat in silence. Once she had drunk her chocolate, she decided to do the first clock round before filling in the Reception reports and backing them up on the computer.

'Why not let me do the porter's jobs while you get on with the Night Manager's duties. We'll get everything sorted far quicker.'

'Thanks, Jimmy, that would be a real help.'

They both got stuck into their various tasks, and Jimmy was right, it didn't take them long at all. It was now 1.45am, and he knew exactly what would get them through the rest of the night shift. Food! Without saying anything he dashed off and made some bacon sandwiches. As Hannah emptied the bins in Reception the aroma of freshly grilled bacon wafted through. She smiled. Jimmy certainly knew how to lay on the charm!

'I thought food was the way to a man's heart. Women are quite happy with jewellery.'

'I'd be more than happy to get you some jewellery. Perhaps a ring, a special one with a meaning.'

'The bacon's fine, Jimmy, and a mug of tea. Thank you!'

'Whoever would have thought we'd end up working together! Even when we first met I'd never have thought this would happen, but you have to admit it, we do work well together. I only moved here to win you back, you know, and that still stands, but I really love this job. I know you and Glenda thought I'd soon get bored of it, but in fact it's just the opposite. I love how you leave me to get on with things and there's no one breathing down my neck. This is a lovely place to live too, the beach, the views, the local pubs. All I need now is...'

'...a good night's sleep. You've been such a terrific

help to me tonight. I really would have struggled without you. The hot chocolate, the bacon sandwich, and most of all your company, Jimmy. But let me get one thing clear – you cheated on me and that still hurts. You brought a girl home and took her to our bed. Did you honestly think I wouldn't find out?'

'I don't know what came over me. I suppose I was flattered that this girl fancied me. She offered it on a plate, but what can I do? I can't turn the clock back, but I really wish I could. There are no excuses at all, but I hope you can find it in your heart to forgive me. Hannah, you know how good we are together, and now we've found ourselves in such a fabulous place, think how lovely it would be to settle down and have a family here. Please, Hanny, give me a second chance.'

'Night, Jimmy. Thanks for staying and helping me out, but I think you should go and get some sleep now.'

Chapter 39

It had been a long night for Hannah, fuelled by adrenalin to keep her going, and with a full day ahead, three restaurant shifts, it was set to continue in the same way. Glenda had offered to return for the Night Manager duty if Ken was still off sick. It was now five-thirty and the early morning cleaner was due in at any minute, the daily newspapers would be arriving and so too would the breakfast chef. Hannah was just unlocking the main doors when she heard the sound of a vehicle drawing up outside. Hopefully it would be the newspapers, so she could put them outside the rooms before the rest of the hotel woke up.

'Morning, Hannah. You're in early.'

'Hello, Mr Dove. Yes, but it's such a long story, what with staff off ill and everything.'

'Oh dear. I've just noticed Tristan's car in the car park, meaning he must have had too much drink to drive home. That would also explain why he's left his phone. I'll take it and return it at some point.'

'I'll just get it for you.... There you go, Tristan's phone. Have a nice day.'

'Owe you one, Hannah, and now I think it will be a most productive day.'

Sorry, Tristan, but I hope for your sake there isn't any evidence of your shady dealings on that phone of yours.

The morning just flew by for Hannah, breakfast went smoothly and the restaurant was laid out for lunch. Ken had phoned to confirm that he was well enough to return to work later. He'd had a 24-hour bug, but felt so much better now. Glen had offered to come in on his day off to run the dinner shift, so that Hannah could leave at six.

As Hannah was going through the lunch bookings, her pager bleeped calling her to Reception as someone was asking to see her. It was now 11.45; she would have expected Tristan to have been there before nine, asking for his phone.

'Hello, Tristan, are you looking for your phone? We did find it.'

'Oh, thank goodness for that. My whole life is stored on that phone.'

'Yes, we found it last night when we were tidying up. I guessed it was important, and as I couldn't contact you, I thought I'd best get in touch with Emmi, but I didn't have her number so...'

'I don't need all that, just get me my phone.'

Hannah was raging inside. How rude of him! She then explained how she had contacted Raymond Dove and given him the phone.

'You what? Do tell me you're joking. What right do you have to give him any of my things?'

'When you've calmed down, I'll tell you. He's your girlfriend's father, and come to think about it, isn't he also your boss? I'd say you're very lucky to have such a caring future father-in-law. He picked your phone up earlier this morning, perhaps about five hours ago.'

'This is the second time you've stitched me up, young lady, and I'm telling you there won't be a third. You've well and truly overstepped the mark.'

'Am I missing something here? You've lost a phone and we've gone out of our way to get it back to you through a close acquaintance. I hardly think that's overstepping the mark at all. Now, I need to get on, Tristan. Have a nice day.'

Who needed sleep with all this excitement going on! The annoying thing for Hannah was she probably wouldn't find out if Raymond had found anything interesting on the phone. Lunch and the afternoon shift flew by and it was nearly time for

Glen to come in. Hannah was now beginning to flag. She'd been awake for more than 30 hours, and had lost count of how many coffees she'd drunk in that time. Actually, she'd really enjoyed the hot chocolate Jimmy had made her. She also realised that he was truly sorry for all he'd done. Saying sorry was easy though, if he'd thought anything of her, surely he wouldn't have done it in the first place.

'I'm here now, Hannah. You go and get some sleep, and leave everything to me. No need for you to worry now.'

'Thanks, Glen, it's so kind of you to give up your day off for us.'

'Not a problem. You'd have done exactly the same. We work as a team, remember, but more importantly, you're a good friend.'

Hannah gathered her things together and headed down to Luckett House where there'd be other problems to sort out. Not that she knew the full extent of it yet, but it involved Susanna and that was quite enough. She walked round the rear of the house, hoping to find Betty, Josie and Margaret in the garden with a bottle of wine, but could only see Margaret sitting there with Bonkers.

'Hi, Margaret, all by yourself?'

'Yes, love, I'm looking after Bonkers. Josie's not feeling very well so she's having an early night, and I haven't seen anything of your Nan all day. I think she's in though, I heard the television.'

'I'll pop in and see what she's up to. Does Josie need anything?'

'No, I don't think so. She said she just wanted a good night's sleep. I think I'll take a walk down to the quay and give Bonkers his last run for the day. He can stay with me overnight.'

Hannah couldn't wait to have a shower, put some music on and relax for the evening. Betty would certainly hear her music, and just as likely call in on her first. A quick glance at her phone showed a text from Carl saying he would be taking a few days off to go and stay with Mike in London. There was another one from Olivia asking when she was free for a catch up, but the best one was from Raymond Dove. All it said was 'thank you'. How mysterious! Hannah wondered exactly what he'd found on Tristan's phone. All very secretive.

'Hannah, it's me.'

'I'm just in the shower, Nan. Give me two minutes. Oh, there's a bottle of wine already open. Help yourself.'

That was helpful. Hannah wouldn't have to go to Betty's now, but should she ask if everything's okay, or just play things by ear? Once showered, dried, and dressed, Hannah found Betty sitting in the conservatory with the doors open wide, enjoying the last of the evening sunshine. She broke the silence by chatting about Josie not feeling too well, hotel gossip, the weekend in London, and just about anything apart from Robert and Susanna's stay. Betty had spent the afternoon cooking, so she went back to her kitchen to fetch them both some of her leak and potato flan, with salad. So far, so good...

'There you go, darling. Sorry, the pastry's a little caught, but I'm sure it will taste fine.'

'It looks lovely, Nan, and here's another glass of wine. While we're eating, you can tell me all about your weekend with Dad and Susanna, or should I say the problem that's worrying you. Just what is that stepmother of mine up to now?'

'Is it that obvious?'

'Yes, but I suppose I knew that if they were coming for the weekend, things wouldn't be straightforward. Come on, Nan, spill the beans.'

Hannah had a feeling this was serious. Betty seemed to be rather stressed, but why? Surely it didn't have anything to do with her. For one, she didn't have any money to lend them.

'Well, you know that I agreed for my assets to go to their children once I'm gone, as well as any spare money after Josie and Margaret buy the flats, it seems they're not happy with that. Susanna's come up with another plan. I didn't tell them how much I'd be giving them, you see. After all, I do need to keep some back to live on myself, but she says that living in that small house is causing far too many arguments. She also said that if they have to live there for much longer, the best thing they could do is split up and for your dad to move out.'

'Nan, that's nothing short of blackmail. What does Dad have to say about it all?'

'Nothing, darling. You know as well as I do that those children are his life. The last thing he would want to do is split up.'

Hannah was furious. She was right, Susanna was blackmailing Betty. There seemed to be only one solution to this. The flat Hannah was living in had to be sold. There was no way she'd be able to afford to buy it, and without a sizeable deposit there'd be no opportunity to get herself a mortgage. There seemed to be little option, but to move back to the tiny staff quarters in the hotel.

'Darling, I'm so sorry that it's come to this. I was holding back from telling you everything, as I really don't know what to do.'

'There's only one thing we can do, and that's to sell the flat, but I'm telling you this, Susanna will never be happy. It will be one thing after another and deep down I think Dad knows it. Come on, Nan, let's have another glass of wine. I'll speak to Dad tomorrow.'

Chapter 40

It had been a few days since Betty had dropped her bomb shell. Hannah hadn't seen her as she'd made herself busy at the hotel while Steve and Tom had been adding the finishing touches to the garden. She knew Betty would understand, but today was her day off and Hannah knew she couldn't really avoid her, plus Steve and Tom would be working at the hotel. She had made arrangements to meet up with Olivia in the evening, a nice cosy celebration at the pub in Saltmarsh Quay. Hannah had no idea exactly what Olivia was celebrating, but for now she knew she needed to put on a brave face, act as though everything was normal in Betty's company and pretend everything was alright. Deep down it was a completely different story. She had to hide her inner rage until she managed to speak to her father, who for the previous few days had been avoiding her calls.

'Morning, Nan. Hi, Margaret and I'm not forgetting you, Bonkers. By the way, how's Josie?'

'She's still not very well, I'm afraid. Actually we were just discussing what we should do as she's not eating very much and looks dreadful. Should we give Richard a call? We're sure she can't have told him she's so poorly, and the other thing is she hasn't seen a doctor.'

'Oh dear, that's quite a dilemma. She might be annoyed if we phoned him. Look, why don't I take Bonkers for a walk on the beach and then pop him up to her and see what happens from there? It's possible she might open up to me a bit more.'

As Hannah went to put on her walking gear, Bonkers saw her get his lead and became so excited to be going out. Hannah realised he'd need a long walk to channel all his energy. The tide was out. If she headed down the hill to Luckett Quay she would be able to walk all the way along the beach to Saltmarsh Quay and then back up the coastal path when the tide started to come in.

'Right, you. Let's go for a long walk and wear you out. See you two later.'

As she headed down the hill to the beach she glimpsed back at the house. Even though she'd only lived there for a relatively short time, she knew how much she would miss it. Renting somewhere else wouldn't be a problem, but it would be nice if whoever bought her flat was able to get on well with Betty, Josie and Margaret. She was just about to let Bonkers off his lead for a run, when she noticed someone heading towards them on horseback.

'Hi, Hannah! What a lovely day! I didn't know you had a dog. Isn't he gorgeous?'

'Hello, Emmi. How's it going? He looks as if he's been enjoying himself.'

'Oh, yes, he always gets excited once he spots the sea, a little paddle and he's happy. You know, I could do this all day long, no worries just me and the horse.'

'A young woman like you shouldn't have any worries. An exciting new career on the horizon, not forgetting a handsome boyfriend.'

'Well, I'm looking forward to working at the stables as I've got so many exciting plans for it, but sadly no boyfriend. Tristan and I have split up. It's sad, but I think it's for the best.'

'I'm sorry to hear that. I thought you two seemed so suited to each other.'

'Yes, I thought so too, but my father's found out a few home truths about Tristan. Anyway, enough of all that. Have a nice walk, Hannah, and once I get settled at the stable you must come up and start riding again. See you soon.'

That was interesting, obviously there must have been a few things said about Tristan which Raymond Dove didn't like. Hannah and Bonkers headed along the beach towards Saltmarsh Quay which was far more crowded. She put Bonkers back on his lead, just in case he had any ideas about running up to some of the families enjoying the beach and stealing their sandwiches. Carefully she weaved her way through all the children playing, walked up to the sea wall and the little café which did lovely bacon sandwiches to take away. They also put bowls of water outside for passing dogs, and by now Bonkers was bound to be very thirsty.

Sandwich bought, and the lady serving behind the counter gave Bonkers a dog biscuit, which he gulped down in one second flat. Sitting back on the harbour wall, Hannah started to think about what she was going to do. The obvious thing would be to move into the staff quarters at the hotel, but it wouldn't be an ideal arrangement with Jimmy there. Of course, an alternative option would be to tell Betty that she wanted to stay and Susanna could just get lost, but that would only cause extra problems between Betty and Robert.

'Come on, Bonkers, let's head home and see if we can persuade your mum to see a doctor.'

Heading through the town, Hannah heard someone shouting her name. It wasn't a voice she knew well, but one that she instantly recognised. Surely it's too early for her to be drunk, she thought, and as she turned round, there was Jane, Carl's mum.

'Hello, nice to see you, Mrs Fern.'

'I can't say the same to you, but perhaps you'd explain exactly what's happened to my son. He goes off to London for a couple of days with you and comes back a completely different lad. And another thing...'

255

'Yes?'

'Now I'm even more confused. He's back in London again, so how come you're here. I thought you were the one leading him astray.'

'Look, Jane. I haven't seen Carl for more than a week, but he did seem happier than he's been for a long time. Now, was there anything else?'

'Well, what's that got to do with it?'

'Sorry, I just thought that every parent would want their child to be happy. Goodbye, must dash.'

Hannah carried on up the coastal path until she arrived at a seat with a sea view. She ought to text Carl and tell him what had just happened as she didn't want to put pressure on him to tell his mum about being gay. For the first time since moving here, she realised how much she missed the bright lights of the capital. Yes, there were lots of work problems, but nothing compared to the worries she was now facing.

'Come on, Bonkers. Why don't the two of us just run away from it all?'

Reaching the top of the coastal path, Hannah noticed Glenda clearing away some glasses from the outdoor tables.

'Hi, Glenda. Why are you doing that? We're not short staffed, are we?'

'No, not at all. I just needed to get out of the building and scream before I did something I know I'll come to regret.'

'That's unlike you, Glenda. What on earth's so bad at the hotel to drive you to screaming point?'

'Take a look in the car park. Notice whose car's parked there? And guess what? He's here for a whole week. Yes, Tristan has arrived with Mrs Van Lincoln. I didn't recognise the reservation as it was only booked in the name of Lincoln. She's only been here for half an hour and she's already complained about the room. Now she's demanding to see you.

Apparently there's something she wants to question you about, but I've told her that you're not in until tomorrow.'

Hannah was fuming mad to see Glenda so distraught. She knew exactly what Tristan's grandmother wanted to speak to her about, but luckily neither of them could prove anything.

'Right. I know it's my day off, but I'll go in to see her on my terms. I'll do the dinner shift. No way will I allow the staff to be put through the wringer by her. Do me a favour, tell Glen he can have the night off. Hey, look, what's going on over there in the car park? It looks like Tristan's given his car keys to someone else and they're driving his car. Did you notice that chap who just got out of it? Look, there's a sign on the door, something to do with 'leasing'. You don't think he's having it taken away from him, do you?'

Hannah headed back to Luckett House with Bonkers and quickly phoned Olivia to cancel their plans as she was going in to work instead. They'd rearrange their get together for a couple of nights' time, no problem.

'Hi, Margaret. How's Josie?'

'Not well at all. I've made her phone the doctor, and to be honest she seems relieved I've made her do it. One thing though, she doesn't want to let Richard know she's unwell, and she's asked the doctor to come here for a home visit. She looks dreadful, Hannah. Your Nan's with her at the moment helping her to wash. I really do think it's serious.'

'Can I leave Bonkers with you as I've got a few problems to sort out at the hotel? Promise me you'll keep me updated with any news though. You can phone me at any time.'

Hannah showered and headed back to the hotel via the back door to prepare herself for the onslaught of Mrs Van Lincoln. She knew it was best to get this over and done with before dinner was served, so she had a quick look in the restaurant diary to see the time Mrs Van Lincoln was booked in for and whether it was a table for one. No, it was a booking for two, which meant that Tristan would be there too. Looking through the restaurant booking lists, Hannah could see it was going to be a busy night ahead. She was just about to close the diary when she noticed another name – Dove. Flash bang wallop, there was her answer.

'Hi, Mr Dove. It's Hannah from the Saltmarsh Cliff Hotel. I'm so sorry to bother you, but we haven't got a note of the number of people for your booking tonight. Thank you, and like I've said, I'm sorry to bother you. Yes, it's been a bit of a stressful day, but not really a hotel problem. Just one which goes by the name of Van Lincoln. Oh, I forgot. Of course you know of her, she's Tristan's grandmother. Really, I didn't know that! So, he no longer works for you and he's not going out with Emmi either. Sorry to have bothered you, Mr Dove. We look forward to seeing you and your guest later tonight.'

Job done! And it certainly was a flash bang answer, but the wallop will be on Tristan. Time to enter the lion's den!

'Is that Mrs Van Lincoln? It's Hannah here. I've just come on duty and I've been told that you want to see me. How can I help? Yes, in the lounge in twenty minutes. By the way, it's lovely to have you back at the hotel.'

Hannah then went and warned Glenda, who had already been in contact with David. He'd said that if she dare raise her voice to any member of staff, she'll be told to leave. Hannah decided to take a notepad with her as she could already see that it might come in handy. To her surprise, Mrs Van Lincoln was ready for her in the lounge. Hannah would have had money on it that she'd have been late and kept her waiting.

'Good afternoon, Hannah. Thank you for seeing me at such short notice and on your day off too.'

'Not a problem, but it's not my day off. The staff must have made a mistake when telling you that. I do apologise, now how can I help you?'

'Oh, no, my dear. It's more of an introduction really. As you live in Luckett House, I thought it only right and proper to let you know we're going to be neighbours. I'm moving to Luckett Quay.'

'Neighbours? I don't understand.'

'Let me explain. You know the house which has been demolished and is in the process of being rebuilt? The one just up from yours? Well, I've bought it! I'm so excited about it all. Can't wait to live here and be part of this lovely community.'

That took the wind right out of Hannah's sails. There wasn't very much more she could say, but she desperately hoped her expression didn't give away her true feelings about having Tristan's grandmother as a neighbour.

'How lovely for you, Mrs Van Lincoln. I'm sure you'll enjoy living in such a beautiful part of the country. Now, was there anything else I can help you with?'

'No, my dear, that's all. I'm sure a happy welcome awaits me on the Quay. I just wish I could find the person who stopped me from buying a different property though. I'd love to thank them as they've done me such a huge favour. Isn't it strange how things work out? By the way, do you think I could cancel my dinner reservation for tonight and just have a light snack in my room instead? I've such a lot of paperwork to sort out, it's all such a mess, and I hate leaving my room untidy for the cleaner. Plus, you never know what they might take it upon themselves to read or even throw out, and we can't have that, can we, dear? Have a pleasant evening, young lady.'

259

Chapter 41

Mrs Van Lincoln's impending move to the quay was the last thing on Hannah's mind. Today she could do little more than focus her thoughts on Josie. The doctor was calling back during the morning as he was concerned about her. Josie had changed her mind and allowed Betty to call Richard, and he too was due to arrive at some point during the morning. Hannah was going to take Bonkers out for a long walk to try and wear him out a little, but he too wasn't quite himself, as if he knew something was amiss. After all, animals have a built-in capacity to react to human emotion, but after a great deal of persuasion and bribery, he did decide to go out for a walk. Once he was on the beach chasing after his favourite ball, it wasn't long before he was back to his usual highly spirited self.

Life was going to be so perfect once the flats were finished and they had all moved in, but now cracks were appearing. First, Susanna, and now poor Josie, and to add to the worries, Mrs Van Lincoln's plans. Hannah thought it best not to be present when Richard arrived. It had only been a short time since he had seen Josie, but Margaret was worried about how he would react to his mother's rapid decline in health. As the tide was out, Hannah decided to walk round the bay to Saltmarsh Quay and perhaps call in on Olivia until picking the boys up from school.

'Hi, are you sure it's alright to bring Bonkers in? I'm so sorry about cancelling last night, it's just...'

'Hannah, you've worn yourself out. You need a break; it's been one thing after another – the height of the holiday season at the hotel, co-ordinating everything for the builder, dealing with Betty, Margaret and Josie, not to mention the hassle with

Jimmy. You really do need to look after yourself.'

'I suppose you're right. I do seem to be pulled in all directions at the moment. It's just that Josie not being well is the only thing I can't put right and that's so frustrating. I know last night was important to you, and I'm sorry I couldn't celebrate with you. Anyway, what was the special occasion? Shall we make another date of it?'

'My divorce came through yesterday. I'm now officially single, no longer married to that lazy so and so. It won't make too much difference to my life really as he'll always be Sam and Ben's dad, despite not seeing them for years. To be honest, Hannah, I don't really know why I considered it a cause for celebration.'

'Of course it's a celebration. It's a brand-new chapter of your life! It's probably a good thing I was unable to celebrate with you last night though, as you need to do this in style. I'm not suggesting a party, but it's a significant milestone and you ought to invite a few others, especially Carl and Tom.'

Olivia and Hannah then spent the best part of an hour discussing ways of celebrating Olivia's new marital status. They also had a laugh about Mrs Van Lincoln, and apparently Olivia had spotted Tristan driving a dilapidated run around, so it did look like his flashy car had gone. Hannah felt much more positive now, and set off back to Luckett House.

'Right, I'd best be going. I expect Bonkers is hungry as he's getting rather fidgety. Let me know which night your mum can have the boys and then we'll check with Carl and Tom. I know we laughed and joked about your divorce, but are you really alright with it all? Do you miss him?'

'I'd be more sorry about it if he'd been a good father to Sam and Ben, but being that he can't even be bothered to see them for years, no, I'm not. He's best out of our lives. Tom's been more of a father to

261

them than he ever was. Are you alright, Hannah, is something the matter?'

'Oh sorry, I was deep in thought there. I've just thought of something which was so obvious, I wonder why I didn't think of it before. I'll be off now, but don't forget to ask your mum, will you? See you later, Olivia. Come on, Bonkers, we're going home.'

Why hadn't Hannah been able to put two and two together earlier? It seemed so obvious, but it wasn't until Olivia had actually said that Tom had been more of a father to the boys that she realised that they were perfect for each other. Of course, neither of them could see it, but it would be another problem ticked off and the boys loved him.

'Come on, Bonkers, let's get back and see how your mum's doing.'

Hannah walked up the coastal path towards the hotel, but just as she headed towards Luckett House, an ambulance overtook her on its way to the hospital. She didn't need to be told who the patient was; her immediate reaction was to cuddle Bonkers. She felt herself shaking with nerves, what should she do? Richard was following the ambulance in his car, but he hadn't noticed her. Hannah wanted to turn round and go back to the beach rather than face an upset Betty and Margaret.

'Hi, Nan. I've just seen the ambulance. How is Josie?'

'Oh, darling, it's not good news, I'm afraid. The doctor is concerned about her stomach, but she's in good hands now and we all need to remain positive. Now Richard's here, he'll see to everything. Now, come here, Bonkers, let's have a cuddle and then I've got a treat for you.'

'Whoever thought a dog would become so important in all our lives, Nan? I've heard of people sharing cars, but never a dog.'

'Yes, I don't know who's the luckiest, us or

Bonkers! By the way, are you hungry, Hannah? Why don't I cook us something and ask Margaret if she wants to join us? She'll be so worried about Josie as well.'

The three of them tried to make conversation over the quick meal Betty had put together for them. It was difficult though, as they were all very worried about Josie. Richard had promised to call them with any news, but it had been more than six hours now. Did that mean things were going well or not? Eventually Margaret checked her watch and decided to go back up to her flat as it was getting late. Betty soon followed and it was suggested that Bonkers could stay with Hannah as she would be up early for a morning walk along the beach.

It was still a beautiful evening even though it was late. Hannah made herself a cup of tea and sat looking out to sea. The garden work was progressing well; the seating areas were completed as was most of the planting. Oddly, the garden was a subject they hadn't discussed over dinner. Perhaps that was because they were looking forward to Josie being there to celebrate the new garden with them. As she called Bonkers in for the night, Hannah heard a car pull into the driveway. It had to be Richard. Should she go to the front door to meet him or pretend she hadn't heard the car. Bonkers barked.

'Hi, Richard. How are things? Would you like a drink or something to eat perhaps? You must be exhausted. Such a long day.'

'I had a sandwich at the hospital, thanks, but a large glass of something would be perfect. Bonkers, have you missed me? I bet you're missing your mum.'

They went through into Hannah's flat and she poured them both a glass of red wine. Richard looked tired and drawn. What should she say?

'Thanks, Hannah. I hope Bonkers has been

behaving himself. He hasn't been too much trouble for you, has he?'

'No, of course not. None at all, and to be honest he's getting used to spending time with all of us here. I don't think he knows any different now. He's not daft, you know. He gets treats and food from all of us here, so I'm sure we're all on a rota in his head.'

'Hannah, the news isn't good... My Mum's really poorly. They've just diagnosed her with cancer.'

Chapter 42

Hannah had a restless night thinking about Josie. She knew all about that dreadful disease as it had already claimed the life of her mother, but poor Richard. The news hadn't really sunk in properly, he had talked for hours and Hannah had been a good listening ear. It wasn't quite daylight, time for a coffee and head down to the beach with Bonkers before Margaret and Betty came knocking on her door.

Another lovely morning sitting on the rocks while Bonkers ran around sniffing at everything and enjoying the fresh air. Hannah was worried though, not just for Josie and Richard, but also for Margaret and Betty. They were all of the same generation and this would be a major thing for them. Betty was only saying the other day how it seemed like they all had a connection. Luckett Quay was special for them all in completely different ways. Please God, Hannah thought, let Josie be alright.

Time passed by quickly and Hannah needed to be at the hotel for nine o'clock. As she shouted to Bonkers to return from his walk her phone rang making her freeze with fear. Please let this be good news.

'Hi, sorry, Olivia. I'm on the beach with Bonkers and couldn't get to my phone. Is everything alright? He did what? I thought he didn't want to have anything to do with you or the boys, but now the divorce has gone through, he's changed his mind? Just tell him to get lost. It's too late now. You told me yesterday that you had no feelings for him. Yes, I understand he's their father, but for the last how many years.... Look, would you like me to come round? I can leave work by about nine tonight. We need to talk, so don't agree to anything with him, okay? What do your mum and dad have to say about all of this? You really ought to tell them everything, you know. Olivia, I really do have to go to work now, but I'll see you later. Just promise me you won't do anything...'

Back at Luckett House Margaret, Betty and Richard were having a coffee in the garden. Richard seemed a lot better than he had been the previous night, thanks to a bottle of wine and a good night's sleep. Hannah stopped by briefly to get ready for work and Richard was heading off to the hospital to meet with one of the consultants. Margaret was going to look after Bonkers for the day and Betty was working with Tom and Steve on the final parts of the planting. It all felt rather strange to Hannah. There was Josie seriously ill in hospital and life was carrying on as normal. It didn't quite feel right.

Arriving at the hotel, Hannah had a meeting with Glenda to discuss the following month's business arrangements. Jimmy had been invited along to the meeting too, which was a bit mysterious. He didn't usually attend, they simply handed him function sheets and room numbers. What could he add to the meeting? A quick check to see Glen and the team were sorted for the lunch and dinner shift. The diary wasn't looking overly busy for lunch time.

'Hi, Glenda. Everything alright?'

'Come into the office, I've got something to show you.'

Hannah followed Glenda into the office and was given a function sheet for the day. A meeting room had been booked for interviews by an agency which dealt with holiday lettings. There didn't seem to be anything unusual about that, until Glenda pointed out the list of applicants who needed to be greeted and shown in by the hotel receptionist.

'I knew you'd be interested in that. Do you fancy

standing on the Reception when the first candidate arrives for his interview, Hannah?'

Hannah laughed, thought it might be a bit cruel, but nothing more than Tristan deserved. So he's not planning to move away if he's applying for jobs here in Norfolk. Back to the present and Jimmy had arrived for the meeting. He looked a little nervous, but so too did Glenda. Hannah remembered! They were awaiting a conference call from David. There had been an email saying that he would be phoning.

'Do we know what this call is about, Glenda? Normally David just speaks to you and you feed it all back to the rest of us. Oh, the phone's ringing now.'

'Hi, David. How's things?'

'Good, thanks, Glenda. Sorry to interrupt your weekly meeting, but I need to fill you in on a couple of things. Before I start though, what's the latest with the Van Lincoln woman? Have you asked her to leave?'

'Hannah here, David. It's sorted for the time being, thanks. She can stay, but it's a bit of a long story.'

'Okay, well, I won't take up too much of your precious time as I know you're all so busy. The reason for my call is to let you know that Devel has just finished filming a new project and we're going to come to Norfolk. However, we'd really like a break rather than get stuck into hotel work, so I've agreed to spend less time on hotel matters and hand things over to you three. I've talked this over with Jimmy and I'd like him to play a bigger role in the day-to-day organisation. The kitchen's running better than it ever has before, so Jimmy can oversee shifts and become a Duty Manager. That will give you two more time to take on some of my work.'

Hannah thought about this carefully. It would mean that she and Jimmy would be equals, but she quite liked the idea that he'd have to come to her for advice and information.

'So I'd like you two to train Jimmy up on the computer system and all aspects of Reception. He's fine with the restaurant. Any questions, ladies? I really think this will work out well for all of us, the hotel and you three.'

'I'll devise a rota, David, and get Jimmy started as soon as possible. Hannah and I will have him trained up in no time at all.'

Call over, function sheets sorted and Hannah couldn't get out of the office quickly enough. She used the excuse that she needed to speak to Glen about a table booking, but by the looks on Glenda's and Jimmy's face, she could tell that they knew that wasn't the truth. Heading through Reception, she noticed Tristan waiting to go into his interview. He looked different, sad even, hunched up like he was carrying the weight of the world on his shoulders. For the first time ever, Hannah felt sorry for him. They remained silent, not even smiling to acknowledge each other.

Her phoned suddenly bleeped with an incoming text message. It was from Richard telling her that the hospital consultant advised operating on Josie the following morning. They certainly weren't wasting any time, things were looking better than they originally thought. Hannah sent Richard a quick reply sending her love.

The last people to leave the restaurant after lunch were the agency staff conducting the interviews. As the men went to the toilet, the young lady came to ask whether she could take a cup of coffee with her. Hannah went off to get a pot and three clean cups.

'Lunch was lovely, thank you. The view from this hotel is spectacular, a far cry from most of the places we normally go to for interviewers, but then the downside is that no one wants to come here to work. It's very quiet around this part of the Norfolk coast, isn't it?'

'Yes, but you've interviewed a good dozen people today, so surely that's a good sign.'

'Well, it would have been if any of them were any good. Sadly, we've been disappointed by this morning's candidates. Let's hope this afternoon brings someone we're looking for, otherwise we're stumped.'

Oh dear, no job for Tristan it would seem. Lunch over with, time to find Glenda and find out exactly what she thought about the situation with Jimmy. As Hannah guessed, she skirted around the conversation but eventually had to admit that Jimmy was keen to progress in his career, and once trained all of their lives would be simpler. They agreed that once he was up and running, the better it would be for everyone.

All the chefs were off duty. Phil, the kitchen porter, was left to clear up. Hannah made herself a cheese sandwich, picked up a packet of crisps and was heading out of the side door to sit in the afternoon sunshine when Phil called after her.

'Jimmy is sorry for what he done to you, he really is, Hannah; perhaps him cheating was the only way you could both end up here in Norfolk. Life has a very funny way of telling us things.'

'I know he's sorry and would love to turn the clock back, but you know as well as I do that it was wrong. It's just not that easy to put it out of my mind.'

Hannah headed off to the bench overlooking the sea, a quick look at her phone showed a text from Olivia saying Martin was coming around to chat things through. Sam and Ben were staying with her parents, but she hadn't filled them in with the details. Perhaps it would be a good idea if Hannah didn't come round after work after all.

'Not a problem. You know where I am if you need

me.'

She didn't really want to return to Luckett House until everyone else had gone to bed. There were far too many problems, although to be fair they were everyone else's problems she had found herself involved in. She still hadn't come up with an answer to her own problem. The flat had to go on the market and where was she going to live?

'Penny for your thoughts, Hannah. Sorry about my promotion, but you do know that it was nothing to do with me. It was David's idea. I had to email him some new menus I'd put together and then he asked me in for a chat. One thing led to another, but you do realise that he's doing this for your sake. It's to give you and Glenda more time to yourself. The week will now be equally divided between the three of us with Annie doing the odd morning Duty Manager shift here and there which will be a good help.'

'Yes, I know that, Jimmy, but I'm tired now. Things have been getting on top of me a bit recently. I know you're sorry for everything, but I just can't forgive you so easily. Some days I wish I could...'

'So why can't...'

'No, Jimmy, let me finish. I'm glad you've come to Saltmarsh Cliff Hotel. You've done more than turn the hotel around, you've also made my life in the restaurant far simpler and I've really enjoyed having you here. My head's all over the place though. If it wasn't for you, neither of us would be here. Regardless of us being a couple, we've both got such a better life now than when we were in London. I'm sorry, Jimmy, it's me, not you. I'm the problem in all of this.'

Chapter 43

That night Hannah had crept back to her flat without anyone seeing her. Betty had left a note for her to say that Margaret was going to move all Bonkers' food, bedding and toys into her flat and they would all take turns going for walks with him. She had also spoken to Richard who wouldn't be going to the hospital until later the next day as Josie's operation was scheduled for early in the morning.

It was now daylight, and no doubt the start of a very difficult day. Hannah made herself a coffee and sat out in one of the sheltered seating areas, amazed at how much planting had been done in the garden. It now looked finished. Checking her phone she noticed a text from Olivia to say that her evening with her ex had gone alright, no, he didn't stay the night, and yes, she would talk to her parents and explain everything.

There was also a text from her father saying that he was coming down for a couple of days and would it be alright to stay with her. That was an easy one to answer. Yes, of course he could stay. The third text was from Jimmy. All it said was thank you, followed with two kisses. She wished she had been on the beach when reading that one as she'd have liked to have been in a position to scream at him, "Why did you mess everything up?" Bonkers came bounding towards her.

'You wouldn't mess anyone's life up, would you? I'd just give you cuddles and treats and you'd be loyal and true. Hi, Margaret.'

'Are you alright? Was I supposed to hear that?'

'Not really, but it doesn't matter. I just want to scream at Jimmy, but I know I'd wake everyone up. It can wait until later. If you're going to the beach, do you mind if I come too?'

Hannah fetched her shoes and off they headed down the hill. Both of them agreed that having Bonkers to care for was perfect. He was keeping them all fit with the daily walking schedules. Margaret took the opportunity to update Hannah on Josie's condition. Apparently she hadn't felt very well before moving to Luckett House, but had pretended that everything was fine while selling her house in Sheringham and buying the flat. After the tests it was discovered that the cancerous growth in her bowel had grown to the size of a cricket ball. It needed to be cut out before she could have any further medical treatment.

Richard had reported that she was in good spirits taking all things into account, but the recovery and recuperation period would be long and very difficult. Best to take each day as it comes and see how things progress.

'Shall we go and sit on that rock, Margaret? When my mum was ill with her damned cancerous illness, I was so young that so many things were kept from me. I don't blame anyone for that, but my mum put on such a brave face and pretended nothing was happening that we weren't coming to terms with reality. Everything was an act and that wasn't right. Yes, fight it with every ounce of your energy, but don't pretend it's not happening. There was so much wasted time which would have been better used enjoying before it was too late.'

'I agree entirely, but last night I kept thinking how nice it is that Josie came back to Luckett Quay, the place she loved. She's had a wonderful life and a fantastic friendship with Richard. The way she talks about it is more like best friends than mother and son. I'm so envious of them, as I've never had a relationship with anyone like that. I would have loved to have had a child, but not one with Frank. I even worshipped my father until I found out he sold me to Frank. I realise that at the time he thought he was doing the best thing, but no, it turned out not to be. I wonder if he ever fully understood just how many lives he had messed up. Not just mine and Frank's, but Josie and Richard's too. Come to that, all the hardworking chaps he employed as well. His bitterness and anger remained with him until the day he died.

'Do you know, Hannah, I'm now the happiest I've ever been? I feel relaxed, calm and free. I know it might sound daft, but everything looks so much different. I've looked at the sea nearly every day of my life, but since I've been here it's all so perfect, even on a cold, wet, rainy day. I'm just so thankful I've been able to appreciate it before it's too late. Whoever would have thought I'd be able to have a second chance at life. I'm not angry with Frank anymore. I do know that I should have followed my heart rather than my head, but I didn't and that's all behind me now, past history and time to move on. I'm the last person to give advice, Hannah, but perhaps your heart is trying to speak to you about Jimmy and what it says is louder than what your head's telling you.'

'Possibly, Margaret, but for the time being Jimmy's the last thing on my mind. It's all about putting energy into getting Josie better again.'

'That's true, but don't keep putting things off, young lady. Remember to make time for yourself too.'

They wandered back up to the house. Richard's car had gone, but Tom's van was parked up. Hopefully he was by himself and not with Steve as she was sure Betty had said she had put them off for a few days because of Josie.

'Hi, Hannah. Have you got a minute, I'd like to ask you something?'

'See you later, Margaret. Thanks for the chat. You're right, and I'll certainly take your advice.'

'What do you need to know, Tom?'

'It's Olivia. Did you know that her ex is back on the scene?'

'She did mention it. Why?'

'Well, he's got no right to be here. Why hasn't she told him to get lost? I think you need to tell her a few home truths.'

'Tom, it's none of my business. It's her life at the end of the day, and don't forget he is the father of her children. Anyway, you were trying to fix her up with Steve and he's just as bad, if not worse.'

'That was different. Yes I was, but.... Anyway, that doesn't matter. We need to know exactly what he's up to. Has she said anything to you?'

'Look, the best thing you can do is ask her yourself. I'm sorry, Tom, but I'm busy and need to get on.'

Hannah wasn't in the mood for Tom and his questions, or anybody else for that matter. Margaret and Betty had each other for company waiting on news for Josie, and to be honest the thought of having to go up to the hotel was such an effort. Hannah felt irritable and fed up. This wasn't a bit like her; she always managed to see the bright side of things, but today was different. Other people had bad days, today was her turn.

Eventually she got herself ready and headed up to the hotel for her shift as the late Duty Manager taking over from Glenda. It was Jimmy's day off so she would throw herself into everything and hope that the shift would soon be over. Walking across the grass to the side entrance, she noticed Tristan's car. At least he won't be waiting around clicking his fingers, she thought. Perhaps he's visiting Mrs Van Lincoln. Actually, that's one positive thing about the day. She wouldn't have to put up with his antics anymore.

'Hi, Hannah. Another lovely day. Have you been on the beach with your dog? I can never remember his name?'

'Hi, Jenny. Yes, I have and his name's Bonkers.'

Hannah knew what was coming next. Everyone seemed to be asking the same questions. Was Martin back in Olivia's life? Hannah knew she couldn't be rude to Jenny like she had been with Tom.

'I don't know. I really think you should be asking Olivia, but perhaps he's turned over a new leaf in which case perhaps it might be good for her and the boys. I've never met him personally, but one thing's for sure and that's your daughter's a very strong woman. Her head will rule her heart and in this case, that's the right thing.'

'I do hope you're right. Yes, her boys are her life and they will always come first. I'm so glad you're back living here in Norfolk, Hannah. You bring something special to the hotel, but most of all I really think you belong here in Luckett Quay.'

Hannah felt a lot better after chatting to Jenny and yes, she was beginning to feel at home, wherever home would be. Her mood lightened, she put on a smile ready for a busy afternoon and evening ahead. The first hour of her shift was spent checking that everything was organised and everyone knew their roles. Emails answered and a quick check in the restaurant diary before having a sandwich and coffee. Her pager alerted her to call Reception. Tristan wanted to speak to her.

'Hi, what can I do for you?'

'Could we go somewhere quiet for a chat?' He looked so dreadful that his rapid change in appearance baffled her. She dismissed his request, telling him that she needed to check the tables outside on the lawn, but if he wanted to talk whilst she worked that would be better. Tristan looked relieved. Yes, that would be a better option, out of the way of everyone.

'I'd just like to say how sorry I am for everything that's happened. No doubt you'll have heard that I've lost everything, Emmi and my job. I deserved it though. I've treated people very badly. I'm not looking for your forgiveness or anybody else's for that matter, but I just wanted to admit it and tell you I know I was in the wrong.'

'You're right, Tristan. You treated the hotel staff in a disgusting manner, and there's no forgiving that. You should have known better, but let's just say that it's all behind us now, in the past. I can move on from it, but I can't speak for the rest of the staff. Now was there anything else?'

'Well, yes there was actually. Hope you don't think it's a bit cheeky of me, but I was wondering whether you had any jobs available at the hotel.'

Hannah couldn't believe what she was hearing. Was he really sorry for his actions or was this little speech a convenient set up because he was desperate to find a new job?

'I'm sorry, Tristan. Although I can personally put things behind us, it would be like a smack in the face for the staff if I were to employ you. No, there are no positions available at the hotel for you, now or at any future point. You must realise you've put me in a very difficult situation.'

'You what? This hotel is always crying out for staff and you know I'd be a real asset here. With all my business contacts, I'm exactly what it needs. Think of all the customers I could easily be able to bring here. You'll regret your decision, Hannah, but just see – I'll soon get you back.'

'Get me back? Well, that's something to look forward to, and as for your contacts, perhaps they're not the type of people we really need at this hotel. Anyway, haven't you just found the solution to your own dilemma? If you've got so many important business contacts, I'm sure one of them could find you a job.'

Chapter 44

A few days had passed since Josie's operation, she was doing well and the doctors were pleased with her progress. Richard had spent most of his time at the hospital and was hoping that she'd soon be able to return home.

Hannah had been busy working at the hotel. Strangely there had been no further visits from Tristan. Perhaps he had learnt his lesson. Jimmy had started his Duty Manager's training, learning about the computer system on Reception and how to book guests in and out. Glenda had remarked on how quickly he had adapted to his new responsibilities. That was no surprise to Hannah as Jimmy was an expert when it came to computers and technology, but today her mind was on one thing only – her father's visit. This was her opportunity to start the ball rolling. Susanna had laid down the rules. She wanted to move to a bigger property and the only way they could do that was by selling the flat. Hannah had come to terms with that, but the stress it was causing Betty was a major problem.

'Hi, Nan. Dad's sent a text to say he'll be here around six o'clock. I'll try to get back after the Night Manager arrives, so around nine-thirty or so. Glen can then finish off in the restaurant.'

'That's fine, darling. I'll have a lovely meal ready for you. It'll be lovely to chat without Susanna here. Do you think there's any simple answer to all this? It goes against all my principles, you know. She's blackmailing me and that's not right. Why did he ever meet her? I know they've given me two beautiful grandchildren who I wouldn't wish to be without, but they're not being very fair, are they?'

'Yes, I know, Gran. Tell him we'll get the flat

valued and then put it on the market. But I've no idea what would happen to the conservatory. It would need a wall built, and then Josie and Margaret would have access to your half only. What about the garden though? Would that need to be divided up?'

'No, darling, because it's just not going to happen. I've come here for a quiet life. Everything was perfect before Josie became so ill. It's your father's problem and that's what I'll tell him. If she wants to end the marriage because of not being able to have a big house, then their marriage isn't worth saving. It's not just any old flat, it's your home and more importantly, my life is so much easier because you're here.'

'But Nan...'

'No buts, Hannah, it's just wrong and I'll be the first to tell your father so. He's my son at the end of the day, and he needs to understand this move has implications for us all. If he's not happy with that, well, I don't know what will happen but I've made my mind up. Subject closed. I can't believe I even considered giving in to her request. I'm so mad at myself for that. Right, I'm off to the beach with Margaret and that gorgeous dog. See you later, darling. Have a lovely day.'

'I doubt it will be lovely stuck in an office training Jimmy for his new role. I could think of far better ways to spend the day.'

'Oh, don't be too hard on him. He's doing everything he possibly can to please you. He was only saying how this promotion would...'

'So you've been talking to him about me. What else did he have to say, Nan?'

'Well, don't go off on one, darling, but I bumped into him when I was last down in Saltmarsh. We got into conversation and he told me all about his promotion and how he was looking forward to getting more involved in the day-to-day running of the hotel. I'm sure it will all work out for the best, so cut him a bit of slack. He's trying his best. If only...'

'If only I could forgive him, everything would be fine. That's what you were about to say, wasn't it, Nan?'

'That's not what I meant, Hannah. I'm sorry, I didn't want to upset you. Margaret's waiting for me, so I must be going. See you tonight then.'

Everybody seemed to be good at giving her advice on Jimmy. He'd certainly done a good job working his charm on them. Underneath it all he was a nice chap though. Hannah looked at the time and realised she ought to be getting up to the hotel for her training session with him, but was that a car outside?

'Hi, Richard. How's things? Got time for a coffee?'

'That would be great, thanks. Just give me a few minutes to put the shopping away and then I'll be down.'

Hannah made them both some coffee and took them out to the garden. Checking her phone she noticed a text from Carl saying this would be the weekend he'd tell his parents that he's gay. She sent him back a quick message wishing him luck for that.

'All sorted now, Hannah. Just thought I'd best get some good food in the freezer in case Mum comes home soon. At least I'll be prepared for that.'

'How are things, Richard? Will you need to be getting back to London?'

Richard explained that he'd been granted compassionate leave from work for as long as he needed. He'd come to an agreement that he would semi-retire and just do some consultancy and PR work for them instead of full-time design. Hannah noticed how tired he looked. Josie's illness had obviously taken its toll on his health, and Hannah knew it would help if he had someone to talk to.

To lighten the conversation up a bit she

mentioned Carl and his parents and they talked about many different things – Bonkers and how he enjoyed his beach walks, life at the hotel and even things he had heard on the radio whilst driving. Hannah realised this was his way of coping with the situation, but glancing at the time she really did need to be getting ready for work. What a dilemma. She didn't really want to leave Richard by himself.

'Richard, I ought to be getting ready for work now. Are you sure you're alright? I know you've probably spent a lot of time listening to Nan and Margaret telling you things they think you want to hear, but it's perfectly okay to scream, shout and get upset, you know. Josie's your mum, the most important person you'll ever have in your life and no one can ever take her place. Please don't bottle things up. It won't help you or Josie in the long run. I wish I could stay longer, but...'

'I know you've got to get yourself to work, but thanks so much for the coffee and listening ear. I do know what you've been saying is really good advice, and I appreciate that.'

That had been exactly what Richard had needed. He was going to get himself ready to go to the hospital, but promised he'd call Hannah if there was anything else she could do.

Arriving at the hotel, Hannah had 20 minutes to spare before Jimmy would come bouncing through the door like an excited puppy, so she quickly went through the list of things Glenda had left her for the training session. Glenda had suggested that if Jimmy was happy with all he'd learnt on Reception and felt confident with it, perhaps he could now be left on his own with it. There's nothing like being thrown in at the deep end, after all.

'Hi, Jimmy, everything alright? Glenda's left us a list of things to go through if there's enough time. I've organised the restaurant already. Glen will be fine with it all, so I'll only need to pop in and out.'

'Yes, the kitchen's sorted out. They won't need me getting in their way. By the way, you haven't commented on how smart I look in my new uniform. I bet you'd never believe I'd wear a suit, collar and tie.'

'Very smart indeed, Jimmy, but admiring yourself isn't going to get all this training done. Come sit down and we can make a start.'

'Okay, boss.'

For the next few hours Hannah and Jimmy went through the health and safety procedures. He was already very familiar with the fire policy and how to handle chemicals properly, so didn't need to spend any extra time on those. Next they moved onto the hotel filing systems, record keeping and reports and information which David and Devel required. Hannah could tell that Jimmy was keen to learn and was taking everything very seriously, but she was also aware of the looks he was giving her. This was getting quite awkward. She needed the perfect opportunity to complete the training for the day, the hotel was starting to become busy and the receptionist had paged for some help. What could be better?

'Do you want me to go and help with the arrivals?'

'If you feel confident about it, yes, that would be great, Jimmy.'

'Not a problem. I might be a bit slow at it though, so I guess they'll just have to be patient with me.'

'That's fine. I can handle everything else. Why don't you stay out on the Reception desk until dinner starts at seven? Just one thing to remember, Jimmy. Don't forget to ask the guests if they require a table for dinner tonight. We don't want them just turning up as that makes the chefs very angry.'

'Very funny.'

Jimmy went off smiling, and Hannah could feel she was too. Looking at the clock, she didn't have a lot more left to do, so she decided to give Olivia a quick call. Being a Friday teatime, Sam and Ben would be at their grandparents, so Olivia would be free to talk.

'Hi, lovely, okay to talk? How's things? Oh, not a problem. I can call back later if you like. Well, if you're sure you don't mind. I just thought it would be best if I called back as you've got someone there with you. Ah, it's Tom. That's why you're keen to stay on the phone, is it?'

Twenty minutes later and having discussed all manner of trivia and answered a dozen questions about the hotel, Hannah finally managed to end the call. She laughed to herself. Poor Tom. He must have been so annoyed. Checking in on Reception, Jimmy was in his element chatting and joking with the guests and the receptionists. Hannah was proud of him. For someone who had worked in kitchens for a career and never really coming into contact with the guests, he was doing a fantastic job.

The rest of the shift ran smoothly. Between them they dealt with any queries the guests had, clearing tables in the restaurant ready for the busy period and taking room service orders to guest rooms. It was nearly nine o'clock and now Hannah could use the remainder of the shift for Jimmy's bar training. He could stand there, serve guests, chat to them and show an interest in anything they had to say. She'd just have to help the restaurant staff clear up and lay tables for breakfast, but suddenly her phone vibrated. A text from Betty asking whether she had time to call.

'Hi, Nan, is everything alright?'

'Yes, your father's just taken Bonkers out for his final walk of the day, and I just thought I'd let you know that I've told him.'

'Oh, what was his reaction?'

'He just said that his marriage was over. I think I may have upset him even more by saying I was glad about that. Obviously Susanna doesn't love him because the size of a property has nothing to do with it, so this was her way of getting out of the marriage.'

'Thanks for the warning, Nan. Will he be still up when I get back?'

'Yes, I'm afraid so. He thinks he can get you on his side. As I've given the flat to you, he thinks he'll be able to discuss it all with you instead of me. Sorry to have put you in this position, darling, but I'm telling you now, he's not happy about it.'

Chapter 45

Hannah could hear her father in the bathroom. It was only six-thirty in the morning and he'd been asleep when she got back from work the previous night. On the one hand, she wished she could have broached the subject, but now she wondered whether she could stay in bed just that little bit longer before getting up and facing the music. He wasn't aware that the flat hadn't been signed over from Betty yet, so technically the argument wasn't anything to do with her. What should she do? Perhaps she should just get up and get it over and done with.

'Morning, Dad. Sorry, I didn't get to see you last night. It was later than I intended. You know how it is when the hotel gets busy, one thing leads to another before you realise it.'

'Yes, and no doubt your nan's already told you I'm on the war path.'

'War's a vile word, Dad. We're a family and that means getting along with each other in a friendly and civilised way, not war. If this is how you're going to be, I'm not in the mood for it. Now, would you like any breakfast?'

'Sorry, darling. I don't want to upset you or Nan for that matter, but I'm really in a desperate situation here.'

'Let's have a coffee and then we can collect Bonkers from Margaret and take a walk into Saltmarsh Quay for a bacon sandwich. I'm sure we can come up with a plan of action my stepmother will agree to.'

'Did you mean to say the word 'stepmother' differently than the other words in that sentence? I can see Susanna's really got to you.'

'Yes, she has, but for one reason only. She's upset Nan. More to the point, she's upset you too and that hurts me.'

Hannah and her father got dressed and drank their coffee. From the window, Hannah noticed Margaret bringing Bonkers down. It would have been nice if she could have joined them on the walk into Saltmarsh Quay, but she knew that would have meant avoiding the issue and having to deal with it later.

The tide was in, meaning they were unable to walk along the beach. Instead, they'd have to go up and over the coastal path. Bonkers was excited. He thought he was going to the hotel, which always meant a treat in store for him. No hotel visit today though, it was just a walk up one side and down the other.

'Your mum and I used to have lovely times up here when you were little, Hannah. Life was so much simpler in those days. You went to work, earnt your weekly wage, came home, watched telly and had four week's holiday a year. I'd do anything to have those times back again.'

'Yes, Dad, but then you wouldn't have had Pippa and Alfie, and they're a major part of your life now. I know what you mean though. Life wasn't nearly as complicated then, but I was a kid at school with no worries. To be honest, Dad, I had nothing to fret about in London. Here, I seem to have attracted problem after problem, but then I really am fortunate to live in such a beautiful place. Just look at that sea view. How could you ever be unhappy watching that every day?'

'True, but I'm asking you to give that view up. I know it's not fair, but I'm expecting you to move into the staff quarters at the hotel. I can't think of any other way round it. I know I should be the one looking after everyone, you, my mother, my wife, my children but, darling, I really can't cope with all of this. Life's taken over and I've been left behind.'

Robert started to cry; something Hannah hadn't witnessed since the day of her mother's funeral and even then he had done his best to hide it from her. Was all this really over a property he didn't even need? Hannah threw a stick for Bonkers to run after and fetch, giving Robert time to pull himself together. This wasn't going to plan, but then if her dad had been in the right frame of mine, Hannah knew he'd never expect her to give up her home. Thank goodness Betty wasn't here to see this. Was money a problem for Robert or was it something a lot deeper, something which Susanna was controlling.

Hannah gave her dad a hug. That's all she could do given the circumstances, and her way of dealing with things was always the same. Whether it was Carl, Richard, Nan or her father, hugs were her only means of comfort.

'Come on, Dad. Let's go and get something to eat and then we'll start putting a plan of action together.'

They carried on into Saltmarsh and headed to Audrey's boat house. The little café would be open for a full English breakfast. He forced a smile, but it was the smile of a man she loved so much. Hannah could have cried, but when she thought about Susanna, her tears turned to anger. How could that woman destroy her father? She had already lost one parent, she didn't want to lose another.

They ate their breakfast and didn't mention anything about the flat for the next two hours. Hannah chatted non-stop about Josie and the new garden as well as her new job at the hotel and how she was enjoying it. Robert was looking more like his usual self, interested in her life and asking questions. It felt just like the good old days when she was at university and came home for the weekends. They paid the bill and checked the tide. It was going out. It looked like they would be able to walk back along the beach to Luckett Quay. Bonkers would be happy, he loved it when the tide had just gone out, the fresh sea aroma and rolling in the wet, salty sand.

'Hannah, could I just ask you something? Where does Jimmy fit into everything?'

'What do you mean, fit in?'

'Well, he obviously features in your plans somewhere. You keep mentioning him just like you did when you first met him.'

'Oh, no, he's not in the plans at all. He works at the hotel, that's all. We're getting on great professionally, but that's really all there is to it.'

For the next hour they enjoyed throwing the ball for Bonkers and watching him rush off to fetch it. Once back at Luckett House Hannah made them coffee and they joined Margaret and Betty in the garden. Hannah hoped Margaret would stay there, then there wouldn't be any talk of selling the flat. With that, Richard came down. What a relief! The five of them talked mostly about the garden until it was time for Hannah to get ready for her shift at work. Thankfully, Jimmy was working in the kitchen rather than being on the Duty Manager rota, so she could easily keep out of his way. Betty was going to spend the afternoon baking.

'Right, I must be going. Have a nice day, everyone. I'll probably be back quite late. You know what Saturday nights are like. No one wants to eat too early and then they stay in the bar until all hours.'

Walking to the hotel, Hannah wondered whether she should have mentioned her father getting upset, but that would have probably upset Betty and cause even more worry. No, it was his business to tell her. Entering the front door of the hotel, she noticed Carl's car parked in the car park. Oh, dear, he was obviously looking for her, but why hadn't he phoned?

'Hi, lovely. What brings you up here? How did things go, or haven't you told them?'

'Oh hello, I'm just here to book a room for tonight.'

'They took it badly? If my dad wasn't here, you could have stayed with me.'

Carl went on to say that the reason why he was booking a room at the hotel was that Mike was coming to stay, and he didn't think it appropriate to stay at his parents'. He did say that he had told his mum and dad everything and they were fine. There was absolutely no drama, no tears and no shouting at all. 'They had an inkling of course, but were just waiting for me to admit it. As long as I'm happy, they're fine with it and Dad's relieved to hear that I'm not moving away as he thinks I'm a huge asset to the business. I did ask them how long they'd known and Mum said that every time I looked through the Argos catalogue as a child, I really wanted the bright pink bike with tassels on the handlebars. I always preferred the girls' toys and showed no interest at all in sport, not even on the television. I always liked girly things, but they thought it was just a phase and I'd grow out of it. I suppose it's what every gay person dreams of, being accepted and treated normally by your family without any upsets or arguments.'

'Come here, let's have a hug. I'm thrilled to bits to hear that good news. It makes such a lovely change. Got time for a coffee?'

'Yes, I think so. I'm not picking Mike up from the station just yet. By the way, we're eating here at the restaurant tonight and wait for it … with my parents.

'Oh, I think the last time I saw your mum at the hotel...'

'Yes, she did mention that she had a few words

with you, but that was because she thought you were after me instead of planning my future. I've told her the story about our first trip to London, so I think she's forgiven you. Talking of London, she's over the moon to learn that Mike lives there. Probably planning lots of sightseeing and shopping trips. Well, that's all my news for now. I suppose yours isn't so positive.'

Hannah spent the next hour filling Carl in on everything going on in her life, the whole lot, including Olivia, her dad, and poor Josie.

'Oh dear, what a week! But you've missed out Jimmy.'

'No, I haven't left Jimmy out as there's nothing to tell as far as he's concerned. Now, I suggest you go and pick up Mike. I don't envy him by any stretch of the imagination as once your mum starts planning, something tells me there'll definitely be three in this relationship.'

'Very funny, but I'm still not going to drop the subject of Jimmy, you know. Okay, yes, you're right. I'd best get going. Make sure my room's ready for me when I get back and put a 'Do not disturb' sign on the door as I've not seen him for a whole week.'

'Too much information, thank you, Carl!'

They both laughed, hugged each other, and Carl went off to the station to collect Mike. Hannah had a quick walk round the hotel checking on each department to make sure everything was running smoothly. There were only a few check-ins as most guests were staying for the weekend and had already arrived. Housekeeping had had a relatively easy day with the cleaning and in the kitchen everything was being prepared for the evening meal. Thankfully, no sign of Jimmy. It was his break time.

Hannah carried on towards Reception to check on the on-duty receptionist before the lunch shift started. Saturdays was generally a quiet day apart from the guests handing in their keys before going out for the day and then collecting them when they got back. The phones don't ring much either, all is normally peaceful. Hannah was just going through the following week's reservations on the computer when Mrs Van Lincoln headed towards the desk.

'Morning. Off out anywhere nice?'

'Yes, thank you, Hannah. I'm off to Norwich to look at sofas for the new house, and as you're probably aware it's taking a lifetime to get finished.'

'Oh, you'd better get Tristan cracking the whip.'

'He's the reason it's taking so long. He's not my favourite friend at the moment, so hopefully he's keeping out of my way for a while. See you later.'

Hannah wondered what all that was about. At least he'd be keeping away from the hotel while his grandmother was a guest though.

'Hi, Hannah, the lads in the kitchen just said you're looking for me.'

'No, not you in particular. Just checking everything's okay for the lunch and dinner.'

'All sorted. Thanks for your time and patience with the training yesterday, Hannah. It means such a lot. How do you think I'm picking everything up?'

'Fine, Jimmy, but do you feel confident about all your new duties? Is there anything you feel we need to go back over?'

'Not workwise, Hanny, but I'd like us to go back to the way we were.'

'Jimmy, we're here to work, and it's Hannah now, okay?'

'Sorry. Okay, I'll have a think about anything I may need further help with and let you know. It's only a week or so before Glenda goes on holiday for three weeks and it will feel strange just having the two of us running the place. It will seem just like our own hotel. To tell the truth, I'm looking forward to it.'

Chapter 46

It was Hannah's day off and she was planning to spend it with her dad and Betty. However, on arriving home after her shift she'd discovered he'd left her a note and gone. He was sorry for all the upset he had caused, but couldn't see a way to resolve it. What could he say or do? Betty was adamant that the flat was hers. Hannah knew that once Dad returned home to Susanna, life would be difficult for him. She made herself a coffee, noticed that Margaret, Betty and Richard were out in the garden and went out to join them. It was a gloriously sunny day, and she wondered what Betty would like to do now Dad had gone. Unfortunately, she got in first...

'Darling, would you mind if I went with Richard and Margaret to visit Josie today?'

'Of course not, Nan.'

Richard piped in. 'It was my suggestion, Hannah. I just thought it would be good for Mum to have some female company for a change. She must be fed up with seeing me all the time. I've also suggested we stop off on the way back for a bite to eat somewhere.'

'Bonkers had a good run this morning, so he should be exhausted and sleep for most of the day, but would you mind just keeping an eye on him while us oldies are out of the way? Why don't you enjoy yourself and have a party, a fun Sunday, invite your friends over,' Margaret continued.

'Thanks, Margaret. I might give Olivia a call and see if she's free to pop round with the boys. We could have a barbecue out in the garden. I'm sure they'd love that.'

The three of them went to get ready for going to visit Josie while Hannah made herself another coffee and thought about ringing Olivia. It would be nice if Carl and Mike popped in too, and feeling a little guilty, perhaps she ought to invite Tom. Instead of phoning him, she sent him a brief text, adding a PS – 'Bring a friend.' Never know, he might turn up with a girl. If they were all able to come it would be the beginnings of a lunch time party. Was there anyone else she could invite? Should she invite Jimmy? Although he was working today, there was no real reason why he couldn't pop in between the lunch and dinner shifts.

It was now half-past ten. Richard, Margaret and Betty had all left for the hospital and Hannah had gone to the little shop in Saltmarsh Quay to buy some more items for the barbecue. She had burgers in the freezer already, but needed some fresh bread rolls and sausages. She also needed some drinks, wine and beers, but no doubt everyone would bring their own.

As she was putting her shopping in the boot of the car, she saw Emmi coming towards her in her riding gear.

'Hi, Emmi. Off out with the horses? It's a lovely day for it.'

'Hi. I was intending to, but it looks like one of the horses has a problem with his leg. Look, he appears to be lame. Can't go riding now, what a shame.'

'Fancy coming over to mine at lunch time? I'm having a little barbecue with a few friends over. You're welcome any time after one o'clock, but don't bring Tristan. He isn't welcome.'

'Don't worry, I definitely won't be bringing him. I'm not even allowed to talk to him because of the legal situation between him and my father, but thank you. I'd love to come. What should I wear though?'

'Whatever you like. You'll be the most glamourous person there, whatever you wear.'

Hopefully after a drink or two, she'll let the cat

out of the bag and talk about the legal situation. It would be nice if she and Tom got a little friendly with each other. She could do with a good man in her life rather than a good for nothing like Tristan.

Back at Luckett House, Hannah began the food preparation. Pesto potato salad, crunchy coleslaw... She suddenly remembered it had been years since she had cooked on an open barbecue. That had been Jimmy's domain and since being back here, Josie had taken over, but it couldn't be that difficult, surely.

Checking her phone, she noticed several texts. Tom had replied saying he'd be there around two o'clock as he needed to go and price up a contract in Cromer first. Carl had said that as Mike didn't need to catch the train back to London tonight he had decided to stay until tomorrow. Jimmy had confirmed he could come, but he'd have to finish the lunch service first, so it would be nearer three o' clock by that time and could she wait for him. No way would that happen. Jimmy was a guest, and that's how it would stay. This was Hannah's get together after all.

It was now a quarter to one, and Hannah had organised everything for her guests, placing cushions in the garden seating areas, putting on some music and making it all cosy and welcoming. Bonkers was taking full advantage of being out in the garden, happily running from the sunshine to the shade and back again. It had the makings of a good afternoon. Last minute plans were always the best!

'Hi, Sam. Where's Ben? Oh, there he is with your mum. Now, I've got a very important job for you boys. There's someone who's going to be very excited to meet you two.'

'Who, Aunty Hannah?'

'Bonkers, the dog! He's so looking forward to playing with you. His box of toys is out on the patio.

Do you think you'd be able to keep him amused for the afternoon?'

That was the last they saw of the boys and Bonkers for a couple of hours. Hannah poured herself and Olivia a glass of wine and they chatted about everyone and everything except her ex-husband. No doubt Tom would bring the subject up though. Next to arrive was Carl and Mike. Carl took control of the barbecue and started to tell them all about his mother and how she'll be the best dressed woman in Norfolk, now she's come to terms with having a gay son. Bonkers started to bark. He'd heard a car pull up on the driveway. Hannah looked out and saw it was a taxi and getting out of the back seat was Emmi, dressed up the nines as if she was going to a Hollywood Premier. Olivia and Hannah both looked at each other speechless. This was a lunch gathering in a Norfolk garden, not the Oscars, but if that's how Emmi preferred to dress, she was welcome. Then they caught sight of who she had brought with her. Also dressed to impress was Britney.

'Hi, you two. Don't you both look lovely! So colourful and the rhinestones really do shine in the sunshine. Please come in and go through into the garden. I'll introduce you to everyone in a minute, but can I get you both a drink first?'

Hannah noticed they'd both brought a bottle gift bag with them. She guessed it would be Prosecco and she was right. She poured them a glass and heard her phone bleep with another text message. Glen. He was warning her that Jimmy had juggled the chef's rota and was taking the evening shift off. This wasn't really what she was hoping to hear. Carl introduced Mike to everyone. Emmi had known Carl for years. She recalled a story from their youth.

'We could have only been about seven or eight years old. You always liked to come and play at my house. I thought that a bit strange as you were the only boy, but we had this game where we'd bring all our dolls out to you and you'd play the part of a doll doctor and repair them all. I remember Mum saying how you'd always love playing with the dolls more than the girls did.'

'Only because you had the best dolls with fabulous clothes and beautiful long hair. At that age I realised I shouldn't really be playing with dolls, so that's why I pretended to be the doctor. One day I pulled a leg off one of the other girl's dolls just to let people see me mend it, but my favourite thing was doing their hair. I used to have such fun doing that until I was forced to do more boyish things like play football and go to Cub Scouts. I hated both of them so much and was always jealous of you girls playing with your dolls.'

Everyone was laughing in a sympathetic kind of way. Bonkers barked again. Was it Tom arriving? Yes, and he'd also brought a guest with him, although not one who was overly welcome. Flash Steve. Hannah wasn't worried though. She knew there'd be no way he'd even think about chatting her or Olivia up, not when there were two Hollywood starlets there dressed to kill.

'Right. Burgers and sausages are ready. Plates, Hannah?'

'Yes, sorry, Carl. Everything's on the table in the conservatory. Just go and help yourselves everyone, but please don't feed Bonkers. I don't want Josie to come home from hospital and find her dog is twice the size, so if I catch you two boys feeding him a sly sausage, there'll be no ice cream for you later.'

'Okay, Aunty Hannah. We promise.'

'Hannah, you don't mind me bringing Steve along, do you? You said I could bring someone with me, and while we were in Cromer he asked what I was doing for the rest of the day.'

Hannah didn't really think it was okay, but she'd let him see that two can play games.

'Not a problem at all, and from the look of it he's enjoying himself. He must be spoilt for choice with both Emmi and Britney here. It's perfect actually. Once he's chosen which one he wants, you can double date. Wouldn't that be sweet!'

Tom's face was a picture. He didn't look at all amused. Emmi didn't appear to be at all interested in Steve, unless she was playing hard to get. She was enjoying herself laughing and joking with Mike and Carl instead.

'Why did he bring him, Hannah? He knows we both can't stand him, but then who knows what goes on in Tom's head? He's always been a mystery to me. One minute he acts like my father and the boy's grandfather, and another time we're more like brother and sister. He's been questioning me about the boys' dad coming back on the scene too. He does baffle me sometimes. I don't know, is that someone at the door, Hannah?'

Suddenly Hannah remembered. Hadn't Tom and Jimmy fallen out over her? She had forgotten about that. She went to let him in, but really shouldn't she be putting him off?

'Don't panic, everyone, the chef's arrived. I'll soon get the burgers and sausages up and running.'

'Hi, Jimmy. No need for you to play chef here, you're a guest like everyone else. The food's all taken care of, so why don't you go through into the garden and I'll bring you out a drink. I presume that will be a soft drink as you'll be going back to work in a few hours, won't you?'

'Actually, I'm off tonight. One of the lads needed a few hours off at lunch, so I've got him to do the evening shift. I'll have a beer, please.'

It was an interesting afternoon. Jimmy tried to show Carl how to cook burgers and sausages properly, but soon walked away downhearted. Tom had realised it wasn't such a fun lunch as he'd thought and soon went and played ball with Sam, Ben and Bonkers. Hannah kept topping everyone's drinks up and Olivia helped to collect the dirty plates. Steve's phone rang; he seemed excited to chat to whoever had called him.

'Hannah, my cousin's just arrived in Norfolk and wants to meet up while he's in Saltmarsh. Is it alright if I invite him over?'

What could Hannah say? Did they really need more male testosterone in the place?

'Of course, that would be lovely. Tell him he'd be most welcome.'

Half an hour later the doorbell rang. Steve's cousin had arrived. Olivia opened the door and welcomed him in, blushing as she did so. Hannah could instantly see why. He was handsome, absolutely gorgeous, everything a woman wanted in a man, and she could feel herself turning red as she went over to introduce herself. He was carrying a bouquet of flowers and a bottle of wine.'

'Hi, I'm Hannah. Nice to meet you.'

'Thanks for inviting me. I'm Pete. I spoke to Steve yesterday and he said he didn't have any plans, so I thought I'd surprise him. I've brought you some flowers and a bottle of wine as a thank you gift. Hope that's okay. There wasn't a lot of choice over in Saltmarsh.'

'They're lovely, but you shouldn't have.'

'Of course I should. It's rude to turn up at a party and not bring a present for the host.'

What lovely manners, Hannah thought to herself. She took the flowers and the wine to the kitchen to find a suitable vase, and pour Pete a drink. Both Emmi and Britney immediately pounced on him, and to Hannah's surprise, so did Olivia. Within a few minutes Carl and Tom were offering him food, and the party atmosphere had improved. The star of the show seemed to have arrived, but perhaps the lovely thing was that Pete himself hadn't realised it.

'Scuse, me, mister. Do you play football? Me and my brother, Sam, do? Do you want to play, cos Tom's not that good at it?'

Pete made an excuse to the girls and off he went followed by Emmi and Britney who wanted to watch him play football. Tom wasn't impressed, neither was Jimmy. He couldn't understand how Hannah could enjoy Pete's company.

'I owe you a big thanks, Tom. I was a bit peeved that you brought Steve with you, but we'd have never met Pete otherwise. Lads, do help yourselves to the beers. I'm going to go and join the girls. Suddenly this game of football has got very interesting, if you know what I mean!' Their faces were a picture. Steve then came over and explained that Pete was in Norwich as he had a job interview the following day.

'Wait till I tell the girls. Pete could be a permanent fixture here in Norfolk. How exciting is that!'

The following morning Hannah was still smiling; she had never seen one group of lads so jealous of one guy. Of course, it didn't help that the girls were aware and played on it even more just to annoy them, but the guy in question was lovely despite not realising it himself. They were all wishing Pete well for his job interview, but today was a new day, and a completely different one. Josie was due to be discharged from the hospital. One of the problems was that she wouldn't be able to manage the stairs, and she would feel so isolated, but after Richard, Betty and Margaret had got back from the hospital the previous night they had come to a decision that Hannah should move up to Josie's flat while Richard and Josie stayed in hers until Josie recuperated a little more. That would mean she could have easier access into the conservatory and garden. Richard was grateful for this.

Hannah had transferred her clothes and bits and pieces downstairs, beds had been changed and Richard had swapped the food in the fridges over. Now he was going to the hospital to collect Josie, and Hannah was ready to go to work for the late shift. Unfortunately for her, she was shadowing Jimmy for the entire shift and she knew it would be a long one. It didn't help that they had quite a lot of check-ins. Hannah just felt it was going to be one of those evenings.

'Right, I'm off, Richard. Hope today goes well. Do give my love to Josie as it'll be late when I get back. I'll see her in the morning.'

'Well, it's not going to be easy, Hannah. For a start Mum won't be in her own home. Sorry, I know that sounds really ungrateful of me, but she's bound to be a bit frustrated as she won't be able to do much. On top of that, we don't really know what the future holds. If I'm honest, I'm beginning to feel like I've got a double personality; the Richard you see here, the real me and then the other one who's rushing around happy with Mum as though nothing's happened. I don't think she'll be able to cope with all this too well, and I'm not sure I will either.'

'I know it's going to be difficult, but don't forget you've also got Nan and Margaret. They'd like to help, even if it's just with the little things, so please do ask.'

'Yes, I know, and I promise you I will, but I don't know if I'll be able to cope, I really don't.'

'No, Richard. As long as you're here in Luckett House, you'll be positive about things. If you feel you need to scream and shout, take Bonkers out for a walk on the beach. Believe me, we find that works best. When I need to vent my frustrations, Bonkers doesn't even flinch. Honestly, you'll feel better soon, I promise.'

'What do you have to scream about, Hannah?'

'Men, Richard, or should I say boys who should be acting their age. Anyway, that's a long story and not one I really wish to go into now. Go and collect Josie and we'll all take one day at a time.'

'Thanks, Hannah. It does feel like Mum and I have found a lovely new family with you, Betty and Margaret. We're so lucky to be living here.'

'And the three of us can say the same having you and Josie here.'

Richard perked up a bit and began to look a lot better. As Hannah waved him off, Betty, Margaret and Bonkers came back along the path. The minute Bonkers spotted her, his tail started to wag and he bounded up to meet her. Margaret asked after Richard because he'd been so quiet and at one point in the hospital could well have been mistaken for the patient. Betty warned Hannah to be prepared for a shock on seeing Josie again as she'd lost a lot of weight and still didn't look very well. Hannah checked the time. She had to be getting ready for work, otherwise she'd be late.

'By the way, darling, I forgot to ask. How was your barbecue party yesterday?'

'It was fun, thanks, Nan. Very funny actually, but let's just say for all the wrong reasons. Some people left very happy indeed and others... Well, let's just say that they had the smile wiped off their face.'

'Oh, dear, that doesn't sound too good.'

'It was, Nan, believe me!'

Up at the hotel, Hannah's first task was to go through the day's check-ins. They all looked straightforward, no VIPs, no children. Housekeeping would have all the rooms ready for two o'clock and there were only two left. Next job was to check the restaurant and kitchen before taking a look at the emails.

'Hi, Hannah. I'm raring to go. By the way, next time you hold a barbecue, promise me you'll let me take care of the cooking. Those lads weren't very good at grilling burgers.'

'Oh, do be quiet, Jimmy. All the food got eaten, didn't it? Everyone had a lovely afternoon, so let's forget about all that and get down to some work.'

Hannah didn't feel too kindly disposed towards Jimmy. Of course the food was alright. It was simple enough to grill burgers and sausages on a barbecue. The thought of all the hours she'd have to spend with him was a depressing one. Could she find a job which would keep him out of her way for a few hours, and suddenly she thought of it. The emails! One of them was from David. He was requesting a report on all the outdoor tables and seating. He did say to ask the maintenance man, but who would know? This would teach him a lesson for criticising the cooking.

'So, Jimmy, this is what David's asked for. Are you sure you're up to it as I don't mind doing it if you think it's too complicated?'

There was no way Jimmy would do a poor job. Hearing the words 'report for David' was enough to set him off for the next three hours. Hannah did feel slightly guilty, but he'd do a good job and David would be impressed. Later he could start his restaurant training as he'd need to learn how to manage it and as Reception would be busy and she'd have to stay on the desk, Glen would have to train Jimmy. Hannah smiled to herself. Well, he shouldn't have criticised the boys' cooking!

For the next few hours Hannah started work preparing for Glenda's holiday. She worked from the back office in Reception, so she was available if it suddenly became busy with the phone calls.

'Ah, what have I done to upset you, Hannah?'

'Nothing at all, Glen, why? Oh, have you just seen what I've written on top of the restaurant booking list for tonight? You'll be fine. He's only training, learning the system. I think it will all be a big shock for him, especially when the chefs start shouting for the waiting staff to take the main courses out, and the guests are still eating their starters. Anyway, I thought you'd relish the opportunity to boss Jimmy around!'

They both had a good laugh about that, and Hannah's phone then bleeped with a text from Richard to say that Josie was home and Margaret and Betty were helping her into bed. She was very tired from the ordeal of the journey home and having to walk, but everything was going to plan.

'Right, Hannah, that's all done. What's next? I've made a list of the benches and the tables. The chairs are all okay, apart from the two which I've put in the maintenance room.'

'Now you'll have to detail it all in a report and email it over to David. Do you need a hand with that?'

'No, no, I'm perfectly capable. Once I've done that, do you want me to stay on Reception for check-ins?'

'No, you can report to Glen in the restaurant. He'll spend the dinner shift explaining the routine to you. Just a word of advice though. Be careful in the kitchen, the chefs can get a bit grumpy.'

Jimmy didn't reply, but headed off to write up his report. Hannah smiled, but realised that he would eventually have the last laugh as once his training was complete, they'd both be on an equal footing.

The evening shift was flowing smoothly. It was nearly nine-thirty and everything in the restaurant was running to plan. Glen had no problems with Jimmy as he seemed to be a natural, chatting away to customers about the food, pointing the fishing boats out to the diners. He certainly didn't need any more training.

There were only two more rooms to check-in; a couple on a three-night break who had already phoned to say they'd be late leaving London, and a business room for one. Hannah was now sorting through some of the following day's reservations on the computer when someone walked through the hotel entrance door. That someone was looking even more gorgeous than he had done the day before at her barbecue, if that was possible! In came Pete wearing a dark suit, white shirt and black and yellow tie.

'Hi, Pete, what brings you up here to the hotel? Nice to see you again.'

'Hello, Hannah. Nice to see you too. Sorry, I didn't put two and two together when you said you worked at a hotel. I didn't dream it would be this one. I've got a reservation here. The company I had the interview with today have asked me back again tomorrow, and they've booked me a room here because I said I had family nearby. Not that I'm really going to let Steve know I'm here. One dose of him in a week is enough. Sorry, that's your friend and my cousin, I'm talking about there.'

'He may well be your cousin, but I don't think I'd describe him as my friend, Pete.'

'I can imagine. I'll say no more.'

Hannah went through the motions of checking Pete in, pointing out where the fire exits were, the breakfast times and everything else he needed to know.

'One more thing. Can I book you a table for dinner? I'm afraid it does close in about twenty minutes though.'

'That would be great. I'm really hungry and I need to wind down after the day I've had today.'

'Shame you didn't know you'd be staying here earlier. You could have invited Emmi to dinner. I'm sure she would have enjoyed that.'

'Oh, please, Hannah, give me some credit. Do I look like the kind of guy who'd want to spend time with Emmi or the other one for that matter? What was her name? It was like a pop star's name, wasn't it?'

'Yes, kind of. It was Britney.'

'Sorry, but I really prefer intelligent conversation over dinner, and sharing it with someone I'd like to know a lot better. Would you be allowed to leave that desk and join me for dinner, Hannah?'

Chapter 48

Hannah would have loved the opportunity to have had dinner with Pete, but unfortunately she was on duty and getting familiar with guests was very much frowned upon. However, she did happen to linger around when he was leaving the restaurant and they were able to chat for a while. She learnt that he was being interviewed by a large accountancy company in Norwich. How she wished he'd get the job. It would be lovely to meet someone who wasn't part of her past or from the local towns. Although she wouldn't change her job or her home for anything, having a bit of fun away from the area would be perfect, she thought to herself. Perhaps it was a pipedream though, after all it did depend on whether he was the successful candidate for the role and of course he'd make more friends in Norwich.

Back to real life and her thoughts turned towards Josie. Hannah hadn't been able to see her since her discharge from hospital, but today she had to prepare herself for that. She knew it wouldn't be easy, but this was yet another occasion where she had to be brave and remain positive for Richard's sake. She would use Bonkers as the perfect excuse to pop downstairs. It felt strange not being in her own flat, but hopefully everything was more convenient downstairs for Josie and she would learn to cope with it. Before knocking on the door, Hannah decided to go to Betty's and catch up with the news.

'Hi, Nan. How are you? Has anyone taken Bonkers for his morning walk yet?'

'No, not yet. Margaret was going to, but he's refused to leave Josie's side since she's been home. He wouldn't have even eaten if Richard hadn't taken his bowl into the bedroom.'

'How sweet! How is she, Nan?'

'Okay, I think. Well, she's looking a lot better for being at home. Obviously yesterday was a long day for her and she was tired, but Richard told Margaret that she was comfortable and had a good night's sleep. The district nurse is scheduled to call in this morning, so why don't you pop in too? First of all though, I was thinking of holding a little party before the weather starts to change, a sort of garden warming party. What do you think?'

'That would be a great idea, and if Josie could get involved, it would give her something to focus on. By the way, have you heard from Dad since he left?'

'No, I haven't, but it's not him I'm waiting to speak to. Before long Susanna will be on the phone bending my ear about moving. Anyway, I'm ready for her. Hannah, darling, you and I haven't spent any time together lately. How about we do something on your day off?'

'I'd love that, Nan, but it won't be until next week. I'm sure we'll sort something out though.'

Hannah hugged Betty goodbye and went down to see Josie. She was sure she'd be able to persuade Bonkers to go out with her for a coastal walk. Once he smelt the sea air there'd be no stopping him.

'Hi, Hannah, do come in. How's things?'

'Fine, thanks, and how's the patient today? I've heard you've also got a very stubborn dog who won't go out for a walk anymore. Margaret might take no for an answer, but I'm afraid I won't. Coming to get you, Bonkers.'

Richard led the way into the bedroom where Josie was resting. It all felt rather strange to Hannah as this was really her flat.

'Hello, Hannah. First of all, thank you so much for letting me stay here. I doubt they'd have let me out of hospital if they'd have known about the stairs. Oh, look, Bonkers has managed to get up for you.

307

Margaret and Richard haven't been able to coax him away from my bedside since I've got back.'

'Well, Bonkers. I think that might be about to change. I'm just as stubborn as you, so don't give me that look. Where's that wagging tail?'

Hannah really appreciated Bonkers being in the room because it was such a shock to see poor Josie looking so dreadful. However, she was very positive in her thinking, chatting about moving back upstairs although Hannah wasn't too sure that would ever happen. Between them, they persuaded Bonkers to go out for a walk, and to be honest, once on the coastal path with all its familiar smells, he was soon back to his normal self.

The early morning cloud was now beginning to fade away and it had the makings of a beautiful sunny day. Hannah wished she could stay on the beach all day, but sadly it was a working day and she needed to be at the hotel. On a positive note, it was Jimmy's day off so she wouldn't have him to contend with, and Mrs Van Lincoln was due to check out. Sadly, so too was Pete.

'Come on, Bonkers, we've just enough time to walk to the other end. There's your ball, go fetch.'

For the next half an hour they both had fun playing together with the ball and sticks which Bonkers kept finding. Hannah looked at her watch and decided that she'd best start making her way back home. Surprisingly, Bonkers came running back the moment she headed for the path. Normally, he had to be cajoled and tricked to return, but perhaps he knew it was time to go, and was missing being with Josie. Hannah quickly glanced at her phone. There was a text from Olivia asking whether she'd be able to meet up the next day and another from Carl with the same question, but before replying to either of them she'd have to juggle a few things round at the hotel.

As they neared Luckett House a car had pulled up onto the driveway. It was the district nurse arriving for Josie. Hannah let her in and then took Bonkers out into the garden, where Betty and Margaret were enjoying a coffee.

'Hi, Hannah, can I get you anything to drink?'

'Coffee, please, Nan.'

'I see you've had more luck with Bonkers than I did. He wasn't having any of it earlier today, but I expect he's realised that Josie will be here when he gets back. He must have been so upset when she wasn't around. Oh, just look at him. How he loves that spot in the garden. Talking of the garden, Betty tells me we're going to have a welcoming garden party. Isn't that exciting?'

'It is, and I'm leaving it entirely in your hands. I want you three lovely ladies to organise it as a surprise, if that's alright.'

'Fine by me, but I doubt Josie will be able to do too much. I haven't mentioned it to Richard, but I do think we have one very sick lady there.'

'I was thinking the same thing. Have they mentioned whether she'll need to go back into hospital for chemo or radiotherapy treatment? It's so sad, isn't it, Margaret? Just when we've all got so much to look forward to.'

'It certainly makes you stop and take stock of life. I so wish I'd done that years ago, all those wasted years with Frank. I wonder what kind of life I would have had if I had... No, I mustn't go down that path, but I will say that I've never felt so good as I do now.'

'There you go, darling, one coffee and a nice piece of cake to go with it.'

The three of them sat in the sunshine talking together for the next hour, but there was a sombre mood about their chat. Life hadn't really turned out how they had planned when they had moved here, and this was going to affect them all. Eventually

Richard joined them as the district nurse was leaving and Josie had gone back to sleep. Hannah felt she had to lighten the mood, but didn't quite know what to do. It was important to remain positive and show a united front.

'Come on, everyone, let's get our thinking caps on,' said Betty, getting a note pad and pen. 'We need to plan this garden party. Do we want to have a theme? I was thinking an afternoon party would be better than a barbecue.'

'Nan, you've just said it, a garden party just like the Queen gives on the lawn of the palace. Nice little sandwiches, quiche and cakes followed with plenty of tea. A good old-fashioned afternoon tea party with perhaps some wine. Every party must have some alcohol, after all. Anyway, I must get ready for work now, so I'll leave you lovely ladies to your planning. Don't forget the entertainment though.'

'Entertainment! You don't generally have entertainment at an afternoon tea gathering, but what a clever thought. Why not have a tea dance? Darling, that's a fabulous idea. Have a good shift at work, see you later.'

That had given them all something to concentrate on and it was good to see Richard getting involved with it too. Back at the hotel, Mrs Van Lincoln had checked out, but unfortunately so too had Pete, although Hannah noticed an entry in the handover book to record that Pete had left a belt in his hotel room and they had left a message on his answerphone to ask whether they should post it to him. Hannah had a quick catch up session with Glenda who had suggested that Jimmy should be left in charge for his first solo Duty Manager shift, but one of them could be on call should he have any problems. Hannah agreed, planning that for the following evening. She could then spend the evening at home but be ready to pop in if she was needed.

The shift was going well. Hannah had spoken with Olivia and Carl and they were coming around to hers for dinner tomorrow, although she did warn them there was a possibility she could be called away if Jimmy couldn't cope with the hotel duties alone.

All the new check-ins had arrived, so Hannah sent the receptionist off for her break. As she was checking the following day's business, the phone rang. Immediately she recognised the caller as Pete. He was returning the call about his belt, asking if it was possible for it to be kept safe until the weekend when he could collect it. He was returning on Sunday as he would be spending Monday with the company in Norwich.

'That's fine. We'll have it put into your room for your arrival. It will be nice to see you again.'

'Thank you, and it will be good to see you too, Hannah. You don't happen to have Sunday night off, do you? I was hoping we could have dinner together.'

Chapter 49

Hannah spent a relaxing and uninterrupted evening with Olivia and Carl. She was tempted to ring Glen at the hotel to see if everything was running smoothly, but she decided against it, it wasn't fair. Jimmy seemed to be coping well, and as she hadn't received any calls during the evening, it was safe to assume he was coping well and everything was in hand.

The one thing she didn't mention to Olivia and Carl was her forthcoming dinner date with Pete on Sunday. She thought about it once or twice as his name had come up in conversation, but something stopped her and she brushed it aside. At one point, however, she did notice Olivia giving her a quizzical look, probably wondering whether something was going on.

As it was only 10.30pm, Hannah knew the Night Manager would now be on duty so it was safe to pour another glass of wine. It was a bit breezy, so she dressed up warmly and took her glass down to the sheltered part of the garden. It was strange having to go the long way round, but she didn't want to disturb Josie and Richard. Something stirred in the bushes, she heard the rustling of leaves and was at first rather startled, but then she saw the familiar wagging tail and realised it was Bonkers. Richard was there too.

'Hi, Richard. How's Josie been doing?'

'Good, thanks. She's eaten well and we've spent quite a while chatting. You've had a busy day, haven't you? I noticed you had some friends round earlier, not that I was being nosey of course.'

'Yes, it was Carl and Olivia. They finished off a couple of bottles of wine, but I couldn't have any as I was technically on call for work. Jimmy's done his first solo Duty Manager shift, so I thought it best to remain sober in case I heard from him with problems from the hotel. Now I'm having that well-earned glass of wine as everything appears to be fine.'

'Isn't Olivia the one with the little boys?'

'Yes, I was worried about her recently as her ex-husband appeared for a couple of days. He hasn't had anything to do with them for so long, I didn't want him thinking he could just swan back and everything would be forgiven. I think she pointed out that she wasn't a free meal ticket and that he'd have to go out to work and put in an effort. That seemed to frighten him off again. To be honest, I don't think Olivia wanted him back anyway; it was just her way of making sure he'd go for good.

'Carl's got himself a new chap who lives in London and his parents are fine about it all. I'm so pleased for him as it was difficult for him to tell his mum. You wouldn't believe how protective she's been with him growing up, but I think she knew all along really. Now she's planning trips to London with them, and Carl and his dad seem much closer too. He always loved working in the family business, but didn't think he could be gay and still be a builder, probably scared about the reaction from people. He has been on the receiving end of a fair few comments, but he now realises that the secret is to stay one step ahead and join in the banter. He did also say that since Frank died the working relationship is so much better. He wasn't a very nice person by all accounts. Oh, I'm terribly sorry, Richard. I've just remembered. He was your dad.'

'Well, I know I'm his flesh and blood, but I've never had a dad. It even sounds odd talking about it, but he was never a part of my life and I'm actually grateful for that. Josie and I haven't missed out by not having him around. It's nice to see the scrapbooks and to keep them for nostalgia, but I don't really feel any kind of family connection towards him.'

'So you've not had a father in your life. Have you ever had a partner?'

'Oh, you're opening up a real can of worms there, I wouldn't know where to start. Me and men! My story's the complete opposite of Carl's. I worked in the fashion industry, which as you know, employs many gay men. In fact, we outnumbered the straights, but that doesn't answer your question, does it? Yes, there's been a few over the years. Some lasted months, and a couple even lasted for years, but the truth is I was such a workaholic that anyone I was in a relationship with knew they came second to that. I know that sounds bad, but I was always honest with them. I've paid the price though. The consequence is that now my career's over, I've only got myself to blame.'

'Your career's far from over, Richard. You've still got so much to give.'

'No, I don't. I'm only there because of a contract that had been signed years ago by the lovely Gina and in a way I'm thankful I'm not there. I need to be here with my mum as she needs me now. Hand on heart, I wouldn't want to be anywhere else. This isn't going to go well, Hannah. It's just the start. They've removed a massive tumour from her bowel, but the cancer's still there and I just need to accept that every day she's with us is a blessing.'

With that, Richard broke down and cried like a baby. What could Hannah do apart from hold him and be there for him? It brought back sad memories for her, just like her own dad waiting for her mum to pass away. He'd put a brave face on things for a while and then there were moments when everything got too much and it all just fell apart. This was so sad, but Richard had to understand that he had

314

support, not just because they all lived in the same house, but because they all cared for him and Josie.

'Richard, can I ask you about those scrapbooks? Do you think it would be nice to show them to Josie? She wouldn't need to know who put them all together, but she's so proud of you and all you've achieved.'

'I've spent quite a bit of time looking through them while Mum's been in hospital. It was nice to have something to take my mind off it, and interesting to look back at all the work I've put in. I'm sure Mum would love to see them, but I'll think about showing her when the time's right. Anyway, enough about me. What's new with you, Hannah? How's the hotel and I don't mean Jimmy.'

'Jimmy's working hard, being careful to say and do the right things. I know people think I should give him a second chance, and there have been times when I've considered it, but I'm happy with life at the moment. Why rock the boat? I love my job and I want to pour all my energies into it, so Jimmy's definitely a no-no.'

'That sounds just like my story. Where did throwing myself into work get me? Lonely and by myself, and I can tell you that it's not always such a fun place to find yourself. Think about it, coming home to an empty house night after night, cooking a meal for one and then sitting there by yourself with only the television for company. No one to discuss things with, and then at the end of the day going to a cold, empty bed. Eventually you'll come to a point where the novelty wears off and you realise it's such a lonely existence.'

Chapter 50

The next few days passed by in a bit of a daze for Hannah as she tried to think things through. She needed to be there for Richard, Betty and Margaret, although she was pleased to see how much stronger Josie was getting. She had even managed to get out into the garden several times despite it being very tiring for her. Josie loved sitting by her bedroom window with its view up the hill towards where her family home used to be. The house itself had now been demolished and in its place stood a modern mini mansion, but the lane itself and the trees were just as she remembered from her happy childhood days. Richard had spent long periods of time discussing special times spent there, the family occasions and memories would always remain in her heart.

Richard had planned to return to London later during the week, so Betty was going to stay with Josie. He needed to check his flat and pop into the fashion house as well as getting a bit of time to himself. The future was uncertain. Hannah had a feeling that he'd think about closing down his life in London. After all, his life would revolve around his mother more now, so it made sense to concentrate on life in Norfolk.

But this evening Luckett House and the problems of its residents were taking a back seat. Hannah was going out on a date with Pete, and she had kept this a secret from Betty and Olivia for fear of inviting bad luck. She hadn't felt this way about a date for years. Actually, come to think about it, she had never felt this way about a date as she and Jimmy had tended to spend their time with university friends. No, this was different. Pete had invited her for dinner in a very upmarket restaurant in Burnham Market and this meant she had to look her best.

How to get out of the flat without anyone seeing her and asking questions was another matter to contend with. For this reason she had arranged to meet Pete at the top of the hill just before it turned into the hotel. It was a cool evening and she had decided it would be better to be slightly late instead of having to stand around and wait for Pete, but it would be chilly later, so she was taking a pashmina with her. Normally she would have taken her faithful Levi jacket, but this was special. She needed to make a good impression, and a pashmina would complement her new dress perfectly.

Glancing at the clock, Hannah saw it was 7.25. Richard had just come in from the garden with Bonkers. Her stomach was tying itself in knots, but this was understandable as she was about to head out on a real date with an extremely nice man.

'Hi, Pete. Sorry I'm a bit late.'

'Not a problem. Wow, you look lovely.'

The minute Pete had noticed Hannah walking along the last part of the lane, he stepped out of the car to open the door for her. Not only was he good looking, but he had such chivalrous manners. Dressed smartly in a crisp white shirt with a casual jacket and trousers, he looked every inch the gentleman.

It was only a ten-minute drive to Burnham, but Hannah had prepared herself well for the date by checking out the restaurant online and acquainting herself with the menu choices. Pate for starters, followed by the sea bass would be ideal, but of course she hadn't let Pete into this little secret.

'Oh, by the way, I've brought the belt you left in the hotel.'

'Thanks. I'd forgotten all about that. Just throw it on the back seat. How has your day been? Hope you haven't had to work all day.'

'I only had to do the early shift, but it was pretty quiet. Just guests checking out after weekend breaks. It should all pick up again tomorrow. Oh, sorry, Pete. I forgot to ask. Did you get the job you were interviewed for in Norwich?'

'Yes, they did offer it to me, but I need to decide whether I really want it or not. Ah, here we are, I've seen such good reviews about this restaurant. Most said that they didn't feel rushed to finish their meals for the next customer.'

So he doesn't know whether he'll accept the job or not. Wonder why that is. It's a bit strange to go to the trouble of attending an interview if you don't know whether you want the job or not. So tonight could be a one-off if he ends up living in London. That's not really a good start to the evening, but I'll have to put that to the back of my mind. Perhaps I could persuade him to take the job!

Pete parked the car, came round to the passenger side of the car and held the door open for Hannah. They then headed into the restaurant where they were shown to a little drinks area where their order was taken and they were handed a menu. Hannah looked at it and pointed out various things just to make conversation as she had already chosen her meal in advance. Two other couples were studying the menus. They had acknowledged Hannah and Pete, but did not engage in further conversation. Hannah looked around. All clear, no one there she recognised! The barman returned with their drinks, both a gin and tonic, and the start of a lovely evening.

They were then led into the private dining room, a real couples' restaurant. Hannah was glad she had gone to the extra trouble of buying a new dress for the occasion. She would have felt so out of place wearing any of her day-to-day outfits. Yes, this was very special indeed. It was the type of restaurant where waiters pulled out the chairs for you and also placed napkins on your laps. But was it too posh? A gorgeous restaurant was one thing, but this was quite another. Hannah wanted to get to know Pete a little better and she was beginning to think it would be rather difficult in this atmosphere.

'Is everything alright, Hannah? Would you prefer red wine with your meal?'

'Oh, no, it's fine. Everything's lovely, thanks. It's such a beautiful place. I was just admiring the splendour and taking it all in.'

That was a far different answer than the real thoughts in Hannah's mind. If truth be known, she would have rather been in a nice cosy pub restaurant. The starters arrived, and she was glad she had ordered the pate because it came with a selection of homemade bread rolls. She would have loved to have eaten them all, but she had to keep up an appearance and that would have seemed greedy.

Pete had ordered a delicious looking mushroom starter. Soon they both started to relax in each other's company and Hannah soon began to feel a lot more comfortable. Whether that was down to the alcohol, she wasn't really sure but she did feel that Pete was interested in her as they chatted about their lives. She explained how the house and area had always been a part of her life, but she'd never dreamed of living and working in the area. She also briefly touched on the subject of Jimmy, although she wasn't aware of how much Pete knew about that. By the time she had stopped talking, they'd nearly finished their main course, which was just as beautiful as the starters.

Hannah was just about to ask Pete about his life when she noticed the manager showing a couple to their table. Was 'couple' even the right word? The woman must have easily been in her 50s, and the man? Well, that just happened to be Tristan.

'Something wrong, Hannah?'

'No, it's just that I know one of the two people who have just come in. Thankfully, he hasn't seen me though. Ah, that's good he has his back to me.'

Hannah continued to tell Pete the story of Tristan, which he found quite amusing. The waiter came to clear their plates and asked whether they'd like a break before ordering dessert.

'I've told you all there is to know about me, now tell me about yourself, Pete. Where were you born?'

'You'd like to know where I was born, rather than where I live now or where I grew up?'

They both laughed. Pete told Hannah that he was born in Manchester, but had never lived there. His parents just happened to be visiting the area when he was born a few weeks prematurely. He had been brought up in Suffolk, the neighbouring county to Norfolk, and that's where the connection had first been made. His family were scattered across both counties. Pete had gone to university in London and hadn't left the capital on starting work. He loved his job, loved the city atmosphere, but just felt it was time to make a fresh start before getting stuck in his ways and becoming bored.

'So you're thinking about the Norfolk job because you have family here?'

'No, not really. Norwich is just a nice city and the job looks exciting. It's something I think I'll be able to really get my teeth into, but I haven't made my mind up completely yet.'

'I'm sorry, Pete. I am listening to you, but that chap I know who came in with the older woman. They're holding hands and she's just stroked his face. Isn't that all a bit odd? Yes, you do need to make a decision soon, but it's best to just go with your heart, I think. Excuse me for a moment. I'm just going to the ladies, but if the waiter comes back, could you order the lemon pavlova for me, please?'

Hannah made her exit, thankful she didn't need to walk past Tristan's table. On her way back, and out of sight of the dining room, the restaurant manager asked her if everything was alright with the meal. Hannah told him how wonderful it all was, but also added how embarrassed she was because the lady with Tristan had said good evening to her, but she had forgotten the lady's name.

'You mean Mrs Camilla Rugstool?'

'Yes, that's it, thanks. I knew her name was Camilla, but couldn't recall her surname.'

Back at the table the desserts had arrived. Pete brought Hannah up to date on what had happened during her absence. The woman had dropped her napkin, the man had got up to pick it up and she thanked him with a kiss.

'Nothing surprises me about him, but to give him his due he was very much down on his luck a couple of weeks ago and now look at him dining out with Camilla Rugstool.'

'Are you sure that's who it is?'

'Yes, I told the restaurant manager a little white lie, and he told me her name.'

'Now you realise who she is, you'll understand just how well that chap has done for himself.'

'Sorry? I haven't heard of her before. Should I have?'

'Rugstool Estates. Her family own a huge part of Norfolk. They're one of the wealthiest families in the whole county.'

'That makes sense. He's just like a little field mouse which gets in everywhere. What a smarmy so and so. Anyway, just like all the other times, he's sure to mess up on the way. Mark my words. Hopefully she'll keep him away from the hotel though.'

After desserts they had coffee together. As Pete

was driving, he had declined more alcohol but felt relaxed enough to open up more about himself. Hannah got the impression that although he and Steve were cousins, they didn't see each other regularly. She also realised that he wasn't in the habit of dining at such upmarket restaurants.

It was now getting late and as Pete had an early start in Norwich the next day, he paid the bill and they made their way to leave. Luckily enough Tristan and Camilla had already left so there would be no awkward moments.

As they drove back to Luckett Quay, Hannah considered inviting Pete in. She would have loved to, but it was Josie's flat after all, and anyway, Pete did need to be up early in the morning. There was also the question of whether Betty would see them both.

'Thanks for a lovely evening, Hannah. I've really enjoyed tonight. However, there's something I do need to tell you, and it's something I ought to have mentioned earlier. I didn't think you'd go out with me if I told you I'm married. Well, it's just on paper really as I'm going through a divorce. I'm sorry, I should have been more up front about this, and the real reason why I can't decide on the job in Norfolk is that I have a daughter to consider.'

Chapter 51

'Damn, what a waste of a night out,' Hannah heard herself saying, although deep down she knew that was far from the truth. She'd had a lovely night out, the best she'd had for years, but why had Pete spoilt it by telling her that he was married with a child? However, perhaps it was to his credit that he had been honest. Many guys in similar circumstances certainly wouldn't have mentioned it.

Anyway, today was a new day and best to put it all behind her. Even if Pete were to take the job in Norfolk, did she really want a relationship with someone carrying such a lot of baggage with them? Hannah knew it was wrong to think like that, a child can hardly be considered baggage, but she just felt as though it would be far too much hassle what with everything else in her life at the moment.

She needed to see if Richard was up as she wanted to take Bonkers out on the beach for some fresh sea air, and if the tide was out they could walk over to Saltmarsh Quay for a bacon sandwich. That was exactly what Hannah needed. She wasn't overly hungry after the wonderful meal at the restaurant the previous evening, but a bacon sandwich would go a long way in helping her to deal with her problems.

Once down on the beach Bonkers did his normal running around and sniffing at everything, but once he realised they weren't just staying on Luckett Beach, but going for a longer walk around the cliff, he looked at Hannah as if to say thank you. There were always more dogs to run and play with over in Saltmarsh and throwing sticks and teasing Bonkers took Hannah's mind off everything. She felt so blessed to be able to do this at any time she wanted and it was on her doorstep. There had still not been any word from her dad or Susanna but Nan had been adamant that there was no way she'd be selling Hannah's flat. Yesterday she'd even commented on the fact that supposing it had been her who had been taken ill instead of Josie. It would have been such a relief to know that Hannah was living next door.

'Come on, Bonkers, this way. Hope we're not too early for the sandwich. I don't need to be at work until two o'clock so we've got the whole morning to ourselves. What do you think of that then? You haven't got a clue what I'm talking about, have you, Bonkers? I bet you'd quickly understand if I said the word 'bacon' though.'

Hannah put Bonkers back on the lead as they got nearer to the quayside and headed up to Audrey's Boathouse where the little café had not long opened. Bonkers was allowed in if he behaved himself, so Hannah ordered the sandwich, a large black coffee and an extra slice of bacon just for him, and went to sit down with one of the daily newspapers from the table. She felt quite isolated from the rest of the world, she hardly knew what was happening in London, let alone abroad, so it was nice to relax with her coffee and sandwich and catch up with world events.

Everyone was friendly here, they loved to make a fuss of Bonkers and Hannah whiled away the time easily. She was just deciding whether the tide would be out long enough for them to be able to walk back along the beach or whether they'd have to take the coastal path to the hotel and back down the other side, when two voices said hello. It was Tom and Steve who had passed by for a sandwich before starting work.

'Hi, how are you two?'

'Fine thanks. Is it your day off?'

'No, Tom. I'm working the late Duty Manager shift today, so I thought I'd take Bonkers out for a long walk and have a little treat.'

'Really? I'm surprised you've got room for any more food after last night. Pete told me about it this morning. He said it was the best meal he'd had for ages. Did you have a nice time? Pete's a nice lad, you know, not loud and cocky like I am.'

Tom's face was a picture. How dare she go out on a date without first checking with him. He needed to get over it. Hannah just wasn't in the mood for this.

'Yes, the food was lovely and we had a wonderful time. Such a gorgeous restaurant, but a bit on the posh side. I felt a bit out of place if I'm honest. I'm more at home in the back room of a pub than a five-star restaurant, but yes, we had a lovely evening.'

'Well, you made a good impression on Pete. Something tells me he'll be accepting that job offer today.'

'Come on, Steve. If you don't stop chatting away, we won't have time for that bacon sandwich before work. See you later, Hannah.'

Grumpy so and so, or should I say jealous so and so. I'm going to have to sort this out once and for all. I know I've said that before, but this time I mean it.

Hannah decided to return via the coastal path as it was a bit of a gamble to bank on the tide being out long enough for them to walk along the beach. As they were walking up towards the hotel, they recognised someone coming the other way. Bonkers was getting excited, it was Margaret!

'You've been out early today. Couldn't you sleep? To be honest, neither could I what with Josie being constantly on my mind. Have you got a minute or two for a chat? Where were you off to last night? I must say you looked most glamorous. Special night, was it?'

'Thanks, Margaret, but it's a bit of a long story, and yes, I did have a lovely evening. Where did you see me though?'

'I was just shutting the window when I noticed you going up the lane. You looked so beautiful in that dress and pashmina. He was a very lucky man to be out with you. Anyway, I really wanted to talk about Josie. She's so poorly these days. Although I've known of her for most of my adult life, and we lived together in the house, we never discussed Frank.

'I'd put him to the back of my mind, but sooner or later I know she'll want to talk about him. Seeing her suffer is so painful, that I don't really want to be alone with her, and Richard will be going back to London soon. She's spent so much time talking about her childhood living here on the hill, and the conversation is moving on through her life, so the next thing will be Frank and how she fell in love with him. The thing is, greed overtook his life and I've said it so many times, that man ruined so many lives including his own. It's not easy to discuss it all with her.'

'Margaret, I don't think any of this is really about Frank. It's more about getting to a point in your life when you reminisce about the past. Josie just wants to live her life through her memories and I doubt whether Frank will play too much of a part in those. We'll just have to listen to her and help her to create some more. She needs you and me, as well as Richard and Bonkers, so let's just take one day at a time and help her in whatever ways we can.'

'Do you really think it's as simple as that? I understand what you mean though because I'm just the same. I often think of happy times before Frank and then skip the decades in between and concentrate on times when we've walked Bonkers on the beach or sat out in the garden with perhaps one glass of wine too many. Those are the things which are special to me, and I'm so grateful that I've been able to do them. It would have been very sad indeed if I'd have passed away before having this wonderful opportunity to live here in Luckett House.'

'And we're going to have many more lovely times with Josie, and into the future too, but we have to remain strong. This is a time of reflection for Josie, so let's make some lovely memories for Richard. He needs us, Margaret, but the truth is, we all need each other.'

'For such a young girl, you have such a wise head on your shoulders, Hannah. That man last night was such a lucky chap. He'll hold onto you if he's got any sense.'

But that would only be if I wanted him to keep hold of me. Perhaps this head isn't as wise as you think. Maybe I want something that my head tells me is wrong.

Chapter 52

Richard had gone back to London for two nights, so Hannah had popped in to say goodbye to him before going into work. She could tell that Josie was putting on a brave face by saying how much better she was feeling, but this was an act to make Richard feel happier about leaving her. Margaret had taken Bonkers for a nice long walk and now it was time for Betty to take over. Things would be different now as she informed Hannah there'd be three days and two nights of fun before Richard's return.

With Glenda away, Hannah was in charge of things up at the hotel. It didn't really feel any different though as she was used to sharing responsibilities, but this time she had Jimmy's support. Her first jobs were to check through the reservations for the following days, look out for any VIP special requests, and then check each department. Rather than have a ten o'clock meeting with heads of department, Glenda and Hannah preferred to personally walk around the building and visit each department to talk to the teams. It also gave her an opportunity to ask if there were any maintenance issues. If so, she could mention them to Bill, the maintenance man, and the jobs would get done quicker. Bill was known to be something of a shirker, and Glenda and Hannah knew that this approach worked best.

Off to the kitchen. Thankfully, Jimmy was on the late shift, and unavailable but everything seemed to be fine. There were a few fish dishes which were not on the lunch menu, but apart from that everything else seemed to be in order. Into the restaurant for a quiet lunch before the hotel started to get busy, and finally back to Reception, where once again everything was working well. Most guests had checked out and the new arrivals listings looked straightforward. Now to the emails with some toast and a large coffee.

The first email was from David saying that he was aware that Glenda was away and that Hannah should not hesitate to contact him if she needed anything and that he would back her in the event of any issues. The remaining emails were either general sales-y type junk or things which Reception could easily handle. Hannah was feeling quite pleased with herself. There had been no hitches or issues to contend with and the morning had gone well. With that, there was a knock at the office door, Jimmy had arrived.

'Hi, aren't you a little early? You're not due on duty until half past two. What can I do for you, Jimmy?'

'I had to come in to phone a large meat order through and so I thought I'd come in for a chat if you aren't too busy, that is.'

'Actually, I think I'm a bit ahead of myself. Just need to check outside in the gardens, so we can chat whilst I check the bins and outside furniture, if you like.'

Jimmy's face immediately lit up. Perhaps he was pleased that she hadn't given him the brush off like she normally would have done, but things were different now he was a hotel employee. He was part of the team running the hotel and that meant being in contact with Hannah. They chatted about business matters, profit and loss budgets, which he needed help with, and also about how to work out costs. Hannah was smiling to herself; this wasn't quite the Jimmy she remembered.

'Hope you don't mind me saying, but you do seem to have matured quickly. Don't take that as a patronising comment though, Jimmy, I really didn't mean it that way.'

'No offence taken, Hannah. It's just that I have you to thank for all this. Your work ethic is so precise and thorough, and you never cut corners. I started to realise that when we were in London, but working here I've noticed it more. The thing that comes across more than anything else is that life is so much easier when everything is done correctly and methodically. Working here is never a chore, it's actually really enjoyable.'

'That's great to hear. To be honest, I doubted whether you'd stay. I knew you'd get the kitchen organised, but after that I thought you'd be leaving.'

'Oh, no, I'd have stayed even if David hadn't given me all this extra responsibility. I want to build a strong team and take the restaurant forward, but now with the duty management shifts I've realised that I want to make this hotel one of the best in the area.'

'I'm proud of you, Jimmy. I really am.'

'Thanks, so much, Hannah, it really means so much to me. Things could easily have been so different, couldn't they? I could have been a real disaster, but thankfully everything seems alright now. You do realise that the main reason I came here was to win you back and tell you that I haven't given up on that.'

'That's enough now, Jimmy. My pager's just gone off and I need to get back to Reception. I'll see you at handover time. Enjoy your morning off.'

The pager couldn't have been better timed and they went their separate ways. Hannah felt good remembering the first time she'd met Jimmy at university. Life was fun then, they didn't have a worry in the world apart from big dreams. They were going to travel the world and have fun. Life hadn't quite worked out the way they'd imagined. After university they'd needed to get jobs and pay their way, and to be honest they then started taking each other for granted. Hannah did wonder whether things would have been different if they had only just met now that Jimmy was more mature. Yes, she thought to herself. That would have been good.

The pager message was to tell Hannah that a man in the lounge wanted to see her. Was it Tristan? He'd be the last person she'd want to see. Perhaps he'd seen her with Pete in the restaurant the other evening. Or had he found something else to moan about it. If so, she could always bring Mrs Rugstool into the conversation.

'Oh, Carl, sorry, I wasn't expecting to see you. Do you have time for a coffee?'

'Yes, if it's no trouble.'

Hannah went off to get the coffees, wondering why Carl wasn't at work and why he was dressed so casually. Maybe he was going to London to see Mike.

'Here we go. One coffee and some homemade biscuits. What is it, Carl? You look like the cat that's got the cream.'

'I am! And I can't wait to tell you. I nearly did when we were with Olivia the other day, but I didn't want to put the kiss of death on it before things were finalised.'

'Slow down, Carl, I'm a bit confused, but do tell me everything before you burst and make a huge mess on the carpet.'

'Okay. Well, I've bought a cottage down in Saltmarsh, and I'm so excited about it all. Yes, it's a bit of a mess at the moment. It needs a complete refurb, but that's the exciting part, getting to choose everything from scratch. I wanted to mention it weeks ago, but I was so afraid that something would fall through. Look, I've got the keys today, and apart from Mum, Dad and Mike you're the first to know, and I have you to thank for all this.'

'Me? How do you mean, me?'

331

'Well, none of this would have happened if you hadn't encouraged me to come out and showed me that I can be exactly what I want to be. Mike is just as excited about it as I am. He can't wait to come here at weekends and just get away from London. He's also hoping to be able to work from home some days. It sounds so funny, I can't believe, it, I've bought myself a home.'

'I'm thrilled to bits for you both, but if you two are going to be spending time here in Norfolk, how is your mum going to take the news? She had her heart set on going to London at weekends.'

'There's nothing to stop her from still going, although Dad must set her a budget! Anyway, hopefully I'll be able to get most of the work completed in two months. I'll need a new kitchen and bathroom and the whole place decorated throughout. Oh, I'm so excited about it all.'

'And so you should be; you really deserve it. Now, I'm sorry but I'm going to have to get some work done. There's my pager going off again. No doubt you need to go and change clothes seeing that you have a whole cottage to pull to bits. I'm really looking forward to seeing your new party house. We could do with a good rave up.'

'Sorry to bother you, Hannah, but Mr Dove is on the phone and he's asking to speak to you personally.'

'Hello, Mr Dove ... okay, sorry, Raymond. That's no problem at all, a table for four at eight o'clock. Would you like me to reserve your favourite one at the side of the room? Ah, okay, you'd prefer the one in the middle by the window. I'm off tonight but Glen and the rest of the team will be here. Yes, no problem. I know I can relax when he's running the shift. Have a lovely evening.'

That's a straightforward booking. He hasn't asked for any extras, so it can't be a celebration or anything. Right, now to get the lunch service started as the bar looks like it's getting rather busy, and lots of people are taking snacks out onto the lawn. Hannah realised how much she'd miss all this at the end of the summer when guests wouldn't be able to enjoy a drink in the sunshine.

It would be the same at Luckett House if it wasn't for the conservatory. Although, what with living upstairs in Josie's flat she wouldn't have quite so much opportunity to use it. Hannah paused to check her phone. A text from Betty to reassure her that everything was fine and she was preparing lunch for herself and Josie to enjoy in the garden.

Within no time at all it was two-thirty. Jimmy was ready to take over the reins as Duty Manager. He did look quite suave in his new suit, but there again Hannah had always considered him sexy even in his chef whites. It was a quick handover, as there were only six arrivals due, and unless they all arrived at the same time the receptionist would be quite able to cope by herself. Hannah mentioned that Raymond Dove would be dining during the evening, but Glen could easily manage that.

'So, off you go, Hannah. Don't worry about anything here. I'm fine with it all.'

'I think I'll wait until Glen comes in at five as I'd like to go through some rotas and bits and pieces with him, but I'll leave you to it, Jimmy. You're sailing the ship now. Talking of ships, do you remember when we were on holiday in Spain and we got stuck out in the waves when we hired a pedalo for the afternoon? Wasn't it embarrassing having to be rescued by helicopter, but I can see the funny side of it now, of course.'

'Oh, yes, that was such a lovely holiday. All our holidays were special, Hannah, it was only our jobs which got in the way. Perhaps we could have a holiday together again some time, just as friends, you understand, no strings attached.'

'Just as friends, Jimmy? Holiday, alcohol, summer sun, no, I really don't think that would work out. Anyway, I can't see David letting us both take leave at the same time, leaving Glenda completely by herself here, so that's a real non-starter.'

Hannah's meeting with Glen was successful with the pair of them finalising a whole month's restaurant rotas and organising the function diary. A quick call to Betty to see whether she needed her to pick anything up on the way home and that was that, all finished for the day. Josie had tired herself out being in the garden, and was now having a rest, and Betty was reading her book. Bonkers was up with Margaret, so everything was fine back at Luckett House.

As they walked through the front door, she noticed the mail sitting on the hall table. She picked up all the envelopes and went up to the flat to relax for the evening with a glass of wine. Curiosity got the better of her – who was the post from? She could see that two of them were general reminders and credit card offers, but the third was handwritten in an unfamiliar style.

Inside was a small piece of paper with no more than a sentence on it.

'I know you're seeing my husband and while I don't have a problem with it as we're getting divorced, I think you should know that you aren't the only one he's seeing.'

Chapter 53

The handwritten note was still lying on the side where Hannah had left it the previous evening. She had to admit she was somewhat surprised about Pete seeing other women, but seeing that he was so nice and genuine, perhaps it was true. The real question was whether Hannah was overly bothered about it. At the end of the day, did she really want to get involved with a man with a daughter and a soon to be ex-wife?

As she wasn't due on duty until the late shift, Hannah was going to sit with Josie while Betty and Margaret took Bonkers out for a long walk. She was really looking forward to it. Betty had sent a text to say that Josie had had a good night's sleep, but to be aware that a nurse might call in. Hannah heard Betty, Margaret and Bonkers going out. Bonkers must have been pulling on his lead, keen to get out, as they were both having problems trying to restrain him. Hannah went downstairs to Josie's. It felt strange knocking on her own front door before letting herself in.

'Hi, Josie. It's only me. Nan says you've had a good night. Where are you? I thought you'd be in bed. That's great, you're out in the conservatory.'

'Yes, I thought instead of getting dressed, I'd use my energy to come out here. I'm trying to set some kind of a routine. You know, meals at a certain time, naps in the afternoon, etc. I would offer you a coffee, but I'm afraid you'll have to make it yourself.'

'No problem. Would you like one too?'

'I'd prefer a nice cup of tea, if that's alright?'

'Of course. Just give me a couple of minutes and I'll bring them out.'

'Thanks, dear.'

As Hannah went into the kitchen to put the kettle on, she was pleased to see Josie looking better than the last time she'd seen her. Her face had more colour to it, and there was even a sparkle in her eyes.

'There you go, one cup of tea just how you like it. Now, can I get you anything else? Something to eat perhaps?'

'Oh, no, I'm fine, thanks. Your Nan's been feeding me so well lately. I've been looking forward to you coming as I feel I can really be myself – no putting on an act like I do for your nan and Richard. I know I shouldn't have to, but I do it for their sake really. It stops me from shouting and screaming, but with you I know I can say and do whatever I please.'

'Do whatever you want to, but remember they're always there for you whatever mood you're in.'

'Yes, I know, dear, but all this is so difficult for me to get used to. I'm not the kind of person who gets upset when asking for help, but I hate being in this situation. I'm not in control and it's not easy having to rely on everyone for things. On a positive note though, I'm so thankful to be back on the hill here in Luckett Quay and so relieved that I wasn't diagnosed with this dreadful illness a year ago, because I wouldn't have had the energy to move here. Neither would I have been able to cope in that house in Sheringham. You see, Hannah, everything happens for a reason. I truly believe that.'

'Oh, yes, definitely. So do I, Josie. This house is a wonderful example of that. Would it all have worked out if Jimmy and I hadn't split up, or Dad had persuaded Nan to move? I know it sounds stupid, but Luckett House has some sort of homely power. It draws you in and looks after you. I don't think I'll ever want to leave here.'

'I agree. I've read so many stories over the years about people who have been diagnosed with cancer. The first thing they say is that they're going to fight it and win. I understand that now. I was just the same, it's not going to beat me, you know. I'll fight it all the way, yet when it came to starting this battle, I didn't know how to do it. I just didn't have the energy to fight. Then I came here, you very kindly let me live in your flat, and it suddenly dawned on me. I'm going to fight to get back up those stairs and live life in my own home. I know I could do it even now, but in my present state I know I'd be stuck up there.'

'Yes, but Josie, don't you think that's the lovely thing about living here. We all gel so easily. On paper you wouldn't think it would work out so well. After all, how many young women live with their grandmothers? Then there's Bonkers. He's more than happy to be with any of us. He's even got a bed in four different homes now.'

'He also loves being able to eat from four different food bowls and running it all off on the beach. Yes, dear, I know that whatever happens with this nasty disease, both Bonkers and Richard will always have a home here. Not that he mentions it greatly, but I think he's had enough of London. The fashion industry is beginning to lose its attraction for him, but I'm so proud of all he's achieved. I'm sure there's so much in his life he hasn't even told me about because he's too modest to share everything.'

Hannah immediately thought of the scrapbooks which Frank had compiled. They'd certainly lighten up Josie's heart, but would Richard want her to see them, particularly since they were from Frank?

'So, Hannah, my dear, come and fill me in on all your news. Is that nice gardener still interested in you? I guess he could be a little staid and perhaps dull and boring, but I'm sure he'd make a wonderful husband and father.'

'You mean Tom, and yes he is although I do wish he'd stop it. We could be really great friends, but I've seen a side to him I must say I'm not happy about.

337

Recently I went out to dinner with someone else, and okay, that's quite another story, but when Tom found out he became really moody and weird about it. He even begrudges me spending time with Carl, and that's totally stupid because he's gay.'

'Do you think he just wants to be your best friend, but you've misread it and think he wants more? It seems like the two of you aren't really on the same page, but enough of Tom, tell me about this date. Who is he and do you think it's serious?'

'Pete. Handsome, gorgeous, fit, caring, treated me like a princess, but – and it's a big but – married with a child, and forgot to mention it until the end of our dinner date.'

'Oh, I am sorry. Some men can be right...'

'Tell me about it, but I did have a lovely evening and more importantly ate some delicious new foods, so it wasn't a wasted night. At the moment though I haven't got time for a man, let alone embark on a new relationship. There's just too much going on.'

'Yes, your nan did mention all the trouble with your dad and his new wife. She sounds to me like a very selfish woman. Strikes me your father would be better off without her, although there are the children to consider. Do you still have problems up at the hotel too?'

'No, not anymore. Everything's coming together well there actually. The hotel has a good staffing team and the owners are happy with how everything's progressing. So at least that's one area that's going in the right direction.'

'So when you say there's too much going on, I hope you're not including me in that. Please, dear, don't put your life on hold for me, I beg you. I know you're a tower of strength to Betty, Margaret and now Richard, but what will be, will be. The doctors aren't sure whether I'll recover properly from this cancer, you know. After my operation, they'll have to

338

decide whether I'm to have chemo or radiotherapy, so it's all a waiting game, but I'll tell you something now. Coming back here has helped me to put my life in order. I'm in a good frame of mind mentally, although I have to admit that Richard troubles me. If he wasn't here, I wouldn't have a problem knowing my life will be cut short. I've had such a blessed life thanks to him. He's brought me so much joy and happiness, but I know that he'll be devastated when I have to pass on.'

Hannah could see that Josie was getting upset, so she handed her a tissue and comforted her. She didn't know what to say. Betty or Richard would surely have had the right words for this occasion, but perhaps Josie didn't want to hear it.

'You know, Josie, there is an answer. Perhaps all those who say they're going to beat it, have it spot on. You're going to beat it too, you'll stay here, get better and enjoy life here at Luckett House.'

*

Jimmy had completed a smooth handover with Hannah. Tom and Steve had been tidying up the garden, but wanted permission to cut back some shrubs. It was best they waited until Glenda came back from holiday before dealing with all that, which meant that Hannah didn't need to get involved. It was a quiet lunch shift, even the bar meals had been a bit slow.

Raymond Dove had cancelled his dinner booking, but rearranged it for this evening. Jimmy had laid the same table as he had originally reserved, and signed off for the end of his shift before two whole days of freedom.

A quick look at the arrivals list showed only a couple of check-ins. All very straightforward. The majority of the guests had booked dinner for seven o'clock and then there was a second sitting at eight. Hannah counted how many covers there were for the night, and her finger stopped at the name 'Raymond Dove'. Apparently he was booked in the restaurant all night. Why? There was also a table for two booked in for nine o'clock under the name of 'Mrs Rugstool'.

Should she tell Raymond that Tristan would be in the dining room? But it occurred to her that if she hadn't have had dinner with Pete, she wouldn't have known anything about Mrs Rugstool. No, it wasn't her business to mention it. However, it would be interesting to see how Tristan would react. Would he put on his normal self-importance stance or be like he is when with his grandmother, unable to say boo to a goose?

It was ten to seven. Hannah had given the receptionist a break, the kitchen was ready for its evening guests, and now she thought it best to give the restaurant staff a little pep talk.

'There's something you all ought to know about tonight. One of the richest women in Norfolk is dining with us. I would imagine there'll be quite a healthy tip for us if we do everything well. However, there's a but – it's possible she'll be dining with someone we've found rather difficult to get on with. Yes, Tristan. I know we thought he'd left the area, but sadly it's possible he may decide to throw his weight around tonight. We'll just have to play it by ear and see how it goes. As your boss, I think it's only fair that I serve him. I know it's not something you'd all welcome doing, but if it wasn't for his dining partner here tonight, he'd be out of here the minute he opens his mouth. We just have to bear with it, I'm afraid.'

The shift was going well. Raymond Dove, his wife, Emmi and another man whom Hannah did not recognise had all arrived for the evening. She took their pre-dinner drinks order from them and handed them the menus. The waiter from the bar brought the drinks over while Hannah looked at the clock with worried thoughts. It was now a quarter past eight. Hopefully, Tristan wouldn't be early. Most of the guests had already arrived, some were eating their starters, but quite a lot were already on their main courses. Hannah was aware that it could get to a point where only the Dove's, Tristan and Mrs Rugstool would be left in the dining room at the end of the evening. That could be fun...

The Doves were ready to order and Hannah was all smiles, complimenting Emmi on her beautiful new dress. Raymond introduced the young man dining with them as Jesse, Emmi's new boyfriend. He was going to be helping Emmi with the stables.

'Before I take your order to the kitchen, have you decided on the wine yet?'

'Yes, thank you, Hannah. A bottle of the house red, please, and also one of the white.'

As Hannah turned to go towards the kitchen, she noticed one of the waiters approaching her followed by Mrs Rugstool. She was alone though, and as Raymond saw her, he stood up to acknowledge her presence.

'Camilla! How lovely to see you! It's been ages. You know my wife, don't you? This is my daughter, Emmi, and her friend, Jesse.'

'Raymond! Yes, it's been ages, years in fact. Gosh, just look at your little girl now. What a delightful young lady.'

'Thank you. She's a chip off the old block, just about to start her own business – a riding stable here on the quay. Are you dining alone? Why not come and join us? Hannah, my dear, would it be possible to add an extra table onto the end of ours for some more space. Camilla and her guest will be eating with us tonight. Also, can you delay serving our meals until they've ordered?'

Oh, dear, there's going to be fireworks here soon, Hannah thought to herself, but she was keen not to miss a second of it. What would happen next? With the help of a waiter she moved a small table to the end of the Dove's one. In walked Tristan, head held high without a care in the world. Hannah was shocked to see Raymond take Camilla Rugstool to one side away from the table and whisper something to her. There followed a few words and pointing of fingers as Camilla called Tristan over. The next thing Hannah noticed was that he'd handed Camilla a set of keys and walked out. With that, Raymond Dove beckoned Hannah over.

'Hannah, my dear. I'm so sorry to be such a nuisance, but could you take one of the covers away, please. I'm afraid that Mrs Rugstool's guest has had to leave in a hurry. Isn't that a shame?'

With that he smiled and winked at Hannah, Oh, how happy he looked, but it wasn't just Raymond Dove who was enjoying this. All the staff had wide grins on their faces too.

Chapter 54

Hooray! It was Hannah's day off, and the first one she'd had since Glenda had gone on holiday. With Glenda's return, the pressure on all of them had diminished and everything was ticking along quite nicely. Both David and Glenda were delighted at how things had run to plan. Glenda especially, as she didn't have to face hundreds of emails on her first day back at work. Hannah had dealt with them all until the previous night and Jimmy had been a major help. There were only a few housekeeping aspects he had yet to learn, but he had impressed everyone with his willingness to share the load, even helping to clean out rooms when they were short of staff. Glenda had found the incident with Tristan quite amusing, and was surprised to hear that he hadn't been seen at the hotel since – and that was more than a week ago.

Hannah put the hotel to the back of her mind. It was her day off and she was going to enjoy it. A girly night with Olivia as the boys were staying with their grandparents. First she'd take Bonkers for a walk with Betty, but she also wanted to have a chat with Richard about Josie's check-up at the hospital. Checking her phone, she saw a photo message from Carl. Every day he sent her a photo showing the updated renovations on his cottage, even if it was just a plastered wall or a pot of paint. Clearly, he was still on cloud nine with it all. Today, it was sparkly new taps which were still in their box awaiting installation.

There was another text from Olivia saying how much she was looking forward to their catch up, plus one from Susanna asking when it would be convenient to talk on the phone. Hannah really couldn't be bothered to get involved with her today, so briefly replied that any time after 10am over the next few days would be fine, although if truth be told, she didn't want to speak to Susanna at all. She headed down into the garden.

'No, no, Bonkers, not yet, you'll just have to wait a bit. I'm going to have a coffee and catch up with your dad. Hi, Richard.'

'Hello, stranger, not seen you for ages. Betty told me that you were working extra hours.'

'Yes, I was, because of staff holidays, but I've got two whole days off now and can't wait to catch up with friends and enjoy myself over some wine. I wanted to ask you, how did Josie's hospital appointment go yesterday?'

'Actually, it went far better than we hoped for. The consultant was very happy with her progress. She's put on a bit of weight and there are no complications from the operation. There's no need for her to go back for another month, and there was I thinking the worst. I suppose I was just recalling our last appointment. Mum's very tired today though, but that's to be expected. We'll just plod on and take each day as it comes. Some days are better than others. Sometimes she's full of energy, but other days she's very washed out.'

'And how are you, Richard? Are you finding things easier now, and what's happening in London, if you don't mind me asking?'

'No, no, that's fine. I think I've sorted out the London part of my life. I've agreed to take a pay cut, so that I'll only need to work there for about ten hours a week. It'll basically be just checking things before they go into production, and it'll do me good to keep the brain cells occupied. I've realised that I can only live from one day to the next, and if I'm honest I didn't think Mum would be as well as she appears to be now. At the moment it's quite relaxed, thank goodness, and I can cope with that.

'You've obviously been busy at work, but how's the situation with Jimmy now?'

'Jimmy's stepped up to the mark in his new roles so isn't as keen on me anymore, which I'm quite pleased about. He's had so much to learn that it's helped to take the pressure off things, but our working relationship's good. We know each other's strengths and weaknesses, and actually it's been nice having him around these last two weeks while Glenda's been on holiday.'

'Sounds great. I'm pleased for you. By the way, I didn't get round to thanking you for everything you did for Mum while I was in London. She enjoyed you calling in for a chat, and I really appreciate you being there for her.'

'Yes, we had a good time and I think it did us both good. I know it's not my place to say this, but you know those scrapbooks that Frank put together? I really do think it would help if your mum was able to see them. She's so proud of you, you know, but she told me that you're so modest about your success that she can't really share it with you. She doesn't have to know where the scrapbooks came from, but just think about it for her sake. Now where's your lead, Bonkers? I think it's time we gave Betty a shout.'

Richard didn't reply. He knew his mother was proud of him and smiled. He'd think Hannah's suggestion through. She was right, Josie had no reason to know that Frank had put the books together. Perhaps it was a good idea to share them.

'Are you ready, Nan. Bonkers is so excited to get out for his run. I think the tide's in, so did you want to go down to Luckett beach or up and over to Saltmarsh Quay? You decide.'

'I don't mind at all, darling, but there's no rush so let's go over to Saltmarsh and perhaps have some lunch in the pub. They're quite happy to allow dogs in, but as the weather's nice, we could sit outside.'

'That's a lovely idea, but whether Bonkers will be happy going the opposite direction to the beach remains to be seen.'

They headed up the hill and Bonkers enjoyed his walk as usual. Perhaps he thought they were going to the hotel and he'd be in line for an edible treat, but that was the last thing on Hannah's mind though. She had completely switched off from work and had no intention of being anywhere near the hotel. She mentioned having received a text from Susanna, and Betty said that she'd spoken to Robert a couple of times since his last visit and there was no mention of money at all. He'd only spoken about what he and the children had been up to. No doubt Susanna had something more to say when she planned to speak to Hannah. She needed to be well prepared.

As they reached the top of the hill before turning down the coastal path, Hannah spotted Emmi coming towards them on her horse. Bonkers was always fascinated by horses; he couldn't understand why they didn't want to play with him.

'Hi, Emmi. Lovely day for a ride out, isn't it? Not too breezy.'

'Yes, it is. Sorry, I haven't got a lot of time really as Jesse and I have a lot of things to sort out in the stables. Did you know it's completely mine now? If you ever fancy getting yourself a horse or going for a ride, you know where to come.'

'That's a nice thought, Emmi, but at the moment I've hardly enough time for myself, let alone a horse. By the way, Jesse seems a very nice man and his love of horses gives you so much in common. I think you make a lovely couple.'

'Oh, no, you've got the wrong end of the stick there. We're not a couple at all. He's so not my type. We're just good friends. Actually, I'm sworn to secrecy on this, but I am seeing someone else.'

'Please tell me it's not Tristan.'

'Of course not, he was such a scum bag. That reminds me, wasn't it funny how he quickly left the restaurant the other night? I wonder what Dad said to Camilla. Whatever it was she didn't seem at all happy, did she?'

'You can't leave me guessing, come on spill the beans. Who's your secret new man? We won't tell a soul, will we, Nan?'

'Promise you'll keep it to yourself. I don't think he'll be too pleased if news gets out.'

'Don't keep us in suspense, Emmi. Who is he? We're dying to know.'

'It's Pete, the lovely man who was at your barbecue. He's going to be working in Norwich, but for the time being we're meeting up at a hotel. Once he's settled, he promises we can go public on it. He's such a gentleman.'

'How lovely. I'm so pleased for you, Emmi, but we shouldn't keep you talking. Jesse's probably wondering where you are.'

Hannah was surprised that her immediate reaction was not anger and a need to shout bad words, but no, perhaps Pete was too good to be true. Just another Tristan, it seemed, but with far better manners. Poor Emmi, she thought; I wonder what her father will think about it.

'Darling, what on earth was all that about?'

'Whatever do you mean, Nan?'

'Pete. The moment she mentioned his name, your attitude changed. The expression on your face was a picture.'

Hannah smiled in a strange way and explained the whole story to Betty, making it sound more like a scene from a film script than real life. They both laughed.

'Yes, but just think how lucky you were. Your

date could have been in a dreadful pub instead of a classy restaurant. I think you were the winner actually. Now, talking about food, let's get a move on. Bonkers isn't impressed with us stopping to chat and leisurely strolling along.'

Once they got down onto Saltmarsh beach they spent time throwing the ball and playing with Bonkers just to wear him out, before even thinking about getting anything to eat. Betty suggested a walk around town before heading to the pub. Hannah had no idea why, although she had noticed that Betty was quite restless. She and Bonkers stayed in the pub garden while Betty went to the bar to get a menu and some drinks, a gin and tonic each instead of their usual half a lager.

'There you go, darling, one gin and tonic, and look who I've just bumped into. Jimmy! He was just wandering past the pub and waved to me. As he's not working until tonight, I've invited him to join us for lunch. You don't mind, do you?'

It was very awkward for Hannah to refuse being that Jimmy was already there chatting about the hotel with Betty. Was this all set up, she wondered? But by who, Jimmy or Betty? The good thing was that he wouldn't be able to stay too long, so perhaps she could tolerate it.

Lunch was spent casually chatting with Betty asking Jimmy lots of questions about his new role, and all of them discussing Luckett House. Eventually Jimmy said his goodbyes and headed back up to the hotel, leaving Betty and Hannah to walk back to Luckett Quay via the beach.

'Well, wasn't that lovely?' Jimmy seems to be settling into his new job well and from all accounts the owner is happy with his progress. I'm so pleased you two are getting on so well together and all that silly nonsense is in the past.'

'Silly nonsense, Nan? You do know that Jimmy

had sex with someone else in our bed! I'd hardly call that silly nonsense. Who's to say it was the only time, and for that matter, was she the first? I suppose we'll never know the answers to those questions, will we?'

They walked back in subdued mood, hardly speaking except to talk to Bonkers. Hannah realised that she shouldn't have snapped at Betty, but... Oh, never mind. Up until that point it had been a very pleasant lunch, and she did have an evening with Olivia to look forward to.

'That was lovely, Nan, thank you. We need to do this more often. We've walked in a full circle and Bonkers is exhausted. Look at him, he's worn out. I don't think he'll need another walk today, do you?'

'Yes, it was good until I spoilt it by opening my big mouth. It was just...'

'Oh, don't worry about it, Nan. You didn't spoil it, but I just don't feel able to forgive Jimmy.'

'Why should you? He was in the wrong and he doesn't deserve you. Anyway, darling, however you deal with it will be the right way and it's nothing to do with anybody else at the end of the day.'

*

'Hi, Hannah. Come in. You've no idea how much I've been looking forward to our evening. No children, no men, and lots of unhealthy food and booze. What more could we possibly want?'

'You're right there, Olivia, no men. I've well and truly had enough of them for the time being.'

Olivia poured them both a large gin and lemon, opened up a selection of snacks and put some background music on, before settling down for a good catch up with her friend. There was lots of talk about Josie and everyone at Luckett House as well as Hannah's dad wanting Betty to sell one of the flats and Susanna's phone call. No doubt it would be about her wanting a bigger home and how nothing was going to stop her from getting it.

'So tell me about the ex-husband. What was all that about him turning up out of the blue? Why now, after the divorce has gone through? Surely he's had plenty of time before this?'

'Oh, that's just typical of him. No thought for anything but himself. I thought it best to hear him out though just for the boys' sake and I'm glad I did because it just reinforced my view that it was right to get divorced. I think he'd have loved to get his feet back under the table and just sit there while I go to work and clean the house and it wouldn't have surprised me if he offered to look after the boys while I get an evening job too. Anyway, I'm pleased he didn't see them as do you know, he didn't even mention them. They're his children and he didn't even talk about them, how disgusting is that? No, I've made my mind up, it's the single life for me.'

'You say that know, but don't you think it would be nice to have a man about the place?'

'If I need any jobs done, Tom's quite capable. Plus, he takes the boys out and does all the male things with them. I'm very lucky in that respect, Hannah.'

'But wouldn't you prefer him to be here on a permanent basis, as in being your other half?'

'I don't think he's interested in me in that way. It's you he wants to settle down with; it always has been.'

'He might think he does, but what you have to remember is he's a man and they don't have a clue about what they want. Look at your ex for example.'

'He knew what he wanted alright. Someone to bring the money home so he could sit on his backside and do nothing all day.'

'That's different. I'm telling you, Tom really doesn't have a clue.'

'Anyway, that's enough about me. What's happening with Jimmy? Is he still trying to win you back? Mum said how well he's doing at the hotel. Perhaps it's not my place to say but she also said that she thinks it's just like the two of you are a couple running your own business.'

They chatted about how Jimmy was really good at taking on the responsibilities of Duty Manager, and how Glenda's life was so much easier now. On a professional level everything was working well, but Hannah knew that she had to be careful. If she showed him the slightest bit of affection, Jimmy would jump at the idea of getting back together.

'I did think I might have found myself someone else, you know. He was charming, a real gentleman and so hot. We went out for a posh dinner date and it was a special evening and he was very respectful. I really thought it was the start of something, but he forgot to mention one important thing.'

'Married? Am I right?'

'Kind of. Separated, but aren't they always? Thing is, he's seeing Emmi now and he's told her not to mention it to anyone.'

'Interesting! Who is it? Anyone I know?'

'Pete, the hot chap from the barbeque. You know, slimy Steve's cousin.'

Olivia was shocked to hear that. They'd both thought Pete had come across as a real gentleman. After a lot more gins and a couple of pizzas and ice cream, Hannah and Olivia felt more relaxed; quite merry even.

'If only we were in London now; we could go out dancing and it would be the perfect end to the evening. Don't you miss being in London? Are you sure you don't regret moving here?'

'God, no. Yes, I enjoyed living there, but now I'm really happy with my job at the hotel. No two days are the same, and now one of the downsides has finally left town, hopefully for good... Oh, I don't think I've told you about Tristan and the way he was

351

marched out of the hotel, have I? With any luck, he's out of Norfolk too.'

'He hasn't left Norfolk at all, or even Saltmarsh Quay for that matter. Didn't you know, he's working in the pub down on the quay?'

'No. Nan and I were only in there at lunch time, and we didn't see him.'

'You wouldn't have done, because he's washing the dishes in the kitchen now.'

'Oh, my goodness. To go from dating one of the richest women in Norfolk to scraping dinner plates. How the mighty fall. To think, some of that could have been down to me. I feel bad now.'

Hannah and Olivia saw the funny side of that though and continued to chat about men until there couldn't have been one in Saltmarsh they hadn't mentioned. All of them came with baggage of some sort or the other, apart from Carl of course, who despite being perfect, was sadly out of the question. By now they were quite giggly and rather tipsy, putting together a list of attributes for the ideal man / husband. Hannah thought he'd have to be good looking, fit, fun to be with, not clingy, but adventurous, quite naughty and enjoy doing things on the spur of the moment.

'Your turn, Olivia. What does your ideal man look like?'

'Oh, that's easy. First and foremost he has to like my boys and want to be with them. He has to be good around the house, caring and kind. I don't need him to be the best-looking guy in the world or the most ambitious, but obviously he needs to turn me on. So just a normal kind of guy who likes kids really.'

'Olivia, you do realise the perfect candidate is right under your nose. You've just described Tom!'

Chapter 55

Hannah felt rough the next morning and also somewhat confused as to where she was and what had happened. It slowly dawned on her that she'd spent the night on Olivia's sofa and they'd both had far too much to drink. Trying to be quiet so as not to wake Olivia, she wandered past her room to the bathroom. It was nine-thirty in the morning, and Olivia's room was empty. When Hannah finally managed to get to the kitchen to put the kettle on, she noticed a scribbled note left for her. 'Thanks for a fun evening. I'm off to work. Speak later. Olivia.'

Two large coffees and a couple of paracetamols later, Hannah slowly began to feel able to head back to Luckett Quay. Thank goodness it was another day off work. She would listen to Betty and Margaret's plans for their party, although in the back of her mind she couldn't help thinking there was something else planned for the day. With no rush to get back, she decided to walk down to the harbour for a coffee and a bacon and egg sandwich – anything to soak up the previous night's alcohol. She left Olivia a quick thank you note and headed out for some fresh air.

'One large bacon and egg sandwich, please.'

'Not got your dog with you today?'

'Just me today, but with a very bad hangover I'm afraid. I never want to see another alcoholic drink again.'

'Wish I had a penny for everyone who came in here and said that, I'd be a very rich man.'

Hannah laughed as she tucked into a very welcomed sandwich. She felt so much better now, and seeing as it was now nearly eleven o'clock she started her walk along the beach to Luckett Quay. Perhaps she might bring Bonkers out for a run along the coastal path later, she thought. Staying the night at Olivia's had meant that her phone had died, she obviously hadn't taken her charger out with her so was unable to check for any messages, but there was an unfamiliar car parked outside Luckett House. Must belong to one of the nurses calling in on Josie, she guessed.

First things first, put the phone on to charge, take a shower and have some more coffee. As she was getting ready, and the phone slowly began to spring to life, Hannah heard the bleeping of texts or emails coming in. Opening the lounge window for some fresh air, the sea breeze wafting through her flat made her feel so much more alive. She glanced at the phone and noticed that all the texts and missed calls were from Betty. Why? Instead of reading the texts, she thought it best to give Betty a call.

'Hi, Nan, is everything okay? Sorry I didn't pick up, but I stayed overnight at Olivia's and my phone battery died. Oh, no, I knew there was something I had to do today, but it all slipped my mind. Give me a few minutes to get dressed and I'll pop down.'

So that's who the car belongs to, but why is she here. I thought Susanna was going to phone, not pay a personal visit. If she's taken the time to drive all the way here, it's clear she means business, that's for sure.

'Hi, Susanna. What a surprise! We weren't expecting to see you today. If you'd have mentioned it earlier, I would have made sure I was here.'

'I thought it would be better to come to Norfolk than to try and explain everything over the phone.'

Hannah could see Susanna was nervous and starting to get upset, but that was the complete opposite to Betty who somehow was far more relaxed. She realised this was likely to be a personal discussion between her Nan and Susanna, but felt she should still offer support.

'There we are, three coffees. I would have suggested sitting outside in the garden, but I notice Margaret's already out there, and I'm sure you'd sooner have a private conversation.'

Betty meant business. She was obviously none too happy about Susanna turning up out of the blue to catch them unprepared and was beginning to feel slightly sorry for her. Having a bigger house must mean so much more to her than Hannah realised. She would hear her out and listen to all she had to say.

'I know it's not right to turn up her without any notice. I should have phoned first to let you know I was on my way, but I didn't feel it would be easy for either of us to talk about this over the phone. You both know what this is all about. We need a bigger house; our current one is far too small for the four of us and Robert's too old to take out a larger mortgage. I'm afraid my only option is to come to you for help.'

'Do you mean help, or money?'

'Yes, Betty, I mean money.'

'Well, Susanna, although I could help you financially, I doubt it would be anything close to the amount you'd require. Since moving here, and especially with dear Josie being so ill, I've rethought my priorities. It's so important to have help and support available when you need it, and for that reason I won't be asking Hannah to move out. If she ever does decide to move with her work, I'll have to cross that bridge when I get to it.'

'I thought that would be your attitude, but it's a bit of a lame excuse if you ask me. I'm very sorry to hear about your neighbour and her poor health, but you'd still be able to find help even if Hannah wasn't here. That's why I've driven all this way. After all, it's only fair to tell you to your face. If you can't help me, Betty, I'm afraid I'm left with no choice but to end the marriage and separate from Robert. That house is far too small for a growing family. Can't you possibly see the seriousness of the situation and reconsider?'

'That's extremely sad and not a nice position for my grandchildren to be in, but it's clear to me that you don't really care for my son. If you did, you wouldn't care how big the house is. It's about love at the end of the day, not bricks and mortar, love.'

'But I do love him...'

'Like I said, if you really loved Robert, you wouldn't be contemplating leaving him. Now, I've nothing more to say on the matter, so do excuse me. I have to pop in on Josie and see how she is today. Have a safe journey home, but please remember whatever you decide to do, we'll always be family.'

With that, Betty went into Josie's without even a second word or a glance at Hannah leaving Susanna to pick up her bag and go. Yes, it was by no means an ideal situation, but what could Hannah do? Susanna was issuing an ultimatum, a form of blackmail: if you don't buy me a house, I'll leave Robert, and that showed her true colours. To be honest, he'd be better off without her. Hannah knew she'd have to phone her father and tell him all about Susanna's conversation with them. She even wondered whether he knew anything of Susanna's visit to Norfolk at all.

An hour and a half later and she finally ended the call to her dad. Hannah was right, he was totally unaware that Susanna had driven down to see them. She'd made an excuse, wanting him to take the children to school, but somehow he wasn't surprised. She would end up disappointed though. With his wage having to fund two homes there'd be a lot less for family luxuries.

Hannah went to find Betty in the garden, who was now relaxing with both Margaret and Josie. They were all laughing and joking about something and Josie looked well. There was a definite colour to her cheeks and she seemed to have far more energy than usual.

'Hey, what's going on here? I moved here for a quiet life, you know.'

'Hi, Hannah. Sorry, but Margaret was just telling us about someone she met on the lane today when she was out with Bonkers.'

'Oh, and who was that?'

'A Mrs Van something or other. The woman who's going to be taking over the house at the top of the hill. She says that once she's moved in, we'll all have to get together and form a Luckett Quay Group. I told her that it's possible she could be invited to join if she passes the criteria.'

Hannah joined in with the amusement, explaining to them about Mrs Van Lincoln and the problems they'd had with her at the hotel.

'Seeing that I'm having such a good day, and it's now mid-afternoon, I quite fancy a glass of wine. I haven't had one for weeks and weeks.'

'Oh, not for me, thanks. I'm still recovering from last night, but I'll go and get it for you. Red or white, and by the way, where's Richard today?'

'Both please! Just bring the bottles and the three glasses from the kitchen. Richard's gone into Norwich to do some shopping actually. Do you need a hand?'

'No thanks, Nan. I'll also fetch a pen and notepad to jot down some ideas for your party.'

'Oh yes, the party to end all parties. Rock 'n' roll.'

'I hope not, Josie. I was thinking more a cucumber sandwich and glass of sherry type party.'

'Very funny, Margaret.'

Hannah fetched the wine, glasses and a notebook. She was surprised how well the party planning was going being that Josie hadn't been well enough to help, but everyone seemed to have their roles organised. Josie would co-ordinate things, ticking things off the list as they were completed. Margaret was responsible for the guest list as having lived there all her life she'd know exactly who to invite. Hannah had to give Margaret the names of guests she'd like to invite, and Betty was in charge of the catering. Not that she was going to do it all herself. Jimmy had also been roped in to help, but Hannah was fine with that. She'd leave them to it.

'So what part do I play, ladies?'

'Hannah, you and Richard can do the decorations. Yes, you two can make sure the garden and patio are decorated, but first we'll have to come up with a theme we're all happy with. Can you think of anything?'

Hannah was happy with her role. Richard, being creative, was sure to come up with something good. Who could she invite though? Some of her friends were already on Margaret's list, but what about Glen, Emmi, and Mr and Mrs Dove? She would also have liked to invite Glenda, but unfortunately with Hannah and Jimmy both off work at the same time, she would have to be on duty at the hotel.

Betty brought the party meeting to a close as by now it was coming up to six o'clock. She would cook them all some dinner while Hannah took Bonkers down onto the beach for a quick run around. Margaret decided to go with them, leaving Josie to rest and Betty to cook. All sorted!

'Look, there's something I'd just like to say before the three of you go, and that's a big thank you. On paper, living together like this would be difficult what with the situation regarding Frank, us being elderly, and you so young, Hannah. But it's all working well, and in fact it's the perfect arrangement. So thank you all for the support you've given me over the last month or so. I know for a fact that if it wasn't for you three, I wouldn't be here to tell the tale. You've given me the strength to keep going and not give into this cancerous illness. I do realise that I'm not quite out of the woods, but every day is a bonus and that's the attitude I shall continue to adopt. I shan't worry about the future anymore, apart from our party, which of course I have every intention of being here for. So, off you all go before we all end up in tears.'

Josie was right, they all were close to tears! Hannah and Margaret changed their shoes and headed down to Luckett Quay with Bonkers and as usual they headed to the rocks while Bonkers happily ran around sniffing at everything.

'Oh, Margaret, what a year it's been. If someone had told me this is where I'd be twelve months ago, I'd have laughed at them. I'm so lucky, a fabulous new job and lovely home, special friends, and before you say it, my own freedom. Perhaps I'm one of these people that has no need for another half. I'm happy just as I am.'

'You may well be right there, Hannah. Perhaps that's what I should have done all those years ago, but the past is the past and I think we spend far too much time dwelling on things gone by. If Frank never came into my mind again, I know I wouldn't be disappointed.'

'I know what you mean, but I bump into my ex every day at the hotel, so it's not that easy to forget.'

'You could easily put everything that happened between you to one side, and just see what the future holds though. Come on now, it's time we were going. I wouldn't be surprised if your nan and Josie have opened another bottle of wine. Mind you, that would be an ideal opportunity to toast the future, wouldn't it?'

Chapter 56

It had been a few days since the meeting to discuss the party and as things had been very quiet at Luckett House, it had given Josie time to focus on the many things on her mind. Richard had joined in as well and they had set a date for a Sunday afternoon in September, which was actually only three weeks away. Hannah was now taking more of a back seat in the organising as she'd made her guest list, but if there was anything unforeseen she was more than happy to help out.

At the hotel thoughts turned towards Christmas. They were holding the first of the pre-Christmas meetings to discuss plans for the festive season; everything from decorations, party nights, food, but most importantly of all how to attract guests and fill the rooms at a good rate. They'd set the whole day aside for this, leaving Annie to concentrate on duty management for eight hours. At some point during the day there would be a conference call from David, and as it was Hannah and Jimmy's first experience of Christmas at Saltmarsh Quay, Glenda was going to run through the successes and disasters of previous years.

Four hours later and they had made good progress. They had covered the rooms, as there were already quite a lot of repeat bookings for the three-day Christmas package, food and menus had been selected, but bookings for the party nights were a bit slow. They would have to advertise the events well. Jimmy needed to plan both lunch and dinner menus for three weeks in advance of Christmas and they agreed that there would be set menus for any bookings of eight or more. They were just debating whether to change the afternoon tea menu when

David emailed to see whether it was convenient to call.

'Hi, everyone. Hope all's going well, and you two new additions to Saltmarsh Hotel aren't too overwhelmed with the Christmas plans. I won't take up too much of your precious time, so here goes. Well, let's start with rooms, then the restaurant and then finally the kitchen.'

The whole thing took nearly two hours, but at last they had crossed all the Ts and dotted the Is.

'So, Glenda, what do you say to that? Done and dusted in less than two hours, that's a record for us. Last year it took us two days, didn't it? Those two youngsters are certainly cut out for success. Thank you, all three of you. I can see I'm not going to be needed so much at Saltmarsh Quay, so before I end off, are there any questions or issues I need to look at?'

'No, I don't think so. Everything seems to be taken care of, but I'm concerned that although Friday and Saturday party nights have a good take up, Thursday bookings are a bit on the low side.'

'Cut it back to just the two nights then, Glenda. Contact those who have booked a Thursday night and see if they're happy to move it to a Friday night instead. It's not the end of the world. By the way, are there any more problems with that horrible man, Raymond Dove's relative?'

'A lot has happened but thankfully he's no longer coming to the hotel. As for his grandmother, she's moving into a house down the hill, so I can't see her bothering us anymore. By the way, Mr Dove is spending more time here than ever as he loves chatting to Jimmy and Hannah.'

'That's great, Glenda. Oh, before I forget, make sure you give him a good bottle of whisky for Christmas. We could do with more guests like him coming through the door. Anyway, the bookings for

September are looking good, we should beat our targets again. I'm beginning to think that young couple sitting there with you are bringing us good luck.

'One more thing, I've secured a deal with the owner of Clock Manor in the Cotswolds. Well, deal's probably not the best word to use, but I've managed to get him to agree to us giving him four nights' accommodation and food in exchange for him doing the same for the four of you. That means you all get a night away as a thank you from Devel and I. Although I should add, you all can't take advantage of that offer at the same time otherwise we'd have some staffing difficulties. Would you be kind enough to explain this to Annie for me? By the way, the Clock Manor is extremely posh and perfect for romantic getaways. Enjoy!'

With that David, ended his call. Glenda explained that he'd done something very similar the previous year as a gift to the Heads of Departments. Glenda had passed this gesture on to her parents which they'd really appreciated. Although Hannah was grateful for David's kindness, a romantic night in a hotel wasn't the kind of thing she could do with. Perhaps she'd gift it to Carl and Mike, or anyone else in her life who would benefit from it. Now she had to get ready for dinner service, which hopefully would all run to plan, before the three of them would go their separate ways. They set a date in their diaries for the next Christmas meeting and set off for their duties.

'Hey, Hannah...'

'I know exactly what you're going to say, Jimmy. David called us a couple, didn't he, but didn't mean it like you imagined.'

'I wasn't going to mention it actually, but I noticed you pick up on it. I was going to ask you to tell Betty that I'll pop down tomorrow afternoon to discuss the party food with her, if that's alright.'

Hannah felt herself blush with embarrassment, but after all, that's what Jimmy would say. As she headed for the restaurant she noticed Raymond Dove saying goodbye to someone in the lounge. Shaking hands formally, it seemed very official.

'Hi, Hannah, do you have a minute to spare? I've some news you might find rather interesting.'

Hannah waited until the other man had left and then sat down with Raymond. He explained that he had just had a meeting with his lawyer to discuss Tristan. They'd agreed that rather than take him to court, it would be far more sensible just to let him off as they didn't want to drag the Dove name through the court system. The bargain would be that by not taking the matter any further, Tristan must agree not to come back to Norfolk again.

'By the way, he's not even washing the dishes in the pub anymore. Once I mentioned a few things to my lifelong friend, his landlord, Tristan was out on his ear. He didn't even finish his shift.'

'Oh, dear. I've actually felt quite sorry for Tristan. Don't know why I should, but perhaps it's because I do try and see some good in people.'

'I can assure you, Hannah, there's not much good to be found with that one. Anyway, before I go, my wife tells me we've been invited to your garden party. We're really looking forward to that. Bye for now.'

So Margaret's invited the Doves! But poor old Tristan. Wonder what he did that was so bad. I doubt I'll ever find out.

The restaurant was now ready for the dinner shift. Hannah had about half an hour before the guests were due to arrive. Just enough time to ring the Clock Manor to try and put a little plan into action. With a little thought and a few white lies, one of her problems could be solved once and for all!

Chapter 57

The party was now only a week away, and everything down to the last blade of grass had been discussed and organised. There were going to be between 40 and 50 guests, a real cross mix from various backgrounds. Workmen who had worked on the conversion were invited, alongside Josie's friends from Sheringham, Margaret's friends and family, and people who Hannah had got to know since her move. Reluctantly, Betty had invited Robert and Susanna, but they had not responded.

Everyone had been told to arrive at any time after 1pm, and it would be an open house for them to come and go as they pleased. Today, Hannah was catching up with Richard to discuss the decorations, but first she needed to make another phone call, hopefully the last one, to Clock Manor.

'Hi, Jenny. It's me again, Hannah. Thanks so much for all you've done so far. Now, I know this might sound a little bizarre, but I'm just checking you've received my card to put in the room with the champagne and chocolates. Today's the day!'

'Yes, all sorted. I'm going to be here until six o'clock as I've got an appointment with a wedding couple at five, and that should only take about an hour. If they get here before five, I'll get Reception to page me and explain the situation. Now, let me just get the story straight. They think you and a friend are coming, but in a different car. Obviously you're not though! They'll get shown to the room – oh, did you know it's one of our best rooms with a four-poster bed and all the trimmings? By the way, what do we do if they refuse to share the same room and ask for an extra one? We're full tonight. I know you're hoping they'll fall into each other's arms and live happily ever after, but...'

'Just hand them the card, please, Jenny, and preferably to the man, Tom. Everything will be fine, I'm sure, but if not, they can take it out on me when they get back. Oh, talk of the devil. Olivia's just ringing me on my mobile. Thanks, again, Jenny.'

'Hi. Just to let you know we're just leaving. I'm so nervous as I've never done anything like this before. Can I just run through the list again to make sure we get this right? I understand why you and Carl can't arrive at the same time as the staff mustn't know that we're mystery guests. So we need to mark the car park out of five, as well as the entrance and the check-in. What happens if anyone gets suspicious though?'

'Don't worry, they won't. Now, have a safe journey and remember before you check-in, go to the bar and have two large gin and tonics. Well, you could have a couple each. You don't have to restrict it to one! Look, Olivia, I need to go. Have a lovely time.'

'We will, but you'll also be with us, won't you?'

'Yes, bye for now.' What on earth had Hannah done? It was one thing to set someone up on a blind date, but quite another to send two friends halfway across the country, book them a hotel room and expect them to sleep together. However, it was too late now, everything had been organised, and now Hannah had to think about the party decorations.

'Morning, Richard. Where's Bonkers, and how's Josie today?'

'Margaret's already taken him out for a walk while Mum's still asleep. I know she's been thinking about the party a lot and it's making her quite tired, but it's good to have something to focus on. Anyway, how are you?'

'Okay, I think. It's just that I think I might have made a big error of judgment and may lose two of

365

my best friends over it. I won't bore you with the details, but I'll just have to see how it all pans out. Right, I'm ready to start making the party decorations, but I'll have to warn you, I'm no expert with the sewing machine.'

Richard laughed, but didn't reply. He made them both a coffee and then went to get something. Hannah was expecting it to be boxes of craft materials, but all he had was a file from which he proceeded to show her some website photos of beautiful garden parties. The table centres were stunning, brightly coloured tablecloths with matching bunting and a three-tiered cake stand. Everything looked so perfect, but Hannah definitely knew her limits. She couldn't possibly copy these decorations, they were far too ornate.

'I'm sorry, Richard, but we've only got a week. I'd need a year to make a few tablecloths, let alone all the bunting. I'm not too good at craft things like this, you know.'

'Hey, who said anything about making them? These are just some ideas, and if you're happy with them, I'll order it all. Hey presto! On the morning of the party it will all be delivered.'

Richard explained that all they needed to do was agree on the colour scheme and quantities. What a relief for Hannah, but also very generous of Richard as hiring all these decorations certainly wouldn't be cheap. It was a lovely thank you present to them all for making him feel so welcome at Luckett House.

'You didn't actually think we'd be making all the bunting, did you? All we have to do is decorate the garden when the goods arrive, but first we just need to choose a colour, and then I'll go into Norwich and order everything today.'

'If you're sure! I do feel slightly bad about all this, as I've not done anything to help with this party. Everyone else has really thrown themselves into it, when all I've done is point at some pictures!'

'But knowing you, you'll make yourself busy on the day of the party, checking everything's going to plan and all the guest have plenty to eat and drink.'

'I suppose so, and yes, that has made me feel a little less guilty.'

By lunch time everything was completely organised. Richard was going to order everything and Betty and Margaret were going to Norwich with him. They both fancied a new outfit for the party and Hannah was staying to look after Josie who had just woken up.

'Good morning, or should I say afternoon? So it's just you and me, isn't it, Hannah? Well, what do you have planned for the rest of the day? For a start, fill me in with all the hotel gossip and how your new job's going. I know you like talking about everything that goes on, unlike Richard. When he used to come and visit me from London, I'd always ask him about his job, but it was like pulling teeth just to get any answer out of him even though he had such an exciting job.'

Richard looked at Hannah and knew exactly what she was thinking – the scrap books! He helped Josie to get comfortable on the sofa in the conservatory with Bonkers curled up beside her whilst Hannah went off to make her a cup of tea. Betty and Margaret joined them, excited to be going shopping for clothes, and joking that they had the perfect companion to go with. They were confident that Richard certainly wouldn't let them buy anything that wasn't one hundred per cent right for the party. Richard then walked into the kitchen.

'I've left the scrap books on my bed. I think it'll be best coming from you, as I know Mum will get upset. If I'm not around, she won't try and put on a brave face and it's only fair to tell her who put the scrap books together.'

The three of them set off for Norwich, leaving Hannah to take the tea into the conservatory for herself and Josie. The last thing she wanted to do was upset Josie, but she knew that Richard would prefer her to mention the books. He was far too modest to blow his own trumpet and didn't want to be present when his mother went through them. On the other hand, if something happened to Josie and she'd not had a chance to see them, Richard would be upset. So it had to be done. Richard, Betty and Margaret would be away for a good four to five hours, so there'd be plenty of time for Josie to see the scrapbooks and compose herself for Richard's return.

'Everything, okay, Hannah? You seem to be in a world of your own. Is something the matter? Hope it's not that lad of yours again?'

'He's not my lad in the way you're suggesting, but you're right, I do have something on my mind which I need to tell you about. To be honest, it's not me that should be doing this, but it's unlikely you'd find out by any other means, and that would be a real shame.'

'I'm confused. Whatever's wrong? Come on, you can tell me – what's the problem?'

Hannah started at the very beginning, explaining that Margaret had left a case for Richard. Opening it, it was a huge shock for him and something he struggled to get his head around. Scrapbooks from school days right up to a couple of years ago. However, she failed to mention that Frank had stopped doing them when Richard's career was going through a difficult period.

'You're telling me that Frank followed all of Richard's career, and he...'

'Yes, he collected all these from trade magazines and newspaper articles, and there's so much in there about Richard's awards. I suppose you'll be eager to see them all, but there's several, so it's going to take a long while.'

Hannah went to get them but thought it wise to leave out the early pictures of Richard as a schoolboy. She'd start with the ones where he had moved to London.

'They're a bit mixed up, I'm afraid, but I'll put them in order starting with the earliest one first. If I move the coffee table across, you can move them from the sofa to the table when you've finished looking at each one.'

Hannah thought it best to leave Josie to go through the scrapbooks by herself, so she made sure she had a box of tissues at the ready and decided to go and sit in the garden and check the emails from her phone. There was yet another photo from Carl showing the taps which were now fully installed on the bath. The bathroom fittings were ready to fit and then the room just needed decorating. Hannah was pleased for Carl, his cottage was coming along nicely. There weren't many emails to answer, but rather than disturb Josie, she used the excuse of getting some food or drink. It had been an hour since she'd left Josie, a cup of tea would perhaps be welcomed.

'How are you doing? Can I get you anything?'

'Sorry, darling? What did you say?'

'Would you like a cup of tea, or a sandwich perhaps?'

'No, I'm fine, thanks. These books are amazing. I can't get over just how successful Richard's been. I know he's had a good job and was very well-respected, but I had no idea he'd won so many awards. I haven't even started on the articles yet, as I've been looking at all the photos. Why hasn't he ever told me about any of this, I wonder. I know he's not one for boasting, but if he's not going to shout about his career, I certainly am. He's so modest, isn't he? Hannah, if you have things you need to do, you can leave me, you know. I don't really need babysitting. I'll be quite alright until the others get back.'

'It's okay, Josie. You carry on with the scrapbooks and I'll take Bonkers down to the beach for half an hour. Oh, look, I've only to mention the word 'beach' and he's wide awake and ready to go. Are you sure you'll be alright?'

'Of course. Now don't you worry about me, where did I get to? The nineteen-eighties.'

Despite being the middle of the afternoon the beach was so quiet as most of the holiday makers with children had left for the school term. The coastline was busy with older, retired people and lots of bird watchers, taking on a completely different atmosphere. The tide was slowly beginning to come in, but Hannah still had time to sit on the rocks for half an hour and throw Bonkers' ball for him to run after and fetch. The sun was bright in her line of vision, and she didn't notice someone join her on the rocks until it was too late.

'Hi, Jimmy. What brings you down here? I thought Saltmarsh was your stomping ground.'

'I've just finished my Duty Manager's shift and handed over to Glenda, but I felt I needed a bit of fresh air. Can you believe we travelled to so many distant places, when we had this beautiful outlook practically at the bottom of your nan's garden? Bit silly, weren't we?'

'No, I don't think so. We had lovely holidays actually, we worked hard and deserved to get away and see the world. I certainly don't regret any of it, but don't forget, we were younger then and wanted different things from life. Remember, the parties in Ibiza, the ski lodges in Switzerland and even the theme parks in Florida? To be honest, even working and living here, I'd still appreciate my holidays away.'

'Yes, but not with me.'

'You're wrong there. I'd love to share holidays with you but...'

'I know, Hanny. I messed up, didn't I? Can I ask you something though? Do you feel more grown up since moving here? Like you've left the carefree young person behind you and become an adult? I do, and actually I'm quite enjoying it.'

'Yes, but that's probably because you've got a responsible role at the hotel now.'

'You could be right.'

'Look, Jimmy, I really ought to be getting back now. Nan, Margaret and Richard have gone to Norwich to get things for the party, and I'm supposed to be keeping an eye on Josie while they're away.'

'Oh, I understand. There goes your phone. You'd better answer it.'

The first was a text from Olivia. All it said was 'thank you'. The next one was from Tom. 'How could I have been so blind, thank you'.

Her ploy had worked. Her two best friends were now an item. Hannah smiled to herself, forgetting Jimmy was still there until he asked if everything was alright.

'Everything's just perfect, thank you, Jimmy.'

Chapter 58

'Morning, Hannah. Thanks so much for staying with Mum yesterday. I've been so silly not showing her the scrapbooks, haven't I? I guess I just overthought everything. Yes, she was somewhat emotional, but nothing like I thought she'd be. You know, we didn't even put the TV on last night. She just wanted to go through all the books again and talk about the events, the clothes and all the celebrities I've met over the years, and we only got up to the eighties! Luckily, there was no mention of Frank. I was dreading that, as I thought it'd be a real problem, but no, everything was fine.

'Anyway, we've got all the decorations booked to arrive the day before the party at no extra charge. That'll give us Saturday to get everything ready without having to rush.'

'That's great, because I'm doing an early shift on the Saturday and won't be back until about half past three. So you all had a nice time in Norwich, love the outfits Nan and Margaret bought themselves.'

'Yes, we did enjoy ourselves, but one thing I found quite sad is that when Margaret was married to Frank, he'd blow loads of money in the pub each week, but tell her she couldn't spend much. He'd only allow her into Marks & Spencer when they were invited to a wedding. I'm so glad he wasn't part of my life, and yes, I know it's wrong to speak ill of the dead, but he really was a horrible man.'

'Everything happens for a reason, you know, Richard. Look how happy she is here. Having said that though, Jimmy doing what he did, wasn't so that we could both move here, you know.'

'I wasn't going to mention that, apart from saying that perhaps you could be friends as well as just work colleagues. You could go out for a drink together or maybe a walk. Surely that wouldn't do any harm?'

'Richard, that subject is over and done with, so back to the party business, please. Oh, sorry, there's my phone again, and this time I think I need to answer it.'

'I'll make some coffee and find us some biscuits while you do that.'

The conversation didn't take very long, and by the time Richard came back, Margaret and Betty had arrived, so he needed to make two more coffees. Hannah was miles away, thinking about her phone call with Olivia. She was so happy for her and Tom, but somehow the picture Olivia had just painted couldn't be correct. Wasn't Tom rather boring? From what Olivia had described, he was more like a wild animal. So much so, that the guests in the next room were banging on the wall to get them to quieten down, and that was at two in the morning! Tom, wild? She wouldn't be able to look him in the eye ever again!

'Come in, Hannah, 'we're all here.'

'Sorry, Nan. I was just thinking of something I've just been told. Now, where were we? What else needs doing? Oh, morning, Josie, you're up early.'

'Hello everyone. I'm glad you're all here as I'll be able to tell you all my news at the same time.'

'You sit here, Mum. I'll make you a cup of tea.'

'Thanks, darling. Margaret, I have to thank you for giving Richard the scrap books. Fancy him keeping all those fabulous things he's done in his career a secret. I'm so happy I know about it all now and that's the most important bit.'

'Here you go, Mum, one cup of tea. So what's this news you have for us all then?'

'Actually, it's more of a request really. Now I'm feeling so much better, I wondered whether I could move back upstairs to my own flat. I know it's going to be a busy week with the party and everything, but I do feel so much more capable now, and it's only fair that Hannah has her home back. What do you all think?'

They all thought it would be fine at the moment, but what would happen should Josie fall ill again? She would be stuck up there with no access to the garden or conservatory. Hannah kept quiet, but secretly she couldn't wait to have her own flat back. Everyone agreed to Josie's suggestion and said that if that was what Josie really wanted, they'd all help to make it possible.

'Could I make a suggestion?'

'Of course, Margaret.'

'I've been thinking. Sometimes I do struggle to carry bags of shopping up the stairs. I'm fit enough to go and walk Bonkers on the beach, but I do find stairs quite difficult to manage these days. Why don't we have a stair lift installed? It would be so convenient for all of us at some point, so shall we enquire about it? What do you think, Josie?'

Everyone agreed it was the ideal solution and Richard would take over the reins to research local companies and gather quotations. They all started to discuss the party, checking over the lists and making sure that everything was in hand. There wasn't much that could now be done before the actual morning of the party, so Hannah decided to make a start on tidying up and packing away some of her things in readiness for her move back down to her own flat. After that she'd have to think about getting ready for work.

'Oh, by the way, Hannah. I've heard from your father. He and Susanna are coming to the party and arriving on the Saturday. They've asked if they can stay with you, but it will only be the two of them as the children are going to Susanna's mother's for the night.'

'Hmm, well, that's something to look forward to, I don't think! Thank goodness we'll all be busy preparing for the party. Right, I must get on. See you all tomorrow for the move, if you're quite sure about this, Josie. I really don't mind staying upstairs a little while longer if it helps.'

'No, no, dear, I think it's the right time to move back, and just think, when we have the stair lift working, I'll be able to fly up and down at any time. Now, don't you worry about cleaning the flat. We can get that done tomorrow. Have a good time at work.'

The flat wasn't actually all that dirty. Hannah had really only used the kitchen to make drinks, and she spent so much time at work that it was only a question of tidying up and getting her things together. They could give it a good clean through in the morning.

Once at the hotel, Hannah had a quick handover with Annie, checking all the arrivals and the restaurant diary. It looked to be a straightforward shift. Hopefully Jimmy would be running the kitchen tonight and Glen was on duty in the restaurant. Paperwork completed, nothing important outstanding, all was running smoothly, but what was that strange phone call about? Someone had phoned to ask who the Duty Manager was and were there any non-resident guests dining in the restaurant that evening? They had refused to give any information about themselves and had hung up the phone when the receptionist suggested transferring the call to the Duty Manager. How very odd.

It was now nine o'clock and the diners had been checked from the restaurant list. Everyone was booked in and no more guests were due in. Hannah left Glen and the team to finish off in the restaurant and decided to get on with some of the reports David had requested and look over the banking paperwork.

With that her pager went off. Reception were asking her to go to the restaurant urgently as there was a problem. She wondered whether it had anything to do with that strange phone call earlier, but as she headed through the lounge and towards the bar, she heard raised voices. One of them was Glen's and suddenly she recognised the other one.

'Excuse me! What's all the shouting for?'

'Here she comes, jumped up little busybody. Glorified waitress who thinks she's important.'

'Hello, Tristan. First things first, could I please ask you to keep your voice down. Our guests would like to enjoy dinner in peace. Now, how can I help you?'

'Yes, I want that table over there, the special one that's always reserved for the Dove's, but those people there are refusing to move.'

'Can we just go into the bar and chat about this, please?'

'Chat with you? The nasty so and so who ruined my life?'

What should Hannah do? Should she call the police? Tristan was drunk and making a nuisance of himself in public. But why was he there? The restaurant guests looked very uncomfortable with the situation, especially now that Tristan had pulled up a spare chair and placed it at the table he wanted to sit at, despite the fact that there was already a family dining there. All Hannah could think of was how thankful she was that the restaurant wasn't fully booked. If he had done this earlier, at seven-thirty, it would have been so much more unpleasant.

'I'm asking you to leave now, please. Otherwise I'll have no option but to call the police.'

'There's no need for the police, Hannah. We can sort this out ourselves.'

With that Jimmy and one of the other chefs appeared and literally lifted Tristan off the floor and carried him out of the hotel. Hannah thought it was just like watching a scene from a movie. She instructed Glen to fetch all the guests a drink of their choosing and go and apologise to everyone. Jimmy and the other chef had gone back to the kitchen, reassuring Hannah that there was no way Tristan would ever return to the hotel.

Hannah had mixed feelings. In some respects she did feel some sympathy for him, but he'd been one of her biggest problems since arriving at the hotel. Perhaps she should try and have a personal talk with him. She made a big pot of coffee and headed outside to see if he was still around. It would, of course, be better to say goodbye on a more friendly note, if possible. There he was, sitting at a picnic table outside.

'Thought you might like a coffee, and I've brought enough for two. Can I join you?'

'You want to have coffee with me after everything that's gone on?'

'Yes, Tristan, strangely enough I do. Call me stupid or daft if you like, but I'm here now. So what does the future hold for you? I'm told you'll be leaving Norfolk.'

'Driven out, you mean. That's the reason I'm going. I have little choice in the matter.'

'A new start somewhere else can often be a blessing in disguise, you know. You've upset a lot of people around here, so wherever you do end up, please try and be civil and polite to people. It helps in the long run.'

'Me being rude to anyone isn't the reason for me leaving. Anyway, I expect old Dove has probably told you everything.'

'Actually he's only said that you won't be around anymore.'

Tristan started to become quite upset. Hannah had to remind herself that he had tried to con Betty into selling Luckett House for a ridiculously low amount, so no, she wasn't going to let emotion get the better of her. He didn't deserve any sympathy.

'I only wanted to be successful and have people look up to me, to be respected. The irony is that quite the opposite happened. Everyone despised me. I thought I was clever finding out Raymond Dove's business and giving information to other people, but I didn't realise that it made me look underhanded. Trust is important, and now there's not a businessman in the area that would give me a job, even though they've likely made a lot of money out of the information I've given them. I thought I was so clever, but I've learnt my lesson.

'Do you know what, Hannah? What's even worse in all this is the way in which I've treated people. I've failed. Look at how I treated Emmi, your staff, and my family. They've all given up on me, and I can't say I blame them.'

'That in itself is a positive thing, Tristan. So many people never even realise they've made mistakes. Hopefully now you can just move on in life, but do things properly this time. Find a job, work hard and perhaps you'll then find yourself a nice girlfriend and settle down. I'm sure you can easily do that. You're a handsome man who could charm the birds out of the trees. You need to use that charm to your advantage and sort your life out.'

'After all the hassle I've caused you, you're being nice to me?'

'Tristan, just go and take on the world, but this time play by the rules rather than breaking them. I really do wish you well even though, yes, you have caused me a lot of stress. I guess every town has a bad apple. Good luck.'

Chapter 59

Hannah and Josie's plans to swap flats and return to their own homes did not go to plan, although Josie had insisted it all happen before the party. However, she hadn't felt too well and now, with it being the eve of the party, there was just too much to do.

Bonkers had already had his coastal walk, Josie was sitting in the conservatory, Margaret and Betty were both busy baking and Tom was due to arrive to tidy up the garden and help with the outdoor decorations. Hannah hadn't caught up with Tom since she had gifted her spa and hotel retreat to him and Olivia. Neither had she discussed it in detail with Olivia, as both her boys had been in the room when she had phoned.

She had, however, spoken to Jenny, Olivia's mum at the hotel, who couldn't wait to tell Hannah that Tom had been staying the night. She'd found out about it from the boys who had let the cat out of the bag. She'd later questioned Olivia about it, and she had confirmed it. Yes, she and Tom had enjoyed a wonderful weekend away at a luxury hotel. Both Jenny and her husband were absolutely thrilled to bits. They'd always considered Tom to be more of a father to Sam and Ben than their real father. It would be interesting to hear what he has to say about it, if anything, while he's here today.

'There you go! That's the last of the bags. Richard, I've just got to take a few bits out of Josie's fridge. Are you sure this move is the best thing to do? You will be able to cope, won't you? Margaret did mention that you have a couple of companies coming to quote for the stair lift. The good thing about Luckett House is that it's old and had rather a winding staircase. Anyway, enough of this chit-chat.

I ought to get this finished.'

'Thanks, Hannah. It was so kind of you to let us swap flats while Mum's been so poorly. Actually, I think it's had a positive impact on her recovery. Looking back, whoever would have thought she'd still be with us. I know we're not quite out of the woods yet, but every day's a bonus. We just have to take one day at a time, that's all we can do, isn't it? Is that my phone or yours?'

'Mine, but it's just a text from Dad to say that he and Susanna are just leaving. That's going to be fun. Just have to sort out the food in the fridge and then we're all done.'

Glancing out of the window, she noticed Tom getting out his van. Thankfully, he was by himself rather than bringing Steve along with him to help with the gardening. There was something different about his appearance, Hannah thought, and then she realised he'd had a modern haircut. No doubt that was Olivia's doing! Just time to pop in to Betty's to see how she was getting on with the baking before greeting Tom.

'Hi, Nan, how are you doing? By the way, Dad just sent a text. They're just leaving.'

'That's rather early, they'll probably arrive here by lunch time and you know what that means – we'll have nearly a whole day with her. Not quite what I had planned, but perhaps we can drag out the party preparations for a bit longer and keep ourselves occupied. I know that doesn't sound like a very nice thing to say, but she was the one who stormed out of here last time.'

'Yes, I know, and that's exactly what we'll do, make sure we keep ourselves busy. Right, I'm off now, got a few more things to move in and then I'll have to sort my flat out ready for them to stay.'

Richard had given her flat a thorough clean and tidy up, so all she had to do was make up the beds.

Before doing that, perhaps there was time to go and speak to Tom. Should she mention his new hairstyle, or Olivia? Actually, no perhaps it was better to play the whole thing by ear.

'Morning, Tom. Thanks for coming over, Nan really appreciates it. She would have done it all by herself, but with all the baking she's doing today, she's a bit hard pushed and anyway, you'll do a better job.'

'It's a pleasure. I can't believe how the garden's come on in such a short period of time, but both Betty and Margaret seem to be keeping on top of the pruning and weeding. Looking forward to the party tomorrow? Olivia and I can't wait. Hannah, we really can't thank you enough for all you did for us.'

'I didn't do anything more than point you both in the right direction, and to be honest I wish I'd knocked your heads together months ago, but I'm really happy for you. You've got so much to look forward to together and also with the boys. Come here, give me a hug.'

'Aww, that's nice. Thanks, Hannah. I know I was a bit of a fool really, but I think we were both nervous about making the first move in case we'd misread the situation and made a big mistake. That would have ruined our friendship, you know.'

'Yes, but that's all in the past. Now it's time to look to the future and new beginnings.'

'If you don't mind me asking, Hannah. Couldn't you find it in your heart to forgive Jimmy? Perhaps I should be banging your heads together. I'm sure he wouldn't do anything so stupid again.'

'And on that note, you've got gardening to be getting on with, and I've got beds to make up for my guests. See you later, Tom, and thanks again for coming over to tidy up. You and Olivia have always been special friends to me, and I couldn't be happier for you.'

Beds made, clothes put away, it was as if the flat swap had never happened. Now it would only be a question of time before her dad and Susanna arrived. Hannah was still rather surprised that they'd actually accepted the invitation to the party. She would have thought they'd have concocted some silly reason to miss it, although perhaps they had some news to share. Were they going to separate? No, if that was the case, surely they wouldn't arrive as a couple. No doubt everything would soon come to light.

'Nan, they've just pulled up onto the driveway. Let's greet them together, have a quick chat over a cup of tea and sandwich and then we can make our excuses. With any luck, they can go out somewhere for the afternoon and evening.'

'Yes, darling, and then tomorrow we'll be busy with the party. They'll have gone home before you even know it. It's dreadful for me to think like that, but I'm not in the mood for Susanna, and come to that, your father too. What's the expression? He needs to man up?'

'You're so funny, Nan. Right, here we go.'

Everyone was all smiles, just as if nothing had happened the last time Susanna was here, but Hannah had an inkling that she was up to something and soon they'd be finding out exactly what that was.

Betty went into the garden with Susanna while Richard took their bags into Hannah's flat. Hannah made a big pot of tea and took Betty's previously made sandwiches out of the fridge. As she was carrying the tray out, she noticed that her father had some sort of file in his hand.

'Here we go. A range of freshly prepared sandwiches, courtesy of Nan. How was your journey, Dad?'

'Fine, thanks. We're both looking forward to this party, aren't we, Susanna?'

'Yes, and I can see how busy you all are

382

preparing, so we won't get in your way, but before all of that, we have some news of our own.'

Hannah knew there was something in the offing, but now she got the impression it was to be good news. Robert broke the silence, explaining that they were going to be moving into a four bedroomed detached house. Both Betty and Hannah sat there listening, yet wondering how they'd be able to afford it, but apparently Robert had studied a map and calculated exactly how far he was prepared to travel to work. From there they looked at houses in a given radius. For the same price as their three bedroomed house, they could afford a bigger property in a different area. The one they had found did need a few repairs carried out, but nothing major, and it even had a good school practically on the doorstep.

'I'm very pleased for you all, but are you sure you'll be happy there, Susanna?'

'More than happy, Betty. I know I've given you a lot of hassle, but it really was all to do with space, and not about not caring for Robert as you thought. I realise how harsh it sounded at the time, but...'

'...that's all in the past, and now we live for the future, don't we, Hannah!'

Hannah smiled to herself because her past was with Jimmy, but could he also be her future? Everybody else's life seemed to be moving forwards, while hers stayed the same.

Chapter 60

Although it was only six o'clock in the morning, Hannah was already up and out on the beach. Bonkers was with Richard and Josie, and Hannah was grateful for time alone, away from the talk about Susanna's new house and the chaotic buzz of the party preparations. She sat on the rocks, poured herself a cup of coffee from her thermos flash and thought how lovely it was to have time to herself and enjoy the peace and quiet of the beach.

Today was quite a special day. Everything that had happened since she had arrived at Luckett House was now coming to a conclusion. It was a strange way to think about it, but that's how Hannah saw it. Arriving with Betty, not knowing how they could save Luckett House, having the idea to divide it up into flats, getting the job at the hotel and then getting back together with old friends, Olivia and Tom. Then there was the wonderful way that had panned out, finding Brian the builder who had led her to meet Carl, but most importantly Betty selling the two flats to Margaret and Josie. In spite of their connection, that was the most special thing, and today was really the icing on the cake. All their friends coming together to share the day, say thank you and mark the start of their new lives.

'Hello, Bonkers, and who are you with today? Oh, it's Richard. I thought it might have been Margaret.'

'No, she's busy preparing the food. I'm surprised to see you down here alone. Don't tell me you're avoiding Robert and Susanna?'

'Got it one, Richard, but I also just wanted a little peace and quiet before the party starts. Oh, don't take that personally. I didn't mean it like that as such; you know I love your company and the friendship that's developed between us. We do seem to be rather similar.'

'That's because we appreciate living here after having spent time in the non-stop London lifestyle. If you're not working, you're commuting and the days are long. That's what we have in common, Hannah. As I was walking down here I was thinking about how long we've all been planning this party and now the day's finally arrived. Most importantly, my mum's still here to see the day. I don't know where she's got her strength from, but she's a real fighter. She does understand how poorly she is though, and I think that's why she insisted on moving back upstairs. She knows she'll have to rest far more. I just hope today's one of her good days and that she'll be able to enjoy seeing all her friends.'

'Yes. I think Josie's illness has made us all evaluate our lives and count our blessings.'

'That's one of the reasons I'm only going to be working a few hours a week now. I'm also thinking about selling my home in London. I'll be able to buy a lovely little cottage here with the money and actually live quite comfortably. How about you? Do you think you'll stay at Saltmarsh Cliff Hotel, or do you think you'll eventually get bored of it and look for bigger and better hotels to work in?'

'I've no idea, but at the moment I'm more than happy here. I don't think I could move far away from Nan. She's been so good to me, not just with the flat, but with everything throughout my life, especially since my mum died. I'm hoping to be able to support her as she gets older, but for now, I think I need to get back up the hill. There's a party happening and my names on a 'to do' list. I'll leave you to your walk with Bonkers. If that doesn't wear him out, Olivia's two boys will certainly do it.'

Walking back up the hill, she pondered over Richard's question. Would she stay in Luckett Quay or would she eventually prefer pastures news? Perhaps she ought to be considering her long-term plans, but life was good and she knew she was blessed to be living in such a perfect place as Luckett House.

With the four flats having a kitchen each, and with it, four ovens, Hannah was thankful that she didn't need to become involved in any of the cooking. Her role was tables, chairs and the little bar, outdoor work, wiping down surfaces, straightening the bunting which Richard had strung up, and making sure the garden and patio looked perfect.

Carl had sent a text asking if there was anything he could do to help. Hannah thought perhaps he could man the bar for her. He'd enjoy doing that, and it would enable him to introduce Mike to everyone. It was now half past eleven. Betty had sent Robert and Susanna out to the little shop in Saltmarsh Quay to collect some fresh strawberries and raspberries for her pavlova. Richard was helping Josie to get ready and Hannah was putting the little tablecloths on the outdoor tables, when Margaret called her in.

'Is something the matter?'

'No, not at all. We're all done and before we both go and get our glad rags on, we thought a little sherry would be the order of the day. I was wondering if you'd join us?'

'I haven't had a sherry for years, but I'll have a quick one with you. I must go and have a shower before I doll myself up too. Are you sure there's nothing else you'll need me to do, Margaret?'

'It's all in hand. We just need to warm a few things up and put the fruit on the desserts and that will be everything completed. Jimmy will be coming in to organise the serving, so we won't have to do a thing. You don't mind him being here, do you, Hannah?'

'Of course not. He's part of our Norfolk life; it's

good that he's here.'

Hannah noticed Margaret and Betty give each other a knowing look. They toasted each other's happiness, downing the sherry in one and then they all went off to get ready for the party. Robert and Susanna had returned and were heading to the bedroom to get changed. It was a lovely sunny September day and Hannah hadn't fully decided whether to wear shorts or a dress. Thinking about it, shorts at a posh garden party probably wouldn't be quite right. It would definitely have to be a summer dress.

Dressed and ready to party, Hannah was the first one in the garden. The guests should be arriving in about an hour, so she put the finishing touches on the table decorations and waited for Margaret and Betty to come down.

'Wow, don't the three of us look posh, Nan?'

'The word you're looking for is glamorous. Isn't that right, Betty? We're all looking so glamorous.'

The three of them laughed together, posing in their finery when out walked Josie, helped by Richard. He led her to one of the comfortable chairs and the three of them joined him for a glass of champagne. There wasn't a dry eye between them, emotions having got the better of them all. Josie leaned in towards them and touched each of their hands in turn. She tried to talk but the words were not forthcoming. Hannah didn't know what to say either, but eventually Margaret took over.

'So here we are. Twelve months ago none of us would have dreamed that this party would have happened. Frank was alive then, and life was so different. Hannah would have been in London. I know people say it without really thinking, but everything in life certainly does happen for a reason.'

'Yes, and if I had to be ill, there was no way I would have moved from Sheringham. No, this is our time. Let's raise a toast to us.'

'Thanks, Josie, you're right there, it is our time, and it's all about Luckett House. It doesn't matter how the house is divided up, it will always be full of love. We were all meant to be here, and that's a wonderful thought.'

'Down on the beach this morning I was thinking about our journeys. This party represents all of us getting here, and tomorrow is the real start of our lives. No more dwelling on the past. Frank's no longer with us, Josie's getting stronger by the day and it's time to enjoy the future here in Luckett Quay, but before any of you mention it, Jimmy was part of my past in London and I'm not sure if he's part of my new life in Norfolk or not, but here's to the ladies of Luckett House.'

Yet again there wasn't a dry eye. But with the arrival of Carl and Mike it was time to get the party started.

'Wow! Don't you ladies look fabulous! Now, where's this bar you'd like me to run? I'm so looking forward to this, but hopefully no one will ask for a cocktail as wine and beer are my specialities.'

When Hannah showed him to the bar, they both had to laugh. It measured no more than two foot in width and four foot in length, and all the drinks were on a table behind it. Anyway, it was adequate for their party, they didn't need anything larger. Hannah poured Mike and Carl a glass of wine and insisted they sat down and chatted with Josie, Margaret and Betty for a while.

Good timing, as Susanna suddenly appeared with Robert and Richard. Hearing the word 'house' mentioned more than once, Hannah decided it was time to mingle and quickly left in the opposite direction. Carl put some background music on the CD player as friends and family arrived and everyone started to relax and enjoy the afternoon. That's a familiar noise, Hannah thought to herself. The sound of the back gate and the scamper of paws. Sam and Ben were shouting and chasing after Bonkers. Hannah didn't know who was the most excited, the boys or the dog!

'Hi, you two. Love your dress, Olivia, and look at you, Tom. New clothes to go with the slick haircut. Very smart!'

'I've a very good reason to look smart these days, don't I?'

'You certainly do, and you both look so great together. The bar's open, so why don't you go and get yourselves a drink while I go and check that everyone's having a good time?'

Hannah didn't recognise all the guests who had been invited, but coming towards her was a family she certainly had got to know over the previous few months. Raymond Dove, his wife and Emmi were chatting to Carl.

'Isn't this lovely, such a beautiful home now. Brian and his team have done a marvellous job with it. By the way, I would never have knocked this house down. I know some of the houses are practically falling down and that's why there are new properties on those plots, but that's not my business. I love restoring and refurbishing older properties just like this. I'm actually doing the one up at the stables for Emmi.

'Oh, and there's some positive news about our mutual friend, Tristan. I've met up with a couple of other businessmen he was involved with and we're trying to deal with the chaos left behind from his shady deals. We're going to use our connections to take legal action. To be honest, we've come to the conclusion that Tristan either really didn't have a clue what he was talking about, or thought that everyone else was born yesterday and would be taken in by his fancy talk. Anyway, the main thing is that he's long gone now.

'Now, I think I've taken up far too much of your precious time, Hannah. Go and enjoy your party and thanks for all you've done for me.'

Both the garden and the conservatory were full of people laughing and joking together and it made such a beautiful picture. Hannah was just about to tell Sam and Ben that it wasn't really a safe place to be kicking footballs about, when she saw Jimmy bringing the food out. She hadn't even noticed he was there before now, but he too had made such an effort with his clothes. He was wearing a lovely shirt that she hadn't seen before and looked quite handsome.

'Caught you looking!'

'Sorry, Carl, what did you say?'

'I saw you eyeing Jimmy up there. Mind you, he does look irresistible, don't you think?'

'You're right, he does look good, but then he always did. I was a very lucky girl at university. Lots of the other girls were jealous of me, but thanks for not giving me a lecture about him. I know everyone means well, but it does get rather tedious after a while.'

'You two look in deep conversation. Can I join in, seeing that I'm one of the original HOT members?'

'Of course. Olivia. Carl and I were just saying what a lovely party it is, and as for you you've given Tom a whole new makeover.'

'I wouldn't really say it was down to me, but I'm so pleased about it. He's a different person lately, stopped moaning about this, that and the other. Well, actually I suppose we've all changed since you've arrived, Hannah. Isn't that right, Carl? Now we just need to sort you out, young lady.'

'Oh, I don't need any sorting. I know exactly what I want. Now, if you'll all excuse me, I need to go and be the hostess with the mostess.'

The afternoon flowed by effortlessly without any more in-depth conversations. Margaret and Betty made sure Josie was comfortable and not getting too tired. Susanna had asked whether it was alright to stay another night so that Robert could enjoy the afternoon properly with a few drinks. She also commented that she'd never realised how lovely the view from the garden was. Perhaps that was because she'd never taken the time to appreciate Luckett House. Everything had generally been about her, but maybe a leopard could change its spots.

It was now nearly six o'clock and quite a few of the guests were preparing to leave. Others had pushed chairs and tables together to make bigger groups and everyone had enjoyed the food. Jimmy was clearing the buffet table away, and the only one still full of energy was Bonkers. Hannah decided to get his lead and take him down onto the beach without anyone knowing apart from Richard in case he thought Bonkers had run off by himself. They often joked about that, why on earth would he, when he gets fed in four different homes every day.

Bonkers was more in the mood to fetch sticks than run around. Perhaps he too had been worn out by the day's excitement. Sitting on the rocks, he nuzzled his face into Hannah. They both closed their eyes and all that could be heard was the sound of the tiny waves lapping the shoreline. This was definitely home. Why would she want to be anywhere else other than this little spot of paradise? She couldn't be any happier.

'Hi, mind if I join you, or would you prefer to be alone?'

'No, I'll budge up, there's room for three. Jimmy, thank you for all you've done today. We really appreciate it.'

'I've really enjoyed being a part of this special day, and in particular being with you, Hanny. Could

I give you a kiss?'

She didn't answer, just closed her eyes again to block out the rest of the world. The party was the end of one chapter in life, and now this was a new beginning...

THE END

Printed in Great Britain
by Amazon